Shop till You Drop

A DEAD-END JOB MYSTERY

Elaine Viets

D0053180

A SIGNET BOOK

SIGNET
Published by New American Library, a division of
Penguin Group (USA) Inc., 375 Hudson Street,
New York, New York 10014, U.S.A.
Penguin Books Ltd, 80 Strand,
London WC2R 0RL, England
Penguin Books Australia Ltd, 250 Camberwell Road,
Camberwell, Victoria 3124, Australia
Penguin Books Canada Ltd, 10 Alcorn Avenue,
Toronto, Ontario, Canada M4V 3B2
Penguin Books (N.Z.) Ltd, Cnr Rosedale and Airborne Roads,
Albany, Auckland 1310, New Zealand

Penguin Books Ltd, Registered Offices:
80 Strand, London WC2R 0RL, England

First published by Signet, an imprint of New American Library,
a division of Penguin Group (USA) Inc.

First Printing, May 2003
10 9 8 7 6 5 4 3 2

For Anne Watts and Thumbs,
who both enjoy curling up with a good book

Acknowledgments

I want to thank my husband, Don Crinklaw, for his patience. When I asked him "Do you think it would sound better if I changed the 'a' to 'the'?" he actually gave me a serious answer.

And my pitbull agent, David Hendin.

And my enthusiastic editor, Genny Ostertag, who keeps dreaming up dead-end jobs for me, so I can have the job I really want.

Thanks to the Penguin Putnam copy editors and production staff, who were so careful.

So many people helped with this book. I hope I didn't leave anyone out.

Thanks to Joanne Sinchuk and John Spera at Murder on the Beach bookstore in Delray Beach, Florida. They encouraged me to write a Florida series. I hope they like this one.

Thanks to Jim Brennan of Brennan Thomsen Associates Inc. Carolyn Cain, author of *The Secret at the Breakers Hotel* for her knowledge of home fires, which she gained the hard way. To Valerie Cannata for her courtroom information. Thanks also to Sarah Watts-Casinger, who saved Thumbs from a life on the streets. And Jinny Gender, Karen Grace, Kay Gordy, Debbie Henson and Janet Smith for their help and encouragement.

Shannon May gave me her South Beach expertise. I

appreciate the help of Ann Meng, broker, Buy the Beach Realty Inc.; Art Rosen Real Estate, Yolanda at the Florida Center for Cosmetic Surgery; M. Diane Vogt, author of *The Silicone Solution*; and premier Internet researcher Martin Walsh.

Thanks to John R. Levy and mystery lover Debra Davis at Shelton Ferrari in Fort Lauderdale, which has a splendid Barchetta.

Rita Scott does indeed make cat toys packed with the most powerful catnip in kittendom. They have sent my cats into frenzies of ecstasy. Read all about them at www. catshigh.us.

Ed Seelig at Silver Strings Music gave me a "Clapton Is God" T-shirt. It is one of my treasured possessions.

Julie Dost let me wander around her weight-training class like a zombie. Her workouts jar something loose in my brain that helps me write.

Thanks to Detective RC White, Fort Lauderdale Police Department (retired), who answered countless questions on police interrogations and procedures. Any mistakes are mine, not his.

Jerry Sanford, author of *Miami Heat* and federal prosecutor for the northern district of Florida, answered many complicated legal questions.

Thanks to Merrilyn Rathbun, research director at the Fort Lauderdale Historical Society, and Florida expert Stuart McIver, who has written too many books to list here.

Thanks to the librarians at the Broward County Library and the St. Louis Public Library who researched my questions, no matter how wacky.

Special thanks to librarian Anne Watts, the person who lives with Thumbs the cat. Thumbs is a real six-toed cat, although his own coat is a richer brown. He agreed to go gray for his role in this series.

Chapter 1

On Wednesday, Helen met a woman who could not frown.

The frownless female was another amazing customer at Juliana's. The store was on Las Olas Boulevard, the fashionable, palm-fringed shopping area in downtown Fort Lauderdale. After working two weeks there, Helen thought she'd seen every kind of expensive kept woman.

The woman who could not frown did not seem all that different from the other customers who were buzzed inside. You could not simply walk into Juliana's. The elegant green door was locked to keep out undesirables: sunburned tourists in "I Love Florida" T-shirts, harried mothers with sticky-fingered children, and the hopelessly unfashionable.

This exclusive policy was never stated, but everyone on Las Olas knew it. Some women walked on by, never ringing Juliana's doorbell. They knew the green door would not open for them.

Woe to those who tried and failed. A woman turned away from Juliana's might tell herself that the clothes were overpriced and made for skinny little bimbos. That was true. But it was also true that Ms. Reject had been publicly branded as without style, and worse, that Juliana's could not help her.

This added to the thrill of those who were admitted by Christina, the head saleswoman. When the green door swung open, some women had the same celestial look of relief and joy that wavering saints must wear when admitted into heaven.

But Brittney, the woman who could not frown, did not register any emotion at all, not even when she squealed "Christina!" and air-kissed her.

Brittney was a longtime customer and a big spender. Helen could tell that by the way Christina had moved across the room, like a quick cat pouncing on her prey. She even hugged Brittney. Christina only touched people who spent lots of money.

As they stood implant to implant, Helen thought the two women looked enough alike to be sisters. Both had long blonde hair (dyed), plump pouty lips (collagened), and sapphire blue eyes (contacts). It went without saying that they dieted to starvation.

They were dressed alike, too. Both wore casual clothes that cost a fortune and stayed in style about two and a half seconds. By next season, Brittney would have given her thousand-dollar outfit to the maid, and Christina would have sent hers to the consignment shop.

Before she worked at Juliana's, Helen had only seen these styles on MTV. Christina and Brittney wore low-rise pants tight enough to show the freckles on their butts, high heels and low necklines. Both bared their shoulders and flat tummies pierced with silver rings.

But Christina looked like Brittney's older sister, although Helen suspected they were the same age. Brittney belonged in those revealing clothes. Christina looked a little too old for them. Maybe it was the lines running from her nose to her mouth or the fine furrows in her forehead. The nights she spent crawling the South Beach clubs were starting to show in Christina's skin.

Brittney didn't have any wrinkles, and she hadn't had a facelift, either. Helen had worked at the shop long enough to know what good and bad facelifts looked like.

"Let me see. Let me see," Christina said, examining Brittney's smooth oval face. "It looks perfect."

"It worked," Brittney said, in a soft, sultry voice that sounded like a sigh in a seraglio. "I've met a wonderful new man. He has a house in Golden Beach."

Golden Beach was aptly named. Oceanfront homes there started at just under three million dollars. Brittney had a rich catch. She presented Christina with a small gold gift bag, packed with crimson tissue paper. "I brought you a little present."

Many of Christina's customers brought her little presents. Helen thought they were trying to curry favor, so that green door would always open for them.

Christina's long, slender hand rustled around in the tissue paper like a small predator and pulled out a Movado watch with a mother-of-pearl museum dial and a matching lizard strap. "Pink! The new color. Although my favorite color is green," she said, and laughed.

Brittney did not laugh. Maybe she couldn't, Helen thought.

"Come on back and sit down," Christina said, as if she was inviting a friend into her home for a chat. Helen was relieved when she saw Brittney head for the sitting area. Juliana's sales associates were only allowed to sit if a customer sat first. If there were no customers, they had to stand. The owner spot-checked the security camera tapes to make sure that rule was followed.

Christina offered Brittney a drink.

"Evian, please," she said, in that velvet whisper.

The super-skinny ones always wanted water. Christina hurried to the back room for Evian water. Helen and Brittney strolled past a single Hermes scarf draped on a mahogany sideboard that had once been in a Rockefeller mansion. ("This isn't a rummage sale," Christina had told Helen. "Never put out a pile of anything.")

They passed two pale blue six-hundred-dollar blouses on a dark, sleek wood rack. Hanging next to them were the matching jackets. They were two thousand each.

Brittney spotted a spaghetti-strap knit top on a rosewood wine table. It was a turquoise knit edged with hot pink crocheted lace. Made of viscose and polyester, the scrap of cloth weighed little more than a Kleenex.

"How much?" Brittney said. Juliana's never used price tags.

"Three hundred fifteen dollars," Helen said. She could

say that now with a straight face. When Helen first saw the top, she thought it looked like a Kmart special, and that polyester and viscose belonged on trailer trash. Now she knew what it could do for the right woman. So did Brittney.

"It's adorable," she said, and draped it over one arm.

"We have the pants to go with it," Helen said. Brittney didn't reply. Her attention was captured by a snakeskin handbag. "How much?" she said, stroking it with exquisitely manicured fingers.

"Four fifty," Helen said.

Brittney draped the turquoise top over the snake bag and carried both to the back of the store. Three black silk-satin loveseats formed a triangle in front of a gilt-framed triple mirror. Behind the loveseats, on a black marble pedestal, was a porcelain vase filled with fashionable flowers that looked like sex toys and bath brushes.

Helen, a solid size twelve, sank into the loveseat. Brittney was so tiny, she barely disturbed the surface. Even her couch doesn't wrinkle, thought Helen.

Helen wanted to hate Brittney, but she couldn't. She liked the woman. There was something winsome about her. Brittney didn't ignore Helen, the way some customers did. While she waited for Christina to return, Brittney said, "I'm sorry, I didn't catch your name. You are?"

"Helen Hawthorne. I'm the new sales associate."

Brittney held out her hand, and Helen shook it. It felt soft but strong. Brittney's skinny arms were corded with high-priced gym muscle.

"How long have you lived here?" asked Brittney.

This was the polite greeting in South Florida. Almost no one was from here. No one you wanted to know, anyway.

"Not too long," Helen said.

"She moved down here from the Midwest," Christina said, coming back with Evian and a chilled crystal goblet.

"Oh," Brittney said. No one ever cared enough to ask where in the Midwest. Fort Lauderdale was a suburb of New York, which had no interest in the nation's boring midsection. The Midwest was the land of pot roasts and pot bellies. No one went there. No one would pry into Helen's secret.

"And what did you do there?" Brittney said. Helen knew

how to stop that line of questioning. She gave her real job title. "I was a director of pensions and employee benefits."

She could see Brittney's eyes getting a glaze on them like a jelly doughnut. But to be sure, Helen started reciting her job description. Even Helen could not endure the whole thing: "I planned and directed implementation and administration of benefits programs—"

"How nice," Brittney said, hurriedly cutting her off. Helen relaxed. There would be no further questions about her past.

But Brittney ambushed her with "Why are you working in a dress shop?"

"Working here has given me a new challenge and a chance to brush up on my people skills," Helen said, hating herself for slipping into corporate speak.

Like all good liars, Helen stuck to the truth as much as possible. Serious jobs in Lauderdale were far outnumbered by dead-end jobs in shops and fast-food places that paid six or seven dollars an hour. Even Brittney, who'd never held a serious job in her life, knew that. It was why most of Juliana's women dated rich old men.

"I was lucky to find this job within walking distance of my apartment," Helen said brightly.

Some luck, she thought, resentfully. I make six seventy an hour, no benefits, no commission until I've worked here six months. Helen wanted her wages to be in cash, off the books. She made thirty cents an hour less than the standard sales associate. The store owner explained why he was stiffing her. "I'm not taking out any deductions, so you're really making more. You understand that you'll have no Social Security, no health insurance, and if I fire you, no unemployment?"

Helen had understood. She wanted it that way. She did not want her name turning up in any computer database. She did not want the court tracking her down. But the irony didn't escape her. She'd fled St. Louis because she caught her husband—make that ex-husband—Rob with a younger woman. A woman who looked a lot like the customers at Juliana's.

I used to make six figures, she thought, and now I'm selling bustiers to bimbos.

Christina directed the conversation back to Brittney, as was proper. "Let's get a look at your new, improved face," she said. Brittney put her face up expectantly, as if waiting for an expert's approval. Helen thought she'd never seen a more perfect oval. There was not a wrinkle, line, blemish or enlarged pore. The skin was smooth and velvety, the striking sapphire eyes large and clear and fringed with dark lashes. The effect was stunning and slightly scary. There was an odd deadness in this perfection.

"Doctor Mariposa did a splendid job," Christina said, admiringly.

"I can't thank you enough for sending me to her," Brittney said.

Christina shrugged. "I know all the good ones," she said. "And all the bad ones, too. Did you see Tiffany's eye job? She didn't consult me first. The damned doctor's got her so tight she can't shut her eyes any more. Tiffany's happy with his work. I haven't the heart to tell her she looks like she's permanently startled."

"Surgery is so risky," Brittney said. "Thanks for the warning. That way I won't look startled next time I see her."

"What did the doctor do to you, Brittney?" Helen asked.

"Injected my wrinkles with biopolymer," she said, shy but proud.

"What's that?" Helen said.

"It's like collagen, only better," Brittney said. "It's very big in Europe, but it hasn't been approved in the U.S. yet. I've heard Bo Derek had it done. Her forehead used to look like crepe paper."

She said it with wide-eyed wonder and without a trace of bitchiness.

Helen thought that Bo Derek looked darn good, with or without the alleged face work.

"Did you need surgery for this?" Helen asked.

"No, you get it injected into your face. It gets rid of the wrinkles, the ones around your mouth and nose, and the frown lines between your eyebrows. It's cheaper than a facelift. I had the lines around my mouth done for about six hundred fifty dollars and my forehead for another couple of hundred."

"Any side effects?" Helen asked. She was fascinated. She'd never heard of this stuff. She couldn't begin to guess Brittney's age. Was she an old thirty? A young forty?

"None. Oh, your face swells up for two or three days, and it really hurts, but after that, there's nothing. There are no allergies to worry about, because it's a mineral. It lasts longer than collagen. This treatment will be good for five years. Then I'll have to have it done again."

"You're sure there are no side effects?" Helen said. She couldn't believe these injections didn't have some risk.

"None," she said. Brittney thought for a moment. "Well, maybe one. I can't frown any more."

"You what?" Helen was not sure she'd heard right.

"I can't frown," she said. "I don't know if it is permanent or not. But it's not really a disadvantage. You don't get forehead wrinkles if you can't frown."

Now Helen understood Brittney's curiously impassive face. Brittney couldn't move whole sections of her face. Helen wondered if an enormous surge of emotion would show on Brittney's lovely features. What if she discovered her man in bed with another woman, the way Helen found her husband Rob? Could Brittney's face still be distorted by rage? Or would her face always be smooth and impassive, even when she was fighting mad? Would that bottled-up anger hurt?

But then she remembered how Brittney earned her living. Like most of the women at Juliana's, she was probably kept by a much older man, as either a mistress or a trophy wife.

"If I can't frown, that's good, don't you think?" Brittney said. "You don't want those emotions, anyway. They will just give you wrinkles." She was absolutely serious, and sweetly trusting. Helen bit back her sarcastic reply. It would be like hitting a puppy.

"I want Doctor Mariposa to do me," Christina said. "She's the best. She was a top plastic surgeon in Brazil. I don't understand why they won't let her practice in Florida."

If Doctor Mariposa couldn't operate in Florida, some-

thing was seriously wrong, Helen thought. Florida let all
sorts of crooks and incompetents practice.

"It's our gain," sighed Brittany happily. "She can't advertise the regular way, so there isn't a long waiting list. The
only drawback is she wants cash. But she has to in her situ-
ation. She can't keep records."

"Speaking of not keeping things, did you really dump
Vinnie?" Christina said.

"I had to tell him good-bye. It was just too dangerous to
date him any more." Brittney crossed her long legs, and
Helen noticed her cerise Moschino mules.

"How come?" Helen asked.

"Too many of his friends were dying," Brittney said
earnestly.

"They were sick?" Helen said.

"No, silly. They were turning up in barrels in Biscayne
Bay." This was a favorite form of mob body disposal in
Miami. In New York and New Jersey, the home of many
mobsters of Italian extraction, bodies were simply dumped
in the river. Then the dead did not rise until May, when the
water warmed up. But here in Florida, it was always warm.
So the Miami mobsters used barrels. The bodies stayed
down until the decomposition gases caused them to rise and
float.

"Six of them were found dead. Two more are missing,
and the police think they're probably dead."

Helen did not know what to say.

"Vinnie is in construction," Brittney said, as if that explained something. Maybe it did. Construction could be a
rough business in South Florida.

"He's also in import-exports."

Helen had been in Florida long enough to know that was
code for drugs.

"Does he have a boat?" Christina asked, shrewdly.

"Oh, yes. A Cigarette boat."

Helen took that as proof.

"The last ones were Vinnie's good friend Angelo and his
date, Heather. They turned up dead last week. Now the FBI
has been following me around, asking me questions and

making my life miserable," Brittney said. She looked like an indignant Barbie doll.

"The FBI are everywhere. Two of them even rang my doorbell at seven a.m. They asked if they could come in, and I had to let them. I couldn't have the neighbors see me with the FBI. But I didn't offer them coffee or juice or anything."

Brittney acted as if she'd punished the agents severely. Helen listened, spellbound.

"See, Vinnie and I had dinner with Angelo and Heather about a week before they died. We didn't know they were going to die, of course. They seemed just fine. Heather was wearing the cutest Dolce & Gabbana outfit—the black one that was in the last issue of *Vanity Fair*. D&G is so hot. Angelo must have really loved her," she said, and this time, the sigh was sad.

"After their bodies were discovered, the FBI showed me the grossest pictures. Polaroids of those poor dead people. They were in awful shape from the water and the sun. Heather had always taken such good care of herself, too.

"That FBI agent said, 'Did you have dinner with these people Wednesday, August first?' I looked at those terrible photos and I said, 'Would I have dinner with someone who looked like that?'" Brittney was trembling with indignation. "That's when I told Vinnie that I couldn't see him any more. It's too dangerous to go around with him. That's why he has a wife."

"Vinnie's married?" Helen blurted. Christina frowned at her, and Helen felt like a hayseed from the Midwest, as she often did at Juliana's. But Brittney was not offended.

"Of course he's married," she said. "His wife knows we date." Helen thought "date" stood for another four-letter word.

The doorbell chimed. Christina buzzed the green door, and it swung open to admit a young Asian woman with straight black hair down to her size-two tush. She was accompanied by a forty-something boyfriend with a bull neck and a bald spot. He had one hand possessively on the small of her back.

"You wait on them," Christina said. "I'll take Brittney."

The long-haired lovely was named Tara. Her boyfriend

was Paulie. Paulie had her try on everything in the store and made crude comments like "Those pants really show off your ass." Tara simply smiled and tried on more short, tight clothes. Paulie dropped nearly nine thousand dollars, a sweet sugar daddy indeed.

After the couple left, Christina congratulated her warmly. Helen barely heard her. She couldn't get the woman who could not frown out of her mind. Helen was haunted by Brittney's sweet nature and her oddly immobile face. She did not know why such a lovely creature would go out with a mobster. Brittney did not seem to understand that dumping Vinnie might not be enough. If all the mobster's friends were dying or disappearing, then she might be in danger, too.

She wondered if Brittney would live long enough to get wrinkles.

Helen was not really surprised three weeks later when she read in the paper that the body of a ninety-eight-pound woman with blonde hair and sapphire-blue contacts was found in a barrel in Biscayne Bay.

But she was surprised whose body it turned out to be.

Chapter 2

Thursday was Helen's worst day since she fled St. Louis. It was raining that morning, a hard tropical downpour. A relentless wind drove the rain under her umbrella. Helen was soaked by the time she'd walked to work. Her black silk Ungaro suit was wet and wrinkled. Her hair was damp and frizzy. She squished watery footprints across Juliana's freshly vacuumed carpet.

"You look like a bag lady," Christina said. "You can't wait on customers dressed like that." Christina's own clothes — white Chanel pants and an Italian knit top — were perfectly dry. Her blonde hair curled obediently around her shoulders. Maybe she had teleported to Juliana's, Helen thought.

"But if I go home for more clothes, I'll just get wetter," Helen said.

"Then borrow something in the store, and don't get anything on it," Christina snapped. "There's a hair dryer you can use in the stockroom for your damp hair."

Helen dried her hair, then looked for something to wear. Nothing fit. Not one single item in the whole store. She found scores of size twos, fours, sixes, several zeroes, some eights, and one size ten, but no twelves she could wear.

Juliana's women were built like little girls with big breasts. Helen was a big woman. Not a fat woman. At six feet and one hundred fifty pounds, she was slim and willowy by some standards. But in Juliana's she felt like a great galumphing giant. Sometimes she thought that was why Christina had hired her. Even on their fattest day, the teeny customers could feel superior to the huge Midwestern saleswoman.

"I'm not huge," Helen told herself. "Twelve is not a big size for a grown woman my height. And I'm good-looking."

So good-looking my husband of seventeen years hopped into bed with another woman, she thought. And now I'm on the run.

Helen was feeling low. The storewide clothes search depressed her, and the pounding rain didn't help. She finally plugged in the steamer in the stockroom and used it to get the wrinkles out of her suit. Then she reapplied her makeup.

"Much better," Christina said, when the spruced-up Helen emerged from the stockroom. "I'm sorry I grumped at you. You don't have to worry how you look, anyway. I expect this will be a slow day with the rain."

With that, the doorbell rang and didn't stop ringing for the next two hours. They were overrun with customers that morning. Perversely, the rain seemed to bring them out, the way a hard rain brought out earthworms on the sidewalks in Helen's hometown of St. Louis.

And worms were all that came to Juliana's that morning. The little sweethearts with the sunny dispositions stayed home. Helen and Christina waited on complainers, crabs, grumps, and grouches. They brought racks of clothes for customers who didn't like the styles or the prices. They hunted up accessories for women who refused to be delighted by the clever materials and cunning details.

Helen got stuck with two abrasive New York women for over an hour, until she was ready to strangle them with a silk scarf. The funny thing was she liked New Yorkers—in New York. There they were witty and kindhearted, even heroic. But out of their element, they seemed rude and provincial.

The New York women tried on twenty-three dresses, seventeen pairs of pants, fourteen tops, eight sweaters, six belts, and three scarves and dropped everything on the floor. They complained that there weren't enough black styles in their size (New Yorkers always wore black). After all that work, only one of the women bought anything, the cotton-and-spandex pants for a lousy two hundred ninety-five dollars. In black, of course.

Helen was still hanging up their clothes when the doorbell rang again. "Quick, Helen, it's Lauren," Christina said in an urgent whisper. "Now, listen to me. I'm going to let her in and wait on her. Your job is to watch her like a hawk. Make a note of everything Lauren puts in her backpack, but don't say anything about it. Never leave her alone for a minute when she's on the floor. And count everything I take into the dressing room, then count it again when I bring it out, so I have backup. I'll watch her in there."

Helen wondered how Lauren could wear those black leather pants in the humid Florida weather. She had a beautiful lion's mane of tawny hair, green eyes, and a long nose that had to be her own. Most of Juliana's women had had their noses done. Helen admired Lauren's daring move in keeping her oversize schnoz. It gave her face character.

Lauren was the most skillful shoplifter Helen had ever seen. While she talked to Christina about the rain and the fall fashions, she slipped a two-hundred-seventy-five-dollar top, a two-thousand-dollar dress, and a four-hundred-dollar scarf into her black Gucci backpack. Helen would never have noticed the vanishing merchandise if Christina had not alerted her.

Lauren also bought two dresses and a suit. Christina acted as if nothing was wrong. She rang up Lauren's purchases and ignored the bulging backpack. When she left, Christina sighed with relief.

"Lauren is a kleptomaniac," she said.

"A good one, too," Helen said. "I could hardly keep track of everything that passed through her sticky fingers."

"Her husband is a big-time criminal lawyer. Lauren is his third wife, and he really seems to love her, despite her little problem."

"Maybe he loves the criminal in her," Helen said.

Christina smiled. "Whatever. I send him an itemized bill of everything she shoplifts, and he pays it without a whimper. In cash. He has the money delivered by messenger. He's grateful that we don't prosecute her. Most stores do these days, even if he offers to reimburse them double the amount."

"If Saks can arrest Winona Ryder for shoplifting, Lauren doesn't stand a chance," Helen said. "No wonder he's grateful."

Juliana's looked like a battleground after the brutal morning. Shirts hung unbuttoned. A sweater was dropped on a chair. Belts were draped over the sideboard.

Helen stared up at the full-length oil painting of the forties woman in the daring black dress that hung over the sideboard. The woman seemed to survey the disordered store with disdain. Her mouth was a cruel red. Her eyes were dark and hard. She looked like the wicked woman in a noir film, the one who made a fool of the trusting hero.

"Is that Juliana?" Helen asked.

Christina laughed. "Are you kidding? The owner bought this picture at an Episcopalian rummage sale."

"She doesn't look Episcopalian," Helen said.

"She doesn't look like the real Juliana, either," Christina said. "She was a short little woman. Great body, good sense of style, but a face like a frog. Nowadays, plastic surgery would have taken care of her problems." Christina sighed at the thought of the woman born too soon to be saved.

"Juliana was the original owner's mother. Mr. Roget— Gilbert's father—founded the store in 1965 and made a fortune. He had the touch. He knew what Juliana's women liked."

Money, thought Helen.

"His son Gilbert took it over when Mr. Roget died, but Gilbert doesn't have much interest in fashion. He has an air charter business in Toronto. All Gilbert cares about is cashing those checks. He comes down for one week in December, known as Hell Week. The rest of the time, we never see him, thank God.

"Now you know Juliana's big secret," Christina said lightly. "Tell anyone about that painting, and I'll have to have you killed."

Helen laughed, even though Christina's words sounded oddly threatening. Maybe Helen was just tired.

"This is the first break we've had in hours," Christina

said. "Watch the door for me, will you? I'm going to the little girls' room. I finally have time to pee."

Helen carried the pile of pants and tops abandoned by the New Yorkers to the mahogany sideboard and began putting them back on hangers. A wooden pants hanger was missing. Did Lauren shoplift that, too?

Helen went to the front counter to get another hanger out of the box. The bill for Lauren's shoplifting spree was next to the cash register. It was for three thousand six hundred seventy-five dollars—exactly one thousand more than Helen saw Lauren steal.

Helen read the list. It said Lauren had taken a blouse and a belt, along with the items Helen saw her swipe. Maybe Lauren helped herself to them in the dressing room. Except Christina didn't take any belts or blouses into the dressing room. Helen counted all the clothes when they went in and again when they came out.

But she didn't have time to puzzle over the problem. A large woman rang the doorbell. Helen was about to buzz her inside when Christina came out of the back screaming, "Stop!"

"What's wrong?" Helen said, frightened by her desperate shriek.

"Don't let her in. She's fat!" Christina said. She sounded as horrified as if Helen was admitting a serial killer.

"So what?" Helen said. "She's nicely dressed. She's wearing Carole Little."

"Her clothes may be Little, but she's too big. There's nothing she can buy in this store." Christina threw herself in front of the buzzer.

"Those five-hundred-dollar evening purses would fit just fine," Helen said.

"What if she told someone she bought them here?"

"What's wrong with that? She might have a slim sister or a size-six daughter," Helen said.

"What if my Brazilians saw her? They already think Americans are cows."

"Who cares what the Brazilians think? Half the people in Rio live in cardboard boxes. They're really thin, and your

precious Brazilians don't care. Besides, their money is practically worthless."

"Not here it isn't," Christina said. The woman looked in
and tapped on the window glass. She had big brown eyes, a
round pretty face, and curly dark hair.

"Wait, I know that woman," Helen said. "It's Sarah. She
used to live in my apartment at the Coronado. She was nice
to me when I moved in. I'm letting her in. You can fire me
for insubordination." She bumped Christina out of the way
with one hip and pressed the buzzer.

But when the green door swung open, Sarah did not walk
in. She was gone. Instead, it was one of Christina's blasted
Brazilians. Bianca was a preternaturally perky size four who
was married to a Brazilian industrialist.

Christina had told Helen that Juliana's Brazilian women
got plastic surgery done at a much earlier age than Americans. "They start in their twenties. The first thing Brazilians
do is get their large breasts reduced, so they look slimmer,"
Christina said approvingly. "That's a trick American women
should learn. Too often the Americans go for the biggest
fake boobs, and then their clothes never look good on
them."

Bianca had had her thighs and belly liposuctioned, her
nose bobbed, her eyes done, and two ribs removed so her
waist looked smaller, Christina told her. Helen could see for
herself that Bianca's dark hair was streaked with expensive
blonde highlights, and her teeth had been whitened.

Helen examined this monument to Brazilian body sculpting. She thought Bianca looked spooky. She'd seen chicken
wings with more meat on them. Helen felt like a linebacker
next to this smidgen of a woman.

Christina rushed forward to greet Bianca, lips pursed for
an air kiss.

After ninety minutes of nonstop chatter, Bianca bought a
wisp of a painted silk dress and two handkerchief-sized
blouses for thirty-two hundred dollars.

"Send the bill to my husband, of course," Bianca said.
"And, Christina, would you be a dear and ship the clothes to
my house in Rio, Federal Express? I want to wear the dress
Monday night."

"Delighted," Christina said. "But you know shipping is cash in advance. Your husband can pay the taxes and duty on arrival. Let me check the rate." She ran a manicured fingernail down a rate chart behind the cash register and named a hefty sum.

Bianca didn't blink. She pulled a big wad of bills out of her tiny purse and paid.

But the amount made Helen raise her eyebrows. She knew how to crunch numbers, and Bianca's whole purchase, including the box, wouldn't weigh four pounds, max. Christina had overcharged the woman by at least three hundred dollars.

Was Juliana's head saleswoman skimming the extra cash? Did she make more than three hundred dollars from Bianca and another thousand from Lauren that morning?

Helen began to wonder about Christina.

Chapter 3

The rent was due today.

Margery, her landlady, would be knocking on the door in half an hour. Fear cold as cemetery fog settled in on Helen. She didn't have enough money for the rent. She was short by forty-one dollars. Panic seized her stomach, and she felt sick and dizzy. Helen didn't take uncertainty well. She was meant to get a fat weekly paycheck with pension and benefits, not live from hand to mouth.

She remembered her old life in St. Louis with its careless luxuries. Helen never thought twice about the manicures, massages, and hundred-dollar haircuts. She used to pass out twenty-dollar tips like business cards.

But that was before she came home from work and found Rob kissing their neighbor Sandy. Their liplock was so passionate, Helen couldn't have pried them apart with a crowbar. And she had a crowbar right there, next to Rob's electric screwdriver. Helen still remembered how it felt when she picked up the crowbar and swung it as hard as she could—and heard that satisfying crunch. The rest of her memory seemed to come back in flashes: the horrible scene in court, her hurried flight from St. Louis, her long zigzag drive across the country to throw off any pursuers.

And now, the long, slow days in South Florida. Days that were pleasant and sunny, at least most of the time. January in Florida was as close to heaven as Helen was likely to get.

Even today's rain beat January in St. Louis. Back home, Helen would have been scraping ice off her windshield and sliding to work on slippery roads. She'd be shivering in a heavy wool coat and damp smelly boots. Now, after work, she kicked off her suit and heels and put on her cutoffs and sandals.

If Helen was being really honest, the only thing she missed about her old job was the money. Pensions and benefits bored her silly. She was glad she'd escaped that. But when she ran from St. Louis, she condemned herself to the prison of low-paying, dead-end jobs. She couldn't take a decent job. She couldn't have credit cards or a bank account. She would be too easy to trace.

So Helen went from making more than a hundred thousand a year to two hundred sixty-eight dollars a week at Juliana's. After she paid her rent, there wasn't much left for food and electricity and other necessities. And that worried her. All the time.

Helen threw herself wearily on the bed, and the old springs creaked. The lumpy pillows and turquoise chenille spread smelled slightly of the ever-present Florida mold and heat. She liked it. It was a vacation smell. Helen didn't turn on the window air conditioner until half an hour before bedtime, to cut down her electric bill.

She picked up Chocolate, the fat brown teddy bear on her bed, unzipped his back, and felt inside. Choc was a stuffed bear all right. He was stuffed with all her available cash. She counted out the rent money for the tenth time. The bear had not grown fatter overnight. Helen was still forty-one dollars short. She checked her purse. Two dollars and seventy-eight cents. There wasn't a stray penny in the sofa cushions.

It was worse than she thought.

Where did her money go? She'd bought pantyhose on Tuesday. She got a run in her Donna Karan control tops, and nail polish did not stop it. Twelve dollars for new ones. Helen had to have the only job in South Florida that required stockings, and tall women could not buy cheap pantyhose. They weren't long enough. The dry cleaning for her black suit was another job expense. And one night, when she was really feeling wild, she ordered a pepperoni pizza.

Helen had another week until payday. She'd have to dip into her stash.

She patted Chocolate on the back like a burped baby, then pulled down the miniblinds, double-locked the door, and opened the utility closet. Wedged between the water heater and the wall was the old Samsonite suitcase she got for her high school trip to Washington D.C. Inside was a mound of shabby old-lady underwear she bought at a yard sale for twenty-five cents. Helen figured no burglar would touch the cotton circle-stitched bras, snagged support hose, and enormous flower-sprigged panties. Under that graying cotton and stretched elastic was all the money she had in the world: seven thousand three hundred and twenty-four dollars. Minus, after today, another forty-one bucks.

She counted out the money, promised herself that she would replace it this paycheck, and knew she would not.

Helen had arrived in Florida a month ago with ten thousand dollars in cash. It was a shock to learn that landlords here demanded a security deposit plus first and last month's rent. That ate up nineteen hundred fifty dollars. Her worthless car needed eight hundred dollars in repairs, and Helen didn't want to spend the money to fix it. She walked to work and hitched rides to the supermarket with folks at the Coronado apartments. But there were times when her pride wouldn't let her mooch any more, and she took a cab. She'd needed a root canal three weeks ago. That was five hundred dollars, and the pain prescription was thirty-eight dollars. She had no medical insurance, either.

Helen had thought she was lucky when she landed a job at the diner the day she arrived in Fort Lauderdale, within walking distance of where she was staying. The owner was a flabby Greek in a stained white apron who had a mustache like a dead mouse. The man beamed when Helen asked to be paid in cash. His English was uncertain, but "off the books" were three words he understood. Helen made decent money in tips, too. Also off the books.

On the third day, she dropped a trayful of glassware in the kitchen. "I'm so sorry," Helen said.

"Dat's OK. We find a way to make it up," the flabby

Greek said, and he put his sweaty hands right on her breasts and rubbed his gross gut against her belly.

Helen reached behind her, found a meat mallet, and hit the randy Greek on his head. Then she walked out the diner door without collecting her pay.

She pounded the pavement for another ten days before she found the job at Juliana's, and that was sheer luck. Sherry, the previous sales associate, did not show up for work one Monday. Her phone was disconnected, and her landlord said Sherry had moved out in the middle of the night, owing back rent. That happened a lot in South Florida.

Christina had been running the shop by herself for almost a week when Helen walked in looking for work. She was hired on the spot. The money wasn't as good as at the diner, but every time Helen thought of looking for something better, she remembered the Greek gripping her breasts with hands like hairy suction cups.

The suitcase snapped shut with a tired *snick*. Helen felt tired, too. She wanted to put up her aching feet. Her apartment was two rooms, a bedroom that opened onto a patio and a bigger room that served as living room, kitchen, and dining room. The furniture was from the 1950s. Some New York decorator would pay a fortune for the boomerang coffee table and the turquoise lamps shaped like nuclear reactors. The turquoise couch had an exuberant black triangle pattern. But the piece she loved most was a genuine Barcalounger. Lord, that monster was comfortable.

Before Helen could throw herself into it, the doorbell rang. Through the glass slats of the jalousie door, she saw her landlady, Margery Flax, with a tall glass in one hand and a cigarette in the other.

Margery walked into the room like she owned it, which she did. "Here, drink this. You need your Vitamin C," she said, shoving the glass into Helen's hand.

Helen sniffed the glass. It looked like orange juice, but it smelled sort of bitter and perfume-y. There was a lime slice on the rim.

"What's this?"

"A screwdriver," Margery said.

"Only in South Florida do sweet old ladies fix you screw-drivers so you get your Vitamin C," Helen said.

"I'm not sweet, I'm no lady, and I'm not old," Margery said indignantly. "I'm only seventy-six."

"You're right. I was being ageist," Helen said contritely.

"Well, I'm not that young, either," Margery said. "But I don't go on about it."

Seventy-six years in the Florida sun had left Margery's fair skin as brown and wrinkled as an old paper bag. Two packs of Marlboros a day didn't help. Juliana's customers would be horrified by Margery's skin. But Helen thought Margery's lived-in face was attractive. Margery had shrewd brown eyes and straight gray hair that curved at her chin. She painted her toenails bright red, wore a silver toe ring and sexy Italian sandals. "The legs are the last to go," Margery said, and she showed off hers in purple shorts.

Margery was a commanding woman. After ordering Helen to drink the screwdriver, Margery now ordered her out of the apartment.

"It's a nice night. Go on out by the pool and talk to people. Peggy's out there."

"What about Cal?" Helen said.

"Hah," Margery snorted, and blew smoke out her nose like a dragon. "That tightwad. What do you see in him?"

"I like the way he says 'ah-boot' for 'about.' "

"Now, there's the basis for a good relationship," Margery said.

Cal was a snowbird from Toronto. He was forty-five and divorced, with a nicely weathered face and good legs. Helen liked a well-shaped calf, and down here, where men wore shorts to almost everything but funerals, she had much to admire.

"Cal is intelligent and a good talker. I love listening to his stories about Canada."

"Talk is cheap," Margery said. "And so is Cal."

"Oh, Margery, you're so prejudiced against Canadians. They're nice quiet people. They make good tourists. They never kill themselves by diving into swimming pools from the tenth floor, like the drunken college kids at spring break. And not all Canadians are cheap."

"Oh, yeah?" Margery said, cigarette dangling from her lip like a movie tough. "Don't ever go to dinner with him. Listen, sweetie, I've got ads in the paper to rent 2C. I'll find you someone better than Cal." She took Helen's rent money and disappeared out the door in a cloud of smoke.

Helen turned on the fan to chase out the cigarette smoke. Now she would have to go sit by the pool just to breathe. She loved Margery but wished she wouldn't go on about the cheap Canadians. South Florida residents had a love-hate relationship with their Canadian visitors, who showed up about November and went back north after Easter. The Floridians needed their tourist dollars but claimed the Canadians were cheap. Servers called them "special waters," because so many Canadians ordered the cheapest dinner special and drank only free tap water.

Helen opened her sliding glass patio door and stepped into the warm, soft Florida night. She was immediately enveloped in a cloud of marijuana smoke from the apartment next door. Phil the invisible pothead lived next to Helen. She'd never seen him the whole time she'd lived there. In fact, she would not believe Phil existed if she didn't smell the pungent pot wafting through his jalousie doors.

The Coronado Tropic Apartments looked glamorous in the subtropic evening light. Margery and her long-dead husband built the apartments in 1949. The two-story Art Deco building had an exuberant S-curve. The sweeping lines were somewhat spoiled by the rusty, rattling air conditioners that stuck out of the windows like rude tongues. The Coronado was painted ice-cream white with turquoise trim and built around a turquoise-tiled swimming pool.

Cal was sitting on the edge of the pool, his pale Canadian legs dangling in the water. Helen liked it that Cal wore a clean white T-shirt. Too many men in Florida proudly displayed big hairy bellies.

Peggy, in 2B, was sitting next to Cal. Peggy was wearing a black one-piece suit and a green parrot on her shoulder. A live parrot with a pretty patch of gray feathers on his breast. Peggy never went anywhere without Pete, her Quaker parrot. She even took Pete to her office. Pets were strictly forbidden at the Coronado, so when Margery was around, everyone had to pretend Pete didn't exist. It wasn't easy. Pete let out the most ferocious squawks.

Since Margery was not there, Helen gently stroked the bird's soft feathers. The parrot danced back and forth on Peggy's shoulder, flapped his wings once, and settled down. Peggy did not. She grew increasingly agitated as she talked with Cal. "Don't blame me," she snapped. "I didn't vote for him."

"That could not happen in Canada," Cal said. "Our system of government would not permit it."

A voice on the other side of the bougainvillea said, "If Canada is such a great place, Cal, why aren't you there?"

Out stepped Margery, defender of America, in purple shorts and red toenails.

"Well?" she said. She folded her arms and waited for Cal's answer. Everyone knew Cal only went home to Toronto long enough to qualify for his free national health insurance. Then he returned to Florida.

"I never said America was bad," Cal said finally. "I said Canada did some things better."

"Squaaaak!" Pete said. Helen jumped. Everyone else politely ignored the parrot.

"Think I'll turn in," Cal said.

"Me, too," Helen said. She did not like the way Margery had treated Cal.

Helen and Cal walked back to their apartments, palm trees whispering behind their backs. Helen, who could always talk to Cal, suddenly felt shy. He seemed tongue-tied, too. Finally, he said, "Want to come in? I found some Molson's on sale."

"No, thanks," Helen said. "I'm tired, and I have to get up early for work tomorrow."

She studied his face in the fading light. Cal's lips were a little thin, and his nose was a little long to be truly handsome. But the gray eyes were intelligent. It was a strong face, she decided. Manly. His blond hair had gone to gray at the sideburns. It looked distinguished. His neck was just right, not too thick or too scrawny. His shoulders were muscular. She was afraid to consider anything lower. Helen felt too lonely. It had been a long time since she had been with a man, and her ex-husband had hurt her badly.

"Would you like to go to dinner this Saturday night?" Cal said.

Helen thought of Margery's warning.

"Yes, I would," she said, defiantly, as if Margery were listening. "I'd like that very much."

"Good," he said. "I was thinking ah-boot"—There. He'd said it again. Helen loved the way Cal pronounced that word.—"going to Cap's Place. It's an old Florida restaurant from the rum-running days. You can only reach it by boat."

"But you don't have a boat," Helen said.

"They'll send one to pick us up," Cal said.

Suddenly, Helen didn't feel tired at all. She felt like she was walking on richly scented clouds. Not all of those clouds were her neighbor Phil's pot smoke, either.

Chapter 4

On Friday, Helen met Christina's boyfriend, Joe.

She'd heard Christina talking to Joe on the phone almost daily at the store. Helen cringed every time she thought of those conversations. Christina's voice would get little-girl cute, and she'd say, "Whatever you want, Big Beary-Warey. I want what you want. No, no, you're the important one. My opinion doesn't matter. Now, what would you like for dinner?"

Ugh. It was pathetic, Helen thought. So 1950s. She couldn't understand how the clever Christina could abase herself for this man. She hoped he was worth it.

Helen didn't know much about Joe except he'd made a lot of money in real estate. Christina told her that he "owned a bunch of warehouses around Port Everglades," the major Lauderdale shipping area.

Christina was desperate to marry Joe. Helen knew she had a condo in low-rent Sunnysea Beach, but she spent most weekends with Joe in his five-bedroom mansion in Fort Lauderdale.

Ever since she moved in with Joe, Christina had expected an engagement ring. She thought she'd get one for Christmas. Now her birthday was coming up. Joe said he had to be in the Keys on business, but he promised to bring Christina a birthday present from Key West. He said it would be "special" and "just what she'd always wanted."

Joe was also stopping by that morning before he left for his trip. Christina was in a dither at this unusual honor. She'd changed into three outfits before she settled on a dramatic scoop-front, hot-pink Moschino number with purple Fendi mules. Helen thought the ensemble looked hookerish. It was the fashion mistake an unsure woman would make. Christina was not confident of her lover.

Christina kept looking out the front window until she spotted Joe's fire-engine red car as it went down Las Olas. "It's Joe's Ferrari!" she said, as excited as a teenager on her first date. In South Florida, when a man made a lot of new money, he either bought a hundred-foot yacht or a Ferrari.

"It's a Ferrari Barchetta," Christina said, as if that should mean something. When Helen didn't respond, she said, "There are only four hundred forty-eight in the whole world."

"Why did he drive by? There's valet parking right in front," Helen said.

"He likes to use the meters," Christina said. She sounded defensive.

A nickel squeezer, Helen thought. The guy's driving a Ferrari and saving five bucks on parking.

Christina ran to hit the buzzer, and Joe walked through the green door, a conquering hero holding his cell phone like a scepter. Dressed in black Hugo Boss, Joe looked like the high school bully all grown up. His dark wavy hair had a small, angry bald patch on the crown. His face was square and scowling. He had beefy shoulders and an aggressive walk.

Christina seemed to grow smaller around him. She fluttered about, kissing him, patting him, hugging him.

She introduced Helen, then said to Joe, "Do you like my outfit?"

"It's nice," he said indifferently. "But are you getting a gut?" Helen hadn't noticed it before, but Christina had a tiny bulge around the middle. Unfortunately, her revealing outfit showed it.

"Are you?" Helen said to Joe. She knew it was rude, but Helen couldn't stand the hurt look in Christina's eyes. Like a lot of powerful men in Lauderdale, Joe was overweight, but expected the women he dated to be rail-thin.

To her surprise, Joe laughed and patted his substantial stomach. "Yeah, honey, I am. Can't help it. It's generic."

He means genetic, Helen thought. I can't believe Christina wants to marry this dolt.

Joe stayed ten minutes and took three phone calls while he was there. Christina looked crestfallen when he left. "He didn't kiss me good-bye. Why didn't you tell me that the Moschino made me look fat?" she said to Helen.

"Because you don't look fat," Helen said.

But Christina would not be consoled. She weighed herself in the stockroom. "I've gained two pounds," she said tragically, as if announcing she had cancer.

Christina ate one plain rice cake for lunch and drank only water. She was determined to starve the two pounds off by the time Joe came back home.

"My gut is heinous," she said. *Heinous* was a favorite Juliana's word, usually applied to such tragedies as a pimple or a broken fingernail.

Christina took out her anger on the women trying to get into Juliana's. She rejected one because she had on a Tommy Hilfiger T-shirt and another because she wore gold moccasins. A third was refused for a fake Rolex, although how Christina could tell from so far away Helen did not know.

"And look at this one," Christina said, as she buzzed in a blonde with a Juliana's dress bag. "Melissa wants to return a dress. Guess she doesn't know about our policy."

Melissa was a little blonde with large implants, a small chin, and sexy, slightly popped, gray eyes. Her pale, aristocratic, oval face made her look like she'd stepped out of an eighteenth-century English painting, except the upper crust didn't show quite so much midriff back then.

Yesterday, Melissa bought a gold Armani evening gown that bared her bony back and shoulders. A day later, Melissa was bringing it back. The long black bag with Juliana's name in hot pink trailed behind her. Melissa's hair was sliding out of its French roll, and the gray eyes were slightly red. She looked like she'd had a late night.

"I'm returning this dress," Melissa said. "My boyfriend hates it."

The gown had been worn. Helen could see sweat stains under the armpits and makeup on the neckline. Melissa was trying an old retailing scam: you wore an expensive dress to some event, then returned it the next day.

"We have a one-return, no-return policy," Christina said.

"What's that mean?" Melissa said, with an imperious tone to match her aristocratic looks.

"You can return a dress once, but then you can never return."

Melissa looked shocked. Her pale oval face went a shade whiter. She had to make a quick decision. An Armani gown was major money. Melissa would either lose several thousand dollars now or her entrée to Juliana's forever.

"I . . . I think I could persuade him to change his mind," Melissa said. The aristocrat, suddenly humbled, picked the bag off the counter.

"A smart woman knows how to tell a man what to think," Christina said.

Then why did Joe think you were fat? Helen wondered.

As soon as Melissa left, Christina began agonizing again about her weight. "Do I look fat in this outfit, Helen? Is it just my gut that's fat, or am I putting weight on my butt, too? Is that cellulite on my thighs? Do you see any cellulite? Tell me the truth, now." When Helen couldn't take any more, she fled to the back room, saying she had to make a personal phone call.

Helen rummaged in her unfashionably large purse until she found her Filofax and looked up Sarah's home phone number. Helen had rented Sarah's old apartment at the Coronado. They'd met when she was shown the apartment and hit it off instantly. Sarah had left her a meal in the fridge on moving day, a gesture Helen appreciated. They'd promised to get together but never did. Now she owed Sarah an apology for not opening the green door yesterday.

Helen left a message on Sarah's machine and hoped she would call back.

Thank God, two favorites came in that afternoon to distract Christina: Brittney and Tiffany. There were no other customers for almost an hour. The women lounged on the black loveseats, talking like girls at a pajama party about clothes and boyfriends. Juliana's women always had boyfriends, never lovers.

Brittney, the woman who could not frown, wore an ice-blue pantsuit that made her sapphire-blue eyes hypnotic. Her matching sapphire-studded Rolex was pretty hypnotic, too.

Tiffany was the woman with the bad eye job. She did look permanently startled, Helen thought, but it was cute on her. Tiffany reminded Helen of Bambi caught in the headlights. She wore a candy-pink pants outfit with frothy ruffles down the front and around the hips. Her platinum hair looked like spun sugar and her lips were cherry red. Her implants bulged out of her blouse. Tiffany's elderly boyfriend had paid for her D cups, she'd told Helen last week, because "he liked to get his hands on his money."

"You look just like Jayne Mansfield," Helen said.

"Whoth that?" Tiffany said, looking adorably blank.

"A movie star," Helen said.

"Thath nithe," Tiffany said, looking pleased. "What movieth hath thee been in?"

"None any more," Christina said. "She's dead. And why are you lisping?"

"Juth had my tongue pierthed," Tiffany said, and stuck out her tongue to reveal a gold stud. "I thould talk fine in a day or two."

Helen was repulsed. "Why would you want your tongue pierced?" she said.

Brittney snorted Evian water through her nose. Christina rolled her eyes. Helen knew she'd said something hopelessly Midwestern. Only Tiffany took her question seriously.

"The oral thex ith fantathtic," she said, and giggled.

"What?" Helen said.

"She says the oral sex is fantastic," Brittney said.

Tiffany giggled again. "No, my boyfriend thayth that."

Then they all shrieked with laughter like schoolgirls. Helen was actually wiping tears from her eyes. It felt good to laugh this hard. She loved this store. She had to be wrong about Christina skimming money. She had to be.

"Speaking of boyfriends, how's Joe?" Brittney said in that soft, sighing voice, and Helen could feel the mood shift.

"He won't be in town for my birthday. He has to go to the Keys. But we're going clubbing when he gets back."

"Which ones?" Brittney said. "Kiss? Tantra? Rain? I hope he takes you to Mynt. It's the prettiest. They pipe scents like sage and mint through the air conditioner. Did I tell you I saw Queen Latifah there one night? And the Backstreet Boys? Of course Bash is reopening. That might be fun. I partied there one night with Sean Penn."

But Christina knew how to yank the spotlight back. "I was there the night Leonardo DiCaprio whipped off his shirt and danced on a speaker," she said. "*Titanic* had just opened and it was huge."

"Titanic, even," Helen said. Everyone ignored her.

"But that's not the best part. Joe has promised to bring me something special," Christina said. Her voice was too neutral.

"Oooh," Tiffany said. "Ith thith the ring at latht?"

"I hope so. But I'd settle for a tennis bracelet."

"You would not. You want the ring," Brittney said.

Christina nodded. "I've waited long enough," she said. "This is put-up or shut-up time. I'm almost forty. I want to be married."

"It's overrated," Helen said. "I was married for seventeen years."

"Divorced is better than never being married," Christina said. "At least some man wanted you enough to stand up at an altar and say so. No one's ever wanted me that way."

"They juth want uth every other way," Tiffany said, and it sounded sadder with her lisp.

"But not when we're old and wrinkled. Not forever," Brittney said in that caressing whisper, and for once Helen could see the emotion in her beautiful expressionless face.

"It wasn't forever," Helen said. "It was only for seventeen years."

"That's forever for us," she sighed. In seventeen years, Brittney would be beyond the help of any Brazilian doctor.

It wasn't true that no man wanted to marry them, Helen

thought. Lots of interesting, honorable men would want them for their brides. But it was true that no super-rich man would marry them. Helen felt sorry for these waiflike women. She knew they were in a trap of their own devising, but it was still a lonely one. She was relieved when the doorbell rang, and she didn't have to answer Brittney.

Christina looked up. "It's Venetia."

"I have to go. I can't stand that woman," Brittney said.

"Me either," Tiffany said.

Venetia was even thinner than most of Juliana's women. She looked like an articulated skeleton in a Chanel suit. When she stretched out her hand to examine a shirt, Helen thought she could count all twenty-six bones. Venetia's wrist was a collection of knobs. She had a strange, jittery way of moving and an odd dirty look to her skin. Helen was glad that Venetia ignored her.

"I want one of your special purses," she said to Christina, "and I want it now." Her voice was harsh and high.

"I have a lovely little beaded 1920s number."

"Fine. Get it. Right now," Venetia ordered.

While she waited for Christina to return, the stick woman bounced impatiently up and down on one foot, twirled her hair, scratched her arm. Venetia made Helen so nervous that she moved to the mahogany sideboard and started folding a sweater that did not need folding. It was cashmere, light and luxurious. Just touching it was a pleasure, so Helen folded and refolded it while she waited for Christina to return.

Christina had a sideline selling evening purses that she bought at rummage sales and antique shops. She cleaned their delicate silver clasps, restored their beading, and put in new silk linings. They were collectibles. They must be addictive, Helen thought. Some women came in two or three times a month for Christina's purses. Helen could see why. She'd collect them if she had the money. They were miniature works of art.

The women always paid cash, and Helen figured Christina must have some deal with the store owner, where Mr. Roget got a cut. She kept the purses on a special shelf high in the stockroom, so they wouldn't get mixed up with the regular stock.

Christina came out carrying an exquisite little black beaded number with a pink heart in the center and an ornate silver clasp.

"Let me see the inside," Venetia said.

"It's pink silk," Christina said. "The clasp is tricky. I'll open it for you."

But Venetia impatiently ripped the purse from Christina's hands. It flew open, and brightly colored candies scattered all over the carpet.

No, wait. That wasn't candy, Helen thought. Those were pills and capsules. Oh God. Drugs. That's what was in the special purses. She didn't want to see this.

Helen picked up the sweater and, hugging it like a teddy bear, she carried it to the stockroom and stayed there.

What was Christina doing? Helen asked herself. Does she think I'm so stupid I won't notice she is selling drugs and skimming money?

Exactly, Helen decided. I am naive about things like tongue piercing. But I worked in a corporation for twenty years. I know a crook when I see one.

In a way, Helen didn't blame Christina. The head saleswoman made thousands for Juliana's cheap owner and was paid only eighteen thousand a year, plus a miserly commission. There was no way anyone could live well on that money. Not the way Christina had to dress for this job.

Helen would have to make some decisions. Should she say something to the store owner about Christina's drug dealing? He should know if illegal activities were going on in his store. But what if Mr. Roget was getting a cut on the sale of the purses' contents? The store owner hung onto his nickels. Did he love money enough to turn a blind eye to drug sales in his own store? He had the perfect excuse if Christina was caught: he was far away, in another country. How could he know what was going on?

What about an anonymous call to the police? Another bad idea. If her boss was caught dealing, Helen's reputation could be ruined, too. If Juliana's was ever raided, Helen's name could wind up in the newspapers, and that would be a disaster. She had to start looking for another job.

When Helen finally came out of the stockroom, Venetia was gone. Helen's foot crunched on something, and she picked it up. It was a pill about the size of an aspirin, but yellow. It had a designer logo.

Even Helen knew what Ecstasy looked like.

Chapter 5

"Joe's back!" Christina crowed when Helen came into work the next day. "He says he has my birthday present, and he wants to give it to me tonight. We're doing the South Beach clubs first, then going to his house for my present. He says he has something I'll love forever. It's a ring. I know it."

Helen had never seen Christina look so pretty. Her face seemed lighted from within. The deep lines around her mouth were almost erased. Her hair shone like burnished gold.

"Joe's going to pick me up after work," she said. "In a limo!" She was beside herself with excitement.

Helen hoped that Joe really was going to give Christina a ring. It would solve everything. The head saleswoman would marry her rich man and live happily ever after. She wouldn't have to skim money or sell drugs. Helen wouldn't have to worry about finding another job. She could stay at Juliana's.

When she went out for lunch, Helen saw a flyer on a telephone pole that said "WANTED: WOMEN 21 TO 65! Earn $35 an hour. No experience necessary." Helen called the number. A bar on East Sample Road was looking for lingerie models.

"I'm Frank, the owner," he said. His voice oozed out of the phone like oil. Snake oil. "Our customers ain't the youngest, you get my drift. Age ain't a problem, long as you got yourself a good figure and big boobs. Forty's young to them. They don't mind a good-looking granny. Like 'em better than the young stuff, sometimes. Your older gal appreciates the attention and ain't so inhibited, you know what I mean?"

Helen hung up the phone while Frank was still oozing. Once again she felt the Greek diner owner's gut bump against her and his hairy paws on her chest and shuddered. Helen wanted this evening with Joe to succeed almost as much as Christina did.

When the store closed at six that night, Christina was waiting for Joe at the green door.

She was wearing a short black Gucci dress that managed to bare lots of skin and still look sophisticated instead of trampy. Her legs were impossibly long in her sleek Charles Jourdan heels. Her blonde hair was pulled into a low knot. Christina looked confident and ready for her brilliant future.

"How do I look?" she asked Helen.

"Stunning," Helen said.

"Do you think he'll like it?" Christina said, and twirled gracefully. Do you think he'll like me, was the unspoken question.

"He'd be a fool not to," Helen said. But she thought Joe was a fool.

Joe's limousine was a black Mercedes superstretch. The driver opened the door for Christina, and she looked so happy, Helen was afraid for her. The last thing she saw, before the limousine door closed with an expensive *chunk!* were Christina's long, slender legs sliding across the black leather upholstery. They looked white and vulnerable.

Helen hoped that Joe wouldn't disappoint Christina again. She resolved not to say anything to Christina tomorrow, no matter how great her curiosity. She would wait for Christina to tell her.

Helen couldn't spend any more time thinking about Christina. She had her own date with Cal that night. He was picking her up at seven. She was as excited and hopeful as a teenager. Helen tried on six outfits and four pairs of shoes before deciding on a slim black pantsuit and flat strappy sandals. She was determined to look graceful when she climbed into the boat.

She wondered if she should bring some money. Would they split the tab, or would Cal pay for their meal? She didn't know how dating worked any more, but she was not going to ask the women at Juliana's. Helen didn't want their men or their lives.

Money is power, woman, she told herself. Give yourself some. She boldly pulled a hundred dollars out of Chocolate the bear and stuffed it into her little black purse.

Cal showed up at her door in South Florida formalwear: long khaki pants and a blue cotton shirt open at the collar and rolled up at the sleeves. Helen was a sucker for rolled sleeves.

"You look lovely," Cal said, and Helen glowed. It had been a long time since a man had admired her.

"You look pretty good yourself," she said, and felt shy again.

The drive to Lighthouse Point took almost an hour in Cal's dented Buick. On the way, Cal entertained her with stories of his marathon drives from Toronto to Florida, his daughter the marketing expert, and his grandchild, the world's most brilliant two-year-old.

"How long have you been divorced?" she said, finally.

"Almost fifteen years. My ex-wife is a fine woman."

"You don't sound bitter," Helen said.

"I'm not. The divorce was my own fault. I was at the office until late every night, and she found someone else."

Helen was silent for a moment. "What are you thinking?" Cal said.

"How nice it is that you got over your wife. There's nothing worse than spending an evening with the undivorced."

"Are they like the undead?" Cal said.

"Exactly," Helen said. "Like the undead, the undivorced are in a state neither dead nor alive. They're obsessed with their exes and spend the whole evening describing their faults and draining the life out of you."

"You haven't mentioned your ex-husband. I gather you're over him?"

"Yes," Helen said, so abruptly it cut the conversation like

an ax blade. There was an awkward silence until Cal said,
"Here's the parking lot for Cap's."

Cal parked, and they walked a short distance to the dock.
The waterway was lined with high-priced, low-slung homes
and boats that were bigger and whiter than the Coronado
Tropic Apartments. But Helen saw no sign of the restaurant,
and there was no attendant or phone on the deserted dock.

"How does Cap's know we're here?" Helen said.

"They always do," Cal said. "I see the boat now." He
pointed toward an open motor launch heading their way.

"It looks like the *African Queen*," Helen said, as she
climbed into the boat. She admired the open boat's beauti-
fully polished wood. On the short ride to the restaurant, Cal
pointed out the old black lighthouse that gave the point its
name. He ignored the tip jar. Maybe he was supposed to.
Helen didn't know the tipping custom for boats that took
you to a restaurant.

All too soon, the boat docked, and they walked up the
path to the long gray restaurant. Helen saw the waterline on
the building's side from a long-ago flood. A rotund yellow
cat greeted them at the entrance.

"I wonder if Kitty got that fat on Cap's food?" Cal said.
Helen thought it was nice that he stopped to pet the cat.

Helen liked everything about Cap's: its timeworn wood,
the bare yellow light bulbs in white porcelain sockets, even
the sound her sandals made on the uneven floors. She examined the photos of Floridians from around 1900, young
men fishing in heavy wool suits. "How could they stand
those clothes down here?" she asked Cal.

She'd never had salad with fresh hearts of palm before.
She liked its odd nutty taste. She had the pecan-crusted
mahi-mahi. Cal had the blackened grouper. They both ordered Key lime pie.

When the check came, Cal presented it to her with a
flourish. "You pick up this one," he said. "The next dinner
is on me. I'll take you to another Florida favorite, Catfish
Dewey's. I have to be in Tampa all week. Could you go next
Saturday?"

Helen was so surprised, she agreed. Good thing she'd
brought that hundred bucks. The dinner cost seventy-two

dollars. She couldn't afford it, but she was tired of worrying about money. It had been a wonderful evening.

"Maybe I'm the tightwad," she told herself. But another part answered, "Cal was supposed to buy the dinner. He invited you. Remember what Margery said about never going to dinner with him?"

Cap's boat brought them back by moonrise. The black waterway was sliced by the blinding white, rotating, lighthouse beam. The wedding cake yachts were lighted now. The interiors were molten gold against the dark velvet sky, but Helen saw no people inside.

Helen shivered in the chill night air. Cal put his arm around her, but she still felt cold.

On Monday morning, Helen didn't have to ask how the evening went. Christina's face said it all. She looked tired and old. Her hair was limp and unwashed. She had an ugly zit on her chin. She had no ring on her finger.

Christina slammed down the phone on a good customer. She broke a nail. She yelled at the florist that the flowers weren't fresh enough. And she rejected one would-be customer after another, like a Roman empress sending slaves to their deaths. Their fatal fashion errors ranged from cheap shoes to bad pants. Helen prayed for the day to be over. She was afraid no one would get into Juliana's today.

But Brittney wafted through the green door at eleven, looking gorgeous in a red floral Diane vonFurstenberg dress and incredibly high Sergio Rossi heels. She put her dainty foot right in her pretty pink mouth.

"So, what was the surprise from Key West?" Brittney said in that caressing whisper. "Did Joe give you a ring? A tennis bracelet?"

"A goddamn cat," Christina snarled. "All that for a fucking cat."

Helen had never heard Christina use those words before.

"But you like cats," Brittney said. "You've been saying you wanted one for months."

"And Joe's been saying he's going to get me a ring for months. Instead I got a counterfeit cat."

"It's not a real cat?" Brittney looked confused. Helen did, too.

"Of course it's real. But the dumb shit thought he was buying me a real Hemingway cat. You know about them?"

Helen and Brittney both shook their heads no.

"Ernest Hemingway had a bunch of six-toed cats at his house in Key West. The house is a museum now, and their descendants are still at the Hemingway Home. Those cats live like kings. They're a tourist attraction.

"Joe paid fifty bucks to a guy in a Key West bar who supposedly sold him a real Hemingway cat. But the Hemingway cats aren't for sale. The Hemingway Home doesn't adopt out the kittens, either. I knew that. Everyone knew that except Joe, who was so stupid he bought a cat in a bar. I told him he was an idiot. I was so pissed, I grabbed the cat and left. Now I'm stuck with this counterfeit six-toed cat."

"It could still be a real Hemingway cat," Brittney said. "Maybe it's one who climbed over the fence to meet her boyfriend."

"Then she got screwed and abandoned, too," Christina said. Tears glittered in her eyes.

"There, there, baby, don't cry," Brittney cooed. "You'll get wrinkles. No man is worth that. I know you like cats. You've probably fallen in love with this one already. I bet you even have some pictures to show us."

"Well, a few Polaroids," Christina said, sniffling.

She pulled two out of her purse. At first Helen thought Christina was showing her a picture of a plush toy. The cat had a cuddly body that made her want to pick him up and hug him. His golden-green eyes were wise. His gray striped tail was majestic. The cat's dignified manner contrasted with his comical fur coat. His gray tabby stripes were interrupted by big white patches, like blank spaces.

Then Helen saw the paws. That cat had the biggest front feet Helen had ever seen on any cat anywhere. On the front paws, the sixth toe stuck out like the thumb on a mitten.

"Those are the famous six toes," Christina said. "I'm calling him Thumbs."

"Big Foot would be more like it," Helen said, then regretted it.

"He's adorable," Brittney squealed. "I love him. I wish I had him."

"You do?" Christina said, surprised.

"I'll give you a hundred bucks for Thumbs," Brittney said.

"He's not for sale," Christina said.

"Two hundred," Brittney said, briskly upping the bidding.

"Nope," Christina said.

"I'll give you five hundred," Brittney said. "Cash."

"I'll get your five hundred some other way," Christina said, rather nastily. "I'm keeping this cat."

Helen wondered if Brittney had staged the cat auction to make Christina feel better. Or did this absolutely perfect female fall in love at first sight with the oddly imperfect feline?

For whatever reason, Christina now wanted Thumbs. "He's the only man I'm sleeping with now," she joked, "and he's always faithful."

That relationship would outlast Christina's romance with Joe. Christina couldn't stop seething over her disappointing evening. The more she talked it over with Brittney, the more determined she was to end it.

"I'm dumping that man," she told Brittney. "I can't wait any longer. It's time I found someone who wants to marry me. I'm telling him tonight."

Maybe Christina secretly hoped Joe would apologize and promise to marry her. Or maybe she wanted to dump him first, before he dumped her. But Christina didn't even get that pleasure. Joe broke off their relationship—by cell phone—before noon. He told her good-bye. Christina told him to take a flying leap. It was a sad and sorry end to her hopes of yesterday.

Now all Christina wanted was revenge.

"I still have Joe's Neiman Marcus charge card," Christina said. "I'm going to call and charge a diamond tennis bracelet. I'll get it one way or the other."

" 'Diamonds are a girl's best friend,' " Brittney whispered. Helen thought she sounded a lot like Lorelei Lee, the character who first said those words.

Christina didn't score the tennis bracelet. The crafty Joe had canceled that card.

"I've got one Joe doesn't know I have," Christina said. "It's an old MasterCard. He thinks it was maxed out. But I know it still has two thousand dollars left. I was saving it for a rainy day. Well, it's pouring now."

"You go, girl," Brittney said.

As a test, Christina tried for a five-hundred-dollar cash advance at the ATM across the street. She came back waving the money triumphantly.

"The spree is on. I have fifteen hundred left," she said. "Now we have to decide how to spend it fast."

"That won't get you a decent tennis bracelet. Or even any serious clothes," Brittney said sadly.

"I'm spending this on something more lasting than clothes," Christina said.

Good, thought Helen. Finally, a sensible decision. "You could get a computer for that," she said.

"Waste of time," Christina said.

"Staring at the screen gives you heinous wrinkles," Brittney said.

"I know! I'll spend Joe's money on my biopolymer treatments. I'll have Doctor Mariposa fill in all my wrinkles. Joe can buy me a new man."

"Brilliant!" Brittney said.

Dumb, Helen thought.

She listened distractedly as Christina called the doctor and made an appointment.

Brittney applauded. Helen was appalled. She'd learned a little more about biopolymer injections since she'd first met Brittney. They'd been featured in a TV exposé. "You don't want to do that," Helen said. "That stuff is illegal. The doctor is injecting liquid silicone right into your face. If your body rejects it, you'll have these lumps on your face. Haven't you seen the stories about it on TV? It left those women horribly disfigured."

"It worked for me," Brittney said with a seductive hiss, like the snake in the Garden of Eden. Her flawless face was

Christina's temptation. She wanted to look as young and beautiful as Brittney.

"You are lucky, Brittney," Helen said.

"So am I," Christina said, defiantly. But Helen knew she was not.

Chapter 6

The rest of the afternoon, Christina and Brittney plotted revenge against Joe. The two women huddled on the black love seats like sorceresses casting spells, furious and beautiful and frightening. If Joe, or any other man, had walked into the store, they would have torn him apart with their teeth and nails.

At least they can't turn Joe into a toad, Helen thought. He already is one.

Helen didn't want to listen to their plots. But their soft, insinuating whispers were somehow louder than ordinary conversation. Helen caught about every third sentence, no matter how much she tried to block it out.

She heard them say, "Turn him into the IRS . . . reward . . . How about Immigration? No, not them. Bad idea. . . . Some guys in Miami would like to know what he's up to, though, and they aren't as nice as the IRS. . . . Brittney, what about your old boyfriend, Vinnie? . . . When I finish, Joe will wish he was never born."

Helen wished a customer would come in, but no one did. She wished the phone would ring. That wish was granted. Even better, the caller was Sarah, the woman Christina had declared too fat to enter Juliana's.

"I'm sorry I didn't get back with you sooner," Sarah said. "I was on vacation at Atlantis in the Bahamas."

"Very chic. Also, very expensive. Did your boyfriend take you?"

"What boyfriend?" Sarah said. "I took myself. I met a guy while I was there, though."

"Anything serious?"

"No, thank God."

Juliana's world of desperate, dependent women fell away. Helen was talking with a working woman now. This was her world, and she knew the rules.

"If you can afford Atlantis, you must be doing well," Helen said. "Where are you working?"

"It would take too long to explain. Why don't you come to my place on the beach for dinner tonight?"

"I'd love to, but my car's in the shop," Helen lied. She was too proud to admit she didn't have the money to fix it.

"Then I'll pick you up after work," Sarah said. "I'm doing research at the downtown library this afternoon. I can swing by Juliana's on my way home. I'll fix dinner. Nothing fancy. Do you like Florida lobsters?"

"Love them," Helen said. "I think they're tastier than Maine lobsters. What can I bring?"

"Just yourself."

Helen walked over by the Federal Highway and spent her lunch money buying flowers from the young Cuban woman who sold roses and sunflowers on the street corner. She'd fill up on rice cakes.

At six that night, Sarah pulled in front of Juliana's in her new green Range Rover and honked. Helen ran out with her flowers. She invited Sarah inside, but was relieved when her friend said no. Helen didn't want to argue with the witchy Christina about the fat and unfashionable.

Sarah lived in Hollywood, a beach town between Fort Lauderdale and Miami. Hollywood Beach was lost in the Fifties. The beach was lined with pastel two-story motels and tiny Deco beach houses. Sarah lived next to the Bel-Aire Beach Motel in a five-story condo right on the ocean.

The condo was pretty, but the ocean view was stunning. The turquoise-blue ocean melted into the deeper blue sky streaked cerise and gold by the sunset. The sunset turned the sand a golden pink.

The beach was nearly empty. But below Sarah's deck was a wide strip of asphalt with a continual parade of people. "They are my entertainment," Sarah said. "It's better than TV."

While Sarah and Helen ate chilled lobsters and salad on the deck, they saw a man ride by on a fat-tired bicycle, a big blue macaw sitting solemnly on his handle bars. He was followed by a woman in a motorized wheelchair, sailing majestically down the boardwalk. Her black-and-white Boston terrier stood in the front of the vehicle like a figurehead on a ship. A Cuban family giggled and ate drippy ice-cream cones. Roller bladers in black spandex skated around children on scooters.

"This is charming," Helen said. "And there's not a liposuction or a facelift in the bunch."

"Not around here," Sarah said, patting her generous tummy. A charm bracelet jingled cheerfully on her shapely wrist. "Want to go for a walk after dinner?"

They joined the throng, passing dozens of little restaurants: Angelo's Corner, Ocean Alley, and Istanbul, a Turkish restaurant.

At a T-shirt shop, they read the shirt slogans. "We divorced for religious reasons. My husband thought he was God," one said.

"That describes my ex," Sarah said.

"Mine thought he was the devil in bed," Helen said. "I came home from work early one afternoon and caught him with our next-door neighbor. Right in the act."

"That must have been awful."

"It was. I never realized Rob had such a hairy butt," Helen said.

"I hope you screwed him back in the divorce," Sarah said.

"I just wanted to get away from him," Helen said, truthfully. "Listen, I need to apologize about what happened at Juliana's last week. There was no excuse. It was rude."

"It wasn't your fault. I know the store doesn't want a large woman like me in there," Sarah said. "I'm bad for Juliana's image." Helen looked at her curly-haired friend in her cool white linen jacket and felt worse.

"That's stupid. I'm sorry."

"Don't be," Sarah said. "It's not important to me. I heard you were working there, and I wanted to stop by and say hello."

"So what do you do these days?" Helen asked. They'd talked too much about her.

"As little as possible," Sarah said, and grinned.

"No, seriously."

"I live on the beach. I made some money in investments, and I don't have to work fulltime. I take a few consulting jobs when I feel like it. But I'll never have to wear pantyhose again. And you know what? I don't miss the office one bit. I originally moved to Florida to take care of my mother. She had cancer. I nursed her for two years. She died in February of 2000."

"I'm sorry," Helen said.

"I am, too. I miss Mom. When she passed away, she left me some property, including this condo. I wanted to live here, but her tenant's lease wasn't up until last month."

"So that's why you left the Coronado," Helen said.

"Yeah, I liked it there, but I wanted my own place. I sold Mom's other property and sank the money into Krispy Kreme stock."

"Doughnuts?"

"I love those suckers. You can tell that by looking at me," Sarah said. "When I bought it, all the financial advisors said that Krispy Kreme was expected to be a poor performer, but I thought anything that good was sure to succeed. I put all my inheritance into Krispy Kreme stock. Bought it at the IPO price of twenty-one dollars."

"Did you just say *IPO*?" Helen said. "The women I hang around with now think that's a French designer."

"Nope, it was a tasty deal," Sarah said. "Stock shot up like a rocket. I sold it when it hit sixty dollars a share. That was a good time to get out. It started tumbling soon after. I kept a few shares for sentimental reasons. Then I took most of that money and sank it into adult diaper stock."

"From doughnuts to diapers? Why?" Helen said. "That's a weird choice."

"Not at all. When my mother was sick, I couldn't get this

one brand, because it was so popular. I had friends on the lookout for it all over the country. They would ship it to me, I figured anything so in demand was only going to go up. Besides, none of us boomers are getting any younger. Adult diapers are a growth industry. So I bought diaper stock and made more money. Then I sold it again.

"I only bought companies I liked—and sold what I didn't. It was such a satisfying way to do business. When my old ink-jet printer died, I bought this highly recommended laser printer. It was a turkey. I was on the phone all day, arguing with customer service. I sold that stock the next day. Good thing, too. The company announced major lay-offs a month later, and that stock went down the tube."

"They all went down the tube after September eleventh," Helen said, with a sigh.

"I was mostly out of the market by then and into nice, safe T-bonds," Sarah said. "I hope you weren't caught in the crash."

"I had airline stock," Helen said. "And Enron."

"Oh," Sarah said. There was nothing else to say. Helen didn't mention that the stock market crash made it hard for her to pay her lawyer. That's where most of her money went—to the man who abandoned her in court.

The two women watched a father and his son fly a dragon kite on the sand. Some college kids were playing Ultimate Loop Frisbee.

"So you owe this fabulous life on the beach to Krispy Kreme doughnuts?"

"That's right," Sarah said. They looked at the sea and sunset. The evening clouds were whipped-cream mounds tinged with lavender. The air smelled of salt and coconut suntan oil.

"All this talk of Krispy Kreme is making me hungry," Sarah said. "Want to go on a doughnut expedition?"

"Sure! Let's make you richer," Helen said.

Imagine, someone who didn't agonize about eating a doughnut, Helen thought. She had to get out of that store and spend more time with normal people. She wasn't sure the Coronado crowd counted.

The closest Krispy Kreme was twenty minutes away. As

Sarah's Range Rover pulled into the lot, the neon sign was flashing.

"Fresh doughnuts!" Sarah said. They raced for the store, laughing all the way. Inside, Helen breathed in the sugary, grease-perfumed air. They ordered a dozen glazed and ripped open the box in the parking lot. When Helen bit into the first warm glazed doughnut, she said, "I've died and gone to heaven."

"So what's it like working with Charlie's Angels?" Sarah said, through a mouthful of doughnut. "How can a smart woman like you stand those bimbos?"

"They're not bimbos," Helen said, wondering why she was defending them. "That's the sad part. They're smart. I would have hired any of them at my old company. The problem is they don't value their intelligence, and neither do their boyfriends. Beauty and money are the only standards that count. In their world, Albert Einstein would be pitied as a guy with a permanent bad hair day."

Both women reached for another doughnut. "OK, they're not stupid," Sarah said between bites. "They're shallow, which is worse. You're too smart for them, Helen. Let me make some phone calls. I know several companies that would love to hire someone like you."

"No!" Helen said, hoping she didn't sound as panicky as she felt. She couldn't work for a corporation. The court would find her for sure. She could never tell Sarah why. Instead, she gave her another half-truth.

"I'm burnt out," she said. "I hit my head hard on the glass ceiling at my old job. I was sick of the pointless meetings and memos. I'd rather work at Juliana's. Except something odd is going on there."

Sarah was a good listener, or maybe Helen was high on sugar and grease after rice cakes, the only snacks Christina allowed in the store. By the fourth doughnut, Helen was talking about Christina's suspected skimming and the purse full of pills.

At the half-dozen mark, Sarah looked serious. "Helen, something is way off in that store. You've got to get out of there. You saw that woman skim thirteen hundred dollars in one day."

"But I'm not sure I saw anything. That's the problem," Helen said, waving a half-eaten glazed. "I have no proof. Maybe Christina saw Lauren shoplift that blouse and belt and I didn't. Maybe there's some FedEx rate I don't know about."

"And maybe she's selling candy in those purses," Sarah said. "Bull. You're a numbers hound. If you could figure out actuarial tables, you can spot a scam. You may not know about implants and eye jobs, but you know Christina is crooked. She's skimming and dealing drugs. You'd better get yourself a new job."

"Why? What's the use?" Helen said, hopelessly. "The only job I could find that paid anything was a lingerie model in a geezer bar. The good jobs are rare. They have so many people after them, I don't have a chance.

"I guess I need to try harder, but I can't seem to get up the energy to look for another job on my day off. I'm tired all the time. I have to stand all day. My feet hurt and my back hurts. When I get home, I just want to go to bed." She downed another doughnut for comfort.

"I said I'd help you find a better one," Sarah said, chomping yet another Krispy Kreme. Helen backpedaled furiously, while reaching for one more glazed doughnut. The dozen seemed to be disappearing fast, but Helen could not remember how many she'd eaten.

"I'm just whining," she said. "I really don't want to go back to an office. Juliana's pays the rent. The work isn't that bad. At least I don't have to say, 'You want fries with that?'" It was hard to say with a mouth full of doughnut.

Sarah did not laugh. Instead, she dropped her doughnut and fixed Helen with her serious deep brown stare. "Listen to me, Helen. Christina is ripping off some rich, powerful people. They won't take it kindly if they find out what she's doing. She's mixing sex, money, and male egos. Mark my words: Murder's next."

"That's ridiculous," Helen said. "I appreciate your concern, but you've had too much sun." She reached for another glazed doughnut. They were all gone.

Sarah would not hear of Helen taking a cab home. She drove Helen to the Coronado.

As Helen settled into her creaky bed, she decided she liked Sarah a lot. But the woman had a melodramatic streak. Murder at Juliana's, indeed. Christina would wear flip-flops first.

The next day, Helen heard Christina plotting a murder. For a lot of money.

Chapter 7

Niki was the first person at the green door that morning, her long brown hair waving in the breeze like a dark banner. She was beautiful, but Juliana's was used to beautiful women. Niki's beauty was in her perfection. Her eyes and her lips and her cheekbones looked sculpted and covered with skin as unblemished as acrylic. She was the perfect high school cheerleader, all grown up.

A man walking by in ugly plaid shorts stared at the beautiful Niki so hard he tripped and fell against a parked Porsche. The outraged owner gave the bedazzled man the finger.

Niki looked luminous in the sunlight, the perfect advertisement for Juliana's. Even at a distance, Helen recognized Niki's white silk Joop halter top, tight white Dolce & Gabbana pants, and gold-trimmed D&G mules.

Christina buzzed Niki into the shop. She wafted in on a cloud of perfume so strong, it made Helen's eyes water.

"In that outfit you look positively bridal," Christina said. "How's Jimmy? Are you here to buy more things for your wedding?"

"What wedding?" Niki said, and burst into tears.

"There, there, sweetie, it will be OK," Christina said, and put her arms around Niki. They were both so thin, they looked like a pile of broomsticks.

"It won't be OK," Niki said. "The wedding's off. All because of that bitch Desiree."

"The skinny blonde chick with the fat lips?" Christina said, handing her a tissue. "She's had so much collagen, she looks like Daisy Duck."

Niki only sobbed harder and blew her perfect little nose. "That's what makes it so awful, Christina. I've done everything right, and then she comes along with those stupid lips and outsize tits, and he falls for her. It isn't fair!"

Niki's own chest implants were impressive. Desiree's mammaries must be mountainous, Helen thought.

Niki tried to stop crying, but she couldn't. She seemed to be in real pain as she told her story. The perfume cloud covered her like a pall.

"I just found out about them last night. Jimmy told me he had to work late. I could have gone to dinner with my girlfriends, but I stayed home, gave myself an herbal mask, and went to bed early. One of our friends called this morning. She said she saw Jimmy and Desiree dancing together at our club. She said everyone saw them."

Some friend, Helen thought.

"I called Jimmy at work," Niki said. "He didn't even bother to lie. He says he's going to marry the bitch. We were supposed to go to a party at the Bee Gees' place on Star Island."

"Which Bee Gee?" Helen said, star struck.

"Robin, I think. Not Barry. And Maurice is dead. It was going to be fabulous. Now he's taking her."

"Oh, sweetie, that's so terrible," Christina said. Niki cried harder. Christina handed her another tissue. Her grief seemed to intensify the perfume until it was almost liquid.

"Jimmy says I can keep the condo in the Towers and the ring, but he wants his freedom."

He bought his freedom at a high price, Helen thought. Condos in the Towers started at one million, and that ring had a rock the size of Delaware. Little jilted Niki would be well fixed.

"He doesn't mean it," Christina soothed. "You've been engaged for four years. This is just a passing fling. Nervous

bridegrooms do dumb things. Jimmy will get tired of Desiree and come back to you."

"He won't," Niki sobbed, and Helen had never heard
such despair. "She's younger than me. She's blond."

"She's bleached," Christina said. "Anyone can be blond
these days."

Helen thought this jab at Desiree was unfair, since
Christina owed her own blondness to the bottle.

"She's never done anything. I've been in *Playboy*," Niki
said proudly, and sat up straight, so that her imposing implants stuck out farther. The movement unleashed another
choking cloud of perfume.

"That's how you and Jimmy first met, wasn't it?"
Christina said.

"Yes," Niki said. "He saw my picture in *Playboy*. He remembered it for six whole months. He recognized me at a
South Beach club and introduced himself."

Helen hoped it was her face Jimmy recognized.

"It was love at first sight. Jimmy was so proud of me.
When we started dating, he bought a hundred copies of my
Playboy issue and gave them to all his friends and business
associates."

To show them what he was getting, Helen thought.

"That's how his wife found out about us. She saw the bill
for all those back issues on his credit card. She was so mad.
She said she'd take him to the cleaners. Poor Jimmy had to
hide things offshore and everything. The divorce took four
years. I went through hell. Now he's marrying that bitch on
the beach in Belize next month."

"I hope the sharks get her," Christina said.

"I want her dead before that," Niki said, her eyes suddenly hard mean slits.

"Don't you want *him* dead?" Christina said. Good question, thought Helen. That's who I'd want to kill if Jimmy
dumped me right before the wedding.

"No, I want her dead," Niki said. Her words were a vi-
cious slash. "Maybe when she's dead, he'll come back to
me."

Niki wrapped her pipestem arms around herself and
rocked back and forth, spotting the black silk-satin loveseat

with her tears and sending waves of perfume rolling through the store. It was time for serious grief counseling.

"Helen, would you unpack that Blumarine jeans stock for me?" Christina said. "I'll take Niki back and show her some pretty new things to make her feel all better. She'll have herself a new man in no time."

"I don't want a new man. I want Jimmy," Niki wailed, like a spoiled child.

Christina herded her gently toward the dressing room, a good-hearted but firm nanny. "Come on, sweetie. I have some lovely white wine. Would you like a glass of wine? Or maybe some Evian?"

That was kind, thought Helen. Smart, too. Niki would buy up a storm in her shattered state. Christina was hauling half the store into that dressing room.

Before Helen could unpack the jeans, the doorbell rang. Helen recognized a regular, Melissa, and buzzed her in. Melissa was the blonde with the eighteenth-century face and the twenty-first-century boob job. Good thing she'd persuaded her boyfriend to let her keep that Armani gown. Now he wanted her to get "something cute" for a barbecue.

Melissa tried on a long strapless tube of ruched material in lavender. It looked smashing with her blonde hair. If you were more than a size four, you'd look fat as a French bonbon. This four hung on Melissa.

"You need a size two," Helen said. "I know we have one somewhere. Let me find it for you."

The top wasn't in the shop or the stockroom. It must be in Niki's dressing room, thought Helen, along with most of the other clothes in the store.

Helen was about to knock on Niki's door when she heard Christina say in a low voice, "I'll need fifteen hundred down and fifteen hundred when the job is done."

That's what a hit man cost, Helen thought. Everyone in South Florida knew the price of a hit man. It was always on the news for some murder trial or other. But they can't be talking about a hit man in a Las Olas dress shop. Niki must want some sort of body sculpting. Juliana's women often resorted to surgery after they broke up with a man.

"I want her dead and him back in my arms!" Niki wailed.

"Shhh! The others will hear you. If you're serious. I'll need the money in cash tomorrow."

Cash? Hit men didn't take checks. But some of the doctors Christina recommended for her regulars took cash only. Like Doctor Mariposa, the illegal Brazilian face fixer.

Niki lowered her voice so much, Helen only caught the words "next Saturday." She couldn't figure out the rest of their conversation. Niki's voice was too soft, too clogged with tears and anger. Christina's was too cautious. But the two women seemed to have reached some sort of agreement. Niki raised her voice a notch. "I want her dead. And I want the Chloe jumpsuit and camisole."

Had the woman just ordered a camisole and a killing in the same breath? Helen wasn't sure what she'd heard, but she couldn't knock on Niki's dressing room door now. Helen was so rattled, she grabbed the first thing she saw off a nearby rack and went back to Melissa.

"Uh, sorry, we don't have that size two after all," she said. "But I thought you might like this instead for the barbecue."

Melissa looked at her strangely. Her slightly popped eyes bulged a bit more. No wonder. Helen was holding a green Versace evening gown.

"Er, I'm sorry," Helen said. "I don't know what's wrong with me."

"We all have those days," Melissa said. "Anyway, while you were gone, I tried on this top. I really like it instead."

Helen finally noticed what Melissa was wearing: a skintight black top slit up the side and laced with slim satin ribbons.

"Very sexy," Helen said, and it was.

"It's only two hundred and fifteen dollars," Melissa said. "Rick gave me five hundred, so I can keep the change."

Change, Helen thought. Melissa's change is more than I make in a week. And I'm working at a place that could be arranging contract killings.

She rang up Melissa's purchase in a daze, all the while trying to understand what she had heard. Helen knew Christina fiddled with the books a bit, but she wasn't a murderer, she told herself. Of course, Christina did arrange things. Face lifts. Designer drugs. Collagen injections. Contract killings.

Should she go to the police? But what would she tell them? All Helen knew was that the supposed victim was named Desiree. She didn't know her last name or where she lived. Did Desiree live in Fort Lauderdale? Boca? Miami? South Florida covered three counties and had millions of people.

Helen needed more information. She waited until Niki left, looking hopeful. Even her perfume seemed lighter. Then Helen walked back to Niki's clothing-crammed dressing room and began delicately digging.

"Was Niki really a *Playboy* centerfold?" she asked. She could still smell Niki's powerful perfume.

Christina was putting a skinny belt through the loops of a pair of flared pants. "No, just an inside feature. And that was five years ago. Old news now. You ask me, she showed too much and got too little. Niki couldn't turn the exposure into a modeling or movie contract. All she ever did was snag Jimmy."

"And now she's lost him," Helen said. "Poor Niki. She was a wreck. Whatever you did for her, she left here smiling."

Helen waited for Christina to say Niki was getting some high-priced plastic surgery. Instead, she started buttoning a sheer pink blouse with dozens of slippery pearl buttons. "I guess I said the right thing," she said. "Maybe I should be a shrink."

Christina did not mention the three thousand dollars. Helen knew she'd heard her say, "I'll need fifteen hundred down and fifteen hundred when the job is done."

"What's Jimmy do for a living?"

"He has some T-shirt shops," Christina said. "But I think they're a front for something else, maybe money laundering. He's known as Jimmy the Shirt."

"Sounds like a mob name," Helen said. "Desiree is the perfect first name for a femme fatale. I hope her last name isn't something disappointing, like Potts. And please don't tell me she lives in an apartment complex in Davie."

"I don't know where she lives," Christina said, coldly.

"But I know you better quit standing around yakking.
There's stock to put away. Here. Hang these up." She thrust
an armload of blouses at Helen.

Christina had effectively cut off any more questions. Was
she being a boss? Or was she trying to shut Helen up?

No, it couldn't be true. Niki didn't come here to buy a
murder. This wasn't happening. Helen couldn't say anything
to anyone, not even her friend Sarah. She knew what Sarah
would tell her: Get out of that place now. Find another job.
It was good advice. She would look for work on her next
day off.

Besides, Niki could still change her mind and call off the
murder, if there really was one. If Niki came in tomorrow
with the money, then Helen would call the police, no matter
how crazy she sounded.

Somehow, Helen got through the next day. She watched
the green door constantly and jumped every time the doorbell chimed. But Niki never showed up with a cute little bag
full of money. She never showed up, period. Helen began to
relax. She'd misheard. She'd misunderstood. This was what
she got for listening at doors. Everything was going to be
fine. It would be better than fine.

Chapter 8

"Do you even know what a Sapphire martini is?" the young man demanded in a supercilious voice. His pretty pink choirboy face was disfigured by a nasty sneer.

If this rude young man had applied to Helen for a job, she'd have shown him the door. Instead, she was asking him for work, and she knew she didn't have a chance.

"Uh, it's blue?" she said uncertainly.

"It's only like the unofficial gay drink," the choirboy said, pitying her ignorance. "If you want to tend bar on Las Olas, you'd better know what gays drink. And straights, too. Do you put coffee in a mudslide? Can you make a margarita? A rum runner?"

The choirboy kept hitting Helen with questions he knew she couldn't answer. Then, when she was thoroughly beaten, he returned the job application she'd painstakingly filled out. "Come back when you know one end of the bar from the other," he said. His tone implied that would be the thirty-first of never.

Helen's confidence was going downhill as fast as a real mudslide. She used to evaluate intricate pension-payment plans. Now she did not know what kind of gin went into a martini.

Helen was determined to find another job. She would not work for a thief and a drug pusher. So on her day off, Helen put on her black suit and went looking for work. Instead, she found a series of humiliations.

Helen didn't want to dip into her precious stash to fix her car, and that made her search harder. She had to find something within walking distance of her apartment. This morning, she'd already walked three long miles in the hot sun. Her feet burned from the sunbaked concrete sidewalks. She had a blister on her right heel. Her suit was sweaty, which meant another dry-cleaning bill.

After the choirboy sneered her out the door, Helen approached the next place warily. This bar looked like some place where Myrna Loy would drink, right down to the chrome cocktail shakers. It was dark and cool inside, and Helen was grateful for that. At least she'd get to sit down while she was being insulted.

The bar was opening for the day, and the bartender was busy cutting up limes and lemons for garnish. She was a cheerful blonde with sunfried skin and a smoker's rasp. She gave Helen a club soda on the house and some free advice.

"You're wasting your time looking for a bartender's job around here," she said, her voice like an emery board on the eardrums. "You have to know somebody to get these jobs. You might want to go to bartender's school. We hire some of the promising graduates."

Helen thanked the woman and wondered how much bartender's school would cost. An MBA was not much good to a mixologist. She'd better give up on bartending.

But Helen could—and did—read, and in South Florida, that seemed a rare skill. Maybe she could sell books. Helen tried Page Turners, the snooty Las Olas bookstore, next. The store manager didn't look old enough to go into the bars that had rejected Helen. But he turned her down, too.

"We're not hiring at present," the underage manager said, "but we will be happy to take your application."

The kiss-off of death. How often had Helen heard those words in human resources? At least he didn't say she was overqualified for the job, another inhuman human resources phrase. The underage manager added a new twist of the knife.

"We are expecting openings soon on the night shift," he

said. "We pay six seventy an hour. The night-shift book-sellers are expected to clean the store and the toilets."

"Toilets?" Helen said. She'd thought book selling would be genteel, if underpaid.

"Yes, but you can also take home the leftover café sandwiches," he said.

Helen wondered if she'd have any appetite for them after cleaning the toilets. The manager was wearing a white shirt and silk tie. Would she have to dress up in a skirt and heels to clean toilets, like a woman in a 1950s TV commercial?

Helen thanked him and walked next to the headquarters of an elite maid service. If she had to clean commodes for a living, she might as well get a job where she wouldn't have to dress up.

For six dollars an hour, Helen could clean toilets all day for the maid service. But it would help if she knew Spanish, the manager said. Then she could make six twenty-five and be a team leader. Helen didn't speak enough Spanish to order a taco in a Mexican restaurant.

Terrific. In two years, her career options had slid from director of employee benefits to toilet team leader—and she wasn't fully qualified for that job.

By three o'clock that afternoon, her job hopes were in the commode. Helen decided her battered psyche could stand one more interview. She'd remembered enough about job searches to save the best for last.

The ad she saw in the paper was intriguing: "Job opportunity in the food service industry," it said. "Enjoy fresh air and sunshine in a casual beach-like atmosphere. No experience necessary. Generous tips for willing workers. Transportation provided."

No experience. Transportation. She was willing if they were.

Helen had called that morning and made an appointment for three-thirty. But when she saw the office, her spirits fell even lower. The office was on a seedy street off Las Olas. Many of the buildings on the dismal little street were abandoned or boarded up, slated to be torn down for a new high-rise.

This office was clearly temporary. There was no com-

pany name on the door, no secretary in the waiting room.
The only furniture was two white plastic lawn chairs. The
mint-green walls were decorated with dirty handprints and
Snap-On Tool posters of busty women. Helen did not think
they created a professional workplace environment.

The inner office door opened and a hard-faced young
woman with spiky cranberry-red hair came out. She was
bursting with health. She was also bursting out of her short-
shorts and white halter top. "Bye-eee, boss. See you tomorrow," Miss Cranberry said.

"Show up dressed for work," a man's voice called out.
"Not that outfit. The one we discussed, yes?"

There seemed to be some professional standards, Helen
thought, and her dying hopes fluttered a little.

The man who came into the waiting room had luxuriant
hair everywhere but on his head. He had little patches of hair
on his fingers, little bushes in his nostrils and ears, a dark
pelt on his arms and a thick curly black mat on his chest.
Gold chains were tangled in his chest hair, and Helen wondered if he'd have to cut them out. But by the time the hair
finally made it to his scalp, it was thin and straggly. It
seemed exhausted.

The hairy man did not introduce himself. He lumbered
back into his office like a bear into a cave and sat down behind a card table piled with papers and Manila folders.

"Come in, come in," he said. "Glad you could make it.
Take a seat, yes? Take a load off those pretty feet. Nice
heels. You can wear those to work, yes?" He had some
kind of accent, but Helen couldn't place it. Latin? Latvian?
Russian?

"What kind of work is it?" Helen asked, sliding into another lawn chair.

"Food service, like the ad says," the hairy man said,
hands drumming on the paper pile.

"What kind of food?" Helen said. Why am I interviewing
him? she wondered. Was he testing her people skills?

"Hot dogs," he said. "All-American, the hot dog, yes?
You will serve them at lunch time under a big sun umbrella
to hungry men. Good tippers. And we pay seven dollars an
hour."

That was the most she'd been offered all day. "Plus benefits?" Helen said, hopefully.

"Many benefits," he said, smiling. He had another patch of hair under his lower lip. "Fresh air. Sunshine. You'll meet many fine gentlemen."

"Don't women eat lunch, too?" she said.

"Some," he said, and shrugged.

"And it's on the beach?"

"On a roadside, but like a beach," he said. "We will take you and the food cart there in the morning and pick you up in the afternoon. Now take off your blouse, please, so I can see if you are qualified for the job."

Helen was sure she'd heard him wrong. "Your blouse," he repeated, pointing a hairy finger at her chest. "You will unbutton now, please?"

Helen picked up her purse and stood up. "I'm at a loss to see what removing my blouse has to do with a food service job. I am terminating this interview."

"Do not be angry, dear lady. You seem to have a nice shape, but I need to see how you would look in a bikini. That will be your job uniform, yes?"

"No!" Helen said.

Searing anger fueled her long walk home. Food service. Fresh air. Beach-like atmosphere. Horseradish! She was supposed to wear a bikini and sell hot dogs with mustard and double entendres. She'd seen those pathetic women on godforsaken South Florida roads, surrounded by a pack of slavering men. She'd be leered at by truckers and tormented by bugs. How could she let this happen? She'd been a woman with a silver Lexus and a closet full of power suits. Now she was being asked to peddle hot dogs half naked.

She had wasted her time and her day off getting nowhere looking for nowhere jobs. She would have to go back to work for a crook. Helen would never get free of Juliana's.

Chapter 9

Helen put on her St. John knit like she was strapping on body armor. It had cost her two thousand dollars six years ago, and it was still her best-looking suit. Now she wore it like a shield. If Helen looked rich and secure, nothing bad could happen to her.

She was going to work at a shop with deep carpets, soft music, and fresh flowers, but she felt as jumpy as if she were hitchhiking through Skid Row with a suitcase stuffed with cash. The uncertainty was wearing her down. In the short time she'd worked at Juliana's, she'd seen a drug deal, money skimming, and what might have been a murder for hire, except nobody was dead.

Helen dreaded another day alone with Christina. She knew there would be another surprise. But she didn't expect it five minutes after she walked through the green door that Friday.

"Meet your replacement," Christina said. "I'm leaving for vacation after work tomorrow, and you will be in charge of the store. Guess who's going to work with you?"

It was Tara, the cute Asian customer with the crude boyfriend. Tara looked adorable in a blue scoop-neck top with white lace insets down the sleeves, and Brazilian low-rise jeans so lowcut they looked like bikini bottoms with legs.

"I thought it would be fun for a few days," Tara said, flipping her long black hair back from her face. "I know the clothes and the customers. Christina gave me a terrific discount."

Helen couldn't even afford the discount, much less the clothes.

"Paulie loves that discount part," Tara said. She giggled and flipped her long hair to the other shoulder. "He doesn't mind me working for a little while. It's like a vacation."

Some vacation, Helen thought. She eyed Tara's high-heeled sandals. Wait till Tara's little feet started hurting in those shoes.

"I'm doing it under one condition, Christina," Tara said, flipping her hair in the other direction. "You have to find me a maid as reliable as the one you got for Brittney. You know where to get the best. Brittney raves about Maria."

Good lord, thought Helen, another role for Christina: domestic service bureau.

"Do you mind a Haitian?" Christina said. "What about someone who doesn't speak English?"

"I don't care what they speak as long as they scrub my floors," Tara said. "Brittney has a real gem. She pays Maria almost nothing but room and board. The woman is practically a slave." Tara seemed happy to be a slave holder.

"I'll have one for you when I get back from vacation," Christina said. "But we have work to do now. I have two days to train you, Tara, and show Helen her new duties. Then I'm gone until next Friday."

Helen didn't know and did not care why Christina was taking a sudden unscheduled vacation. Christina did not say where she was going, and Helen didn't ask. She wanted that woman out of her sight. Maybe then Helen could figure out what to do about her crooked, drug-dealing boss. Even better, maybe she could land another job.

There were so many new things to learn that Helen did not have time to think, and that was good, too. The day passed in a blur. Christina showed Helen and Tara how to lock up and set the alarm. Helen learned what to do with the invoices and new shipments. Tara learned to size and fold stock and ring up sales. She cheerfully absorbed her new duties and seemed to find them interesting. Tara clearly loved clothes, enjoyed their colors and textures, and had a good eye for accessories.

Helen and Tara both learned to close out the register. They even had the combination to the store's safe. "There's only two of you. I'll just have to trust you," Christina said. "If you steal anything, I'll track you down and kill you." She laughed wickedly.

These new tasks were harder to learn because Christina could not keep her mind on her work. She kept leaving out steps when she explained a complicated procedure on the cash register.

"No, wait, you hit this button first," she told Helen. The cash register made a rude grinding sound, and the drawer refused to open for the third time.

"Damn. I've messed it up again," Christina said. "I can't concentrate. I see Doctor Mariposa tonight. I'm getting my wrinkles injected with biopolymer. It's all I can think about."

"Maybe if you wrote the steps down," Helen said.

That worked. Christina wrote out the instructions and taped them to the register. "That's all you need," she said.

Christina spent the rest of the afternoon examining her face in the triple mirror. "I can't wait," she said. "By eight o'clock tonight, this line will be gone. And this one." Christina pointed to the furrows between her nose and lips. They were getting deeper.

Helen still thought the injections were a mistake, but she didn't try to argue Christina out of them. The woman was determined.

"Wait till Joe sees me," she said. "I'll make sure he sees my new face. I'll buy myself the red Versace that's cut down to my navel and go dancing at all our clubs."

Christina was nearly cackling in anticipation. Her fury at Joe was frightening. Christina's unrelenting anger distorted her face until she was almost ugly. Her nose seemed long and witchlike. Her lips were locked in a snarl. Her eyes were mean slits.

"Tomorrow, you'll see a new me. I'm going to look younger and better," Christina said. "I'll find me a new boyfriend. Better than that jerk, Joe. He'll be sorry."

* * *

But it was Christina who was sorry.

The next morning, Christina came into work wearing a huge Hermes scarf that put her face in shadow. When Christina pulled off the scarf, Helen saw what she was hiding.

One side of Christina's face was grossly swollen. Her cheek was the size of a grapefruit half and covered with knoblike lumps. The other side was smooth and wrinkle-free, turning Christina into her own grotesque before-and-after picture.

Despite the Brazilian doctor's promises and Brittney's testimonial, the biopolymer injections were not safe and simple. Christina's face was a horror show. Helen had braced herself when the scarf came off, but the shock must have shown on her face. Still, she said nothing. But Tara had been expecting a cosmetic miracle. She looked at Christina's bloated cheek and blurted, "What's that horrible thing on your face?"

Tara tried to recover her blunder with, "I mean, your face looks a tiny bit swollen."

"Doctor Mariposa said I had a bad reaction to the biopolymer. She says I should be patient." Christina's voice was mumbly, distorted by the swelling.

"When will the swelling go down?" Helen asked.

"The doctor doesn't know. She said I might have to wait for the body to reabsorb it."

"How long will that take?" Tara said. She looked genuinely concerned.

"Four or five years," Christina said. Tears coursed down her face. The ones on the swollen side slid down faster as they hit the grotesque hump of flesh on her cheek. Helen tried not to stare.

"I look like a chipmunk," Christina wailed.

"You do not," Helen said. It was true. Chipmunks looked cute and cuddly.

Christina spent the whole morning bemoaning her swollen face. When even the biggest spenders came into the store, Christina refused to come out and wait on them. She stayed in the back room and wept until her eyes were red.

Christina called all her friends, except the beautiful biopoly-
mered Brittney, and cried on the phone. She used all the ice
in the store's mini-fridge, making cold packs for her bloated
cheek. By the time she left for lunch, Christina's eyes were
glassy, and Helen suspected she'd been in her special purses
for pain killers.

Helen tried, but she could not feel sorry for Christina.
Maybe your deeds showed on your face, she thought. But
then, what will I look like?

Christina came back after lunch in a vintage black hat
with a wisp of a veil. The hat's brim swooped down on the
right side and cleverly hid the worst of the damage to her
face.

Even Helen had to admit the good side of Christina's face
looked ten years younger. Now the skin was firm and
plump. The trench between her nose and mouth was gone,
and so were the deep frown furrows between her eyebrows.

Christina must have gone home to change. She wore the
hat with a long slinky black top and skinny pants. The Ferragamo pantsuit had such style. Even the buttons were beautiful. That afternoon, Juliana's customers raved about
Christina's chic new look. Those who didn't know any better praised the wonders of her wrinkle injections. Christina
looked almost happy. She seemed to forget the ruined right
side of her face. In the unreal world of Juliana's, half a
youthful face was better than none.

About three o'clock, there was a sudden lull in the stream
of shoppers. Helen and Christina leaned against the counters
for a rest. Tara boldly stretched out on the black loveseat.
She knew the rule that sales associates had to remain standing, but Tara also knew she'd be a customer again. The
owner wouldn't dare reprimand her.

When Tara was lounging out of earshot, Christina said, "I
want to take my special evening purses with me. They're not
store stock. If anyone asks for one while I'm gone, tell her
I'll be back next Friday."

"Fine," Helen said. She was relieved the purses would be
out of the store. She'd been wondering what to do about
them. She was not going to sell pills for Christina.

Christina went back to pack up the purses. She returned

with a white box and a pink bag. "I'm going to run them out to my car on my break," she said, patting the box. "But I like this one so much, I'm keeping it for myself." From a nest of hot-pink tissue paper in the bag, she pulled out a teardrop-shaped purse made of gold mesh.

"That looks like real gold," Helen said.

"It is," Christina said. "This purse is from the early 1940s. Isn't it a beauty? Look at the clasp. Those are real diamonds."

Helen knew better than to open the purse.

Christina was barely back from her break when Brittney was at the door. Helen buzzed her in, and Brittney thanked her in that whispery voice.

Helen could not tell—who could?—if Brittney was angry or happy. But she seemed anxious to talk to Christina. The two women took Evian water and settled into the loveseats for a chat. Tara was busy accessorizing a customer. Helen tidied the shelves under the cash register.

When Helen carried an extra box of padded hangers to the back room, she heard what the two women were talking about: the best way to get even with Joe, Christina's ex-almost fiancé. They'd been having this same conversation since the split, but Christina was still furious.

"Every time I think about what that man did to me, I could murder him," Christina said, raising her voice. Helen nearly dropped the box of hangers. Christina must have seen her reaction, because the two women retired to the dressing room for a private talk. Christina didn't even bother to take in any clothes to make it look like business.

Helen listened at the door. If Christina was plotting a murder, Helen was going to do everything she could to prevent it. Christina kept her voice low, and Brittney always talked in a whisper, so it was hard to hear what they said. But Helen heard this much:

"Do you know what I spend every month?" Brittney said, her voice soft as a sigh. She sounded angry, or maybe she was pleading.

"I need more," Christina said. "They're raising my condo fees."

"I don't have more," Brittney said, the whisper becoming a hiss. "I'm not made out of money."

Then the door chimed, and Helen had to answer it. A woman with extravagant apricot hair wanted to look at evening gowns. By the time Helen had sold her a sleek new design, Brittney was gone.

Helen was not sure what she had overheard. Was Christina reduced to begging for money? There was no time to consider the problem. Suddenly, the store was flooded with customers. They ran her ragged, demanding ever smaller sizes and blaming Helen if they couldn't fit into them. Helen moved in the zenlike state achieved only during the most hectic and miserable moments in retail. While she waited on the rude women, she used most of her mind to daydream about Cal. She was seeing him tonight at seven. She couldn't wait. They hadn't had a chance to talk since their Cap's date last Saturday.

As the unsatisfied women ordered her about, Helen began to paint herself a rosy future with the attractive Canadian. A woman could do worse than spend the rest of her life with a man who told funny stories, she thought, putting blue skies and pink clouds in the picture.

And though it was way too early to think this way, Cal might be marriage material. Helen was not ready to buy a wedding dress or anything. That was silly. But she could sense something solid about Cal, something possible. She wondered if the U.S. courts would track her all the way to Canada.

Suddenly, the flood of customers dried up, leaving behind their wreckage: piles of abandoned clothes and accessories, tangles of hangers, carpets littered with tissue paper, straight pins, and extra buttons. Someone had smeared red lipstick on a white blouse. A shirt reeked of perfume.

Helen was wearily hanging everything up when the phone rang. It was Gilbert Roget, the store owner, calling from Canada. "Is Christina there?" he said.

"I'm sorry, Mr. Roget. She's busy with a customer. Is there something I can help you with?"

"Yes, could you ask her to check an International FedEx shipping bill?" he said. He gave her the number. "Some customer in Brazil is complaining about the high price of a shipment to his wife, Bianca. He called me. Could Christina look into it?"

"Of course," Helen said. "I'll make sure she takes care of it today."

Especially since Christina caused the problem, Helen thought. She's not leaving me to deal with that mess.

Christina was furious. She called Mr. Roget and told him it was a clerical error. But the wily businessman demanded to know who had prepared the FedEx package. Christina had to admit she had. She promised to refund the disputed portion to the unhappy Brazilian. Helen knew the money would have to come from Christina herself.

That's probably why Christina did not even try to be conciliatory when Lauren's lawyer husband called about his wife's shoplifting bill.

"I think I was charged too much," he said. "My wife didn't bring home the blouse and the belt that are on the bill."

"I can't keep track of her purchases once she leaves the store," Christina said. "Maybe she sold them."

"Maybe I didn't buy them," he said.

"Look, buddy, just be glad I didn't have her skinny ass thrown in jail," Christina said, and slammed down the phone.

"Jesus! How much worse can this day get?" Christina asked, fleeing to the back room.

Her question was answered when the pill-popping Venetia came into the store. She was angry and jittery. Venetia demanded to see Christina immediately. Her shrill voice was like an ice pick in Helen's ear. Tara ran back to get her, while Helen kept an eye on Venetia.

Helen could hardly stand to be near the woman. Venetia bounced back and forth on the balls of her feet, picking at invisible lint on her Yves Saint Laurent. Pick. Pick. Pick. Bounce. Bounce. Bounce. Jitter. Pick. Bounce. The whites of Venetia's eyes were bright yellow, the same color as the trim on her suit.

She's definitely strung-out, Helen thought. I'm glad I don't have to deal with her.

When Christina bustled up, Venetia threw the black beaded purse at her. Christina ducked, and it flew past her and skidded across the counter. Christina's hat was knocked sideways.

The delicate little purse looked like it had been mauled by bears. The beading was torn, the silver clasp broken, and the pink silk lining shredded.

"It didn't last," Venetia said in her high voice, and Helen knew she was not talking about the silk lining.

"I'm sorry you're not happy, but that is not my problem," Christina said smoothly.

"Take it back," Venetia said, her eyes wild, her voice nearly a shriek. "Take it back, and give me back my money. All my money. My husband is going through my accounts."

"I cannot do that," Christina said. "There are no returns on special items."

"I want my money!" Venetia screamed.

"I'm sorry. You'll have to leave," Christina said in a firm voice. Tara gasped, as if Christina had produced a flaming sword. She knew Venetia was being barred from Juliana's forever.

"You'll be sorry. You'll be very sorry," Venetia said, as the green door closed on her for the last time.

"Is this a full moon or what?" Christina said to Helen. "Crazy complaints must come in threes, like deaths." She looked in the mirror, and straightened her hat to cover her swollen cheek. "Is it six o'clock yet?"

"No, but why don't you leave early?" Helen said. "We'll close up."

"I'm outta here," Christina said. "I'll see you next Friday. You and Tara can hold the fort."

Helen was glad to see Christina go. She watched her slim figure disappear down Las Olas, melting into the tropical twilight.

Chapter 10

Helen stripped off her blouse and switched on the TV. She wanted to catch the news while she dressed for her date with Cal. As she unzipped her skirt, she caught the words "carjacking of a twenty-three-year-old Plantation woman."

Helen stared at the screen in horror as the announcer said, "Desiree Easlee, who lived in a gated community in suburban Plantation, was shot and killed this morning in an attempted carjacking."

Desiree? Niki's rival was dead? No, it couldn't be. She wasn't the only woman in Florida named Desiree. Helen's skirt slid unnoticed to the floor.

"Miss Easlee was engaged to be married to T-shirt entrepreneur James "Jimmy the Shirt" Dellamondo. The wedding was supposed to take place in Belize next Saturday," the announcer said, and Helen's last hope was as dead as Desiree.

On the screen was a photo of a luscious-lipped blonde in a tight black dress with a zipper up the front. In the next shot, Desiree was in a loose-fitting black body bag with a zipper up the front. Desiree's enormous breasts created a mountain in the body bag.

A dead photogenic bride made good television, and the station had put extra effort into reporting this story. The announcer said the security guard did not have any record of a strange car being admitted to the gated community, and the police had no leads.

No leads, Helen thought. She felt sick and dizzy and guilty. Her head throbbed and pounded with the refrain: Desiree was dead. Desiree was dead. And she did nothing to stop it. Now she had a face to put with her crime of cowardice. An innocent young woman was dead a week before her wedding.

I could give the police a lead. I could tell them who set this up. I know who arranged the murder of Desiree. And why.

On the television, someone was saying that gated communities gave a false sense of security to residents. The people who lived there did not take the same precautions as residents who lived on public streets. A neighbor complained to the TV reporter that the security guard was an old man who frequently slept while on duty.

Another woman, who identified herself as a doctor's wife, defended the gated community. "We have the guard for prestige, not security," the woman said.

Helen could not figure out why a dozing senior citizen was prestigious. But it wasn't fair that the poor gate guard was going to be the scapegoat for this crime. Helen knew this wasn't a carjacking gone wrong. It was a murder for hire. Helen had heard the whole thing being planned and done nothing.

But what could she have told the police? See, officer, there's this woman named Desiree. I don't know her last name or where she lives, but Niki wants her dead before she marries her boyfriend. Niki went to the manager of a dress shop to hire a hit man. At least I think that's what was going on. I couldn't hear them talking too clearly. And I never saw any money change hands.

Helen would have looked like a fool. But Desiree might still be alive.

Now Desiree was dead. Before her wedding to Jimmy the T-shirt baron, just like Niki wanted. Christina had arranged the murder, but there was no way Helen could prove it.

She had a date with Cal in five minutes. She'd have to cancel. But what could she say? This woman I never met was killed, Cal. I should have stopped it, although I don't know how.

There was nothing Helen could have done differently. There was nothing she could do now. She had to pull herself together and quit standing there like a statue wearing an underwire bra.

Helen pulled on some clothes. She had no idea what she put on. Only after she locked her front door did she notice she was wearing cutoffs and a Tweety Bird T-shirt. Well, Catfish Dewey's was supposed to be casual.

She was almost to the pool when she heard Cal say, "Don't you look beautiful?" He whistled appreciatively.

Unfortunately, Cal was whistling at Peggy, not Helen. Peggy was wearing a long, low-cut black dress that showed off her elegant figure and dark red hair. The dress was bare on one shoulder. Peggy didn't have her parrot.

"Where's Pete?" Helen asked.

"He's home alone for the evening. I'm going to the opera, and *Manon* is not a sing-along. There's my ride. Gotta run," Peggy said, as a silver Lexus pulled into the Coronado parking lot.

Peggy didn't run. She glided to the car like a runway model. A man in impeccable eveningwear greeted Peggy warmly and opened her door. He was theatrically handsome, with burnished blond hair hanging over one eye and cheekbones that looked like they'd been chiseled by a sculptor. Helen thought Peggy's escort could be a Calvin Klein model or a member of the Hitler Youth.

And I could be a scrubwoman, Helen thought.

"I've always wanted to ask Peggy out," Cal confided, as they climbed into his rattling Buick. "But she's too expensive for me."

"And I'm cheap?" Helen asked.

"No, no," Cal said, soothingly, "you're just ah-boot perfect." This time, his "ah-boot" failed to charm Helen, and she kept a huffy silence on the ride to Catfish Dewey's.

But she thawed when they got to the old restaurant. Catfish Dewey's was as homey as a basement rathskeller. She felt instantly comfortable with its knotty pine paneling and red-checked tablecloths.

Cal wanted the all-you-can-eat catfish. Helen had no compunction about ordering stone crab claws, the most expensive item on the menu. They still cost less than dinner at Cap's. It was the first time Helen had had stone crab, and she was fascinated. The claws really were hard as stones. Harder. They were like concrete.

"Stone crabs are pretty, don't you think?" she asked Cal, as she dipped the sweet crabmeat in mustard sauce. "Most crabs look like boiled spiders, but stone crabs are pale yellow with flamingo pink splotches and black tips."

"You look pretty cute with yellow on your lip," Cal said, as he delicately removed a blob of mustard sauce with his napkin. Then he launched into a tale about the first time he ate a lobster that had Helen laughing again.

He was delightful, Helen thought, and her anger dissolved. So what if he complimented Peggy? She was getting touchy. That's what happened when you lived alone too long. No, that's what happened when you were rattled about Desiree. But her mind quickly skittered away from that. Catfish Dewey's was overflowing with friends and families dredging fries in ketchup and dipping hush puppies in tartar sauce. There was no room here for carjackings and murders for hire.

Cal and Helen spent the next few hours chattering away, while their tired but efficient waitress hauled out basket after basket of cracked crab and fried catfish.

Finally, Helen had eaten herself into a stupor. She surveyed the mounds of empty crab claws and mustard sauce cups and said, "I think it's time for the check." Cal agreed and signaled the waitress.

The waitress produced that as quickly as the food. Cal grabbed for it and Helen let him. Then he patted his back pocket. Suddenly, he began slapping himself frantically. At first, Helen thought he'd been attacked by an invisible swarm of mosquitoes. Then she realized Cal was patting his empty pockets. Next, he turned his pants pockets inside out.

"I seem to have forgotten my wallet," Cal said. "I'll pay you back as soon as we get home, but would you mind picking up the check this time?"

Helen minded. A lot. But she had been warned by Margery not to dine with Cal, and she had not listened. On some level, she must have been expecting this, because she'd tucked seventy-five bucks into her purse. The bill came to forty- eight dollars and eight-six cents. The waitress returned with her change. Helen was seething, but she wasn't sure if she was mad at herself or Cal.

She left a ten-dollar tip for the deserving waitress, and without a word to Cal, got up and headed toward the door. He could follow or not, she didn't care. She felt strangely light after this decision. Then she realized it was because she'd left her purse back at the table. Helen turned around to retrieve it, just in time to see Cal filching the waitress's ten spot.

"Put that money down!" Helen said. Heads turned, but she didn't care who heard. "I can't believe you'd sink to stealing a waitress's tip."

"I was taking it back for you," Cal said. "If you tip too much, it spoils the help." He was lying, and he knew she knew. The man actually cringed when she approached. Disgusting.

Helen yanked the ten-dollar bill out of his hand and marched over to the waitress, who was staring at them. "Here. This is yours," she said. Helen thought about walking home but decided Cal could drive her. He owed her that much.

All the way home Cal railed about rich Americans who tossed around money in Florida, making life difficult for hardworking Canadians. The value of the Canadian dollar had sunk so low he couldn't afford a decent life. As Cal ranted, he became the aggrieved party. The entire United States was personally depriving him.

Helen didn't answer. She kept remembering her landlady Margery's words: "Talk is cheap, and so is Cal." She had nothing else to say. Her anger at Cal burned away the last thoughts of Desiree.

Back at the Coronado apartments, they both got out and slammed their car doors simultaneously. Cal stomped off to his apartment. He slammed that door, too, so hard the jalousie glass rattled.

Helen didn't want to go inside yet. She was too upset. She hoped the soft, humid night would comfort her. She wandered over by the pool and saw Peggy sitting in a lounge chair by the water. She was still wearing her glamorous black dress, but now she had Pete on her shoulder. Pete looked ruffled and grumpy, but Peggy seemed complete with her parrot.

"Bad date?" Peggy said, sympathetically.

"Unbelievable," Helen said, and gave her the details.

"Oh, I believe it," Peggy said. "I've dated every bum in Broward County."

"But you went to the opera tonight with a wonderful man," Helen said. As soon as she'd said it, she realized Peggy was alone in the dark, just like she was.

"A wonderful gay man," Peggy said. "Troy's partner is in Paris on business. He knows I like opera and can't afford tickets. Troy was kind enough to ask me to go with him. In South Florida, all the good men are either married or gay."

"Is it really that bleak?"

"Yes. Pete's my main man now." The parrot hopped triumphantly back and forth on her smooth shoulder. Peggy, pale and beautiful in the moonlight, looked like a princess held prisoner by a green goblin.

"Then there's no hope?" Helen said, although she already knew the answer.

"Sure there is," Peggy said. "I buy lottery tickets. My plan is to win big and buy me a good man."

Peggy's sad laughter followed Helen all the way to her apartment. As she passed her neighbor Phil's door, she was surrounded by a thick sinsemilla smog. The invisible pothead was burning some fine weed tonight.

Lucky Phil, she thought. He could fire up his dreams whenever he wanted.

Chapter 11

Margery never said "I told you so." Helen's landlady simply turned up at her door Sunday afternoon with a plate of fudge.

"Here," she said. "Chocolate cures almost everything."

"Even stupidity?" Helen said. She bit into a thick dark square. It was bitter chocolate. "Mmmm. My favorite."

Margery's violet shorts were the color of the evening sky. Her red toenail polish was a tropical sunset. Her kind, shrewd old eyes seemed to see straight into Helen.

"Welcome to South Florida, land of deadbeats, drunks, and druggies," Margery said, helping herself to a piece of fudge. "Most of the single men down here are some other woman's mistake. The trick is not to make them your mistake."

"I should have listened to you," Helen said. "I didn't believe anyone could be so cheap. Cal stole the waitress's tip. That's disgusting."

"Canadians are stingy tippers. You've heard the local joke: What's the difference between a canoe and a Canadian?"

Helen shook her head.

"A canoe tips," Margery said.

Helen tried to laugh but she couldn't. Nothing seemed funny right now.

Margery turned serious. "You're a nice person, Helen. I

worry about you. This isn't the Midwest. In South Florida, everyone is running from somebody or something: bad weather, bad debts, a bad life, a bad spouse. Or they've done something bad.

"Nobody has roots here. In the Midwest, if you don't know a guy, you can make a few phone calls and find out about him. Down here, women hire private detectives to do background checks. Too often, they find out they are about to marry a deadbeat dad, a bisexual, or a man in trouble with the law. I know you're running from something, too. I suspect some man hurt you. I don't want you to get hurt again."

"The Midwest doesn't have a lock on morality," Helen said, thinking of her ex.

"I know," Margery said, reaching for more fudge. "But there you can find out about the bad operators a little sooner."

I didn't, Helen thought. She changed the subject abruptly. "What can you tell me about my next door neighbor, Phil the invisible pothead?"

"He's not invisible," Margery said. "I see him all the time."

"I haven't seen hide nor hair of him," Helen said.

"Well, he's the last of the real hippies. He's a little older than you. Has a long gray ponytail and interesting T-shirts. Always pays his rent on time. He's a real Eric Clapton fan."

"He is? I never hear any music," Helen said.

"He uses headphones. Phil is very considerate. But he's not a good man for you, dear. And while we're on the subject of men, no one from St. Louis has been asking for you. I would call you at work if anyone came snooping around. I keep an eye on your place."

Helen had confided to Margery only that she was afraid of her ex-husband, who might come looking for her. She didn't say why. Helen did not mention the court.

"Thank you. And thanks for the chocolate," Helen said. "It's just what I needed. I'll bring your plate back tomorrow."

"Don't worry about Cal," Margery said. "I'll make sure he doesn't bother you."

Kindness and chocolate helped Helen get over her bad

date. But there was no cure for her unquiet conscience. Desiree, the bride in the body bag, tormented her all night.

On Monday, she went back to where Desiree's death had been plotted. What if Niki came in? What would Helen say to her? She dreaded her first day in charge, but Juliana's ran smoothly. Only regulars stopped by, so Helen did not have to worry about barring anyone from walking though the green door.

On her lunch hour, she found a good job prospect. Helen talked with the manager and made an appointment for an interview with the store owner after work. She left Juliana's that evening excited and hopeful.

She was interviewing for a sales associate's job at a Las Olas shop two blocks west of Juliana's. Helen liked everything about it. Pam Marshall, the owner, was a stylish woman in her early fifties, with laugh lines and eye crinkles. She was easy with her age and herself.

Pam's store sold clothes Helen would wear, if she could afford them. Helen saw actual size twelves, even fourteens and sixteens. She liked that, too. She liked sitting in Pam's comfortably cluttered office, drinking fresh coffee with her. She liked the pay best of all: seven fifty an hour. Already, Helen was calculating what she would do with the extra money.

"So when can you start?" Pam asked, taking another sip of her sugar-laced coffee.

Yes! Helen thought, I've got it. "I'd have to give my current employer two weeks' notice."

"Good," Pam said. "I like employees who play fair."

"And—" Helen hesitated, searching for the right words. "I have to be paid in cash only. I don't want to be on the books."

"What about your FICA and taxes?" Pam said.

"If I don't exist, then you don't have to worry about them," Helen said.

Pam leaned forward and looked Helen in the eye. "I'm supposed to cheat the government so you can have a few extra bucks a week? I'm not a chiseler, Helen. I'm a business woman. And I'm surprised at you."

Pam put her coffee cup down and stood up. The interview

was over. Helen slunk away, scalded with shame. This is
what she'd become, a petty cheat. Just like her ex.

She headed for her apartment at the Coronado like a
wounded animal crawling to its cave. Once inside, she had
to get out. The room seemed too small to contain her misery.

If she went out by the pool, she might run into Cal. So
what? she decided. If she couldn't face herself, she could at
least face a tip-swiper. Cal was not going to keep her away
from her favorite place. Helen put on some shorts, squared
her shoulders, and marched out, taking her newspaper with
her. She could always hide behind the job ads if things got
sticky with Cal.

Margery had kept her word. Peggy and Pete were by the
pool, but Cal did not come out that evening. He stayed in his
apartment and cooked up bushels of broccoli and brussels
sprouts. Cal not only came from the English-speaking part
of Canada, but the English-cooking part. He loved over-
cooked vegetables.

"After all, they are cheap," Peggy reminded Helen.

"And obnoxious," Helen said.

The stink of boiled broccoli nearly overpowered Phil's
pot smoke. Maybe Cal would become as invisible as Phil.
Helen suspected he was avoiding her deliberately. She
thought Cal would hide inside and live on broccoli until he
turned green to avoid paying for their Catfish Dewey's dinner.

Helen picked up her paper and studied the want ads. Ma-
rine biologist. Meat cutter. Mechanic. More skills she didn't
have.

"So how is the job search going?" Peggy asked.

"It's not," Helen said.

"You're too picky," Peggy said. "I can find you two high-
paying jobs in no time. Give me those ads."

She took the paper from Helen and started reading. Pete
sat on her shoulder and studied the ads, too. Or maybe he
wondered why someone was holding his cage liner. Either
way, the quizzical green bird made Helen laugh.

"Here's one," Peggy said. " 'Dancer/escort—Twelve
hundred dollars a day. Cash guaranteed. Easy entertainment.' Can you dance?"

"Me? My family's German. Unless it's a tune with a tuba in it, I can't dance."

"Hawthorne is German?" Peggy said.

That was a stupid slip, Helen thought. "No, Hawthorne is my married name," she lied. To distract Peggy she said, "What's the other job choice?"

"Wrestling. The ad says, 'We need athletic females of all types and sizes. Earn one hundred dollars an hour. No experience necessary.'"

Helen pretended to consider the ad. "Where would I wrestle at?"

"The big question is what you would wrestle *in*."

"In?" Helen echoed.

"Want-ad wrestling is generally done in something: Jell-O, mud, Karo syrup. For some reason, the guys at the clubs get off on that. They also get to spray you with whipped cream, but that's extra.

"Of course this wrestling gig could be porn. Then you'd be wrestling in something else—a dirty movie."

"For a hundred bucks an hour? And no residuals?" Helen said.

"Hmm," Peggy said. "Wrestling could be hard on your back. How's your health insurance?"

"Don't have any," Helen said, happy to tell the truth for once.

"Then you need to buy some lottery tickets," Peggy said, and was back on her favorite subject. "The lottery is up to forty-two million. I've got a new system for winning. I've read the interviews. The big winners use family birthdays for their numbers. Those numbers must be lucky. I'm using my mother's birthday and Pete's."

"Awwwk!" Pete said.

"Do you think parrot birthdays count the same as human ones?" Helen said.

"Pete's family. He's closer to me than anyone."

There was a flash of purple, and Margery the landlady charged past the bougainvillea, frightening Pete into a squawking fit that everyone ignored. Helen had never seen her so brilliantly dressed. Margery's evening shorts were deep orchid, her toenails tangerine, and she was wearing purple sandals that ended in big bows at her slender ankles. Helen wished she had the courage to wear shoes like that.

Margery sat down in the chaise longue next to Helen. "Wait till you see who's moving into 2C, girls," she said. "Have I got a treat for you."

"Who?" Helen and Peggy said, sounding like a pair of owls.

With that, the jungle of poolside palms parted, and out stepped Tarzan in gym shorts. Helen expected him to uproot the palms with his bare hands.

Long black hair tumbled past his tanned shoulders. His high Slavic cheekbones gave an interesting slant to his cobalt blue eyes. He was six feet tall and strong, but without the gnarled gym muscles Helen hated. This manly vision was wearing the smallest pair of red shorts the law allowed, with an interesting bulge in front.

"He looks like Fabio," Peggy whispered. "Only better."

Helen could feel the sexual electricity surge across the Coronado lawn. The heavy, humid air seemed about to explode. The fabulous half-naked hunk was heading straight for them. He strode over the grass, an almost unclad colossus. Oiled muscles rippled in his mighty thighs. Helen thought of statues of the winged god, Mercury. Helen thought of things the nuns in St. Louis said were occasions of sin.

"Oh, my," Helen said.

The manly vision stopped in front of Margery's chaise longue. He bent down, exposing tempting tanned crescents of muscled buttock, and gave Margery a chaste kiss on the cheek. She blushed.

"Thank you for everything," he said, looking deep into Margery's eyes. His voice was a caress. He produced a business card from God knows where. "If you ever need me for anything, anything at all, just call this number." The godlike figure disappeared back into the palm jungle.

"Oh, my," Peggy breathed. "I know what I need."

"This is a setup," Helen said, hoping to recover her wits. "He's a Chippendale. You paid him."

"He's paying me," Margery said, smugly. "He's the new

renter in 2C. I made him some of my fudge. Naturally, he was grateful."

"Is he mortal? Does he have a name?" Peggy said.

"Daniel Dayson." Margery pronounced it the way some women would say Matt Damon or Russell Crowe. "He's the most beautiful man I've ever seen, and I'm working on my eighth decade of guy watching."

"Is Daniel straight?" Helen said. It was a sad fact in South Florida that the best bodies usually belonged to gay men.

"That boy has plenty of lady friends, but he needs the right woman," Margery said.

"That's me," Helen said, but she knew it was hopeless. She was too ordinary for a man who looked like that.

"He's got to be a male model. Or an exotic dancer," Peggy said.

"Wrong," Margery said. "He's a fire equipment inspector."

"He's hot enough to inspect my equipment any time," Peggy said, and the three women launched into a deplorable series of jokes involving fire hoses and heat.

When they finished, Helen's stomach hurt from laughing. Her brain sizzled with suppressed desire. "I think I'm more impressed by his steady job than his eye-popping physique," she said.

"I'm not," Peggy said. "Although I admit a man with a job is a rarity down here. But oh, lord, the way that man moves . . ."

"Squaaak!" Pete the parrot said, hopping back and forth on her shoulder.

"Shut up," Peggy said absently, brushing the bird aside. Pete sat in stunned silence. It was the first time she'd ever talked to Pete like that.

Chapter 12

Desiree was dead.

Helen could forget that for half an hour or even half a day. Then she'd see a young woman with blonde hair tumbling down her back or hear a newscaster's solemn voice, and it would come rushing back. Once again, she'd see that shocking news story. First, the bride-to-be in her black dress, then in her black body bag.

Desiree was dead. Desiree was dead. As Helen walked home from work Tuesday night, her feet pounded that rhythm into the pavement.

Helen went dragging into her small, stuffy apartment and threw herself on the lumpy bed, not even bothering to change out of her suit. Her feet hurt. Her head hurt. She felt old and fat and tired. But most of all, she felt discouraged. She'd wasted another lunch hour looking for work. Christina was due back in three days, and Helen still did not have another job. She would never escape Juliana's. She would never get away from her guilt.

Desiree was dead. Desiree was dead. The words pounded in Helen's head until it felt like the whole room was beating to the rhythm.

Then Helen realized the whole room *was* beating to the rhythm. Her landlady was pounding on the door and calling her name. That woman had quite an arm on her. What was wrong now? Did Margery want to raise the rent? Helen straightened her rumpled suit, pushed her hair back, and opened the door.

Margery looked like an exotic orchid in a swirling lavender-print shorts set. Her toes were painted fuchsia. In her hand was a glass plate with one perfect chocolate-dipped strawberry.

"Thought this might cheer you up," Margery said. "You look like forty miles of bad road. You're too young and pretty to be so hangdog."

Margery was smart, Helen thought. Her landlady had seen the slump of Helen's shoulders as she came up the sidewalk and knew something was wrong. Rather than probe with nosy questions, Margery plied her with chocolate. It almost worked. For a minute, Helen thought of telling her about Desiree's death. But then she hesitated, and the impulse was lost. Helen had kept silent for so long, she had lost the ability to confide.

Like all good liars, Helen knew enough to tell part of the truth when possible. So she said, "Work's getting me down, Margery. I feel like a lumberjack around those women at Juliana's."

Margery snorted so hard it hurt Helen's sinuses. "You don't want to look like one of those helpless Barbie dolls, do you?"

"It's not how they look. It's how they make me feel. So Midwestern. So out of it. They're so fashionable. They're so South Beach."

"Helen," Margery said. "Those women are not real South Beach. They're only wanna-bes. That's why Juliana's has to keep people out. Because they're afraid. On South Beach, the doors are wide open. Everyone can walk in and succeed—or fall flat on her face."

"No," Helen protested. "Christina belongs. She goes to all the clubs. She knows the South Beach nightlife. She's seen at all the hot places: Mynt. Pearl. Kiss. Rain. Crobar. She goes to dinner at The Forge. She's been to B.E.D. with four women and one man."

"I don't care about her sex life," Margery said.

"No. B.E.D. is the name of the club. It costs about a thou-

sand dollars to get a good bed, at least that's what Christina
said, but you sit on these big beds, see, and—"

"The guys get to say, 'I went to B.E.D. with four women
last night.' Real sophisticated." Margery sniffed. Helen was
grateful she didn't snort.

"I guess that sounds silly. But Christina was at Bash the
night Leonardo DiCaprio danced topless."

"That's what she says. Maybe she just read about it in
Ocean Drive magazine. But I'll tell you this much, Helen,
even if she was there—she may remember Leonardo, but he
won't remember her. You don't need to know the names of
the clubs. Half of them will be out of business by next week.
Don't let Christina intimidate you. If she was really South
Beach, she'd be in South Beach, not Fort Lauderdale.

"Eat your strawberry. You'll feel better," Margery com-
manded. "I've gotta go."

And she was gone, leaving Helen with one perfect strawberry. Helen ate it in tiny bites, making it last as long as possible. On any other night, it would have cheered her up. But
not tonight. Tonight she had to live with Desiree's death.
Tonight, she also had to live with her past.

As the evening sun sank lower, so did Helen's spirits. In
another hour, she would have to get out the cell phone she
only used once a month and call her family. Helen dreaded
her mother's tears. Not even the call afterward to her
beloved sister, Kathy, would make things better.

It was almost seven o'clock. Time for the call home.
Helen locked the doors, closed the blinds, and opened the
door to the closet with the water heater. She pulled out the
suitcase and rummaged through the old-lady underwear
until she found the cell phone and a piece of pink cellophane
from a gift basket.

Helen didn't have a phone in Lauderdale. She didn't
want to be traced. She'd bought this one in Kansas City and
mailed her sister Kathy a thousand dollars to pay the
monthly phone bills. Helen hoped that would cover them for
a long time. If anyone found out about the phone, it was registered to a false name and purchased in Kansas. She hoped
that would be enough to confuse any pursuers.

Helen braced herself, and dialed her mother's number in

St. Louis. "I will not get angry," she told herself. "I will not shout. Mom belongs to a different generation. She doesn't understand."

"Hello, Mom," she said. Her mother burst into tears. Actually, it was more like a whining wail. It always set Helen's teeth on edge.

The phone call went exactly as Helen expected. Her mother cried and begged Helen to come home and be a good wife to her bad husband. "Think of your immortal soul," her mother sobbed. "The Pope says divorce is wrong."

"So let the Pope live with him," Helen said, then regretted her outburst. She had hurt her mother's feelings again.

"We could get a lawyer and work out the other problem, Helen honey, if you'd just get back with your husband."

The other problem. Helen could not talk about that. She brought out the piece of pink cellophane. It was her escape. She crinkled the cellophane and said, "What's that, Mom? I can't hear you. I have to go now. You're breaking up. I'll call again on your birthday. Bye, Mom."

Helen hung up the phone. The short conversation left her emotionally drained, as tired as if she'd been digging ditches. At least the call to her sister would be easier. Kathy was the only person from her old life who knew where Helen was and how to reach her in an emergency.

Kathy lived in the near-perfect St. Louis suburb of Webster Groves. She and Tom had a new baby, Allison, and ten-year-old Tommy Junior. They also had a big old house that needed paint and new plumbing. Tom's salary was frozen at 1999 levels, and Kathy worked part-time as a checker at Target. But she rarely talked about their money problems.

"Helen, you sound tired," Kathy said, when she answered the phone.

"I've been talking to Mom," Helen said.

"Was it awful?"

"No worse than usual."

"Seriously, Sis, how are you doing?" Kathy asked.

"I'm fine. I like my new life. I like the weather here. I wasted too much time sitting inside in the St. Louis winters. I hate winter. I feel like I got half my life back."

Helen realized, once she said it, that it was true. If she

could just find another job and figure out what to do about
Christina, her new life would be good. She didn't miss her
old life or her old job. Only her old paycheck.

"You know if you're ever in trouble, you can call me,"
Kathy said. "I'll send you money or come get you. I'll hire
a lawyer. I'll post bail if you're arrested. Whatever you
want."

"I know," Helen said. She also knew she'd never call her
sister for help. Kathy had enough problems with her active
family.

They spent the rest of the time talking about Tom and the
kids. Good things. Everyday things. And if Helen were truly
honest, things she never wanted.

"That's the baby crying. I've got to run. Good night, Sis.
I love you," Kathy said.

"I love you, too," Helen said, feeling better, and lonelier,
too. She switched off the phone and buried it in the suitcase.

Chapter 13

Helen made her first executive decision at 10:02 Wednesday morning. She was in charge at Juliana's. She had the power to keep out any woman in the world. The more she refused, the more she built the store's reputation.

The doorbell chimed. Tara said, "I'm not sure we should let this woman in."

"What's wrong with her?" Helen said.

"She's wearing cheap shoes," Tara said. She sounded as if they were contagious. Helen looked. The woman was dressed in real Gucci, but her shoes were third-rate Prada knockoffs.

"Let her in," Helen ruled. It felt good to say that.

"But Christina never lets in anyone with cheap shoes."

"Christina isn't here," Helen said. "I'm manager this week." She buzzed in the woman, to Tara's silent disapproval. Helen felt triumphant when Ms. Cheap Shoes bought an expensive dress.

There was no question about admitting the next woman. She was a professional beauty with artfully tossed long hair. She had dark hypnotic eyes in a pale heart-shaped face. Her white silk shirt looked casual in the way only thousand-dollar shirts can. Her jeans fit like a second skin. Her white calf-skin boots made her legs look even longer and slimmer.

"She's gorgeous," Helen said.

"Her name is Sharmayne. She used to be a model," Tara said. "She is Christina's only failure."

Before Tara could explain, Sharmayne strode in with that look-at-me model's walk and demanded, "Where's Christina?"

"She's on vacation," Helen said.

"Then you'll have to do," she said, imperiously.

Sharmayne pointed to the shirts, skirts, tops, and dresses she wanted to try on. Tara and Helen staggered back to the dressing room under loads of clothes. Five minutes later, Sharmayne stuck her head out the door. "There's no belt on the bottle-green D&G," she said.

"I'll get it," Helen said. She found the belt in the stockroom, knocked once on Sharmayne's door, and opened it. The former model was sitting naked in the silk chair. Helen froze. She had her first female flasher.

Christina had warned her about them. Catching sight of bare breasts and buns was an occupational hazard for the sales associates at Juliana's. The customers had beautiful bodies, and they were used to exhibiting them. Tan lines were rare. Most women didn't cover up when Helen brought in more clothes, even though she always knocked on the door and waited for them to say, "Come in." But there was a kind of naivete to their nudity.

A female flasher didn't show off her perfect breasts or trim thighs. She'd sit in the silk chair with her legs spread like a *Hustler* centerfold, daring the salesperson to stare.

Helen had asked Christina if these flashers were lesbians. "It's not about sex. It's about power," Christina told her. "Flasher women are treating you like a servant, a nothing. They know you can't complain. Do you think Mr. Roget cares if a clerk is harassed by a big spender?"

"So what do I do if I get one?" Helen had asked.

"Pretend she's dressed. It pisses her off."

Helen steeled herself for her first confrontation with a female flasher. Sharmayne is dressed, she told herself. She's dressed in a jumpsuit. She's . . . not sitting quite like a flasher. Her legs are closed. And what's on her thighs? Some kind of weird stocking?

Helen couldn't stop herself. She stared at Sharmayne's

thighs. They were ruined by rippling trenches and craters. The skin over the indentations sagged like an old woman's. Worse, it was flaky-dry and blotchy.

A botched liposuction. Helen had seen those telltale ripple scars before, but never this bad.

"A former model," Tara had called Sharmayne. With those scars, she was banished from the catwalk forever. She could never do anything but the dreariest catalog and department store work. When she saw the pity in Helen's face, she turned defiant. "Admiring your boss's handiwork?" she said.

Helen was speechless.

"Christina recommended the doctor for this liposuction. Said he never made a mistake. Except that day, he did. Turned out the good doctor had a little alcohol and pill problem. I was his wake-up call. He got treatment, and he settled out of court. I had to promise to never mention his name, but thanks to my lawyer, I can afford to shop here for the rest of my life."

Helen could tell that wasn't enough. Sharmayne fed on admiration. Once anyone saw her scars, it was gone. She was a starving rich woman.

"I make Christina wait on me," she said. "Just to remind her. I don't think I want anything today."

Helen closed the dressing room door.

It took Helen and Tara half an hour to hang up all Sharmayne's clothes. Tara was no bigger than a twelve-year-old girl, but she worked like a dockhand, hauling the heaviest loads. She had quit flipping and touching her long hair. She was too busy.

Tara knew how to sell clothes to Juliana's customers, perhaps because she dressed like them. Helen would never have dared wear those snakeskin low-rise jeans or the matching top that bared her midsection. Helen would look like a hooker. Tara looked cute.

Tara admitted the sales job was harder than it looked. "I'm so tired at night I fall straight into bed, and Paulie has to massage my feet." She held up one platformed foot with its shell-pink nails.

Then Tara picked up another blouse and buttoned it on a

padded hanger. "Helen, when I'm a regular customer again, I promise I will put everything back on the hangers."

In the quiet times between customers, Helen and Tara talked. Tara had been a Juliana's regular for six years. She knew everything about everyone, even where Brittney got her endless supply of money.

"That's such a sad story," Tara said. She leaned forward, her long hair forming a dark veil. "She was engaged to this rich millionaire named Steve. . . ."

In Lauderdale, there were poor millionaires, who were mortgaged to the hilt, and those who were solvent. They were the rich millionaires.

"Brittney was supposed to marry Steve. She really loved him. They were going to be married at the Biltmore. A big wedding with a sit-down dinner. We were all invited. I had the cutest hot pink dress with these little spaghetti straps. I couldn't bring myself to wear it after what happened."

Tara looked sad, but Helen didn't know if it was because of Brittney's tragic loss or her own.

"What happened?" Helen prompted.

"Steve committed suicide right before the wedding. No one knew why. Brittney said that he'd been really down, but Steve would not tell her what was wrong. He didn't leave a suicide note. He'd been drinking more than usual. They found his body in a canal near the Seventeenth Street Bridge. He left Brittney everything in his will: a two-million-dollar house in Bridge Harbour, stocks, bonds, and a lot of money."

"If she has lots of money, why did she date a mobster like Vinnie?" Helen said.

Tara looked surprised that Helen would ask. "You have to have a boyfriend," she said.

"What about the Golden Beach guy?" Helen said, remembering Brittney's timely thank-you gift to Christina.

"Brittney didn't fit in with his stuffy old friends," Tara said. "His wife made a terrible fuss. Most wives know their husbands date, and they're grateful they don't have to . . . you know . . . but not this one."

Helen knew, but she was still amazed by Tara's priggishness. She couldn't even bring herself to say something like "sleep with their husbands."

Helen also noticed that Brittney's Golden Beach boyfriend was married, and so was her mobster, Vinnie. Brittney liked other women's men.

Helen enjoyed Tara's stories. They made Juliana's sound like a soap opera. This week was almost like a vacation for her, too. Helen could not forget Christina's skimming, drug dealing, maybe even murder for hire. She'd closed her eyes to that once before, and now Desiree Easlee was dead. But she had only two days before Christine returned. She had to face that ugly reality.

When Helen came back from lunch, she found Tara staring at herself in the triple mirror.

"I need to perk up my tits," Tara said. Her breasts looked plenty perky to Helen, and she said so.

"Do you really think so? I think they are a little droopy. Paulie has a plastic surgeon friend who says he'll work on me for free. He wouldn't make me any bigger, just put a little on top to tip them up again."

"Tara, you're perfect," Helen said. "You saw what happened to Sharmayne. Why would you do that to yourself?"

Tara shrugged. "Everyone gets boob jobs. They're like a visit to the gynecologist or something. Besides, I don't want to lose Paulie."

"Paulie is crazy about you," Helen said. "And even if you did lose him, which you wouldn't, there are other men."

Helen didn't add "other better men, who don't talk about your breasts and buns in public," but Tara heard her unspoken words.

"You think Paulie's kinda crude, don't you?"

Helen hesitated, choosing her words carefully. She waited too long. Tara said, "I'm running out of options, Helen. I got refused at a South Beach club. That's never happened."

"What do you mean, refused?" Helen said.

"I had to wait in line with the tourists and the nobodies, with the people saying, 'I'm the owner's personal trainer.' 'I'm his photographer.' It was humiliating.

"I always get in. I wear the right clothes. I never wear

cheap shoes. This time, the bouncers made me wait. That's never happened before. Not in New York or LA. But it happened in South Beach. I'm losing it, Helen. I have to hang onto Paulie. He has money, and he cares about me."

"Do you care about him?" Helen said.

"I care about surviving," Tara said.

Helen felt sorry for Tara. That's what all this high-risk surgery and dieting was about. Survival. Tara felt she only had one commodity to offer, her looks, and she feared they were fading.

"I came so close to making it," she told Helen. "So close I could almost touch it. Then it all slipped away. It was because of September eleventh. I never told you what September eleventh did to me. I lost so much. I cried and cried until I couldn't cry any more."

"Did you lose family members or friends?" Helen said.

"Worse. It was personal," Tara said. "Paulie and I were supposed to stay with this movie producer in LA. He was giving a big party with movie stars and everything. Then the attacks happened, and we couldn't go. All the flights to LA were canceled for days. The producer was supposed to give me an audition. Paulie was going to put up some money for his movie."

Helen thought she was missing some connection here. Why didn't Tara fly out later for the audition? "Was the producer on one of the hijacked planes? Or was he killed some other way?" she said.

"At the box office," Tara said. "His film had just been released. It was about these terrorists who attack New York, but they used old-fashioned bombs and stuff, and nobody wanted to watch it. He lost all his money. Nobody wanted to see that movie, even on cable. My one big chance, ruined by a bunch of Arabs. I don't think I'll ever get over it."

"You must be scarred for life," Helen said.

Tara missed the sarcasm. She was back in front of the triple mirror.

"Maybe it's this top," she said. "It's heinous. It makes me look fat. Do you think it makes me look fat? Paulie bought it for my birthday. The pants fit like a dream, but the minute I put on the top, I thought, 'This makes me look fat.'"

"You don't look fat," Helen said. "What do you weigh? Ninety-eight pounds?"

"Ninety-six," Tara said. "See? I am fat. I've gained two pounds. You can see it, too."

"Tara, I never said that."

But Tara would not be consoled. She was getting on Helen's nerves. Helen wished there were customers to distract them. It was five-forty-five, and a last-minute rush was unlikely.

Even Tara could see that Helen was eager to leave Juliana's. "You go ahead," Tara said. "I'll lock up." Helen left gratefully, never dreaming what would happen next.

Chapter 14

"This wine is not bad," Peggy the parrot lady said. "What month is it?"

Peggy and Helen were out by the pool after work, sipping wine and slapping mosquitoes. The sort of wine they could afford did not have a vintage year.

"Not sure," said Helen. "I got it in a box at the drug store. I think it has an expiration date, though."

Pete the parrot had his usual perch on Peggy's shoulder. Helen reached out to pet Pete's soft feathers with one finger, and he nuzzled her.

"He's a love bird," Helen said.

"Speaking of love, there he is," Peggy said. "Wouldn't you love to go out with the divine Daniel?"

Daniel Dayson looked even better the second time around. He seemed built on a different scale from ordinary men. His legs were strong as cypress trees. His arms were ropes of muscle. His long black hair rippled past his broad shoulders. Helen did not want to run her fingers through his hair. She wanted to grab it and hold on tight while he . . .

"Hello, Helen," Daniel said. His dark blue eyes seemed to bore holes into her. She could feel her will power slowly leaking away.

"Hi," Helen said. It was the most coherent thing she'd managed to say to Daniel since he'd moved in. What was the matter with her? She was too old to be acting this way.

"Would you like a glass of wine, Daniel?" Peggy said. "It's a fresh box."

"No, thanks, Peggy. Some other time I'd love to, but I have a date." Daniel waved good-bye and walked back to his room. Helen watched his massive glutes move under the thin red fabric of his tiny gym shorts.

"He has a date every night," Peggy said. "Same lucky girl. They usually wind up in his room. I should know. I live right next to him. I never hear a sound except his bed-springs—and the moans. My lord, the way that woman carries on. He leaves a satisfied customer."

"Is that why you offered him a fresh box?" Helen said.

"Helen!" Peggy said.

Peggy and Helen started giggling and couldn't stop. They were laughing so hard, they didn't hear Cal come up behind them. It was the first time Helen had seen him since the disastrous Catfish Dewey's date. Now Helen wondered what she could have seen in Cal. He seemed old and wizened, compared to the magnificent Daniel. She'd never noticed before that Cal's chest was narrow. His legs, which she'd once admired, now seemed too skinny. And was he getting a bit of a dowager's hump at his neck—or a permanent slouch?

"I was in the laundry room. Your boyfriend's laundry is done, girls," Cal said, nastily. "Who wants to fold his underwear?"

Peggy winked at Helen and said, "Oh, me, me, it's my turn." She moaned dramatically and fell backward into the chaise.

Pete let out a startled "Awwwk!" Cal stomped off without a word.

"Men!" Peggy said. "They're all jealous." That caused another fit of giggles. It was broken by Margery, who blew in like a purple tornado.

"Helen, you got an emergency call from the store on my phone," she said. "I think it's serious. First one of those you've ever had."

"Is it Christina?" Helen asked, running for Margery's apartment.

"No, some guy," her landlady said.

Margery's phone was on the TV tray next to her purple recliner. The caller was Paulie, Tara's boyfriend. He sounded panicked.

"Helen? Is that you? Is it OK to call this number? Tara said you gave it to her for emergencies."

"I did, Paulie. What's wrong?"

"Tara hasn't come home yet. It's nine-thirty. Juliana's closes at six. She called me and said she was going to lock up, then stop off at the supermarket. She should have been home by now. If she was going anywhere else, she would have told me. She's very good about that. No one is answering the phone at the store, and her cell phone isn't on. I've already called the hospitals and checked with the police, and she's not been in a car accident. I'll stay here in case she gets home. Could you go over to Juliana's and see if everything is OK?"

"Of course, Paulie," she said. "I'll leave right now."

She hung up the phone. "I'll go with you," Margery said.

"No, stay here in case Paulie calls again. He's a real worrywart. Tara probably went shopping and lost track of the time."

But Helen still ran to the store. She didn't like what she saw when she got there. The lights were on. The alarm system was not. She did not see the "armed" light. She tried Juliana's green door. The buzzer lock was on. She peeked in the window and saw clothes lying on the floor, a chair upended, a box of hangers overturned. She did not see any sign of Tara.

Helen's heart was beating fast. She felt time slow down. Tara! Oh, my God. Where was she? Had she been kidnapped? Killed? Helen unlocked the green door and ran inside calling, "Tara! Tara! Where are you?" She heard a moan coming from a dressing room.

Helen threw open the dressing room door. Tara was lying on the floor. Her top was ripped down the front. A nasty bump on her forehead was rapidly turning purple. There was a small red smear of blood on her forehead. Tara groaned and tried to sit up, then fell back on the carpet as a single drop of blood slid down her face. Her long black hair fanned around her.

"Tara!" Helen knelt down beside her. "Tara! What happened? Who did this to you?"

"Two men," she said, her voice barely a whisper. "They forced their way in. They hurt me."

"Did they . . ." Helen forced herself to say the word. "Did they rape you?"

"No," Tara said. "They hit me—rammed my head into the wall."

"Oh, Tara, oh, no, I'm so sorry. I should have never left you here alone. Don't move. I'll call the police and get an ambulance."

"No!" Tara said, gripping her arm. She really seemed afraid now. "They'll come back and hurt me."

"That's why we need the police."

"Nooooo," Tara wailed, trying to sit up again. "Please, just call Paulie."

"Paulie would want me to call the police, too," Helen said, firmly. "You stay there." She ran to the phone outside the dressing room, dialed 911, then told the operator what happened.

"Have the intruders left the building? Is anyone else in the store?"

"I don't know," Helen said. "I just ran in when I saw the lights on and found Tara and called you. I could look around."

"Stay right there, ma'am," the 911 operator said. "Don't hang up. Keep talking to me. We'll have someone there in a moment."

Helen could hear sirens, then the screech of tires. Two patrol cars pulled up in front of the store, and Helen ran up front to let them inside. The two officers looked enough alike to be twins. Both were about six feet tall with short dark hair and open boyish faces, until you saw their eyes. They had hawk's eyes, alert and watchful. They walked like gunslingers. Helen found that comforting. One had a name tag that said T. Gerritsen. The other one was J. MacWilliams.

The two officers asked Helen to wait outside by the door. "But Tara's in there," she said.

"We know that, ma'am. We need to check things first," Gerritsen said.

The two officers went inside Juliana's, guns drawn. No one had ever entered the fabled green door that way, although a few women must have thought about it.

While she waited, Helen kept berating herself. She should have stayed with Tara until closing. Instead, she let herself get irritated by Tara's silliness. What kind of manager was she? She couldn't even stay another fifteen minutes to make sure Tara left the store safely. If anything happened to her, Helen would have two deaths on her hands—Desiree Easlee and Tara.

She was wringing her guilty hands when Officer Gerritsen reappeared. "The paramedics are on their way. They'll check her out."

Helen saw Tara sitting on the loveseat, talking to the other officer, MacWilliams. She wanted to sink down on the carpet and cry with relief.

"Can I see Tara?"

"In a little bit," Gerritsen said. "We're talking to her now. Do you have the boyfriend's phone number?"

"Yes, sure. I should have called him. I'll do that now."

"We'll do that," the officer said. "We need you to see if anything is missing or damaged. Don't touch anything. Just see if you can tell."

Helen walked around the store, stepping carefully to avoid the clothes scattered on the carpet. There weren't as many as she first thought. Six blouses were pulled off their padded hangers. A few belts were tossed around, along with an Hermes scarf and a Versace evening dress. A chair was overturned, and a box of hangers was spilled on the floor. But nothing was damaged. Even the money was still in the register, about five hundred dollars.

Helen told Officer Gerritsen that nothing was missing up front, not even the cash in the register. "But I'd better check the stockroom, just in case."

Before she could do that, the paramedics arrived. They gave Tara an ice pack to put on her forehead and urged her to go to the emergency room or see her family doctor. Tara refused. She signed a release form, and the paramedics left.

Helen was shocked by her appearance. The bump on Tara's forehead had swollen into a purple knot with green highlights. Her snakeskin top was nearly torn in two and she was missing one shoe. But Tara seemed alert and otherwise unhurt.

The police still would not let Helen talk with Tara. She went to the stockroom to finish the requested check. Everything looked undisturbed. The only odd thing was on the security panel. The store's interior cameras had been turned off. Helen wondered if she or Tara had hit the wrong button and accidentally shut them off.

Helen could hear the police questioning Tara. She was telling her story for what sounded like the second or third time. Helen edged to the door and peeked out at the scene.

"I was getting ready to close," Tara said. "It was almost six o'clock. That's when we close. I was here alone because Helen went home early."

Helen winced.

"Two black men forced their way into the store. They both had guns."

"What did they look like?" Officer MacWilliams said.

Tara pulled her long hair forward until it hid her face. "One man was tall, sort of husky, muscular. I told you that. One was skinny and short, almost as short as me. I couldn't see their faces. They were wearing ski masks and gloves."

In South Florida? Helen wondered. No one on white bread Las Olas noticed two black men dressed like this?

"How did they get in?" MacWilliams asked.

Good question. Tara would have had to buzz them in.

"They knocked on the door and sort of pushed their way in," Tara said, vaguely. "I'm not really sure. I guess I panicked when I saw the guns. They ran inside and started throwing things around. They kept asking me, 'Where is it?' I didn't know what they were taking about."

"Did you see them take anything, ma'am?"

"No," she said.

"What about the money in the cash register? I understand there's a considerable sum in there."

"I didn't get a chance to count it and put it in the safe," she said. "I think the short one was going to the cash register when the tall one started hitting me. He hit me in the head."

"I thought you said he pushed your head into the wall," MacWilliams said.

"He did that, too," Tara said, pulling her hair forward to hide more of her face. All Helen saw now was a black curtain of hair. "I'm sorry. I'm not making sense. My head hurts."

"Just a few more questions, ma'am. When the tall man grabbed you, what did you do?"

"I fought with him, of course. That's how my blouse got torn."

Helen saw that only Tara's top was ripped, the one that she thought made her look fat. The pants that fit like a dream were fine.

"Your nails are pretty long. Did you scratch his face? Sometimes we can get the suspect's DNA from skin under the victim's nails."

Tara held out her hands. Her long fragile fake nails were unbroken. Tara must have realized she didn't look like she'd put up a fight, because she said, "There wasn't much I could do. He was bigger than me."

"What time do you think it was when the tall man hit you?" the officer said.

"A little after six," she said. "That's a guess. I wasn't keeping track of the time. He hit me, and I heard someone rattling the door handle, and then both men ran out the back, and I passed out."

"And you've been unconscious for over three and a half hours?"

"Yes," she said. "I may have awakened once or twice but I didn't really come to until Helen found me."

"The blood on your forehead is fresh, ma'am. You'd think after three and a half hours, it would have dried."

Tara started crying. "You don't believe me," she said.

"I didn't say that, ma'am," MacWilliams said. "Now, you say that your store's security system wasn't on yet, and your security cameras were not working. But the jewelry store near you has a security camera. Maybe it caught the two men as they walked by there."

The little bit of Tara visible behind the curtain of hair seemed to grow paler.

"No," she said. "I don't think they walked by the jewelry store. I think they got out of a cab in front of this store."

"A cab," the officer said. "That's good. Cabs keep records."

"Or maybe it wasn't a cab," Tara said quickly. "No, I was wrong. It was a regular car. A white car. Like those white cabs, except this car didn't have the yellow stripe the way the cabs do."

She's lying, Helen thought. Even I can tell she's lying.

"Did you see the driver?" MacWilliams asked. But before Tara could lie again, Paulie's angry voice thundered through the store.

"What the hell do you mean, why did I wait almost three hours to call someone? Are you questioning me? Me? I been worried sick. Tara told me she was going to the supermarket. She should have been home about seven, seven-thirty at the latest. When she didn't come home, I called the hospitals and the police, afraid she'd been in a car accident. Then I called Helen. Why didn't I just drive over here? Because we live in friggin' Coral Springs. It would take forty-five mintues to get here. Now, do I have to call my lawyer, or are you gonna let us out of this place?" Tara looked up, and her hair fell back to reveal a bruised but hopeful face.

"Do you want to make a sworn statement now?" the officer asked Tara.

"No," Tara said, and put down the black curtain of hair again. "I'm too sick."

"You've badgered this poor girl enough," Paulie said, outraged. He stomped angrily back toward the black silk-satin loveseats. His gut bulged out of a navy golf shirt two sizes too small, but for the first time, Helen liked Paulie.

The officer ignored him and said to Tara, "You will prosecute these men if we find them."

"Damn right she will," Paulie said. "But you jerkoffs

couldn't find your ass with both hands. I don't think you'll ever find them."

Helen didn't think the police would find the two men, either—because they did not exist.

"She's not coming back here tomorrow," Paulie said. He scooped Tara into his arms and carried her out the door. Tara's long hair hung down, a dark flag of surrender.

Chapter 15

"Tara's whole story is phoney as a South Beach boob job," Margery said.

"I was going to say three-dollar bill," Peggy said. "Either way, it's a fake."

Helen felt better. On the walk home from Juliana's, she had begun to doubt herself. What if two men really had forced their way into Juliana's? What if they were connected with Christina and her drugs?

When Helen got home to the Coronado apartments, it was after eleven. A worried Peggy and Margery were waiting for her by the pool. Helen felt so drained, she could hardly walk across the lawn to talk to them.

"You look terrible," Margery said. "What happened? Are you OK? Is Tara OK?"

"Tara was attacked by two men. At least, I think she was," Helen said. "It's all my fault. I should have never left her alone."

They made Helen sit down and drink tea and eat dark chocolate. "You need sugar when you're stressed," Margery said.

Margery gave her a Godiva dark chocolate bar. Peggy brought over a box of Thin Mint Girl Scout cookies she kept in the freezer. Helen ate the Godiva bar in four bites. A half dozen Thin Mints disappeared off her plate, so she must have eaten those, too.

After that jolt of caffeine, she had enough energy to talk about what happened in full detail. Margery and Peggy were as skeptical as the police when they heard the story, and that reassured Helen.

"She's lying," Peggy said flatly. Pete, sitting on her shoulder, squawked his agreement.

"Two black men in gloves and ski masks on Las Olas?" Margery said. "They might as well show up in that getup at a Klan rally. Even crackheads aren't that nuts."

"I know South Florida is full of crazy criminals," Helen said, "but I can't believe two men would force their way into Juliana's and not take any money. There was five hundred dollars cash in the register. And why rob a dress shop, when there are jewelry stores on the same street?"

"Nothing is missing at Juliana's, right?" Margery said.

"Not so much as a scarf," Helen said. "And our internal security cameras were turned off."

"Sounds like Tara faked a robbery," Peggy said.

"But why do that, if nothing is missing? Did Tara want the attention? Or was she trying to hide something?" Helen said.

"Hmmm," Margery said, chewing thoughtfully on a Thin Mint. "I wonder if she was seeing a lover, and the time got away from her. She couldn't explain her absence to her boyfriend, Paulie, so she staged the robbery and blamed those favorite fantasy culprits, the two black men."

"Maybe she just wanted rid of that ugly snakeskin top," Peggy said.

Helen laughed. "Listen, I'm exhausted. Thanks for waiting up for me and for the chocolate. I have to go to work in the morning. I'd better . . ." She stopped dead.

A luminous orange bra and stiletto heels were floating toward them in the darkness. The three women stared in awestruck silence at the approaching bra like it was a 38D UFO.

As it got closer, they saw the glow-in-the-dark bra and heels were worn by a young woman. She had on a thong swimsuit, except the lower part didn't glow. The woman had yards of brown hair, but her suit was spectacularly small.

She looked like Wonder Woman in an orange thong. Helen had never seen any breasts, real or fake, jut out like that.

"Excuse me," the glowing young woman said. "Do any of you drive a green Kia?"

"I do," Peggy said.

"I'm staying at Danny's, and I'm blocked in. Could you move your car? I have to be at work at midnight. Oh, is that your cute little birdie?"

Pete made a sweet chirping sound that Helen had never heard before.

"I'll be glad to move my car," Peggy told her. "Come along, traitor," she said to Pete.

When they left, Margery said, "That's Daniel's girlfriend. That man needs to find a nice girl. He's dating a stripper."

"Are you sure?" Helen said.

"What do you think she is, dressed like that and going to work at midnight? A nurse?"

"I'm beat. I'm not thinking at all," Helen said. "Good night, Margery. Thanks again."

Helen headed to her place, which suddenly seemed far away. She waded through the thick fog of pot smoke swirling around Phil's door, then opened her own apartment. Its familiar smell of tropical mold and trapped heat felt like home.

She was exhausted but jittery from the caffeine in the tea and the chocolate. Helen finally fell into a restless sleep, still worrying about Tara and the strange events at Juliana's.

Helen was awakened by the sound of a key in the lock. Was someone opening her door? she wondered groggily.

She willed herself alert. Wait. That wasn't her door. It was her neighbor Phil's door.

Phil!

He really did exist. Helen scrambled out of bed, determined to finally see the invisible pothead. She didn't bother throwing on a robe over her T-shirt. She ran barefoot across the cool terrazzo floor and flung open her front door, blinking at the bright morning light.

Helen was too late. All she saw was two brown plastic grocery bags disappearing into Phil's place. Nothing else.

She did not even get a glimpse of Phil's hand. One bag seemed to be filled with anonymous canned goods. The other contained the biggest bag of Oreo cookies in captivity.

"Nice shirt," drawled a man's voice. It was Daniel. "Is that Elvis with an American flag? Very patriotic."

Helen blushed. Then she realized she wasn't wearing any underwear and blushed more. The T-shirt was long enough to cover the vital areas, but she was standing barefoot and pantieless in front of the most gorgeous man in South Florida.

Naturally, he had to be dressed. Daniel was wearing a perfectly tailored navy blue uniform with official-looking red patches on his bulging biceps. Helen thought he looked even better in his uniform than he did in his gym shorts.

"Nice uniform," she said. A new record. Now she'd said two coherent words to Daniel.

"Thanks," he said. "I'm off to work. See you later."

Daniel was working on a sunny day, Helen thought, when many single men would be heading for the beach or the bar. But Daniel was different from your average South Florida single man. He had ambition.

She glanced at the kitchen clock. It was only seven-thirty. She didn't have to go to work yet. She went back to her lumpy bed. It squeaked loudly, but it squeaked for her alone.

Daniel is perfect, she thought. Absolutely perfect.

Too bad he already had the perfect girlfriend. Helen remembered Wonder Woman in the glow-in-the-dark bra and sighed.

I can't compete with a woman who looks like that, she thought. The perfect man is one flight up, and he might as well be a thousand miles away. No, a thousand miles would be better. Then I wouldn't know he existed. Daniel is handsome, hardworking, and polite. He's too good to be real, except he is. I don't have a chance with that man.

But Helen's mind would not stay on the divine Daniel. She was filled with a nameless dread. It grew larger and larger and would not go away, not even at work. Nothing bad happened at Juliana's. In fact, Thursday passed swiftly and pleasantly with her favorite customers, and the cash register rang merrily.

But Helen was afraid, and she did not know why. The fear grew all day, sitting on her spirit like some dark un-named monster.

By Thursday night, the fear had a name: Christina.

Did Christina really arrange Desiree's death? Helen had to know. She could not work for a murderer. She would mention Desiree's death first thing Friday when she came back. She could tell by Christina's reaction if she was guilty.

If Christina really killed Desiree, then she would quit on the spot and go to the police. Unless quitting would get her killed, too. Maybe she should continue working there until the police arrested Christina.

Which was more dangerous: staying or quitting? Helen didn't know.

All she knew for sure was Christina would be back to-morrow, and with her would come chaos.

Chapter 16

Helen had dreaded this morning for a whole week. It was the day Christina came back to work.

Then something worse happened: Christina did not show up.

Helen opened the store by herself at nine-thirty. Christina is caught in the Third Avenue Bridge traffic, Helen told herself. She had been held up as much as twenty minutes by that blasted drawbridge. Nothing made Helen feel more like a wage slave than sitting in traffic waiting for some billionaire's hundred-foot yacht to sail under the lifted bridge.

At ten a.m., Helen decided that Christina had been delayed in an accident on I-95. The highway was notorious for bad driving. Everyone on it was either eighty going twenty or twenty going eighty. She turned on the stockroom radio and listened to the news and traffic. No accidents.

At ten-thirty she realized Christina had overslept. She had turned off the alarm and gone back to sleep. Helen called Christina's home phone. It rang and rang in that echoey way that happens only in an empty home. Helen called Christina's cell phone. She got a generic recording: "The subscriber you have called does not answer. Please try your call again. Message DH124."

At eleven o'clock, she called the store's Canadian owner, Gilbert Roget. He gave her some sensible advice.

"Are you there alone, Helen? Then stay at the store until

six and close up. Go by Christina's place tonight, and see if she's sick. If no one answers, call the police and report her missing. And get that girl, what's her name, Tara, back working at the shop."

Helen had downplayed the trumped-up robbery to Mr. Roget. He'd shrugged it off. He thought America was a violent place, anyway. No damage was done, nothing was taken. It was no big deal.

Helen hoped Tara would return. Actually, she hoped she wouldn't need Tara. Suddenly, she wanted Christina back. Helen wanted everything to be the way it was when she first started working at Juliana's. But she knew that was not possible.

"Mr. Roget, I'll be glad to check on Christina, but I don't have a car."

"Then take a bus," Gilbert Roget said. "I'll reimburse you for the fare."

You're all heart, Helen thought. Christina lived somewhere in Sunnysea. A bus ride would take most of her evening. But she was too worried about Christina to argue with the penny-pinching store owner.

"Do you know Christina's address?"

"No, but my secretary does. I'll have her call you back."

The secretary said Christina lived at One Ocean Palm Towers in Sunnysea Beach.

"Are you sure?" Helen said, surprised.

"Yes, in 2200P. That's the penthouse."

The penthouse? Those started at two million dollars. Any high-priced high-rise in South Florida had to have one of these words in its name: One, Ocean, Palm, or Towers. When the first expensive high-rise was built on Sunnysea Beach, the developers used all four of the magic words. They needed them to combat Sunnysea's down-at-heels image. The funky little beach town was mostly 1950s motels, T-shirt shops, bars, and offbeat beach houses. One Ocean Palm Towers was the first grand high-rise condo development in Sunnysea. Those who loved the little beach town were afraid it would not be the last.

After she locked up for the day, Helen walked home. She

found Peggy and Pete the parrot in their usual after-work spot by the pool.

"I'll be glad to drive you to Christina's," Peggy said. "I've wanted to get a closer look at One Ocean Palm Towers, anyway. That's where Pete and I will move when I win the lottery."

Helen noticed that Peggy said "when" she won—not "if." Pete went back to Peggy's apartment with an indignant squawk. Then Peggy and Helen piled into the little green Kia.

Christina's place was twenty minutes and several million dollars away from the Coronado. The marble sign announcing One Ocean Palm Towers was bigger than Helen's apartment. It was surrounded by a forest of palm trees and pricey plants. They drove past a fountain the size of a swimming pool, pushing up a regal plume of water.

"How does the manager of a dress shop live here?" Peggy said.

"Good question," Helen said. "Christina only makes around eighteen thousand a year."

"This looks like about a hundred years," Peggy said.

"One hundred eleven and change," Helen said. She hadn't completely lost her number-crunching skills. "Christina also makes a commission, but that wouldn't cover the monthly maintenance fees on this place."

"Maybe Christina inherited some money," Peggy said.

"In that case, why work at Juliana's at all?"

At the entrance, Peggy started to park the little green Kia between a vintage Jaguar and a silver Mercedes when a doorman came running out. He directed her around the back to the service parking. The Kia wound up next to a plumber's van.

Even the back parking lot had a stunning view of the ocean. Peggy and Helen watched the wild waves crash on the private beach for a moment. Christina could not afford this ocean view even if she skimmed a thousand dollars a week from Juliana's, Helen thought. If she was arranging murders for hire at three thousand each, she'd still have to wipe out half of Broward County. What else had Christina been up to?

Nothing good, Helen decided.

The magnificent marble front with its vigilant doorman was for show. The service entrance door was propped open with a brick. Two Hispanic men in khaki stood outside it, smoking. They nodded politely when Helen and Peggy walked past them into the back entrance. The decor was grimy cinderblocks and unpainted concrete.

"The bucks stop here," Peggy said. "Want to take the service elevator to the penthouse?"

"Let's go around to the front entrance and see if we can talk to a receptionist," Helen said. "Maybe he'll know when Christina is supposed to return."

The doorman looked at Peggy's flip-flops and cutoffs the same way he'd viewed her car. Fortunately, Helen was still wearing her Ungaro suit. He let the women approach the reception desk.

The lobby was slick with shiny polished marble. Helen felt like she was walking across a skating rink. The manager on duty was a pale blond creature in a black suit. Helen was not surprised that his name tag said Mr. White. He looked down his nose at her and said, "Miss Christina left no special instructions with us as to when she expected to return from her vacation."

"She told me she'd be back at work today, and she didn't show up. I'm concerned about her. So is the owner of Juliana's, Mr. Roget." Helen hoped dropping a rich man's name would help her get taken seriously.

"I understand your concern, madam," Mr. White said, "but I cannot open her door."

"Can you let us go up and at least ring her doorbell? What if she's sick and needs help?"

"Each One Ocean Palm Towers unit is equipped with a security system and has a panic button in every room, including the lavatories," Mr. White said. "If Miss Christina needed personal aid, she would contact us. However, to set your mind at ease, I will go up with you and ring her doorbell."

The elevator was paneled like a lawyer's office. They rode to the twenty-second floor in silence. The doors opened on a dramatic view of the ocean, green and turquoise until it faded into the darker evening sky.

"Wow!" Helen and Peggy said together. Mr. White's nostrils pinched in disapproval. People who went to the twenty-second floor were not supposed to be so easily impressed. They stopped in front of white-paneled double doors with a discreet brass plaque that read "2200."

"Well, there are no newspapers piled up on her doorstep," Helen said.

Mr. White looked scandalized. "We would not permit that," he said. He solemnly pressed the doorbell, and they heard the chime echo through the apartment. But there were no footsteps.

"Ring it again," Helen said. Mr. White did. Again, there was nothing but the sound of chimes. Then Helen thought of Thumbs, the cat Christina loved so fiercely.

"Do you know what happened to her cat?" she asked.

"I'm sure she made private arrangements for the care of her animal," Mr. White said. "Now, if you're quite finished."

There was nothing they could do but take the elevator down to the vast marble lobby and walk back out to Peggy's little car.

"I don't like this," Peggy said.

"Me either," Helen said. "Christina has never missed a day of work in her life. If she isn't there, then . . ." Helen stopped, afraid to go on.

"She's dead?" Peggy finished.

"Well, something's very wrong," Helen said, unwilling to jump to that conclusion yet. "Mr. Roget said if I didn't find her at home, I should file a missing person report."

She reported Christina missing to a bored Sunnysea Beach cop. He told Helen that Christina was an adult and could come and go as she pleased. The police could not do anything until Christina had been missing at least forty-eight hours.

"But she was due back today, and she missed work," Helen said.

"Was she known to be depressed?" the officer asked.

"No, Christina was looking forward to her vacation."

"Was she in the process of a messy divorce, or did she have arguments with her spouse?"

"She was single," Helen said. "I thought I said that. Her boyfriend just broke up with her, but he didn't threaten her or anything."

"He have any history of prior physical assaults?"

"Joe? No!"

"Has the subject ever extended a vacation before?"

"No," Helen said.

The cop droned on. "Did she make her return flight? Did she, for that matter, make her flight out?"

"I don't know if she was flying anywhere," Helen said.

"Where was she going on her vacation?"

"I don't know," Helen said, feeling foolish. "All I know is that Christina was eager to leave."

"Then maybe, ma'am, she wasn't eager to come back."

Chapter 17

Another restless, sleepless night. Helen's lumpy bed seemed to be stuffed with cabbages and bowling balls. Any attempt to find a more comfortable position set off a series of lonely squeaks.

At seven a.m., Helen gave up and got up. She told herself she was getting up an hour early because she wanted breakfast by the pool. But she knew what she really wanted: to see Daniel in his dashing blue uniform.

Helen felt guilty thinking about Daniel Dayson. Christina was missing, maybe dead, and she was carrying on a schoolgirl crush. But I can't spend all my time worrying about Christina, she told herself.

A disapproving inner voice lectured her: "Didn't Rob and Cal teach you anything? You know you have terrible taste in men."

But Cal was a harmless mistake, the kind a woman made when she jumped back into the dating pool. She didn't sleep with him or anything. She lost a little money, that's all. And Rob? The pain of Rob's betrayal seemed to be receding in the February sunshine. It was winter in St. Louis, and it was easy for her heart to stay frozen there. But South Florida was so lush and romantic and most of all, warm, that things seemed possible.

Helen dressed carefully, spending extra time on her hair and makeup. Then she poured herself a cup of coffee. It was quarter to eight when she went outside. Margery and Peggy were at the picnic table under the coconut palms.

"You look nice this morning," Peggy said, looking up from her paper.

"He's already left for work," Margery said. Helen flushed. How did her landlady know?

"Daniel is always gone by seven-thirty," Margery said. Her shorts set was covered with purple butterflies. Margery pointed to a white bakery box and a stack of paper napkins on the picnic table. "Want a chocolate croissant?"

Helen did. Peggy took another.

Peggy was dressed for her receptionist's job in a parrot-green pantsuit. She looked like an exotic bird or Pete's big sister. The wild parrots were screeching in the palms overhead, taunting Pete. He ignored them. Pete had no interest in his kind, just as Peggy had no interest in the male species. They were content with each other.

Peggy pointed to her morning paper. "A guy in Hallandale won the lottery," she said. "Twenty-three million dollars. He's thirty years old, and he'll never have to work again. He's going to take the whole thing in a lump sum, so he'll get about half, something like twelve million."

"Why would he do that?" Margery said. "Why not take the payout over thirty years? He'll get the whole twenty-three million, plus interest. It's more money that way. I could understand someone my age taking it in a lump, but he's a young guy."

"No, he did it right," Peggy said. "All the experts say the figures work out in your favor if you take it in a lump sum and invest it. That's how I'm going to do it when I win."

She was serious, Helen thought. "Which lottery game do you play?" she asked.

"Lotto. It has the big jackpots."

"How many tickets do you buy each week?" Helen said.

"Three a day. Twenty-one dollars a week."

Helen whistled.

"That's not much," Peggy said. "There's a guy who comes into the store and buys sixty dollars in tickets every week, and those are nothing but scratch-offs."

"If you invested that money, you'd have something," Margery said.

"If I win the lottery, I'll really have something," Peggy said. "Think about it. A guy right in Hallandale won twenty-three million. The good luck is getting closer. Look at the smile on that man's face. That's the same smile you're going to see on mine."

She passed Helen the paper. But Helen never got to the photo of the grinning winner. She was distracted by the headline on the opposite page: "Body of Unidentified Woman Found in Barrel in Biscayne Bay."

The story began, "Miami Palms police are seeking information to identify the body of a woman found dead in a barrel in Biscayne Bay. The barrel was pulled from the water yesterday by . . ."

Helen could hear Peggy and Margery saying, "Helen, what's wrong? Helen, are you OK?" but she couldn't stop reading. The story continued:

"The woman was between thirty and forty years old, with shoulder-length blonde hair, and was wearing a black pants suit, a police spokesperson said. The deceased was described as being of slight build and about five foot three inches tall. Police said the woman is believed to have been dead about a week. The deceased died as the result of blunt trauma, sources said. Persons with information should contact . . ."

The page blurred. "Oh, my God, it's Christina," Helen said. "She's dead. It's right here in the paper."

"Where?" Margery said, grabbing the paper. Helen pointed to the article with a shaky finger. Margery read it and said, "The dead woman was small, skinny, and blonde. That description would fit half the women in South Florida."

But Helen was having trouble breathing. "No, it's her. I know it. It's horrible. She was beaten to death. That's what 'blunt trauma' means. There's a number to call. Margery, can I use your phone?"

"Sure, dear," Margery said. The landlady put an arm around Helen's waist and helped her to her apartment, as if Helen were an invalid. "Now, calm down. Don't get so upset. If she's really dead, it happened awhile ago, and there's nothing you can do about it. Take some deep breaths. There. Feel better? You don't know anything for sure yet. It still might be someone else. Lots of women wear black in South Florida."

But Helen knew it was Christina. She sat down in Margery's comforting purple recliner and had a sudden overpowering desire to fall asleep, but she knew she'd have no rest until she made that call. Her hands shook so badly, Margery had to dial the number for her.

The Miami Palms officer sounded more professional than the bored Sunnysea Beach policeman. Her name was Sweeney, she said.

Helen told Officer Sweeney about Christina not showing up for work. Sweeney asked many of the same questions as the Sunnysea missing persons officer. Helen had the same embarrassingly vague answers. How could she not know where Christina was going on vacation? she asked herself. Because Christina did not want to say. And I did not want to know.

"What was the subject wearing when you last saw her?" Sweeney asked.

"A black pantsuit with a long slinky jacket," Helen said.

"Do you know the brand name?"

"Ferragamo," Helen said. "I'm sure it was a Ferragamo. It was new."

Officer Sweeney tried to keep her voice neutral, but Helen thought she heard a heightened interest. She asked Helen several questions about the suit's details, down to the buttons.

"They were black with a gold center," Helen said. "Very distinctive."

"Would you be able to identify them?"

"Definitely," Helen said.

Then Officer Sweeney asked if Christina had any distinguishing physical characteristics, "something that could help us with the identification."

What made Christina different from any other underfed blonde in South Florida? Helen wondered.

"Well, she had her lips injected with collagen."

"OK," Sweeney said, and Helen knew that was no help. Everyone got their lips enlarged these days.

"And, wait, she just had some biopolymer injections in her face. The illegal ones. Something went wrong, and her right cheek is very swollen. It's really big, about the size of a grapefruit half."

"Um, that's not going to help us in, uh, under the current circumstances," Sweeney said, and Helen's stomach lurched. She realized that elegant Christina was gone forever. Did the dead Christina know she looked like something in a horror movie now? How she would hate that. Was that part of her punishment? Good lord, I sound like my mother, Helen thought, and made herself listen to Sweeney again.

". . . We're trying to make an ID on the body," she heard Sweeney say. "Would you know the name of her dentist?"

"I'm not sure she has one," Helen said. "She told me once that she was afraid of dentists."

"What about any surgical procedures? Any recent biopsies? Any blood she was stockpiling prior to a planned surgery?"

"She's pretty healthy," Helen said. "I don't think she's ever had any operations, except for breast implants. But I guess they don't count. Everyone around here has those, right?"

"Actually, that's very helpful," Sweeney said. "Silicone implants have serial numbers."

Then Helen blurted, "That's awful! Her fake boobs are the only way to tell if it's the real Christina."

"I can't believe I said that to the police," Helen groaned.

"You were in shock," Margery said. "Drink this hot tea."

"What time is it?" Helen said. "I have to open the store."

"It's nine o'clock. Are you sure you're well enough to go to work?" Margery said.

"Don't fuss," Helen said. "Work will do me good." She stood up. She still felt wobbly, but she was OK.

"Peggy will drive you there," Margery said. "And don't argue."

Helen did not. She was grateful for both women's help.

She hoped work would keep her mind off the horror of Christina's death.

At Juliana's, Helen opened a box of silk dresses, wrinkled and crammed too tightly into the box. She tried not to think of Christina, her battered body jammed into a barrel. Was she still alive when the barrel was dumped in the bay?

Helen called the florist and complained that the flowers looked funereal. "Send something cheerful," she said. But the funeral Helen was thinking about was Christina's. It would have to be closed casket. I'm burying her too soon. The police don't know. It may not be Christina.

Everything reminded her of Christina. Helen knew Christina had done wicked things, but that's not how she remembered her. Helen saw her sitting on the silk-satin loveseats, laughing with her regulars. She saw Christina finding the perfect dress for a desperate woman, convincing her it was designed to make a man as lovesick as she was. With Christina's magic, it often did.

Helen saw Christina, slim and elegant, in her exquisite clothes. Then she saw her on an autopsy table, wearing a white sheet and a toe tag.

That's when Helen picked up the phone and called Tara. She could not be alone at Juliana's any more. Tara was eager to return to work.

"I'm sorry about Christina not coming back. I hope it's not serious."

"Nobody knows," Helen said. She would not mention the newspaper article unless she had to. That would make it too real. "Do you know where Christina was going on vacation?"

"It's funny," Tara said, "but she went out of her way to avoid talking about it. I figured it was her business and didn't press her. I'm sorry you want me back because there's trouble, but I can't wait to get out of here."

Helen had not mentioned the fake robbery. The subject seemed to have barbed wire around it. Now Tara was whispering into the phone. "Paulie's smothering me. I swear I can't go to the john without him tagging along. He means well, but I'm going crazy. I'll tell him my shrink recommends I go back to work as part of my recovery. And I know! I'll say the cops have a twenty-four-hour guard on Juliana's. You'll back me up on that, right? I'll be in Monday."

"Terrific," Helen said. "I need you."

And she did. All morning long, customers came in and bought clothes as if someone had shredded their wardrobes with garden shears. Everyone asked after Christina. Some brought her little gifts, which Helen put away for when Christina returned. (If she returned.) I don't know for sure the dead woman is Christina, Helen told herself. (But she is.) The ID hasn't been confirmed yet. (But it will be.)

That afternoon, two Miami Palms homicide detectives showed up at Juliana's. They looked like they'd been auditioning for *Miami Vice*. Did anyone still wear pink sport jackets and two-day stubble? The men even looked like Crockett and Tubbs. She wondered which one lived on the sailboat.

"Do you recognize this purse?" Crockett asked her. He pulled out a brown paper evidence bag. Inside was the vintage gold mesh purse with the diamonds on the clasp. The one Christina had showed Helen the day she left for vacation. Helen looked at it and felt the floor slide away. She grabbed onto the counter to keep from falling.

"Where did you get it?" she said. "Did you find it in her home? Or her car? Pawn shop, that's where you got it. Someone stole it and . . ."

Helen was babbling. She knew it, and the detectives knew it, too. They looked at her with the professional sadness of people who have had to deliver too much bad news, and Helen could not lie to herself any longer.

"Christina is dead." She'd said it. Now it was real.

"We found this purse with the body," Crockett said.

How ironic, Helen thought. A fragile vintage purse survived unharmed, but Christina, hard as nails Christina, did not.

"One more thing, ma'am," Crockett said. He showed her a smooth black button. The subtle gold center glowed like a jewel.

The words stuck in her throat. Helen forced them out.

"It's her suit button," she said. "Was she alive when they put her in the barrel?"

"No," Crockett said gently. "She was dead."

Helen felt relieved. She did not ask if Christina had suffered. She'd been beaten to death. "Please don't make me identify her."

"No, you won't have to," Tubbs said. "We'll make the ID from the implants."

Helen felt an irrational anger flare up. "Then why did you have that terrible article in the paper, if you knew about the implants? Couldn't you have traced her that way and saved me this?"

"The implant manufacturer was out of business," Tubbs said. "The records were in storage. We were afraid it would take awhile to locate them. Time is important. The faster we start the investigation, the faster we can find her killer. We have the records now. But your information was a big help."

"Does she have any family to bury her?" Helen asked.

"A sister, Lorraine," Tubbs said. "She lives in Arkadelphia. Once the medical examiner is through, Lorraine will take the body home to Arkansas for burial. The sister is flying in today. We'd like to ask you some questions now, if you don't mind."

Helen locked the green door and put up the "back soon" sign. Then she and the detectives went to the black silk-satin loveseats. Helen sat down, even though sitting was forbidden for sales associates when there were no customers. Let Mr. Roget fire her. With Christina dead, who would run the store?

The detectives asked Helen questions for what seemed like hours. The funny thing was, Helen could not remember any of them later or how she answered. But she remembered being very careful. Helen did not lie to the police. She just did not tell them everything. She did not say anything about Christina's drug dealing and skimming. She did not mention the murder of Desiree Easlee. She told herself she was too disoriented to deal with those matters now. If she said the wrong thing in her shocked state, she could be implicated in drug dealing, embezzling, and murder. After all, they hap-

pened at the shop. She needed time to work out the best way
to tell the police.

After the homicide detectives left, Helen called Mr.
Roget. The store owner made appropriate sounds of horror
and dismay when he learned of Christina's murder, but they
sounded perfunctory to Helen. He seemed more interested in
making sure that Helen and Tara could run the store now
that Christina was dead.

"I'm not sure I want to manage Juliana's, Mr. Roget," she
said, just to see how the old cheapskate would react.

"I'll make it worth your while," he said. "I can give you
an additional dollar an hour."

"That's all? For running a store?" Helen said.

"You'll get your commission after six months. And of
course, I'll keep the same terms, cash only, off the books,"
he said, and it almost sounded like a threat. Helen remembered the Las Olas store owner who wouldn't pay her in
cash. She'd be making seven seventy an hour. She knew
how hard it was to get that money on her terms.

"OK, Mr. Roget. Do you want me to close the store Monday, in honor of Christina?"

"Oh, no, Helen," he said, genuinely upset now. "Don't
close the store. Christina wouldn't want that."

Right, Helen thought. And you wouldn't want to miss a
sale. She wondered if he'd closed the store when his own
mother, the original Juliana, died.

"And Helen," he added, "do what you can to keep the
store name out of the newspapers. We don't want that kind
of publicity for Juliana's, do we?"

Now a new fear gripped Helen, something she'd never
thought of. What if Christina's murder got a lot of press?
What if her own name got in the newspapers? And the two
homicide detectives. Their clothes may have been out of
style, but they looked smart. Suppose they figured out who
Helen was? One phone call back to St. Louis, one story on
the news wires, and Rob would find her.

Helen would have to go back to cold St. Louis. There
would be no evenings spent drinking wine by the Coronado
pool with Peggy and Pete. No purple-clad Margery, dis-

pensing chocolate and sympathy. No glimpses of Daniel, the perfect man.

It was a horrible prospect.

Helen felt sick just thinking about it. She ran for the restroom and threw up. Then she closed the shop for the day. To hell with Mr. Roget.

Chapter 18

When Helen opened Juliana's Monday morning, she thought she saw someone back by the dressing rooms.

"Hello?" she called into the darkened store. "Anyone there?" Helen was frightened. Too many odd things had happened here lately.She flipped on the lights and reached into her purse for her pepper spray. With the spray in her hand, Helen had the courage to walk through the store.

"Hello?" she called again. She looked behind the counter but saw no one. The carpet had been vacuumed last night by the janitor service, and no footprints disturbed the deep pile.

"Who's there?" Her voice sounded like a croak. There was no answer. But she could swear someone was in the store with her.

When Helen opened the dressing room door, she saw it—a flash of blond hair and black. But there was no one in the room, and no way for anyone to run past Helen. There was just an empty dressing room, with a freshly vacuumed carpet, a peach silk dressing gown on a padded hanger, and a pair of tiny black heels in a size Helen could never hope to wear. There was no blonde in black. It was a trick of the room's triple mirrors.

"It's my imagination," she thought. It's Christina, whispered a voice in her mind.

But Christina was dead and had been dead for more than a week. Why would she be in the store now? Yet Helen had the feeling she was there, saying good-bye, walking past the ice blue silk jackets she so admired, caressing the Hermes scarves, drinking in the vibrant D&G colors, reveling in the rioting Versaces, looking at the painting of the make-believe Juliana, and finally, defiantly, sitting on the silk-satin loveseats for the last time.

"Christina, if that is you, I hope you are at peace," Helen said, and she felt foolish when she said it. But then she didn't feel foolish, and she didn't feel frightened any more. She was sure whatever had been in the store was gone. Still, when Tara showed up at ten that morning, she was relieved to see her.

Tara blew in like a fresh breeze. "I'm in black in honor of Christina," she said, solemnly. Helen had called her from Margery's last night and told her that Christina was dead.

Helen almost smiled. She could hardly call that outfit mourning. Tara's top stopped just south of her black bra, and her Brazilian lowrise jeans barely covered her bikini wax, leaving most of her flat midriff exposed. But Helen thought Christina would have appreciated the effort.

"Poor, poor Christina," Tara said. "It's so horrible. I can't believe it."

Her black veil of hair parted, and Helen saw Tara's forehead. Even skillful makeup could not completely hide the ugly bruise.

"How are you?" Helen asked.

"I'm OK," Tara said, and shrugged, baring more midsection. "But I don't want to talk about it."

Helen didn't either. She didn't know what to say or why Tara had faked the robbery. They were both relieved when the doorbell rang. Tara looked out and said, "Do you really want to buzz this woman in? She doesn't look like one of ours."

Unlike Christina, Helen buzzed in almost everyone. The only person she ever kept out was a mother with two little girls, and those children had chocolate ice-cream cones. But even Helen had her doubts about this woman. She was short and stout and wearing a shiny black satin dress with fussy ruffles and rhinestones. Her chubby feet bulged out of patent leather heels. Her gray hair was tortured by a frizzy perm, and her bangs were chopped off straight across her forehead. Her skin was pale white and thickly powdered. Her mouth was a thin, mean line in blood-red lipstick. She didn't look like someone who would shop at Juliana's, and yet she seemed familiar.

"Honestly, Helen, that woman scares me. She looks like a vampire. Do we have to let her in?"

"I think I've seen her somewhere before," Helen said.

"*Halloween II*?" Tara said.

Helen laughed and buzzed in the woman. She bustled in, looked around the room with disapproval, and dropped a shapeless black leather purse as big as a doctor's bag on the counter. Tara stepped back as if it were poisoned.

"I'm here for my sister Leanne's last paycheck," the woman said, her jaw thrust out like a bulldog's. "And don't try to deny it. I've been through her books and I know she's owed one more."

"I'm sorry, but we have no one named Leanne working here," Helen said, more politely than the woman deserved.

"Oh, yes, you do. You just don't know her God-given name. She called herself Christina. She liked that phoney foreign froufrou. Our parents gave us honest, down-to-earth names, Leanne and Lorraine, but Leanne's name wasn't good enough for her. Arkadelphia wasn't good enough, either. She left home more than twenty years ago. Said we were hicks." From the set of the woman's jaw, the insult still rankled. "Then she went and took an Eye-talian name instead."

"Oh, of course, you're Christina's sister, Lorraine," Helen said, and as soon as she said it, she saw the woman had Christina's eyes, without her clever makeup, and her pale skin, powdered into flour whiteness. Her thin lips could have used some collagen.

"The police said you would be in town," Helen said. "I am so sorry. We're all in shock. Christina's death was so sudden, so unexpected."

"I always expected it," Lorraine said. "My sister was a sinful woman. She lived a life of shame and degradation, and God struck her down so she would no longer infect the righteous."

Tara gasped. Helen felt a sudden rebellious urge to defend Christina. "I think you are mistaken, Lorraine. Christina managed a fashionable store and was much loved by her clientele. Many of them were her friends."

"Whores and kept women," Lorraine said, looking directly at Tara, "who use their bodies for shameless display and immorality." Tara backed into a rack of blouses until they almost covered her bare middle.

"I said to Leanne, maybe I don't have your looks, but I have something more lasting, my immortal soul."

"Yes, well, I'm sure in that case that you won't want to stay here any longer than necessary," Helen said frostily. "You wouldn't want to jeopardize it. Let me get Christina's check out of the safe."

Helen came back with the check and a release form. Just because she could, Helen made Lorraine show her driver's license for identification. She saw the birth date. Lorraine was forty-three, only four years older than Christina, but she could have been her mother.

This woman is cold, Helen thought. She finds out her sister is dead, and by the next morning, she has already counted her money and wants her last paycheck.

Lorraine's black purse swallowed the check and snapped shut. "It's not for me," she said, as if she could read Helen's mind. "This money will be used for the Lord's work."

"Will there be a memorial service for Christina here in Florida?"

"No, I am taking my sister away from this Sodom and Gomorrah. She will be buried back home where she belongs." Then the woman's mouth snapped shut, remarkably like her purse, and she marched out.

Tara was weeping and wiping her runny mascara on the back of her hands. Helen handed her a tissue. "Poor Christina," Tara said. "Going back to Arkadelphia. She wouldn't be caught dead in a place like that!"

Helen thought Tara's statement made a weird kind of sense. "Reminds me of what Mark Twain said about heaven for climate, hell for society."

"I see why she never mentioned her sister," Tara said. "I'd want to forget I was related to that, too."

In her mind, Helen saw Christina again, slender, smart, and so sophisticated. Helen understood at last why Juliana's green door had a lock. Christina was not barring all those nameless women with bad T-shirts and cheap shoes. She was keeping out one person only, her terrible sister.

She had lost that battle. Lorraine was taking Christina home — a fate worse than death.

Chapter 19

It was still dark at five-ten in the morning. Helen heard the sound she'd been waiting for, the sliding doors of the panel truck.

She slipped on her cutoffs and sandals and ran outside into the warm black morning. The Coronado apartments were silent. One light was glowing yellow in Margery's kitchen. Her landlady seemed to get by on about three hours sleep.

Helen crunched out to the newspaper box in front of the Coronado. She saw the red tail lights of the departing delivery truck. Helen bought a morning paper, slipping the coins in the yellow metal box with trembling fingers. Her heart was pounding, and her mouth was dry with fear. Her whole future was wrapped in a thirty-five-cent paper.

She spread the paper out on her coffee table. Nothing on the front page. Nothing in the entire front section. She began to breathe easier. Then, when she went through the whole paper, fear gripped her again. There was no story. Helen would have to do this again tomorrow and the day after that.

She took a deep breath, then went through the paper once more, slowly this time. She saw the small headline on page 13A: "Police ID Biscayne Bay Body."

The story began, "The body found in Biscayne Bay Friday has been identified as Christina Smithson, 39, manager of Juliana's dress shop, a longtime retail fixture on Las Olas, police sources said."

The article repeated the awful details but added one thing new. "The murder is believed to have taken place at Ms. Smithson's luxury condo in Sunnysea Beach."

So that's where she died, Helen thought. At home, in a building with a burly doorman and a security system.

She read on. "Sunnysea Beach homicide detectives are conducting the investigation with the assistance of Miami Palms police." That meant Crockett and Tubbs were no longer running the investigation.

"The Downtowner Merchants Association has announced a $25,000 reward for anyone who has information leading to the arrest and conviction of the person or persons who killed Ms. Smithson. Anyone with information is requested to contact Sunnysea Homicide Det. Sgt. Dwight Hansel at 954-555-1252."

Helen's name was nowhere in the story. She nearly cried with relief. She was safe. The TV stations did not have any video of the barrel being pulled from Biscayne Bay, so they weren't interested in Christina's story.

Christina's murder would not be a big story. Helen's name would not be in the newspaper. The court and her ex Rob would not find her. She would not have to go home to St. Louis. Helen felt relieved and guilty at the same time. Christina had been buried twice, once in Arkadelphia and now in the newspaper.

The twenty-five-thousand-dollar reward was a sad commentary, Helen thought. The local merchants association cared more about Christina than her own sister did. Lorraine was giving her nothing, not even a Florida memorial service.

When Helen realized how many people read that little news story, she was even more relieved her name was not in it. At Juliana's, the phone rang nonstop that Tuesday. Christina's faithful customers wanted to talk about her terrible death. Some were sobbing. Some wanted to know about funeral arrangements. Others wanted to make sure that Juliana's was staying open.

"Yes. The owner, Mr. Roget, said Christina would want it that way," Helen said.

"Thank God. I have a party Saturday night," said the tongue-pierced Tiffany, who had finally lost her lisp. "I need a new dress. It's a matter of life and death." But not Christina's life—or her death, Helen thought.

She'd barely hung up when the phone rang again.

"Helen, are you OK?" It was Sarah, the woman judged too fat for Juliana's. "I saw the article in the newspaper. The one about Christina. I'm so sorry. You must be worn to a frazzle. Let me take you to lunch today. Can you get away for half an hour? I'm working downtown."

Helen and Sarah ordered chicken crepes at an outdoor restaurant on Las Olas. The bright flowers, green plants, and pretty wrought iron offered a soothing, sheltered spot to discuss Christina's murder.

"Do the police know Christina was skimming money and selling drugs?" Sarah asked, mopping up béchamel sauce with a forkful of crepe.

"I didn't say anything to them," Helen told her.

"Why not?"

"Because it was worse than I told you," Helen said. "I think she also arranged a murder for hire."

Sarah's crepe landed with a splat on her silk jacket and skidded down her suit. The alert waitress brought Sarah a glass of club soda, and she scrubbed at the stain with her napkin.

When Sarah could talk seriously again, she lowered her voice. "Christina arranged a murder? You heard this and did nothing?"

Helen felt another stab of guilt. "I didn't think I could go to the police. I wasn't sure. I didn't know the woman's name or where she lived. I had no proof, just what I'd overheard, and I didn't even hear the whole conversation. I could have been wrong."

"But you weren't," Sarah said. Helen abandoned her crepe. She'd lost her appetite.

"Helen, you've got to go to the police."

"I don't want my name in the paper," Helen said.

"The best way to get your name in the paper is if the police find out you've been holding back information. You'll look guilty. Come forward now, and you still look like a concerned citizen."

"But what if the police never find out what Christina was doing?"

"Did those detectives look stupid?"

"No. They were very smart."

"Then they'll find out. Besides, it's the right thing to do."

Something in that corny phrase appealed to Helen's Midwestern morality. Maybe it was because Sarah looked so earnest, so honest, she made Helen want to believe in truth, justice, and the American way.

"You're right," Helen said. "I'll do it. I'll call the Miami Palms police."

"The paper says the investigation is being handled in Sunnysea. That's the scene of the murder."

"Then I'll call Sunnysea when I get back."

"Good. And as your reward for being a solid citizen, we'll go out for margaritas after work. Let's go some place close. Maybe Himmarshee Village. I'll come by about six."

The relief was exhilarating. Helen felt as if a backpack full of rocks had been lifted from her shoulders. As soon as she returned to Juliana's, she called the name she saw in the paper, Detective Sergeant Dwight Hansel.

And so, Helen made the biggest mistake since she walked down the aisle with Rob.

Chapter 20

"Are you telling us this broad was running drugs, skimming money, and arranging murders?" Detective Dwight Hansel said.

"Yes, I am," Helen said. And I'm making a hash of it, she thought.

Hansel and his partner, Detective Karen Grace, were at Juliana's within an hour after her call. As soon as Helen saw the tall, loudmouthed Hansel swagger in the door, she knew she was in trouble. She could tell where he spent most of his time. Those massive shoulders and muscled arms were made in the gym. That beer gut came from even longer hours on a bar stool.

His partner, Karen Grace, had strawberry blonde hair and a figure Helen's grandmother would have called buxom. She also had cops' eyes and a way of walking that said "Don't mess with me."

Helen told the two homicide detectives the whole story. Hansel made it clear he didn't believe Helen. "Did you tell the store owner this woman was stealing from him?" he said.

"No," Helen said. "I couldn't prove anything. The shipping charge could have been an addition error."

Helen was sweating now. What if Mr. Roget found out Christina had been skimming? He'd fire Helen for not telling him. It would take weeks to find another job. Helen would fall behind in her bills and never catch up. She'd have to leave the Coronado. With every stupid sentence, Helen saw another piece of her new life slipping away.

"And the drugs? Why didn't you say something about them to Mr. Roget or the police?" Hansel said.

"Uh," Helen said.

"Didn't you say you found Ecstasy, and this Christina sold it to a customer?"

"I wasn't sure. Someone else could have dropped it."

"Really? You got a lot of people dropping drugs in here?"

"No. I'd never seen any before."

Helen felt like she was twisted into a pretzel. She couldn't think straight. Hansel had been questioning her for what seemed like hours, asking the same things over and over.

"What did you do when you overheard this so-called murder being planned?" Hansel said.

"I wasn't sure it was a murder. I didn't know the victim's name. There was no way I could find her."

"You could have come to us. We would have known how to get in touch with Jimmy the Shirt. That's how you find his new girlfriend."

Helen felt the bottom drop out of her stomach. He's right, she thought. I let a woman die because I did nothing. But what if she'd gone to someone like Dwight Hansel? Would he have taken her seriously or shrugged her off as a crazy woman? Helen knew the answer.

"The murderer had no trouble finding Desiree Easlee," he said. "She is dead. We know that much is true. How did you find out about her murder?"

"I saw it on TV," Helen said. She could feel the anger building, the same anger that got her in so much trouble in court. Maybe she'd made a mistake. But she was trying to do the right thing now, and this was what she got.

"And did you tell the police?"

Detective Hansel sounded so snide, so sneery. Just like that sanctimonious judge in St. Louis. Something snapped in Helen. "No, because I knew I'd encounter someone like you," she said.

"Watch it, lady. I can haul you in as a material witness,"

Hansel said. Helen was pretty sure he could not do that. But she was also sure he could make her life miserable. In fact, he was already doing that.

"So what we have here is a criminal mastermind with fake tits?" Hansel said, sarcastically.

"Implants don't lower a woman's IQ, detective — just a man's," Helen said. His partner, Karen Grace, snorted. "Christina was smart and beautiful. How do you think she got that million-dollar ocean-view penthouse?"

"On her back," Hansel said.

"Not at almost forty, detective. You'd better investigate a little better."

"I apologize for my partner. He can be insensitive," Detective Grace said.

"Hey, what is this?" Dwight Hansel said. He sounded indignant, but they might have been playing good cop, bad cop. Helen didn't care. She wanted them to leave.

"We drive all the way over here, and you tell this wild story," Hansel said. "We haven't found anything to support it: no drugs in the woman's condo. No shoeboxes full of cash in her closet. Yes, she had more money than a store manager should, but her sister says she received a nice cash gift from an aunt in Arkansas. A sort of off-the-books legacy before the old lady died. We're not the IRS. We don't care about that. Her sister says this Christina was smart about investing and turned it into a lot of money. And we did find evidence that she knew her way around the stock market."

Lorraine made up that story, Helen thought. Christina's older, colder sister was greedy. Helen wondered if Lorraine had found the cash and hauled it home with Christina's body. Lorraine concocted the story of the legacy, so the police wouldn't look too closely at Christina's bank account. Lorraine wanted to inherit all of her dead sister's money, legal or not.

But Helen didn't say any of that. Who would Hansel believe: salt of the earth Lorraine or Helen with her wild tale of drugs and murder at a dress shop?

"Did you find Christina's cat?" she asked instead.

"Cat? There was no sign of one," Detective Grace said.

"We didn't find no cat," Hansel added.

"She had a cat named Thumbs. It had six toes."

"She must have given it away," Hansel said.

"She'd never do that," Helen said. "Christina loved that cat. Maybe Thumbs ran away when the police opened the door."

"And took its litter box?" Grace said. "I'm telling you we found no sign of a cat. No toys, no litter box, no food or bowls. Nothing."

"Any cat hair?"

"Some. She worked in a public place. She could have brought those hairs home with her. Her condo was clean. Nothing was out of place, except in one room."

"What was in there?"

Hansel cut in. "Can't tell you. It's part of an ongoing investigation."

"Did you find any purses in her condo or her car? She took a box of expensive evening purses with her when she left that last Saturday," Helen said.

There were no purses. There was no cat.

When the two detectives finally left, Helen felt beat up. She was mad at herself and snippy with Sarah when she showed up at the store. "You got me into this, Dudley Do-Right," she said.

"I still think it's better that you went to the police," Sarah insisted, stubbornly. "What if Hansel found out that information on his own?"

"He's too dumb to find anything but the next brew."

"And his partner? Is she dumb, too?"

"No," Helen said. "She didn't talk much, but she didn't seem stupid."

"Then you did the right thing," Sarah said.

But Helen didn't think so. She hardly spoke as they walked around the old Himmarshee Village. It was old for Fort Lauderdale, anyway. The museum buildings hailed from about 1905. The commercial buildings were from the 1920s. Helen could find blocks of buildings much older in St. Louis, but Florida was newly hatched.

A Florida historical district was not a sober affair. Most of the buildings were bars and restaurants, with plenty of beer and live bands. Sarah and Helen stopped at a bar and had margaritas. Helen liked the salty-sweet taste, but she was restless sitting in the dark bar. Sarah didn't want to sit long, either. They saw huge crowds streaming toward Sammy's Good Tyme Saloon.

Helen and Sarah followed the crowd. Every inch of Sammy's was packed. People were hanging off the upstairs decks, sitting on the balconies and staircases. More were crowding the open first-floor windows, watching the party-ers lucky enough to get inside. Sammy's set up auxiliary bars at the entrance, selling beer, wine, and bottled water to those who couldn't get in.

"What's drawing the huge crowd?" Helen said. "A Beatles reunion?"

"Big Dick and the Extenders," said a twenty-something with a luxuriant goatee. "They usually play in the Upper Keys. They're great."

"I've heard of them," Sarah said. "Big Dick is supposed to make Howard Stern look like Miss Manners."

Helen and Sarah elbowed their way in closer to the open windows. Helen liked the music. Most of it was songs from the sixties and seventies, with some hard-driving southern rock. She did not like Big Dick's jokes. She had expected some about sexual organs, considering the band's name. What she didn't expect was how many jokes put down women and how many women laughed at them. They even laughed when he said, "I see a lot of beautiful women here tonight. I see some ugly bitches, too."

Helen felt trapped in a fifties frat house. The audience, mostly young men and big-haired women, seemed to love it.

"Let's get out of here," Sarah said.

"Took the words out of my mouth," Helen said. She was about to walk away, when she saw a tall man in a purple muscle shirt deep inside the bar. He seemed familiar, but she couldn't place him.

"Sarah, wait. Do you know that guy?" she said, pointing him out.

"I can't get a good look at his face," Sarah said. "There are too many people."

A couple in front of them left, and Sarah and Helen

moved forward and pushed their way inside. Helen saw the
guy more clearly now, but she still couldn't place him. He
stripped off his muscle shirt, waved it in the air, and began
dancing like a Chippendale. Muscle Shirt was at least three
beers ahead of his companions. The drunken crowd cheered,
and his dance grew wilder and lewder. Helen saw Muscle
Shirt had incredibly hairy armpits. Then she got a good look
at his face.

"Oh, my God. It's Detective Dwight Hansel," she said.
"The homicide cop who interviewed me today. I've made a
terrible mistake."

The band took a break, and the sudden quiet was thun-
derous. Then the regular barroom sounds started up again—
the clink of bottles, the scrape of chairs, snatches of
conversation: "So I said to her, if you don't like it, you can
haul your skinny ass out of here . . ."

Nice place.

"Let's get out of here before Dwight Hansel sees us,"
Helen said.

"I've been ready to leave for a long time," Sarah said,
starting for the door.

It was too late. Hansel saw them and stepped in front of
Helen. He was standing so close, she could smell the sweat
on his purple muscle shirt. His skin looked slick and slippery.

"You following me, Helen?" he said, pointing to his
chest with his beer. The bottle was sweating, too. "You can
save your energy. I'm going to be following you. In fact,
I'm gonna be all over you like a cheap suit. You know why?
Because I think something is going on in that store. I've
been talking to some people. That Christina was selling
more than dresses. And you're in on it. Or maybe it's the
boyfriend. Hey, I like that even better. You're in on it with
the boyfriend."

"Joe?" Helen said. It came out as a croak.

"Yeah. Maybe you wanted a rich boyfriend for yourself.
So you murdered your friend Christina."

Helen was so insulted he'd accused her of wanting Joe,
she ignored the charge of murder.

"Joe? You think I'm interested in Joe? I wouldn't go out

with Joe if he was the last man on earth. He's even dumber than y—"

She stopped just in time. She almost said "you."

"Than what?" Hansel said.

"Your beer bottle," she ended lamely.

"Joe's smart about money," he said. "He has a couple million in the bank. You're making how much pushing dresses? Maybe you'd rather spend your days sitting out by some rich guy's pool."

"You've got to be kidding," Helen said.

"Oh, no," he said, softly. "I'm dead serious." Then he walked back to his friends and left Helen standing in the middle of the seething crowd of drunks. Helen felt the fear in the pit of her stomach, coiled and knotted and heavy. She'd trapped herself. This man would never believe her.

"Are you OK?" Sarah said.

"No," Helen said.

"What do you want to do?"

"Get another drink," Helen said.

Helen was surprised it was still early when she got out of the bar. Which bar it was, she couldn't remember, and the sign seemed kind of blurry. But her watch, which she could read, said it was only eight-thirty. Helen was tipsy. No, not tipsy. Hammered. Hammered in Himmarshee.

"I can walk home," Helen said.

"You're not walking home in your condition," Sarah said. She held her liquor better, or maybe she hadn't drunk as much as Helen. Anyway, Sarah drove Helen to the Coronado. Helen nearly fell out of the big Range Rover when she opened the door. She walked carefully to her apartment, as if her head might fall off. Then she put on her cutoffs and Tweety Bird T-shirt and poured herself some wine in an iced tea glass. She filled the glass to the brim.

Margery was sitting at the picnic table, smoking Marlboros and reading a paperback. Her landlady's shorts were the color of a new bruise. Her toenails were ruby red. She saw Helen lurch into a chaise longue.

"What the hell is the matter with you?" Margery said.

"I think I made a mistake," Helen said. Her words sounded slurred.

Margery picked up Helen's iced tea glass and poured the wine on the grass.

"Hey!" Helen said.

Margery ignored her. She went into her place and came out with a ham sandwich, a bag of pretzels, and a big glass of water.

"Eat this," she said. "And drink all the water. I'm not making you coffee because that will just make you a wide-awake drunk."

Helen ate. She was hungry and thirsty. Then she told Margery what she had done.

"You made a mistake," Margery said. For some reason, Helen felt better when her landlady said that. "Why didn't you tell me you were going to the Sunnysea police? They have the worst force on the beach. Didn't you hear about the homeless guy who was Tasered?"

Helen looked blank.

"Must have been before you moved here. There was something wrong with the guy. He was mental or on drugs or something, and he went into a Sunnysea café and started tearing up the place. Broke a window, flipped over two tables, scared the owner half to death. The cops were called. Four of them showed up. They held the guy down and hit him with a Taser. A stun gun. The guy died. Some witnesses said the cops were justified. Others thought they used excessive force. One of the papers asked if there was going to be an investigation. Know what the police chief said? 'Why? We didn't shoot him or anything.'"

Helen groaned. She could feel a headache starting. She could feel that heavy coil in her stomach grow tighter. It was squeezing her guts.

"Look, Sunnysea Beach has some good cops," Margery said. "But the city can't afford to pay much, so they can't hire the sort of police you'd get in a richer place. They get young, inexperienced cops who think they know everything. They get rejects from other departments. They get retired guys from up North with attitudes and pensions who don't care any more."

Helen groaned again. Now her head was throbbing, and her guts were in a viselike grip. Snakes of fear slithered around in the pit of her stomach. She had not felt like this since she ran from St. Louis.

"Too late for regrets now," Margery said briskly. "You talked. The damage is done. I'll do my best to protect you. If those cops show up here, you call me. If you need a lawyer, you call me. I know a good one who owes me a favor. If you need any other help, let me know. . . . What the hell is that?"

Margery's head swiveled around like the kid in *The Exorcist*. Helen followed her. They saw Peggy the parrot lady and Daniel the magnificent strolling along the sidewalk.

Helen thought they made a stunning couple: long-legged, red-haired Peggy and Daniel with the rippling muscles and the tiny shorts with the large bulge.

Helen saw the couple was actually a threesome. A grumpy-looking Pete sat on Helen's shoulder. Daniel seemed to realize that Pete was out of sorts, too. He reached out to pet the parrot. Pete clamped down on Daniel's finger and refused to let go. The parrot had a wild, piratical look in his eye.

"Pete!" Peggy said angrily. "Pete! Stop it right now." But Pete hung on. She gently pried his beak open to free Daniel's digit.

"Is that a parrot or a pitbull?" Daniel said.

"Pete's going to his room," Peggy said. "Daniel, I am so sorry." And she was gone.

"Let me get you a Band-Aid. You're bleeding," Helen said. There was a tiny teardrop of blood on Daniel's finger. It was perfect, too.

"You better put some antibacterial ointment on that," Margery said. "Do you have any?"

"Yes," Helen said.

Daniel followed Helen docilely into her apartment. She was grateful that she'd hung up her work suit and put the wine box away before she went out by the pool. At least she didn't look like a drunken slob. With Daniel so near, Helen was sobering up fast.

When Daniel stepped into her apartment, the place suddenly seemed much smaller, and the bed much bigger. The bed was very big. It seemed to take over the apartment. It was pulsating, throbbing, beckoning. No matter where Helen looked, she saw the bed.

Daniel was standing much too close. She didn't want him to do that. No, she did. She wanted him even closer. But Helen was afraid she'd do something embarrassing, like throw herself into his arms and start kissing him. Helen was also afraid to take Daniel into her bathroom, which was the size of a phone booth. She had him sit down on the couch and brought in the ointment and a Band-Aid.

"Would you put it on for me?" he asked. Helen took his wounded hand and held it in hers. Daniel had huge fingers, and Helen wondered if that meant his other appendages were large. Feet, for instance, she told herself, trying to clear her pheromone-fogged brain.

It didn't work. Smearing goo all over Daniel's index finger and wrapping it in a Band-Aid seemed like some arcane aphrodisiac rite, a prelude to passion. Get a grip, woman, she told herself.

"Well," Helen said, briskly. "That's that."

"Thanks," he said, looking deeply into her eyes. "Anything I can do for you?"

Helen studied his face for a smirk. He seemed to be sincere. "For a Band-Aid?" she said, with a shaky laugh. "Don't be silly."

"Then I guess I better go," he said, and moved off into the velvet night.

Helen could not stand to be alone in her apartment. Daniel had overpowered it. He'd overpowered her fears, too. She still felt the fear coiling in the pit. She was still afraid Detective Dwight Hansel would get her. But when Daniel was with her, the snakes stopped slithering.

Helen stepped around her huge empty bed, opened the patio door, and cursed her denseness. Daniel had given her an invitation, and she was too dumb to recognize it. She'd lost her only chance to be loved by a perfect man. She breathed in the soft night air and thought she might die of longing. But women who wore Tweety Bird shirts did not die of anything so interesting.

Helen went sadly, soberly, out to the pool. Peggy was outside again, without Pete. Or the magnificent Daniel. Pete wasn't a pet, Helen decided. He was a feathered chaperone. An earsplitting squawk was enough to discourage most men. If not, Pete literally nipped the romance in the bud.

"I guess I messed up my chances for a date, huh?" Peggy said.

Helen looked at her. "You don't really care, do you?"

"I'd care very much if Pete had hurt Daniel," she said, seriously.

"But you don't really want to date Daniel, do you?" Helen said. "You admire him, like a painting or a statue."

"Helen, I've had too much hands-on experience to get involved with any man again. I'm through with them for good. Pete's the only man for me."

Helen wondered what had happened to make a woman as striking as Peggy live like a nun.

Their purple-clad landlady popped out of the palms like a wild orchid. "What happened?" Margery asked.

"Absolutely nothing," Helen said.

"Good girl," Margery said, approvingly. "Only way to land a man like that."

But Helen was sure she'd made another mistake.

Chapter 21

"If you need any other help, let me know. . . ."

Margery's words haunted Helen as she walked back to her apartment. She passed through Phil's pot fog in a fog of her own. Helen knew she was in trouble. Big trouble. She had angered a homicide detective. If Dwight Hansel looked into her life, what would he find?

Nothing.

Helen had no phone, no credit cards, no bank account, not even a paycheck. Any good detective would be suspicious.

But Hansel was not a good detective. That was Helen's only hope. He was a loudmouth drunk, a party animal. Of course, she'd been poking sticks into the party animal's cage. He could strike back with a search warrant.

But he would not find anything, she thought. There's no trace of my other life except for a teddy bear and some clothes.

And an old suitcase. Containing seven thousand one hundred and eight dollars in cash.

A wild flash of panic ripped through Helen. Buried in her closet was seven thousand dollars she could not explain. She had no bank statements. That cash would say "drug money" to any cop, no matter how stupid. The coil of fear grew heavier. The snakes were slithering in the pit again.

I've got to get that money out of my apartment, she

thought. Helen paced back and forth, asking: Where can I keep that cash?

A safe deposit box? No, that would cost money to rent. Besides, it would leave records. Even Hansel could find a safe deposit box.

"If you need any other help, let me know. . . ."

Margery. Margery would help her. Helen pulled down all the blinds, flung open the utility closet door and grabbed the old Samsonite suitcase wedged between the wall and the water heater.

She looked out her front door. The Coronado apartments were quiet. No one was outside. Peggy's lights were off. So were Daniel's. Cal's were on, but she could hear his TV. And Phil? She sniffed the air, heavy with the sweet, burning-leaf smell of pot. Phil was happily in the hay.

Margery's light was on. Helen carried the suitcase over to her landlady's apartment and knocked lightly on the door. "Margery!" she called in a whisper. "Margery, are you there?"

"Where else would I be at this hour?" Margery bellowed, flinging open the door. "Come on in." She was wearing a purple chenille robe. Her gray hair bristled with red sponge curlers.

"Are you running away from home?" she said. "What's with the suitcase?"

"Margery, can you keep this for me? I promise it's nothing illegal, but I can't . . ."

"The less you tell me, the better. As far as I'm concerned, I'm storing your old luggage. Case closed," her landlady said, patting the suitcase, "and I'm keeping it that way."

Helen's worst nightmare came true. The next morning, Detective Dwight Hansel showed up with a search warrant. But he wanted to search the store, not her home.

Hansel and his partner, Detective Karen Grace, were waiting in front of Juliana's when Helen arrived at nine-thirty. Helen looked like a drug dealer in her heavy black sunglasses, but she was only trying to shield her eyes from the searing sun. Helen was so hungover from her night in Himmarshee she could hardly unlock the door. Breakfast had been black coffee and aspirin. Only then did she have the courage to look in the bathroom mirror. Helen winced at the sight: She looked old enough to be her own mother.

Detective Hansel did not look like someone who had been dancing on the ceiling at Sammy's Good Tyme Saloon the night before. He seemed earnest and sober and eager to nail Helen's hide to the green door. Detective Grace was the same odd mix of don't-mess-with-me voluptuousness. Helen suspected Grace had to watch every bite to keep that lush figure from going to fat. Or maybe not. Working with Hansel could make any woman lose her appetite.

Hansel wanted to search the premises for evidence of drugs. Helen was relieved to see that the search warrant was fairly specific. The police were looking for ledger books, documents, long-distance records, and computer disks that did not relate to the business of the store and also for illegal drugs or narcotics paraphernalia.

No scales and tiny baggies at Juliana's, Helen thought. So far, so good.

Helen called Mr. Roget in Canada and told him two homicide detectives wanted to search the store in connection with Christina's death. Mr. Roget did not understand American law and didn't care to. "Cooperate fully with the police, and call me if there is a problem," he said. Helen was relieved he didn't ask too many questions.

Stay out of the way, she told herself. Stay under the radar. You cannot afford to get noticed by the police. You do not want to go home to St. Louis.

Helen moved to the back of the store by the black silk-satin loveseats, as far away as she could get from Detective Dwight Hansel. He was up front, searching the counter area. Detective Grace was in the back, looking at ledgers in the stockroom.

She asked Helen what she was doing the weekend of Christina's death. Helen told her that she had been on a date with Cal Saturday night. She'd spent the rest of the time at the Coronado, where her landlady watched her like a hawk. Detective Grace took Margery's name and address. She also wanted the names of Juliana's regulars. Helen gave her a list.

Then she gave Helen something. "You were right," Grace told her. "Christina Smithson had a cat. I went back and checked her apartment."

"Did you find Thumbs?" Helen said, hoping the cuddly animal was safe.

"No, I saw the rubbing marks."

"The what?"

"I have a cat named Cookie. Cats mark their territory by rubbing their heads and faces on furniture, doorjambs, and corners. It leaves a dirty gray spot at cat height, no matter how clean you are," Detective Grace said. "I found the rubbing spots at Christina's. There was one near a kitchen cabinet where she probably kept the cat food. Way in the back, behind some folded paper bags, were a few food pellets and a grooming brush. The brush was full of hair. The lab says it's domestic cat hair. She had a cat sometime while she lived there."

It was a small victory for Helen. Detective Grace didn't come out and say it, but she believed Helen was telling the truth—about the cat, anyway. She gave Helen her card and said, "Call me if you think of anything else."

Her partner was another problem. Dwight Hansel treated Helen as if she was lying, and he went out of his way to tell her. "I still haven't found anything to substantiate your story," he said.

Stay polite, she told herself. "I'm sorry," she said.

"I hear women of a certain age can start making up stories," he said. "Has to do with hormones or something. Unless you're just plain lying."

Don't let him rattle you, she told herself. "I'm not lying," she said.

"You were the last one to see her alive," he said. "And that makes you especially interesting to me."

I've got to find out who killed Christina before Dwight Hansel looks into my life, Helen thought. He'll send me home to Rob for pure spite. Now the snakes were slithering in a pit lit by slashes of panic.

At ten a.m., she was no longer alone in her misery. Tara arrived for work and turned pale when she saw the two detectives. Helen thought Tara looked thin and vulnerable in

her tiny tight skirt and lowcut top. Tara kept pulling her long
black hair across her face like a curtain, hoping to hide behind it.

She told Detective Hansel she was a new employee and
had only worked for Christina for one week, which was true.
Tara forgot to mention that she'd been a customer at Juliana's for six years. Helen didn't tell the cops, either. Her
last attempt at being a solid citizen had been a disaster.

The search was swift and efficient. The police took some
papers and computer disks, but it seemed clear they found
nothing exciting. Christina had removed her troublesome
special purses before she left for vacation. The police did
find some tiny baggies, but they held extra buttons. If there
were any stray pills from the infamous purse spill, the cleaning service had vacuumed them up weeks ago.

The two detectives gave Helen a receipt for the items
they took and said they would get more detailed records
from the phone company. Helen wondered if they would
find any suspicious calls and felt another jagged stab of fear.
There was no way she could prove Christina made those
calls, not her.

Helen and Tara were both relieved when the two detectives left but wary of talking about the search.

"Did they bring in the drug-sniffing dogs?" Tara asked.

"No," Helen said.

"We're lucky Detective Hansel is lazy," Tara said. "The
cops did that to a friend of mine. He'd moved his stash, but
the dogs knew it had been there and set up a racket. The cops
made his life hell."

Tara knows about the purses, Helen thought. But all she
said was, "Detective Hansel didn't mention anything about
the two armed men who forced their way in here."

"Oh," Tara said. That single syllable held immeasurable
relief. Both women hoped the poor communication between
the two police departments would keep that event buried.

The awkward silence was broken when the doorbell rang.
Juliana's regulars began stopping by like mourners visiting
a funeral home. They were dressed in impeccable black and
had the air of women at a wake. They knew Christina would

have no memorial service. This was the only way her favorites could pay their respects.

Brittney, Tiffany, and Bianca all showed up, fortunately after the police left. The three chief mourners huddled together on the silk-satin loveseats with Tara, drinking bottled water, remembering Christina, and discussing their favorite plastic surgeries. Helen, mindful that she was not one of them, stood respectfully nearby, feeling like a funeral home attendant. Actually, she felt more like the corpse. She was still hungover from last night.

Brittney was talking about a society dinner party. "The hostess was a rich doctor's wife," she said in a ghostly whisper.

"Aren't they all?" Tiffany said.

"Except for the rich lawyer's wives," Tara said.

"Her penthouse condo cost millions," Brittney said. "It was right on the water. But she has the worst eye job in Lauderdale. When she blinked, one eyelid closed slower than the other. I couldn't stop looking at her. Finally, I had to ask the name of her surgeon. I wanted to make sure I never went to him."

The others shuddered delicately. Tiffany seemed unaware that her own eye job was less than successful.

"It takes such courage to have any work done," said the radically rearranged Brazilian, Bianca. "One slip and you're ugly forever." Helen figured with all the surgery they'd had, these women had the courage of a Roman legion.

They discussed who did the best eye jobs (upper and lower), which plastic surgeons corrected the other doctors' mistakes, and the merits of face lifts versus fat injections.

"Fat injections have less risk, but they only last eight months," Tara said.

"And that's if the doctor doesn't get greedy and dilute the fat. If he does, then it's four to six months," Tiffany said.

"Or if *she* does," whispered Brittney. "Women doctors are just as greedy as men."

"Greed is the one place where women have true equality," Tara said. Helen found that line strangely haunting.

The doorbell chimed, and the women looked up. "Helen, you can't let that one in," Tara said, alarmed. "She's wearing a beige Ann Taylor suit. Christina said anyone who wore Ann Taylor was too boring for words. This woman is definitely too boring for Juliana's."

Helen liked the suit. In fact, she had one almost like it. "She's carrying a Kate Spade bag," Helen said firmly.

"It's last season's," Bianca sniffed. "They sell them at no-name designer sales. Look inside. It will be stamped 'salvage.'"

Helen buzzed in the woman anyway, to the fierce disapproval of the loveseat set. It was not enough for them to be admitted. Others must be excluded. Otherwise, the green door meant nothing.

The Ann Taylor woman only confirmed Helen's poor judgment in their surgically altered eyes. She committed one faux pas after another.

Ms. Taylor asked where the price tags were, and the loveseat women rolled their eyes. Juliana's customers knew price tags were never displayed.

They sniggered openly when Ms. Taylor said, "Excuse me, but someone left her high heels in the dressing room." Juliana's customers knew the shoes were there as a courtesy if they needed to see how a dress looked with heels.

They were not surprised when Ms. Taylor left without buying anything.

Helen sighed and, for the tenth time that morning, wished Christina was there. She always knew what to say to her regulars, how to sell to them, and how to soothe them. Helen liked Juliana's customers, most of the time. She pitied them sometimes, and she always envied their money. But she felt they were from some alien planet. They were so small, so delicate, so dependent on men.

But we're all dependent on men, Helen thought. I could only go so far at my corporation before I hit my head on the glass ceiling, and I hit it hard.

Director of Human Resources was the title with the money and the power. It was the job Helen wanted, but it always went to a man at her company. Helen settled for second best, the duller, safer title of benefits director. Her career was good, but not great. But she had her marriage. Then she found out her husband had betrayed her, and she'd picked up the crowbar that wrecked her life. In court, the judge, another man, decided her awful future.

Maybe we aren't so different after all, Helen thought. But she could never say that to Juliana's women. They seemed to know that Helen's pantyhose had runs in the toes stopped with clear nail polish. They would look at her self-manicured nails and four-year-old Ungaro suit and see no resemblance.

Precisely at one, Bianca, Brittney, and Tiffany rose gracefully from the silk-satin loveseats. Each woman told Helen how sorry she was to learn of Christina's death. Each bought something for a few hundred dollars—a purse or a scarf or a belt—as if she was making a memorial donation in Christina's name. Then they were gone. Helen wondered if they would come back.

Helen knew she was not the right person to run Juliana's. There was something wrong with her. She hated needless cosmetic surgery. Helen thought most people looked better with their original face, unless they were disfigured. To her, the marks of maturity were not disfiguring. They gave people character. So she told the regulars she didn't know who did the best lip work and breast implants. They knew she was lying. These women did not want to hear Helen's lectures on the dangers of silicone and collagen.

When Juliana's regulars wanted biopolymer injections, Helen did not tell them about exotic South American doctors, like Christina did. Instead, Helen gave them the phone numbers of the reporters who investigated the horrific damages. No one took the numbers.

The next afternoon, Helen made her worst mistake. It was with Melissa, the little blonde with the large implants and the sexy, slightly popped gray eyes. Helen knew she'd mishandled the woman, but she felt she had to try to stop her.

"You've taken over for Christina?" Melissa asked her.

Helen said yes.

"Then you must have her list of plastic surgeons. I need my eyes done. I have terrible bags."

Helen looked at Melissa's smooth pale skin. It was flawless.

"How old are you, Melissa?" Helen asked.

"Twenty-seven," she said.

"You don't need an eye job," she said. "Your skin is perfection."

"It's not," Melissa said. She squeezed out one crystal tear. "My boyfriend left me for a younger woman. It's my eyes. I know it. If my eyes were OK, I'd still have him."

"Did you ever wonder if the problem was not your face?" Helen said.

"What do you mean?" Melissa said, suddenly alert and tear-free.

"I mean," Helen said, "that you are beautiful, but you don't believe it. You cannot see yourself as others do. Why let some quack cut on you? He could ruin your looks forever. A therapist would be less painful."

"Are you calling me crazy?" Melissa's eyes were not popped now, but hard and narrowed.

"I'm merely suggesting—" Helen began.

"I'm outta here," she said. "And I'm not coming back. I don't have to listen to some nowhere sales clerk tell me I'm crazy."

Melissa stalked out, slamming the green door.

Another customer lost forever, Helen thought. Soon, the sharp-eyed owner would notice that sales were down. Helen would be out of a job. No one else could take Christina's place. No one else had the right combination of sophistication and sleaze.

Juliana's was slowly dying, and Helen could not prevent that death, either.

Chapter 22

It was two a.m. and too hot to sleep. Helen didn't want to turn on the window air conditioner. Its rattling would only keep her awake. Besides, it was expensive to run. She had to save money.

Helen got up and slid open the patio door. Cool night air poured into her stuffy apartment. She stood in the doorway, letting the tropical night embrace her. Something sweet bloomed in the velvety dark and sent out a heavy perfume. She heard some small creature rustling in the foliage. Unknown insects sang a high-pitched chant.

Then Helen heard another, wilder sound. At first, she thought it was two cats. Then she realized the wild moans were from Daniel's apartment. Some woman was having perfect sex with the perfect man. The stripper with the Day-Glo bra? Or had he moved on to someone else? Daniel had not promised to be faithful. Unlike Rob, her ex-husband.

The moans grew louder, sweeter, and more excited. She and Rob had sounded like that, long ago. Love with Rob had been good, right up until the day she discovered him with another woman. Only later did their love feel wrong. Rob had betrayed her with dozens of women, while Helen foolishly believed he'd loved only her. When Helen finally realized her husband had been unfaithful, she felt as if acid had been thrown on her soul.

In South Florida, she seemed to be healing. Her anger

had faded to a deep, piercing sadness. Her recovery was slow, but it was happening. Around single men, Helen still felt awkward as a teenager, except she had zits *and* wrinkles.

Helen also felt lost. After seventeen years of marriage, she didn't know the rules of the dating game any more. She couldn't even tell when a man was flirting with her. But she wanted to learn.

The extravagant cries from Daniel's room reached a crescendo. Helen shut her patio door and returned to her empty bed.

It was even hotter at Juliana's the next morning. When Helen opened the green door, she was hit with a blast of warm, muggy air.

Tara tripped in behind her on pink flowered mules, fanning herself. "Feels like Sumatra in here," she said. "The air conditioner must be broken."

"Another crisis," Helen said.

"A big one," Tara said. "You can't survive in South Florida without air conditioning."

"Lord, I hope it doesn't need major repairs," Helen said. "Mr. Roget will hit the roof."

"Check the filter first, and maybe you won't have to deal with Old Tightwad," Tara said. "Our air conditioning acts this way sometimes when the filter needs changing."

"Come to think of it, no one's changed the filter since I started working here," Helen said.

Helen opened the utility closet and stared at the air conditioner. It made its usual hum-chugging sound. The large olive green machine had pipes snaking all over. Some were wrapped with black foam padding and silver duct tape. All were thickly layered with dust. A big square vent trailed long wisps of gray dust, like an old man's beard. A box of filters leaned against the air conditioner. But Helen could not see where to install the filters.

"Yuck-o," Tara said, stepping back so she wouldn't get dirt on her pink outfit. "Where does the filter go in that thing?"

"Beats me," Helen said. "I'm wearing a black pants suit. I'll try to change it. You watch the door. There's a pile of manuals back in the stockroom for the cash register and stuff. Maybe I can find one for the air conditioner."

The stockroom was even hotter, but Helen didn't dare carry the appliance manuals into the store to sit on the forbidden loveseats.

Helen leaned against a stockroom table and started shuffling through the foot-high stack. She could feel sweat trickling down her neck. I'll have to send this suit to the dry cleaner, she thought resentfully. Mr. Rich Guy Roget will never pick up the tab. He doesn't have to worry about my dry-cleaning bills, but I'm supposed to save money for him.

Stop this. Start looking for another seven-seventy-an-hour job.

But they are all bad, she told herself.

Then go back to St. Louis and make real money.

That was worse.

Helen began shuffling through the stack again. Juliana's seemed to have saved every appliance manual since the store opened in 1965. There were manuals for outdated cash registers, obsolete clothing steamers, even a long-deceased stereo.

Finally, Helen spotted the instruction booklet for the air conditioner under an old refrigerator manual from 1972. That fridge probably had been junked years ago. Why did Christina keep these things?

The refrigerator manual slipped out of Helen's sweaty hand, and a pink flyer fell out. With a nearly naked woman on it.

Whoa! She was way too hot for a Frigidaire.

The flyer looked like the sort that Las Vegas prostitutes slipped under hotel room doors. Helen had seen them when she attended a CPA convention in Vegas years ago, before it became a so-called family gambling center. The male convention-goers laughed and snickered like school boys at the flyers' innuendoes. Helen was fascinated by the ads. Where she came from, prostitutes didn't advertise like pizza parlors.

This flyer said "Let Jasmine show you the secrets of the Orient."

The woman in the flyer was showing most of her secrets

already. She was a slender, full-breasted Asian with long dark hair. Jasmine's mouth was open and pouty. Her breasts and buttocks were thrust out, bold and inviting. She was both submissive and brazen. It was clear what Jasmine was selling: The string bikini covered almost nothing.

It certainly didn't hide the fact that this was a much younger Tara.

Helen stared at the flyer, until a drop of sweat plopped on the paper. Maybe she'd made a mistake. But the photograph was clear and sharp. There was no doubt this was a younger Tara. The face was a little rounder. The breasts were a little higher. The hair was just as long and black. Too bad, Helen thought, she hadn't used that curtain of hair to hide her face.

There was something written on the flyer in black ink: "Love Will Keep Us Together."

It didn't look like Tara's handwriting. Tara's script was as small and delicate as she was. Besides, she liked to dot her *i*'s with tiny hearts. No, that bold dark scrawl was Christina's. But why would she write "Love Will Keep Us Together" on the flyer? What did it mean? Was it a slogan? Or a song title?

Helen was too hot and sweaty to figure anything out in that airless room. She'd fix the air conditioner first. Maybe she could think better when she cooled down.

Helen hid the flyer under the stack of manuals and began reading the filter-changing instructions. She found the Phillips screwdriver, unscrewed the dust-bearded vent on the air conditioner. Inside, the filter looked like it was wearing an inch-thick blanket of gray felt. Big wads of dark fluff and mounds of dirt spilled out behind it. No wonder the air conditioner wasn't working.

Helen changed the filter, vacuumed the vent inside and out, and while she was at it, cleaned the whole utility closet. All the while, she thought about Tara.

Christina had found out Tara had been a prostitute and hidden the proof in the store. Was she blackmailing Tara? How much money was Tara paying to keep her past quiet? And why . . . ?

"You fixed it!" Tara said. "Cool air is coming out. The store should be liveable pretty soon."

Tara stood silhouetted in the stockroom doorway, a small, slender woman in a fashionably fringed skirt and a shoulder-baring top. Her pink mules were embroidered with flowers. Her long hair was soft and shining. Her skin glowed. She looked sweet and vulnerable, unlike the brazen tart in the flyer. Tara had reinvented herself.

"What's wrong?" Tara said. "You look like you've seen a ghost."

Helen reached for the flyer. "You were a Las Vegas . . . sex worker?" she said, proud she'd remembered the politically correct term for hooker.

She could see Tara's body tense, as if she were turning to stone. "Yes," she said, defiant but also afraid. "So?"

"Is that where you met Paulie?"

"God, no. He thinks I'm a mail-order bride from Thailand. He paid a fortune to get me here. I banked it all."

"You're kidding," Helen said. "Paulie thinks you're from Thailand? With that Midwest accent? Where are you from—Chicago?"

"Cleveland. I told him I'd listened to Berlitz tapes," Tara said.

"And he believed you?"

"Men believe what they want to believe, especially when it comes to sex," Tara said. "I'm the fantasy woman he's always wanted—exotic, quiet, submissive. Paulie really wants a hooker, but he doesn't know it. I give him what he wants. He gives me what I want—money and security. He'd drop me like a hot potato if he knew my past. He thinks I was a virgin when we met."

"How much was Christina blackmailing you for?" Helen said, deciding to bluff.

"I paid her two thousand a month," Tara said. "Recently, she wanted to raise it to twenty-five hundred dollars. I could barely make the two thousand, even with all Paulie gave me. I was desperate."

"That's why you faked that robbery," Helen said. "You were looking for this flyer, weren't you?"

"Yes, but I was also looking for some photos. She has

pictures of me with my clients . . . doing things. She showed me the flyer first, and I laughed and said flyers could be faked. Then it was her turn to laugh. She said she had some photographs Paulie would love to see."

"Photos can be faked, too," said Helen.

"Not these," Tara said, sadly. "I saw them. They're real. I searched the store, but I couldn't find the flyer or the photos anywhere. The search took longer than I expected. I couldn't explain to Paulie why I was so late."

"Why not? You could have said you were delayed by an accident on the road."

"You don't know Paulie. He's so jealous, he'd check. He calls my cell phone if I'm half an hour late."

"So you tossed some clothes around, hit your forehead on the wall, and made up the story about the two men with guns," Helen said.

Tara nodded, the curtain of hair sliding across her face.

"Don't worry," said Helen. "I won't tell the police about the break-in unless I absolutely have to." For my sake, she thought, not yours.

"I didn't kill Christina," Tara said. "You believe me, don't you? I'd be crazy to kill her before I found out where she stashed those photos. If the police find them, I'm in trouble. That's why I came back to work here, to see if they turned up anywhere."

"I thought you and Christina were friends," Helen said.

"We started off that way. Friends, I mean. Then she showed me the photos and asked for money. I was afraid she would tell Paulie and ruin everything. So I pretended we were still friends. It wasn't too hard. I pretended with Paulie, too. Most of the time, I could forget what Christina was doing."

Tara said it without bitterness. Helen wondered if she was faking that, too.

"Where did you find the flyer?" Tara asked.

"In the filter box," Helen lied. "Do you know what 'Love Will Keep Us Together' means?"

"It's a song by Captain & Tennille, isn't it? An old one." She shrugged. Obviously, it meant nothing to her.

"Are you going to tell Paulie?" Tara said. "Are you going to ruin the only good thing I've got?"

"No, Tara," Helen told her. "Your past is your own."

Unless you killed Christina, she told herself.

Chapter 23

Did Tara kill Christina?

Christina had preyed on her friend, bleeding her for money, month after month. Tara had to pretend they were still friends to keep her privileged life. She would only be free if she had those photos. Tara was so desperate, she beat her head against the wall until she bled, then made up the story of the armed intruders.

But Tara still didn't have the photos. She needed Christina alive.

Helen could see a frustrated Tara beating Christina to death with something heavy like a tire iron. But she couldn't see tiny Tara stuffing the dead body into a barrel and then lugging the heavy barrel out to Biscayne Bay.

Tara seemed so delicate, so fragile. But delicate Tara could carry huge armsful of clothes to the dressing rooms. Fragile Tara could lift big boxes of stock. Tara was strong as a stevedore.

Helen wanted to find Christina's killer. She was tired of being afraid. She was afraid Detective Dwight Hansel would discover her past. But she didn't want the killer to be Tara. She liked Tara, despite her occasional outbreaks of silliness.

But how could Helen unravel this mess? She had no detecting skills. She didn't know the meaning of the mysterious words on Tara's flyer, "Love Will Keep Us Together."

They could be a slogan, a song, a code. Or a note Christina jotted down that had nothing to do with anything.

Maybe the key was hidden in those appliance manuals. Maybe there were more blackmail victims. But every time Helen slipped back to the stockroom, the doorbell rang, and she had more customers.

Helen soon saw any search was hopeless while the store was open. She'd wait until this evening. She was itching to read those appliance manuals. She had to know if there were more juicy secrets buried in those dry pages.

The wait was almost unendurable. It grew worse when the last person Helen wanted to see walked into Juliana's— Niki. The woman who paid for the murder of Desiree Easlee now flashed her wedding ring like a trophy. She'd won, although Helen did not think Jimmy the Shirt was any prize.

The bride wore black, a good color for a killer. Even Helen had to admit that Niki made a radiant bride, until you got close. Then her mouth was bitter, and her eyes were hard. But the *Playboy* non-centerfold finally had a man. Helen wondered if he could endure her perfume until death parted them.

"I just heard about Christina," Niki cooed. "It's so terrible. She would have been so happy to know that Jimmy and I are married."

"I thought Jimmy was going to marry Desiree," Helen said. She couldn't resist.

"She died," Niki said, shortly. The perfume cloud around her quivered.

"She was murdered, wasn't she?" Helen said. "It must have been a shock when you saw the reports on TV."

"I didn't. I was devastated when Jimmy . . . well, when Jimmy and I split up. I went home to Mother. I spent the whole month in Athens."

"Georgia?" Helen said. Niki could have driven from Georgia to Florida and back without leaving a trace.

"Greece," Niki said.

That would be a little tougher.

"I flew straight back when I heard about the carjacking. Poor Jimmy was so lonely. He threw himself into my arms and said he still loved me. He admitted Desiree was a mistake. He wanted to get married right away, so we'd never be apart again. We got our license and went to a judge, then caught a plane to Costa Rica. We've been there ever since on our honeymoon."

Clever Niki was telling Helen she had an alibi for both Desiree and Christina.

"How was Costa Rica?" Helen asked.

Niki wrinkled her nose. "Full of bugs. But I don't care. I'm so happy." Her lips twisted into a Lady Macbeth smile.

What woman would marry a man right after his fiancée was buried?

The woman who hired her killer.

Jimmy was another gem. His bride-to-be was brutally murdered, days before their wedding. Her coffin was barely underground before he married another woman. Jimmy had not bothered to mourn his fiancée one week. The "mistake" had been erased.

Niki and Jimmy deserved each other. Helen was glad when Niki finally left Juliana's, even though the bride didn't buy anything. Her perfume lingered like an accusation. Helen felt like airing out the store.

The day crawled forward. Helen and Tara dragged clothes in and out of dressing rooms. Customers dropped ten-thousand-dollar gowns on the floor, left Hermes scarves draped over chairs, and abandoned belts on counters. They bought almost nothing. It was six-twenty when the last customer left Juliana's.

Tara had been pale and subdued all day. She did not speak to Helen, except to ask the price of a Versace shirt. Now Tara said, "I guess you won't want me working here any more."

"Why?" Helen said.

"Now that you know what I am," Tara said.

"I know you're a good saleswoman, and I expect you here at ten in the morning," Helen said. "Why don't you go home before Paulie starts worrying? I'll close up."

"Thanks," Tara said, and managed a weak smile. But she left as if she was escaping from jail. Poor Tara, trying live down her long-buried past. She must have dreaded the day it would be unearthed. Helen knew how she felt. She had her own secrets.

Helen locked the door, closed out the cash register, and put the money in the night safe. Alone at last.

The stack of appliance manuals was sitting in the stockroom, safe and dull as a pot roast. Helen paged through telephone booklets, security system manuals, and light fixture instructions. She shook each one and fanned the pages.

She found six things, but they were hardly fodder for blackmailers. They were harmless articles. Five were the sort of stories proud mothers showed their bridge clubs. The sixth was a routine news story.

Helen found the first story hidden in a computer manual. The pill-popping Venetia was "Local Mother of Year" in the *Golden Shores Gazette*. She was praised as the "spirit of Golden Shores volunteerism," who raised half a million dollars for the children's home. "But she's also the busy mother of two little boys," the article oozed.

Venetia's Adolfo suit could have come from Nancy Reagan's closet. Helen was surprised how attractive Venetia looked when she wasn't twitching.

The puzzle was Christina's bold, black writing on this clipping. She'd scrawled "Mother and Child Reunion." Definitely a song title, a Paul Simon hit from the 1970s.

What did that mean? Why hide this story in a computer manual? It could not possibly be blackmail material.

Next, Helen found a newsletter for a Wichita nursing home. The *Sunny Gables Monthly* had named Cindy Pretters as Employee of the Year.

Despite the big hair and bad makeup, Helen could see that Cindy was Tiffany, before her eye job. Cindy/Tiffany's baggy uniform was a far cry from the clothes she wore now, bought by her rich old boyfriend, Burt.

Even ten years ago, Tiffany had a knack for pleasing older men. She was photographed with four nursing home residents. The three elderly men looked at Tiffany like she'd just let them into heaven. Tiffany's charm seemed to escape the only other woman in the picture. Mrs. Vera Crinklaw, age ninety-two, stared stoically into the camera, as if she'd been forced to attend at gunpoint.

Christina had scrawled another song title on the *Sunny Gables Monthly*: "Silver Threads Among the Gold." Helen's grandmother liked to sing that song. It was even older than the Captain & Tennille hit.

That was two articles.

In a booklet for a battery-operated clock, Helen found the third: a *People* magazine story about the supermodel Sharmayne. She was photographed at an animal shelter benefit hugging her German shepherd, Big Boy. Sharmayne was at the height of her career and her beauty. The disastrous liposuction was another year away. But despite Sharmayne's stunning looks, it was Big Boy who stole the photo. He made Rin-Tin-Tin look like the runt of the litter. His fur was glossy, his bearing noble, his eyes alert and intelligent. No wonder Sharmayne told the magazine "Big Boy is my main man."

Christina's black slashing writing was on this story, too. It was a Nick Lowe song, "The Beast in Me."

The fourth was a business article announcing that Christina's ex-boyfriend, Joe, had paid six hundred thousand dollars for a five-thousand-square-foot warehouse near Port Everglades. This story was so boring, Helen could hardly read it to the end.

In the margin, Christina had written "Gotta Serve Somebody."

A Bob Dylan hit? This made no sense whatsoever.

Story number five was hidden in the instructions for store shelving. It was an article from *Chicagoland Hi-Life*, a magazine devoted to rich people's parties.

"Chocolate Lovers Bash Sweetens Charity," the sugary headline said, but it was the photo that captured Helen's attention. It starred another Juliana's regular, Niki, the perfumed bride from hell, with four female partygoers. The benefit was at a lavish house, and the four women dripped diamonds. Only Niki had no jewelry. She outshone them all in a simple black dress.

Christina had written "Diamonds Are a Girl's Best Friend." Why use this clichéd show tune?

The last article was a short news story about the death of Brittney's fiancé, Steve. The story said his body had been

found by a boater in a canal near the Seventeenth Street
Bridge.

The couple was to be married in June. The story said the
medical examiner found "significant amounts" of alcohol in
the deceased's blood. Steve's death was ruled an accident,
but Helen could see how the suicide whispers had started.

Christina had written "Tiny Bubbles" on this story, Don
Ho's ode to a bottle of bubbly. It was a mean choice for a
man who got drunk and drowned.

Helen looked through the stack of manuals again but
found nothing else. It was almost eight o'clock when she left
the store. On the walk home, Helen puzzled over the articles
and song titles. They were an eclectic collection, from Nick
Lowe to Don Ho. If this was a code, it was beyond Helen.

She had been searching for two hours. Helen knew less
than when she started. She had not found Tara's blackmail
photos.

Where did Christina hide them? The police had already
searched her penthouse. Did that mean the photos weren't
there? Did the police miss the hiding spot? Or did they have
the photos, and they weren't telling Helen? No, if Dwight
Hansel had those photos, he would not miss an opportunity
to torment her.

Tara had searched the store and found nothing. It was
Helen who stumbled on the Las Vegas flyer by accident.

How many other secrets did Juliana's hold?

These questions buzzed around Helen like gnats, irritat-
ing her and refusing to go away. When she finally got to the
Coronado, Helen went out by the pool, looking for Peggy or
Margery. She wanted to discuss her finds, but neither
woman was home.

Instead, Daniel and Cal the Canadian were talking at the
picnic table. Daniel was barechested, and his tanned abs
looked like they'd been bronzed. His cobalt eyes had a
wicked slant in the twilight. His long hair tumbled down his
shoulders like black silk. Next to him, Cal seemed old and
shrunken, juiceless and used up.

"Yes, sir," Daniel was saying. "I agree that the American
medical system leaves much to be desired. But I'm not convinced the Canadian system is a cure-all. I read that in some

Canadian hospitals, patients lie in the hallways because there aren't enough beds. Is that true?"

Daniel was so well mannered, Helen thought. Most Coronado residents walked away when Cal started lecturing on the joys of Canada, but Daniel listened patiently and answered thoughtfully.

Cal growled an answer Helen couldn't quite hear. "It's been a pleasure talking to you, sir," Daniel said. "See you later."

Helen watched Daniel walk to the parking lot. His muscles moved like oiled coils of steel. Daniel was barely out of earshot, when Cal said, " 'Sir'! He says 'yes sir' and 'no sir.' To me!" Cal kicked the picnic table with his sandaled foot.

"But, Cal, you're always complaining that Americans are not as polite as Canadians," Helen said. She enjoyed tweaking Cal. He still had not paid back the money he'd "borrowed" for that disastrous dinner at Catfish Dewey's.

"But he called me 'sir,' " Cal said. "He makes me feel like his grandfather."

Well, you look like his grandfather, Helen wanted to say.

But she didn't, proving that Americans were politer than Cal thought.

The green door did not open quite so often these days. Customers were drifting away, as Helen feared. But not Juliana's small group of regulars. They kept coming back and asking the oddest questions.

"Did Christina give you an envelope with my name on it?" asked Sharmayne, the former supermodel. She waltzed in that Saturday morning and disdainfully demanded to speak to Helen.

"No," Helen said.

"You must have it somewhere," Sharmayne said. "Look again." She tossed her mane of hair like an impatient pony.

"I don't have it," Helen repeated firmly, and Sharmayne knew she'd been rude. She tried her softest smile, the one usually reserved for rich men.

"Christina was going to send me something right before she died. I never received it, so it must still be at the store."

"Maybe it was at her home," Helen said. "In that case, her sister Lorraine would have it, or the police."

Sharmayne blanched. "No," she said. "I know it's here. If you find an envelope with my name on it, send it to me. Don't open it, please."

Don't open it?

Sharmayne saw her silence as stonewalling. "There will be a reward if I get that letter unopened," she said. "A big reward. Very big."

Sharmayne walked through Juliana's, pointing at clothes until she had picked out more than the average woman spent on herself in a year. Helen carried them to the dressing room. Sharmayne stripped off her shirt and began unbuttoning her low-rise jeans. Helen fled. She couldn't stand another look at those ruined thighs with the liposuction scars.

This time, Sharmayne bought. She wanted all the splendid, splashy things, but she seemed to buy them more to stay on Helen's good side than because she enjoyed them.

Tiffany with the bad eye job was the first regular, but not the last, to bring Helen "a little present." She gave Helen silver Elsa Peretti earrings from Tiffany's "because I want you to be my friend."

Niki had given Helen a Movado watch with a charming note: "Time we were friends."

She told Helen, "I'd like to have the same relationship with you that I had with Christina." Niki's words glittered with unspoken meaning and lingered long after Helen got her perfume stink out of the store. Does she want me to find her another hit man? Helen wondered. Christina did not have time to blackmail Niki about Desiree's death, if she in fact arranged it. Something else was going on.

The presents made Helen uneasy, but she kept them. They were no more than tip money for these women. She could pawn the watch and earrings if she ever needed cash fast.

Christina had something on all of you, Helen thought. I can't figure out what. But I'd better find out soon.

Tara did not offer Helen bribes or presents. She seemed grateful for Helen's silence and her acceptance. She worked even harder. She followed Helen around the store like a puppy. Helen knew it wasn't just gratitude that kept Tara at her side. Tara wanted those incriminating photos, and she would not let Helen out of her sight until they turned up.

The only person Helen didn't hear from was Venetia, Mother of the Year and Pill Popper of the Decade. Helen figured Venetia had found a new pusher and was twitching somewhere else.

She was surprised when Joe, Christina's ex-boyfriend, called that Saturday afternoon and asked if Christina had left anything for him.

"Like what, Joe?" Helen said.

"A package, an envelope, a box, I dunno. But I know she was going to give it to me. So you find anything with my name on it, you call me day or night, no problemo, and I'll pick it up. And, Helen, there will be a reward. A big one, you know what I mean?"

"I'm sorry, Joe, but I haven't found anything."

"She had something for me," he said. "I want it. Now."

Joe must have realized that sounded like a threat, because he softened his words. "I mean, I miss her, and it would be nice to have some way to remember her. We were kinda engaged."

"Except you dumped her," Helen said. "If she left you a package, I'd open it carefully. If it ticks, it may not be a watch."

"She always said you were great with the jokes," Joe said. "We split, but it was a misunderstanding. I . . . I loved her." He managed a teary throb in his voice.

Right. You really loved Christina, she thought. That's why you have never said Christina's name, just "she" and "her."

Joe's voice grew softer, more persuasive. It oozed through the phone like honey. The receiver felt sticky. "Look, Helen, let me level with you. That cop, Dwight Handel—"

"Hansel," Helen said.

"Yeah, him. He's on me like white on rice. He thinks I killed her."

"Why you?" Helen said. "Aren't bodies in barrels mob hits?"

"The FBI said this was not a mob hit. It was made to look like one. They're not interested in it. But this Dwight Handel—"

"Hansel," Helen said again.

"Whatever. He's definitely interested in me. I've had to get a lawyer. I'm not supposed to be talking about this, but I've got to have that package. I mean, it like clears my name."

Sure it does.

"Don't you have an alibi for the time Christina died?" she said, fishing for more facts.

"That's just it," he said. "The police can't tell exactly when she was killed. She was kinda messed up after being in that leaky barrel for about a week. She was very decompressed."

"Decomposed," Helen said.

"That, too. They coulda figured it out by the stomach contents, but she didn't eat nothing."

And who's fault was that? Helen wondered.

"All they can say for sure is it happened sometime between Saturday after she left the shop and Monday morning. I don't have an alibi. I was alone the whole weekend, kicking back, watching videos and drinking beer."

Joe never spent any time by himself, if he could help it. Helen knew that. Every weekend, he and Christina and a carload of friends went to the South Beach clubs. He couldn't stand to be alone. He might hear his empty head rattle.

"The police think she was probably killed sometime Saturday after she got off work, though, because she got her last cell phone call at six-twenty-two."

"Who called Christina?"

"Me," Joe said.

Helen was relieved when Brittney came into Juliana's about four that afternoon. She was wearing something white and drifting that made her look like a lovely lost soul. White was the color of mourning in some cultures. It certainly looked mournful on Brittney.

Brittney was different from the others. There were no odd

overtones, no presents, no offers of money if Helen found any letters or packages. She wanted to talk about Christina. Helen thought Brittney sincerely grieved for her friend, although she did not look sad. How could she? Brittney could show no emotion.

She was the only one who seemed to care if Christina's killer was caught.

"It's just terrible about Christina," Brittney said, her voice soft and fluttery as moth wings. "What are the police doing about it?"

"They searched her house. Then they searched the store," Helen said.

"They find anything?" sighed Brittney. It sounded so hopeless when she said it.

"They found nothing," Helen said.

But I did, she thought.

Chapter 24

Tara snapped on Monday.

It was almost closing time when she began screaming. No customers were in Juliana's. Helen was grateful for that.

Helen was steaming the wrinkles out of the new stock, a hot, mindless job that had to be done before she could go home. Suddenly, Tara shrieked, "Put on another CD! I can't listen to *10,000 Maniacs* ten thousand times."

Tara's jaw was clenched, and so were her hands. Her rigid arms looked like they were clamped to her body with iron bands. *10,000 Maniacs* could sound a little monotonous if you were in the wrong mood. But Helen didn't think it should provoke a reaction like that. The strain of those blackmail pictures must be getting to Tara.

"Sorry, I tuned it out," Helen said. "I'll find something else."

The store had more than two hundred forty CDs in two tall towers, but the same six seemed to get played over and over. The CDs at the bottom of the towers were thick with dust. Helen reached down and pulled out *Billboard's Top Hits 1975–1979*. No wonder that one was never played. These were strictly moldy oldies. Who wanted to hear Captain & Tennille?

Helen was about to shove it back into the rack when she stopped. One of those ancient hits was "Love Will Keep Us Together." The song on Tara's flyer.

Helen opened the plastic CD case. Inside was the usual
paper insert. It looked too thick. She pulled it out and
opened it. Folded inside were three photos.

Tara was in a big round bed with two men and a woman.
The four were so tangled together, Helen got dizzy trying to
figure out who was doing what to whom.

The other woman was African-American, with a beautiful body. Helen could not see her face. The men were flabby
and white as mushrooms. Helen couldn't identify them, either, although one had an impressive head of white hair. The
other was bald as a baby, but he was doing very grown-up
things.

Only Tara was clearly visible. All of Tara. And she was
definitely not a virgin bride. "Love Will Keep Us Together"
was Christina's nasty little joke. She knew these pictures
would destroy Paulie's love and split the couple forever.

"Find anything?" Tara called back to the storeroom. She
sounded calmer.

"How about listening to Andrea Bocelli?" Helen asked. It
was one of the same six CDs they always played.

"Sure," Tara said. "A little opera will class up the place."

She'll be back here any second, Helen thought. She
shoved the photos into the CD case, and brushed off her
skirt

Helen did not dare tell Tara to go home early. She would
be suspicious. Instead, the two women closed the store together as usual. Tara went to her car, and Helen set off walking in the direction of the Coronado apartments. She waited
until she saw Tara drive toward the highway and disappear
from view.

Only then did Helen turn around and go back to Juliana's.
She turned off the alarm system and the security cameras.
Back in the stockroom, she stripped off her jacket and knelt
before the first CD tower.

Helen pulled a CD from the bottom of the rack and saw
her fingerprints in the dust on the case. She could not leave
fingerprints on blackmail evidence. Oh God, she'd already
left fingerprints. How could she be so dumb?

Helen found a paper towel and cleaned the Captain &
Tennille CD inside and out and then wiped the liner and the

photos, hoping she hadn't left any partial prints on some stray corner.

I need gloves, she thought. But who wore gloves in South Florida?

Wait. There were gloves in the store. Helen opened the second drawer in the accessory cabinet and pulled out a pair of white kid twelve-button gloves. Juliana's customers occasionally needed them for formal evenings. Helen rolled up her blouse sleeves, and carefully pulled on the long white gloves with the tiny pearl buttons. At Juliana's, she thought, you searched in style.

When she found the next set of photos, Helen was glad she was wearing gloves. She didn't want to touch them. They repelled her, and yet she could not stop looking at them.

Helen also understood why Sharmayne wanted her to send that envelope without opening it. The supermodel was wrong. Christina had not put those photos in an envelope. They were in a Nick Lowe CD with a song called "The Beast in Me."

The photos of Sharmayne with that handsome dog Big Boy gave new meaning to the term animal lover.

Niki's crime seemed mild in comparison. The blackmail evidence was hidden in the cast recording of *Gentlemen Prefer Blondes*, which had that old showstopper "Diamonds Are a Girl's Best Friend." Inside was a copy of Niki's arrest record and a short news story. Her mug shot lacked the airbrushed perfection of *Playboy* photography. Niki looked stunned and desperate.

Niki had been arrested for burglary. She went to the parties where the women dripped diamonds and figured out which ones had jewelry worth stealing. Then she passed this information on to two professional burglars. Niki had "cooperated with the authorities," the news story said, and received probation. Niki sold out her friends to avoid prison.

Diamonds were her best friend. Niki was not loyal to her accomplices. Both were sentenced to fifteen years.

After Sharmayne, Niki's sin seemed human and forgivable. But Niki's new husband would not be taking her to any diamond-studded Star Island parties if it was known she liked to help jewel thieves. In fact, the wedding might not have come off at all, whether Desiree was dead or alive. Jimmy the Shirt might have a dubious reputation, but he'd want his wife to be above reproach.

Tara. Sharmayne. Niki. Three song titles down. Four to go.

Helen opened one CD after another before she found the Paul Simon album with "Mother and Child Reunion." By now Helen had caught on to Christina's ugly little jokes. This one would be bad.

It was. Venetia, the Mother of the Year, was photographed with a boy about twelve, and she was not holding his hand. Helen wanted to gag. How could any woman do that with someone so young? The boy wasn't even attractive. His nakedness made him seem newly hatched.

Helen wondered if the photos were Venetia's idea or the boy's and how they fell into Christina's hands. Maybe Christina paid the kid for them. What did she give him— money or drugs? Helen closed the CD case, once again grateful for the gloves.

Helen found one more set of photos that night. She almost overlooked them, but the odd CD title caught her eye: *Celtic Harp on the Prairie*. Helen could not imagine Juliana's South Beach club set listening to "Beautiful Dreamer." It hadn't been a hit in a hundred years. But then Helen noticed another harp song was "Silver Threads Among the Gold." Christina had scrawled that same title on the nursing home newsletter.

Helen opened the CD case gingerly, bracing herself for another stomach-turning sight. When she saw a mug shot and an arrest record, she sighed with relief.

Two gold watches, a Mont Blanc pen valued at six hundred dollars, and a diamond pendant worth three thousand were reported stolen from residents at the Sunny Gables nursing home. Police found these items in a car belonging to Employee of the Year Cindy, now known as Tiffany with the bad eye job. In the mug shot, Tiffany looked flat-faced with shock. Her blond hair was straggly, and her eyes were bloodshot. Helen saw no trace of the big-busted blond beauty who bought so much at Juliana's.

The owners of the pen and the watches refused to press charges after their valuables were returned. But Mrs. Vera Crinklaw was determined to see Tiffany in court over the theft of her diamond pendant. Helen remembered Mrs. C. from the nursing home newsletter. She had refused to be charmed by Tiffany. She knew there was something wrong about the little slyboots, and she wanted public vindication.

Alas, Mrs. C. died of pneumonia before Tiffany's trial. Her heir considered the case closed when he got the pendant back. Tiffany thought she'd got away with it, until Christina. If Tiffany's rich old boyfriend Burt ever discovered her past, she could kiss him good-bye.

Helen now had five good reasons for blackmail. And five good reasons to kill Christina.

She wondered what blackmail evidence Christina had on Joe. She hadn't found any Dylan CDs with "You Gotta Serve Somebody." Nor had she seen any sign of Don Ho's "Tiny Bubbles."

Helen still had another CD tower to search, but she had to leave. It was almost time for the birthday call to her mother in St. Louis. She would be frantic if Helen didn't call on time. She put all the incriminating evidence back in the CD tower. She thought it was the safest place.

Helen felt leaden and tired on the walk home. She'd seen too much. She had nothing to look forward to tonight but a talk with her mother filled with tears and regrets. She stripped off her suit, put on some cutoffs, and sat down on the bed. It squeaked mournfully. She checked her watch. Twenty minutes to go. She'd better get the suitcase from Margery. That's where she hid the cell phone.

Margery was talking on the phone and handed the suitcase to Helen without a word. On the way back, Helen lingered in the warm evening. Palm trees rustled their sultry song. The air was soft and warm and scented with ocean salt and swimming pool chlorine. The setting sun turned the pool a pearly pink. Purple bougainvillea petals floated on the water.

It was so hopelessly romantic that Helen wished for just a minute she was still married to Rob and they were alone in the water and he was covering her mouth with wet chlorine kisses. Rob was a good kisser.

Then she remembered the August afternoon she came home from work early, hoping Rob would do just that in their pool in St. Louis. Instead, she found her husband kissing their little blond neighbor Sandy. That's when she'd picked up the crowbar and changed everything.

Well, there was nothing Helen could do about that now. It was almost seven o'clock. Time for the call home. Helen went inside, locked the doors, and closed the blinds. Then she rooted around in the old lady underwear until she found the cell phone and the piece of pink cellophane. She dialed the number.

"Happy birthday, Mom," she said.

"Happy?" her mother wailed. It quickly turned into a whine. "I should be happy when my daughter is a fugitive? Oh, Helen, why can't you come home? That's the only birthday present I want. I talked with Robbie, and he said he'll forgive you."

"He'll forgive me!" Helen shouted, her anger rising in a red tide. "He'll forgive me! I didn't do anything."

"You wrecked his car," her mother said.

"Of course, I wrecked his car. I found him and Sandy shagging on our patio."

The scene flashed again in front of her. Rob and Sandy were naked on the teak chaise longue, his hairy bottom in the air, her freshly waxed legs waving like antennae. Rob was supposed to be oiling the wood and doing patio maintenance. Instead, he was nailing Sandy. And Rob always said he didn't like Sandy.

Helen had picked up the crowbar she found next to Rob's electric screwdriver. She brought the crowbar down on the chaise with a satisfying *crak!* Rob jumped up off (and out of) Sandy. Sandy scurried behind a pot of pink impatiens for protection, but not before Helen noticed she was not a real blonde.

Rob abandoned his lady love and tried to hide in his Land Cruiser. He scrambled in and locked the doors, but Helen had the crowbar. She still remembered the satisfying sound it made as she destroyed the big SUV. First, she mulched the windshield while Rob cowered in the front seat, arms up to protect his head from flying glass. Next, she broke all the other windows. Then she cracked the headlights and tail-lights and splintered the side mirrors.

She was busy bashing the doors when Sandy crawled to the pile of clothes on the patio and picked up her cell phone. Helen was having so much fun she did not hear Sandy calling 911. The police laughed their heads off when they saw the naked Rob hiding in the car. He tried to get Helen arrested for destruction of property, but the car was registered in her name. After all, she'd paid for it. Rob and Sandy did not press attempted assault charges. Sandy was too afraid her husband would find out how she'd spent her afternoon. He did anyway.

Unfortunately, Helen's insurance would not cover self-inflicted damage. And Rob's photos of the battered Land Cruiser and the police report on the domestic disturbance call did not help her court case.

She realized her mother was still talking. ". . . Everything could be worked out, Helen, if you'd just get back together with your husband."

Helen's hands itched for a crowbar. "He's not my husband, Mom. We're divorced."

"Divorce isn't recognized by the Church, Helen," her mother said. "The Pope said so. If you should ever remarry, you'll burn in hell."

"The Pope's wrong," Helen said. "When I lived with that mooch Rob, I was already in hell. Anything else would be heaven. Mom, don't you remember what my life was like? When Rob quit his sales job, he quit looking for work and lived off me."

"He wasn't living off you, dear. He just couldn't find a job on his level."

"For five years?" Helen said, angry all over again.

"And he did a lot around your house. He remodeled the kitchen and the bathrooms, and—"

Helen interrupted. "Mom, he didn't do anything but tear up those rooms. I had to hire people to finish what he started. I paid for those renovations myself. Meanwhile, he was screwing every woman in the neighborhood."

"Helen, I have no desire to hear that language. And while I don't want to be critical of my own daughter, perhaps if you'd been home more instead of working those long hours, your husband might have been more faithful."

"Mother!"

"Well, men have different appetites than we do, dear. I know you think I'm old-fashioned, but it's true. Robbie could still be a good husband if you'd just come home and do what the judge said."

"Never!" Helen said. "I'll starve first."

"But you don't have to," her mother said. She started her wailing whine again. "Helen, you could have a decent high-paying job—"

"Except I'd have to give half that salary to Rob, Mother."

"Is that so bad, Helen?" her mother said. "It would still be many times more than you are making now."

Helen looked around the musty apartment at the Coronado with the squeaky bed and the turquoise Barcalounger. She remembered her huge St. Louis home with its tasteful furniture. Half the home and most of the contents went to Rob.

Helen had filed for divorce after the Land Cruiser crushing. She was the injured party. But charming Rob had convinced the judge that he was a house husband who made Helen's successful career possible because he stayed home and took care of their household. His many lovers testified that Rob provided invaluable domestic services, while Helen fumed, and her incompetent lawyer told her to shut up.

The judge believed Rob, the man's man. Helen was making six figures, his honor said, because of Rob's love and support. The judge gave Rob half the house. That was bad enough, since Helen put up all the down payment. But then the judge awarded Rob half of Helen's future income, claiming her deadbeat husband made her current career possible "at the expense of his own livelihood."

When the judge said those words, Helen was outraged. Before her lawyer could stop her, Helen grabbed a familiar black book with gold lettering. She put her hand on it and said, "I swear on this Bible that my husband Rob will not get another nickel of my salary."

Later, the book turned out not to be a Bible, but a copy of the Revised Missouri Statutes. But Helen still considered the oath binding.

"Young woman, you will do as I order, or you will be in contempt of court," the judge had thundered.

"I'm already in contempt of this court," screamed Helen. She realized she must have looked like one of those "crazy women's libbers" the judge disliked so much. Rob sat there in his nice suit, kept his mouth shut, and got all her money.

Now she was holding the cell phone and screaming again. "Mother, I'd rather starve than give Rob my money. That's why I left St. Louis and took a dead-end job. Even if the court or Rob finds me, I'm barely making enough to live on, much less having money left over for that mooch."

Her mother wept louder. "Helen, you are cutting off your nose to spite your face. All your education and what are you making now? Seven dollars an hour?"

"Seven seventy," Helen corrected her.

"Doing what?" her mother demanded.

"Never mind what," Helen said. She didn't trust her mother not to blab to Rob. "It's respectable."

"It's a waste. I never thought I'd have a daughter hiding from the law."

Helen wasn't sure how far the courts would go to track down a deadbeat wife. But she knew Rob would go to any length to get her money. Well, he would be disappointed. Helen came from hardworking stock. Her grandmother was a cleaning woman who supported herself with dead-end jobs her whole life. Helen could, too.

"I don't know how you could do this to me," her mother wailed. "I don't even know where you are."

And you won't, thought Helen. Because Rob would charm it out of you.

"I'm in a better place, Mom," Helen said. "I'm happy here. I like it better than St. Louis."

"You hate me. You hate your home," her mother said.

"I love you," Helen said. "Please try to understand." It

was time to bring out the pink cellophane and end this conversation. Helen crinkled it in her hand.

"Sorry, the phone's breaking up. I'd better hang up. I can't hear you, but I love you, Mom."

I can't listen to you, but I love you, Mom.

"You're breaking up. Bye, Mom. Happy birth—"

Helen cut herself off in the middle of a word, to make it seem authentic.

After the call, Helen could not stay shut up with her thoughts. She took the suitcase back to Margery's, then went for a walk on the side streets, where people like her lived, shop assistants, waiters, and retirees.

Darkness was coming on. Cats with torn ears crawled over fences for another night of dangerous freedom. Small things scurried and slithered through the impatiens and palmettos. Lights were going on in the brightly painted cottages, and in their glow, Helen caught glimpses of other people's lives.

The more she walked, the more peaceful she felt. Juliana's and its dirty secrets seemed far way. So did her mother and her rigid morality.

Helen's peace was shattered by the roar of a motorcycle. She did not look up, hoping the noise would soon be gone. But then the motorcycle slowed to a rumble, and she heard a man say, "Would you like a ride?"

Helen looked up and saw Daniel on a black Harley.

He wore his black leather jacket and chaps like a knight's armor. His legs were braced to control the motorcycle, and she could see his muscles flexed through the leather. She felt weak in the knees.

"Come on," he said. "I won't keep you out late on a school night." He smiled so charmingly, she climbed aboard the big bike. He handed her a helmet, which felt heavy as a bowling ball.

Helen settled in behind him, put her arms around his broad chest, and felt how it tapered into his narrow waist. She leaned against him and breathed in soap and sweat and leather. Every time Daniel shifted, she felt him move against her. His body was hard but warm.

They were going too fast to talk, and Helen was glad. She

knew she'd be tongue-tied. At first, she was afraid they'd be killed. Herds of SUVs drove straight at them. Angry pickups roared past. Delivery trucks cut them off. Helen tensed and closed her eyes, expecting to be ground chuck. But soon she saw that Daniel knew what he was doing. She relaxed and began to enjoy being wrapped around a man for the first time in ages. She felt young and carefree.

Half an hour later, Daniel roared into the Coronado parking lot, Helen still clinging to him. They pulled off their helmets together. Helen stayed sitting on the bike, a little dazed. Daniel dismounted and kissed her. Hard. She dropped the helmet and kissed him back, her fingers tangled in his long dark hair, her chest pressed against his black leather jacket.

"I have to leave now," he said finally. "But I want to see you tomorrow night. Seven-thirty OK? We'll go for a longer ride."

"Oh, yes," Helen said, knowing he was not talking about his motorcycle.

Chapter 25

"I have a new system to win the lottery," Peggy the parrot lady said.

"Hmmmm," Helen said absently. She was still dazed by Daniel's kisses. Her lips were swollen and bruised. Her cheeks burned, rubbed raw by his beard, which was pleasantly rough. Like his kisses.

Tomorrow night she would have that perfect body all to herself. If those kisses were any preview, Daniel was even better than he looked.

Helen plopped down at the picnic table and stared into the night, wishing it would go away and become tomorrow, so she could be with Daniel.

"Are you OK?" Peggy said, then looked closer at Helen. "No, you're not. You look like you've been hit on the head with a coconut."

"I went for a ride on Daniel's new Harley."

Peggy whistled. So did Pete the parrot.

"He wants to take me riding tomorrow night," Helen said.

"Well, well," Peggy said. "Are you going?"

"Oh, yes," Helen sighed. "He's absolutely perfect. I think this is it."

"Oh, oh. What kind of protection do you have?"

"Huh?" Helen said.

"I thought so," Peggy said. "Don't pretend he's swept

you off your feet when you wind up in his bed tomorrow night. Do you have any condoms?"

Helen could feel a blush creeping up her neck. "No," she said.

"I have a box I'll never use. I'll get it for you."

Helen was content to daydream in the dark until Peggy returned with the condoms. "Helen, I hate to sound like your mother, but do you know what you're doing? You aren't the type who has casual affairs. You're a serious person. This guy dates strippers. If you just want a good time, Daniel could be fun. But he's not for the long haul. If you're looking for any kind of commitment, he'll probably take off. Can you live with that?"

"Daniel may not be Mr. Right, but he's Mr. Right Now," Helen said. She was surprised to hear herself say that, but she meant it. "I don't care if I only have one night with Daniel. No woman can expect perfection forever. I'll take what I can get."

"Then put these in your purse."

"Thirty-six condoms?" Helen said.

"Hope you use them all," Peggy said, and winked.

"Thanks," Helen said. She went to her apartment as if she were sleepwalking. On the way, she passed through Phil's perpetual cloud of burning hemp.

Phil had his dreams. So did Peggy. Tomorrow, Helen would have hers.

Helen was not sure how she made it through work the next day. She brought the wrong sizes for her customers. She counted out the wrong change. She forgot to buzz in Brittney and left her standing outside the green door tapping her foot impatiently. Tara finally noticed Brittney and admitted her. When Brittney asked about the progress of Christina's police investigation, Helen simply smiled and stared into space, which shocked Brittney. No wonder she left in a huff.

After that disaster, Helen tried drinking black coffee until her nerves screeched like a badly tuned violin. The caffeine did not make her more alert. She picked at her lunch. She said, "What?" when Tara asked her questions. But mostly

Helen stared into nothing, like a woman in a trance. She'd been put into that trance by Daniel's kiss. Only another kiss would break the spell.

Yesterday, she'd been dying to examine the other CD tower. But that was before Daniel. Now she didn't care about Juliana's ugly secrets. All Helen could think about was Daniel, the man with the dashing black leather, the magnificent muscles, the beautiful manners.

Tonight, she had a date with the perfect man. Daniel could ask out any woman in South Florida, but he wanted to spend the evening—and the night—with Helen.

What should she wear on their first date? She mentally went through her closet, discarding one outfit after another as too old, too dowdy, too dull. Helen would have broken into her precious stash and bought something spectacular at Juliana's except she could not wear any of the store's midget sizes.

Helen finally decided on her black pantsuit, which always made her look slim. She had some flimsy French underwear, which she hadn't worn since before her divorce. She wished she had time for a facial, a makeover, a complete exercise program.

That afternoon, Helen jammed the cash register, and it took Tara half an hour to fix it. Then she knocked over Tara's soda and ruined a Chanel scarf.

"You are useless today," Tara said. "It's five-thirty. Why don't you go home?"

"What if something happens while you're here alone? Paulie will never forgive me."

"Paulie will never know. You're doing more damage than an army of looters," Tara said, and pushed Helen toward the door.

Helen went. Maybe Tara wanted another chance to search the store. Helen didn't care. She doubted Tara would stumble on the photos in the CD towers.

Helen ran all the way home. All she could think about was getting ready for her date with Daniel. She took a long steamy shower, washed her hair, painted her nails, creamed her skin, and put on the black French bra that gave her the incredible cleavage. She carefully applied her makeup. But her hands shook so badly, she smeared her dark eyeliner. Helen tried to wipe it off with a Q-tip, and wound up with black raccoon circles around her eyes.

Helen took off all her makeup and reapplied it.

The last things Helen put on were the diamond earrings Rob gave her on their wedding night. They were the only good jewelry she kept from her old life. Her engagement ring had been sold, along with her Rolex watch and the diamond pendant Rob bought her for their tenth anniversary. She threw her gold wedding band in the Mississippi when she left St. Louis.

When she finished, Helen twirled in front of the mirror and decided she didn't look half bad. It was seven-twenty-five. Helen went outside. Peggy and Pete the parrot were out by the pool with Margery. Her landlady was wearing a tie-dyed purple shorts set and magenta suede mules.

Peggy began whistling, "Here Comes the Bride." Margery told her to hush.

"You look lovely, dear," Margery said. "It's about time that boy dated a real woman. What time are you going out?"

"Seven-thirty," Helen said. "Any minute now."

They heard cars squeal into the parking lot and then the blare of police radios. A uniformed police officer went running to the back exit of the Coronado.

"What the heck?" Margery said, and got up.

Another uniform ran to the foot of the staircase. Two men in plain clothes and dark windbreakers that said FDLE walked purposefully up the steps to Daniel's second-floor apartment, hands hovering above their weapons. Helen had lived here long enough to know they were the Florida Department of Law Enforcement. One knocked on the door to 2C and said, "Open up! Police!"

Both men stood back, as if they expected Daniel to blast through the door with a sawed-off shotgun.

"Daniel! He's hurt!" Helen said.

"No," Margery said. She held Helen's arm tightly so she could not bolt toward Daniel's apartment. "Stay here. Stay calm until we know what's going on."

Daniel's door opened, and the two FDLE agents went inside. Helen wasn't sure how long they were in there, but eventually they came back out with Daniel. His hands were cuffed behind him. The agents handed him over to the two police officers. Daniel looked heartbreakingly handsome in black leather.

"Daniel!" Helen cried.

"Awkk," Pete the parrot said, and danced gleefully on Peggy's shoulder. Helen remembered that he'd bitten Daniel.

"Shut up, bird brain," Peggy said.

"What are you doing with that boy?" Margery demanded.

"Sorry, ma'am, he's under arrest," one police officer said. "He's being charged with theft by deception."

"There must be some mistake," Helen said.

"No, ma'am. No mistake. He's being arrested for cheating widows and poor people."

"He's innocent. Daniel, let me go with you," Helen said.

"No! Stay here and call my lawyer," Daniel said. "His name is Steinway, on Oakland Park."

"Oh, shit," Margery said.

"Steinway," Daniel repeated. "Like the piano. Tell him they're booking me at the Broward County Jail. Don't come down there, Helen, please."

"Come on," the police officers said. Doors slammed, tires squealed, and Daniel was gone. The last thing Helen noticed was how dumpy the police officers looked next to the superbly muscled Daniel.

Helen remembered that night in flashes. The FDLE agents had a search warrant for Daniel's apartment. They left hours later, carrying out box after box.

Peggy called Steinway the lawyer.

Margery took Helen back to her own place and installed her in the purple recliner, wrapped in a blanket. Helen started shivering uncontrollably, and Margery made her hot chocolate and chicken soup. Helen took a sip of each.

"There must be some mistake," she kept repeating.

"I'm sure it's all a misunderstanding," Peggy soothed. But Margery stayed silent, and Helen noticed.

"Why did you say what you did when Daniel yelled out that lawyer's name?" Helen asked her landlady.

"Do you really want to know?" Margery asked.

"Yes. No matter how bad it is, I want to know."

"Steinway represents every successful crook in town. Retain him and you might as well announce you're guilty. Except Steinway has a remarkable record for helping the guilty go free."

"Oh, shit," Helen said.

"I could be wrong," Margery said.

"I feel like such a fool," Helen said. "What if Daniel really did cheat widows and poor people? That's disgusting." Then the tears started, and she couldn't stop them. "God punished me for wanting to hop into bed with a man I barely knew."

"Rubbish," Margery said. "Do you think God runs a dating service? She has more important things to do."

"You're right," Helen said. "I sound like my mother."

"God forbid," Margery said.

Helen laughed, then blew her nose. "I wish the cops could have arrested him tomorrow night," she said, and all three women laughed until their sides ached as much as Helen's heart.

Peggy and Margery walked Helen back to her room and helped her undress. She was fine, until she stripped off her top and saw that incredible cantilevered bra. Then Helen started crying again. Margery wrapped her in a robe and rocked her like a child.

"Maybe it's a case of mistaken identity," Helen said, sniffling.

"Maybe we'll know more when we read tomorrow's paper," Peggy said.

Helen thought she'd never fall asleep, but she did, almost immediately. It was a restless, phantom-ridden sleep, haunted by old sorrows. She knew she'd been a fool, and her dreams told her so, until she didn't want to hear it anymore. But she could not escape. She slept on. Only when Helen heard the doors of the newspaper delivery van slam shut at five-ten the next morning did she awake.

Helen rummaged in her purse for change to buy a paper. She had to know what Daniel had done. "He cheated widows and poor people," the police said. But how? She thought guiltily of her ride on Daniel's brand-new Harley. Where did he get the money for that?

When Helen opened her door, Margery was stepping outside. She was wearing her purple chenille robe and red sponge curlers.

"Going for a paper?" she whispered.

Helen nodded.

"I'll go with you," Margery said.

Helen bought the paper but did not open it. They walked back to Margery's. Her landlady poured coffee for them both, then put on her reading glasses. They were ready for the worst. The story was on page 2B: "Police Arrest Man Accused of Fire Safety Scam."

Margery read the story outloud, "Daniel Dayson, 42—"

"He's my age?" Helen said. "I thought he was younger."

"Me, too," Margery said. She cleared her throat and started reading again from the top:

"Daniel Dayson, 42, has been charged with cheating at least thirty Florida restaurants and food-related businesses with a fire-equipment repair scam.

"Anne Watts, spokeswoman for the Florida Department of Law Enforcement, said Dayson allegedly bilked restaurant owners of more than sixty thousand dollars. The FDLE spokeswoman said Dayson would 'go into restaurants, show false ID, and claim to be from the fire marshal's office. Dayson would say he was there to inspect the restaurant's kitchen hood systems and portable fire extinguishers.' "

"The uniform," Helen said. "Daniel wore that tailored blue uniform with the official-looking red patches."

Margery adjusted her glasses and started reading again.

"Dayson would claim that the restaurant's equipment was not working properly and was in violation of the fire code. 'It was quite a scam,' Watts said. 'Apparently, Dayson would tell the restaurants they would have to shut down until the equipment was fixed. This could cost them thousands of dollars in lost business while they contracted with repair people or ordered the proper equipment. Dayson would offer to fix the equipment himself, for cash. Grateful restaurant owners would give Dayson several thousand dollars in cash for repairs that they did not need. Needless to say, he fixed nothing.'

"FDLE investigators said Dayson was also wanted in Georgia, Alabama, and Texas for the same scam. 'The investigation is ongoing,' Watts said. 'Anyone with information on this case should call . . .'"

Margery threw the paper down. "I can't believe I made fudge for him," she said.

I can't believe I wanted to go to bed with him, Helen thought.

She picked up the paper and looked at Daniel's mug shot. Some people look guilty in mug shots. Others look angry, evil, or bleary-eyed. But Daniel looked surprised. Perhaps he thought he could charm his way out of this, too. Even in the harsh light, he was handsome.

At seven a.m., Peggy arrived without Pete to discuss the Daniel disaster. Helen thought she looked naked with no parrot on her shoulder.

At eight, Cal pounded on Margery's door. "Turn on the TV if you ladies want to see your boyfriend," he said. "I always knew he was a crook."

Margery slammed the door on Cal's gloating face, but she flipped on the TV. The women did not see Daniel, but his victims. A Hispanic couple was telling a reporter in halting English that they gave Daniel three thousand dollars for phony repairs to their Hialeah restaurant.

"He had a badge and official papers. He wore a uniform," the husband said. "We were afraid he would close us down."

"It is all our savings," the wife wept.

The other interview was a seventy-year-old Davie widow who ran a doughnut shop.

"He came in here wearing a blue uniform with patches on it. How was I supposed to know?" the widow said, her chin trembling. "Now they tell me that Broward County fire marshals wear a different uniform. Well, it's too darn late. I lost fifteen hundred dollars. He never even did the repairs."

"Imagine picking on an old lady," Margery said. Her red sponge curlers bobbed with indignation.

No one had the nerve to say the "old lady" was younger than Margery.

"Well, he's a first-class con man," Margery said. "He fooled me."

"And me," Peggy said. "And all those poor people."

And me, Helen thought. "I think I'll get dressed for work," she said, and went sadly back to her apartment.

Handsome is as handsome does, Helen's grandmother used to say. There was something small and mean and ugly about Daniel's choice of victims. He went after the old and the poor, after people who did not speak English well, after people who were afraid of official papers.

How could I find a man like that attractive? Helen thought. What's wrong with me? I've made one bad choice after another: first Rob, then Cal, now Daniel.

What had Margery said? Single men in South Florida were all "drunks, druggies, and deadbeats." Except for Daniel, a petty crook who preyed on the old and the helpless.

No wonder Peggy was through with men forever. Peggy would rather play the Florida Lotto, where her chances of winning were one in twenty-three million. Peggy believed those were better odds than the dating game, where she saw no chance at all.

Helen opened her purse, took out the box of condoms, and tossed them in the trash. She wasn't ever going to get lucky.

Chapter 26

"My life," Helen said, "is in the toilet."

She was staring at a blue toilet with a gnarled schefflera plant growing in the bowl. A bathtub was planted with a mass of spiky mother-in-law's tongue.

"Then you've come to the right place," Sarah said.

Bathtubs and commodes were the decor at Le Tub, one of Hollywood's funkier restaurants. Some of the exiled porcelain were planters. Others were painted with slogans: "An inexpensive place for folks with money!" one tub said.

Le Tub's weathered wood booths overlooked the silver water of the Intracoastal. A boy fed his french fries to the fish. Helen watched the sun set. It was hard to take her troubles seriously when she sat between a bathtub and a postcard view.

Sarah looked chic in a gauzy white outfit, and Helen remembered with shame that she was a Juliana's reject. "Thanks for taking me here," Helen said. "I feel better already."

"Good," Sarah said. Her charm bracelet jingled cheerfully, but her bright brown eyes were sympathetic. "I'm sorry about Daniel."

"I feel like such a fool," Helen said.

"Why? The guy was a scam artist who operated in three states. Florida breeds them like mosquitoes. If you got conned by him, you've got plenty of company. At least you didn't give him your life savings."

"I gave him my heart," Helen said, then wished she'd never said something so ridiculous.

"Honey, at our age, that's a gift we've given before. He didn't get anything new."

Helen giggled. A waiter came by, and both women ordered white wine and seafood salads.

"I'm trying to think of Daniel as a diversion," Helen said. "When I was with him, I forgot my troubles."

"But you still have them," Sarah reminded her. "What's happening with the investigation? Who are your candidates for Christina's murder?"

"There are too many," Helen said. "Christina was blackmailing at least five people, maybe more. It was nasty. She could ruin a lot of people."

"Like who?" Sarah said.

"Tara, for starters. Christina had proof that she was a prostitute in Vegas."

"This is South Florida. Would anyone care?" Sarah said.

"Tara's boyfriend, Paulie. He'd dump her in a heartbeat, and he's her meal ticket. Christina was bleeding Tara for two thousand a month, and she wanted more. Tara says she wouldn't kill Christina because she couldn't find the incriminating photos. I think she's telling the truth. Of course, I believed Daniel was the perfect man."

"Enough flagellation," Sarah said. "You're starting to enjoy it."

"Christina also had compromising material on Sharmayne, the supermodel, and Tiffany with the bad eye job."

"The woman was busy," Sarah said.

"I think she may have been blackmailing her ex-boyfriend Joe, too. He's been bugging me for a package he says Christina left him. The creep practically threatened me. The only problem is, I haven't found any blackmail photos for Joe yet. But I still have to check the other CD tower."

"What's his song?"

"'You Gotta Serve Somebody.'"

"Dylan," Sarah said. "Christina had good taste. An ugly sense of humor, but good taste."

"Oh, yeah?" Helen said. "Then why am I looking for Don Ho's 'Tiny Bubbles'?"

"I don't know, why are you?"

"It might have something to do with the death of Brittney's fiancé, except she's not acting like the others," Helen said. "I don't think Brittney was being blackmailed."

The seafood salads were served in paper bowls, with forks sticking out of the top and a pile of paper napkins on the side. They were mounds of fresh calamari, salmon, crab, and shrimp.

"Oh, I forgot Venetia, the jittery drug customer," Helen said. "Christina was blackmailing her, too. That woman is weird enough to flip out and kill Christina, but she's too skinny to hurt anyone."

"Don't be too sure," Sarah said. "I used to work in a hospital. The skinny druggies can get powerfully strong when they are desperate. It took four men to restrain one ninety-pound cokehead at our hospital."

"Then I'll keep Venetia on the list," Helen said. "There's also Niki. Christina knew she'd been a jewel thief. And there was the murder for hire. Except everything went right. Desiree died, and Niki got her man."

"Maybe Christina was blackmailing her for it anyway," Sarah said.

"Maybe. But Niki couldn't have killed Christina. When the murder took place, she says was in Greece."

"That's what she says. I say we check her out," Sarah said.

Their seafood salads were eaten, the sun had gone down, and Helen was shivering in the chill evening air. "Let's go back to my place for coffee and Key lime pie and talk this over further," Sarah said.

Helen had no problem discussing the blackmail business with Sarah. But she would not mention it to her landlady, Margery. Maybe she did not want Margery knowing too much. Her landlady already had Helen's suitcase full of cash.

Helen and Sarah walked along Hollywood Beach until they reached Sarah's condo. Kids pedaled by on low-slung yellow banana bikes, their rumps nearly touching the

ground. Young couples kissed by the ocean. Old couples
walked hand-in-hand on the boardwalk. Tired parents
packed up their beach umbrellas and sunburned offspring.

At her condo, Sarah made coffee and cut two slices of
pie. "I gather you're not going to the police with this new information?" she said.

Helen just looked at her.

"You're afraid Detective Dwight Hansel will make your
life difficult, and you'll need an expensive lawyer, like Joe
had to get."

"Yes," Helen said. It was partly true. The whole truth was
worse.

"Then you'll have to solve Christina's murder yourself."

"I'm no detective. I don't know where to begin."

"Find out who has an alibi for the day Christina died."

"Weekend," Helen said. "Well, sort of. The police think
she was killed sometime between Saturday evening and
Monday morning. Christina's last phone call was with her
ex-boyfriend Joe, about six-twenty Saturday night. She'd
left the store by then. I know for sure that Joe has no alibi.
Niki claims to have one. I can't tell you about the blackmail
victims or Brittney."

"Then you need to know. Invite them all to the store, the
way Nero Wolfe gets people to come to his brownstone.
Then ask where they were the weekend Christina died."

"How am I going to get these women in the store at the
same time?"

"They shop there all the time. Invite them for a special
sale."

"Juliana's never has anything as plebeian as sales," Helen
said. "But we are getting in some lovely new stock. I can
offer them a first look. A special champagne showing. It will
cost me a couple of bottles of bubbly."

"Don't you dare pay for the champagne yourself. Take
the money out of petty cash."

"You're right. I will," Helen said defiantly. "What's old
Tightwad Roget going to do? Fire me?"

Sarah's cell phone rang, and she looked at the caller's
number. "Oops. I have to take this. Make yourself at home."

This might work, Helen thought. She used to analyze financial reports in her other life. Now she could analyze alibis. Helen remembered something else. There was a twenty-five-thousand-dollar reward if she caught Christina's killer. She didn't have to bring in the killer at gunpoint. Just give the police information leading to the arrest and conviction.

Sarah's call was taking longer than she thought. Helen read an old *Best Friends* magazine she found on the coffee table. She was halfway through a story about theater cats when Sarah came out of her office and caught Helen in mid-yawn. "I'm tired, too," Sarah said. "Take the magazine. I'll drive you home."

The more they talked about the special showing on the drive home, the more enthusiastic Helen became. "I'll hold the champagne showing in two days. Tell them it's a one-time-only offer. I'll start calling first thing tomorrow. There's just one problem: How am I going to get these women to talk about where they were when Christina died?"

"Tell them you know the time of death. They'll jump in with where they were. It will be easier than you think," Sarah said. "Trust me."

"That's what got me into trouble in the first place," Helen said.

The champagne showing had everything a Juliana's regular could want: secrecy, snobbery, and special treatment.

Helen called each woman and made her swear not to tell a soul, knowing she would talk the instant she hung up. Her conversation with Tiffany was typical.

"You have to keep this quiet," Helen said. "I can only invite five special people. I couldn't ask Melissa or Bianca, much as I love them, because, frankly, you're a better customer."

"I won't breathe a word," Tiffany said. "I'm so honored." She was, too. Helen felt a little sad.

Niki jumped at the chance to be one of the chosen. Brittney said she'd be delighted. Even the hard-boiled Sharmayne said yes. That really surprised Helen. But she suspected the women liked the idea they were getting special treatment in a store that prided itself on exclusivity.

Helen's one failure was Venetia. She couldn't reach her

at home or on her cell phone. Helen kept calling every half hour. It was five o'clock, the day before the special sale, when a shrill voice answered the phone.

"Venetia?" Helen began. "This is Juliana's, and we'd like to invite you to a special—"

"I can't believe you'd have the nerve to call here," the woman screeched. "You've ruined my daughter-in-law. Ruined her."

Whoa. Venetia's husband had definitely married someone like Mom.

"Do you know where she is?" the screecher continued. "In a private hospital, trying to recover from the damage you did. She went to your store to return a purse and came home raving. I don't know what you gave her, but it sent Venetia over the edge. We had to commit her that afternoon. She's been there ever since. If it wouldn't bring more shame on our family, I'd call the cops, you heartless—"

"Wait, it wasn't me," Helen said. "I'm the new acting manager."

"Where is that terrible Christina? Did they finally fire her?"

"Haven't you heard?"

"I don't hear anything. I'm trying to keep my son's family together."

"Christina was murdered," Helen said.

"Good," the woman said, and slammed down the phone.

Venetia had an alibi, and it was ironclad: She was in a detox ward when Christina was murdered. But that made Helen one person short for the champagne showing. The solution was standing—or rather, moping—in front of her.

"Tara," Helen said. "I need a big favor. Tomorrow, would you be a customer instead of a sales associate? If you buy anything, you can use your store discount. I'll also pay you for your time."

Tara squealed like a little girl getting a special treat. "That's your idea of a big favor? I've been dying to go. I was thinking of quitting so I could be a customer. I've already got my eye on that new black D&G."

* * *

Helen showed up at the store that Friday morning with three bottles of chilled Piper-Heidsieck Extra Dry for the five women.

"Aren't you going to put out any snacks with that?" Tara said.

"No, they buy more if it's just champagne," Helen said. They talk more, too, she thought.

Tara looked dubious. "Niki doesn't hold her liquor well," she said. "Neither does Tiffany."

"I promise I'll send anyone who gets tipsy home in a cab," Helen said.

At ten-forty-five, while Tara shooed out the uninvited customers, Helen hung an elegantly lettered sign on the green door. It said, "Closed for a special event. Reopen at two p.m."

By eleven-oh-two, all the special guests had arrived. Helen popped the first champagne cork. It was like she had fired a starter's pistol.

The five women bought as if shopping was a competition sport, an Olympic event. They spent like drunken congressmen with taxpayers' money. The clothes Tara bought cost more than Helen made in a year at Juliana's. Niki beat her in the shopping sweepstakes. Brittney spent more than both women combined.

The women spent with style. They tried on dresses that laced fetchingly up the front like corsets or bared elegant backs. Skirts were slit to the thigh. Blouses showed off smooth shoulders or slender waists.

The fabrics were rich or sheer or so frothy you wanted to dive into them.

The colors were edible. Tiffany bought a delectable peach slip dress. It's stylish on her, Helen thought. I'd look like I was in my underwear.

Sharmayne came out in a severe black Chanel suit piped in white, and black ankle-strap heels straight out of a bondage catalogue. The effect was incredibly sexy. Everyone applauded, and Sharmayne did a catwalk strut through the store.

They are so beautiful, Helen thought. They're like flowers in an exotic garden. Except one of these beauties could be a killer. She looked at the gorgeous women laughing and sipping champagne. She wondered which one murdered Christina and let her rot in Biscayne Bay.

She also wondered why she was trying to trap this killer. Was she nuts? The fear began crawling in her guts again. I'm playing Nero Wolfe, she thought, but I forgot he had Archie Goodwin when he sat in a room with a killer. Not me. I'm getting them drunk. I'm unarmed and desperate.

Helen stood at the cash register like a soldier at her post, ringing up one purchase after another, until Juliana's profited more than a hundredfold on the investment of three bottles of champagne. After the buying fever was over, the five women sat on the loveseats. Spent was the only word to describe them.

They were now deep into the third bottle of champagne. Niki had hiccups. She sent out a wave of perfume with each *hic*. Helen thought she'd better pop the question before it was too late.

"I'd like to propose a toast to Christina," Helen said, lifting a champagne flute.

"She would have loved this," Tiffany said, sounding the least bit teary. She finished the glass in one gulp.

"Don't the police know anything about her . . ."—Niki couldn't bring herself to say "murder"—"passing?"

"They know the time of death," Helen said. "They think she died sometime between Saturday evening and Monday morning."

"That's so sad," Niki said. She gave an enormous *hic* and then a delicate belch. "I didn't come back until Saturday. I mean the Thursday after she passed." And interesting slip, Helen thought. Was the date of the carjacking and Christina's murder on her mind? Or did she just say too much?

"I was in Greece," Niki said. It sounded like Griss. "I was having a wonderful time while Christina was getting murdered."

I'd better get a cab for Niki, Helen thought.

"I spent the whole time with Paulie, but I can't say it was all that wonderful," Tara said. The word came out "wunnerful." She moved her head abruptly and slapped herself in the face with her long dark hair.

No way to prove that, Helen thought. And Tara was tipsy, too.

"A girl's gotta do what a girl's gotta do," Tiffany said, and finished off another glass. The champagne should have made her eyelids droop, but surgery had stretched them too tight. Instead, she looked slightly bug-eyed.

"Too bad they don't give Oscars for best performance in bed," Tara said. "Then the world would know what a good actress I am."

Tara wasn't tipsy. She was sloshed. Two cabs, thought Helen.

Brittney adroitly steered the conversation away from the slippery subject of sheets. "Where were you, Sharmayne?" she whispered. "Some place glamorous, I'm sure."

"I was at the Frances Sneed Memorial Scholarship benefit in New York."

"I saw your picture in the *New York Times*," Tiffany said. "You wore your black Vera Wang. It looked super."

"And where was—*hic*—your little puppy, Big Boy, while you were in New York?" Niki said.

Helen felt herself blush at the mention of the dog's name. Sharmayne must have seen her face redden. She stared right at Helen and said, "I took him with me. I never board him at the vet's. Big Boy doesn't know he's a dog. We stayed over until Monday."

Sharmayne knows I've seen those blackmail photos, Helen thought. And she's absolutely sober. The fear snakes in the pit of her stomach slithered nervously.

"How about you, Brittney?" Sharmayne said.

"I was at the Kensington art and jewelry sale in Boca," Brittney whispered. She looked rather like a work of art herself. One of those lifelike people sculptures so popular a few years back.

"Ooh, that's the three-day sale by invitation only," Tara said.

"Right," Brittney breathed. "I stayed at a hotel from Saturday night until Monday morning and shopped till I dropped."

"Lucky you," Tara said. "Three days of bargains."

"Don't you usually go to the Kensington sale, Tiffany?" Brittney said.

Tiffany's eyes bulged like an ornamental goldfish's. She tossed off another flute of champagne before she said, "No, my boyfriend, Burt, was out of town. His big saltwater aquarium broke Friday right after he left. Cracked right down the middle. I spent the whole weekend running around getting new saltwater fish and a new tank and everything. Took me till Monday to get things back together. It was awful. Flish fopping all over the carpet . . ."

The phrase "fish flopping" had defeated her pierced tongue.

"Did you go to Deep Blue Sea for your saltwater fish?" Brittney asked.

"No," Tiffany hiccuped.

"Funny," Brittney said, softly. "They have the best selection."

"Well, I didn't think so," Tiffany said. She sounded flustered, and for a moment Helen caught a glimpse of the straggly-haired girl who swiped jewelry at the old folks home.

"So where did you buy your fish?" Brittney asked. The woman would have made a good prosecuting attorney.

"I don't wanna talk about it," Tiffany said, slurring her words.

She's lying, Helen thought. And she doesn't have an alibi.

At two o'clock, the champagne was drunk, and so were at least three customers.

"Time for me to reopen the store," Helen said. "And your cabs are here. Tara, ready to go?"

"How am I going to explain to Paulie why I'm coming home in the middle of the day?" Tara said.

"Tell him you got the flu," Helen said.

"The wine flu," Niki giggled. Her perfume seemed to be getting stronger as she got drunker. "Gotta queshun. Christina leave anything for me?"

"Some papers?" Helen said, thinking of Niki's arrest record squirreled away in the CD case.

"No, a tape. Wedding songs. I'd like it for sennimen—for stentimen—for pers'nal reasons."

"I haven't found any tapes," Helen said.

"You wouldn't lie to little Niki?" Her face crumpled like a wet Kleenex, and Helen was afraid she might cry. Time to go. Helen loaded Tara, Tiffany, and Niki into cabs, along with their mountains of purchases. Brittney said she could drive herself home. Helen had not seen her drink more than half a glass of champagne.

Sharmayne was completely sober. She was also the last to leave. She stood at the door, hip cocked at an aggressive angle, voice lowered to an icy threat.

"I know what you were doing," Sharmayne said.

Then she slammed the green door in Helen's face.

Chapter 27

Sharmayne was furious. Tiffany was lying. And nobody seemed to have a decent alibi. The champagne showing was a smashing success.

As soon as Sharmayne stalked out the door, Helen called Sarah. After all, this had been her idea. Helen wedged the phone between her ear and her shoulder so she could talk while she cleaned up.

"I'm not sure what I learned, but I've certainly stirred things up," Helen said.

She was enjoying this. Helen was a natural detective—or busybody. That's what they called women back home who watched the neighbors through their miniblinds and pumped the unwary for personal information.

"There's hardly an alibi in the whole bunch. I can't prove if Tara was with her boyfriend the whole time," Helen said. "Brittney doesn't have an alibi, either. She spent the weekend at an invitation-only sale in Boca. She could have slipped out any time and driven back to Lauderdale in forty-five minutes."

Helen carried the empty champagne flutes to the stockroom. She went back for the third champagne bottle and dropped it in the recycle bin. It landed on the others with an audible clank.

"Nice dress shop you're running there," Sarah said. "Sounds like a bar."

"If it was, I'd have some decent bar rags to clean off the table tops. Spilled champagne is sticky." Scrubbing at the rings with paper towels seemed to smear them around.

"Sharmayne is furious with you, but she has an alibi, right? She was in New York."

"But I don't know that for sure," Helen said. "If the benefit was Saturday night, Sharmayne could have come home Sunday and had plenty of time to murder Christina."

"I can check Sharmayne's story," Sarah said. "I have a friend in the travel industry who owes me a favor."

"What if Sharmayne used fake ID?"

"Unlikely these days. Even if she did, she was traveling with a German shepherd. That will show up in the computer. She couldn't exactly put Big Boy in a carrier under the seat, could she?"

"What about Niki?"

"It's even less likely she'd fake an international flight. I'll check on her, too."

Sarah called back in an hour. "Bingo," she said. "Sharmayne traveled under her own name. She flew out of Fort Lauderdale at 10:22 a.m. Saturday and returned Monday at 4:57 p.m. The dog went by crate. No other hits for a woman passenger with a large crated dog during that time.

"Niki's in the clear, too. She left for Greece the Thursday evening before Christina disappeared. She flew nonstop from Miami to Madrid, then to Athens. She did not come back until the Thursday after the carjacking. Christina was already dead."

"She died the same day as Desiree. How's that for irony?" Helen said. "We're making some progress. Niki, Sharmayne and Venetia are definitely out."

"Unless one of them hired a hit man," Sarah said.

"Who would they go to—Christina?"

"No, most of them have mob boyfriends."

"That's why Christina was blackmailing them," Helen said. "We've just gone in a circle. Those three are in the clear. I still have to deal with the lying Tiffany. I'll call her in the morning when she sobers up."

"Good idea," Sarah said. "When she's hungover and remorseful, she may tell you more."

"After I close the store, I'll take another look at those CDs. I'm starting to get somewhere. I'll solve this yet."

But Helen never got a chance. She was interrupted by a death threat. It was almost six p.m. when the phone rang.

"Juliana's," Helen said. No servile "How may I help you?" The store's name was a statement and a challenge.

A muffled voice asked, "Where is it? Where's the stuff?"

"What stuff?" Helen said, puzzled. Was this a wrong number?

"You know," the voice said. There was no menace to it, and that made the low, flat voice more frightening. Helen couldn't tell if it was a man or woman. Had the voice been mechanically altered?

"I don't know what you're talking about," Helen said.

"Yes, you do, Helen," the oddly inhuman voice said. It knew her name. The hair went up on the back of her neck. "I want it, or you're next. You've got a week."

"For what? Before what?" Helen was desperately trying to understand what this crazy person wanted.

"Before you get your own personal ride in a barrel."

There was a click. The silence was so loud, Helen could hear her heart pounding. Thud. Thud. Thud.

Someone wanted to kill her.

Someone wanted to stuff her body in a barrel. She'd never be identified. She didn't have any implants. She'd wind up buried in a potter's field.

Shadows shifted in the store, and Helen jumped before she realized it was only the wind rustling the trees on Las Olas. The corners of the store seemed dark and menacing. The stockroom was a black cave filled with unspeakable secrets.

At six p.m., Helen locked the store and left. On the walk home she kept looking around nervously. A big white Lincoln with tinted windows was crawling down Las Olas right behind her. Helen slowed her pace. The car slowed down, too.

The Lincoln was following her. If she ducked down a side street, it could follow and run right over her. No one would see her die.

Helen had only one chance. When the light changed at

the next corner, she crossed to the other side of the street. The car would have to make a U-turn to kill her. She'd run inside a shop and call 911. Helen wasn't worried about getting hit while she crossed the street. The Lincoln was hemmed in by a UPS truck and a van.

As she crossed, she looked through the Lincoln's windshield, hoping to identify the driver. The sight left her frozen in the middle of Las Olas—at least until the light changed and the UPS truck started honking.

The Lincoln was driven by a woman so small her white head barely cleared the steering wheel. She was old, but determined. No one was going to push her around. She refused to go more than ten miles an hour, no matter how much the cars behind her honked.

That was her hit-and-run killer? Helen felt ridiculous.

A palmetto bug as big as a bagel skittered over her foot. Helen gave a disgusted shriek. That startled an orange cat, and it ran out from behind a bush.

Thud. Thud. Thud. Her heart was racing.

Helen had brought this on herself. She'd stirred things up, spurred on by greed and fear. She wanted the financial ease twenty-five-thousand dollars would give her. She wanted Detective Dwight Hansel and Christina's death to go away. She'd poked and prodded until she found those pictures and arrest records. She'd seen into the souls of five people. Now one of them was looking at her. One of them wanted her dead.

At last, Helen was home. She passed through the comforting smog of Phil's burning weed and locked the door to her apartment. She felt safe. Until she remembered Phil's pot smoke and had another horrible thought.

The caller had not asked, "Where are the photos?" or "Where are the papers?" The inhuman voice had demanded, "Where's the stuff?"

Drugs. The caller could be looking for drugs. That's what Christina was selling in those pretty little purses: candy-colored pills and capsules. She took them with her that Saturday. They disappeared, and Christina was never seen alive again.

Helen knew what drug dealers did when you double-crossed them. She watched the TV news. She'd seen the body bags being brought out, the blood-spattered walls, the tales of torture. They could shoot her knee caps, one at a time. They could give her a Colombian necktie. They could leave her, bleeding and starving, to die in a rat-infested abandoned building.

They'd kill her for sure, slowly and painfully. Because Helen didn't know anything. She didn't even know what they wanted.

Chapter 28

"How much do you want?" Tiffany said.

She stood defiantly under the painting of the cruel-lipped Juliana looking equally tough. No pretty pink ruffles and curls today. She was dressed in dead black, her long blonde hair hanging straight down her back. A Tiffany that Helen had never seen before had walked into the store.

Helen thought Tiffany was soft and yielding, giggly. This Tiffany was hard and determined. It was like finding out that Barbie dolls were made of titanium. Yet this Tiffany made sense. Tiffany would have to be tough to survive in her world—and smart enough to disguise it.

Helen had called Tiffany that morning and said, "Could I talk with you privately next time you're in the store?"

"I'll be there in ten minutes," Tiffany had said. She didn't ask why Helen wanted to see her. She marched into Juliana's wearing sunglasses black as a drug dealer's car windows. Helen recognized the sign of a raging hangover. She also saw a woman ready for a fight.

Tiffany whipped off the glasses and looked Helen in the eye. "How much do you want?" she said.

"I don't want any money," Helen said.

"Don't play games with me," Tiffany said.

"All I want to know is where you were when Christina was killed."

"So you can blackmail me for even more," Tiffany said.

It was weird. Tiffany was furious, but her eyes stayed wide open. They could not narrow. There wasn't enough skin left after the eye surgery.

"How can I blackmail you about that weekend? I don't have any proof."

"Then why do you want to know?" Tiffany said.

"Because I have to know where everyone was when Christina was killed. I've got to solve her murder, or the police will suspect me."

Tiffany started laughing. It was not a cute giggle. It was a harsh barroom bray. "That's all?"

"I swear," Helen said. "I'm not going to tell anyone. Have you ever heard me spread gossip?"

"No," Tiffany said. She looked Helen up and down. "Not with that pudding face. You're from the Midwest. You're too dumb to lie." Somehow, things had reversed. Tiffany was in control.

"I was with the pool boy," Tiffany said, tossing her blonde hair.

"The pool was broken? Not the fish tank?" Helen said.

"No, you moron. We were in bed the whole weekend. I've got an alibi. I just can't use it. I made up that fish tank story yesterday on the spur of the moment, and it sounded like it. Last time I drink champagne before noon."

"Where was your boyfriend, Burt?" Helen said.

"On a gambling cruise. I knew he wouldn't be back until Tuesday. I wanted some romance. I wanted to feel a young man's muscles instead of an old man's flab. Kurt had a surfer's body and sun-bleached hair. He was my age. Actually, he was a little younger, but I don't look my age."

Helen realized she didn't know Tiffany's age. On a good day, Tiffany looked twenty-five. Today, she looked forty.

"I can't believe I'm such a cliché," Tiffany said. "The pool boy. Next it will be the tennis instructor and the personal trainer. Never again. It was the first time I'd ever cheated on Burt, and it will be the last. I only wanted one weekend. Kurt called in sick so he could spend Monday with me, too. It would be when Christina got herself killed. That's just my luck."

"I hope it was everything you wanted," Helen said. She knew about wanting the wrong man.

"Oh, it was. Right up until he left Monday night. Then he asked me for a thousand-dollar 'loan.'" A single tear rolled down her cheek.

Tiffany knew the truth then: Her romantic weekend had been one more service provided by the pool boy.

Helen had bagged four alibis, but she was no longer enjoying the game. Tiffany's single tear left her scalded with shame. Poor Tiffany. It must have hurt when she realized the pool boy was using her the same way she used Burt.

The doorbell chimed, and Helen buzzed in a well-dressed woman and her escort. Helen had never seen the woman before, though she recognized her Ralph Lauren suit. She thought the escort looked familiar, too.

Then she realized that the man and woman were not together. He was homicide detective Dwight Hansel, and he'd bulled his way into the shop. Helen ignored him and settled the woman into a dressing room with enough evening gowns to keep her busy.

Hansel was standing at the counter when she returned. Helen was freezingly polite. "May I help you?" she said.

"Yeah, you can help me," Hansel said, taking out his nail clippers. "You can help me figure out what's going on in here."

Clip. Clip. He was clipping his nails. Gross.

"We sell women's apparel," she said.

"Do you now?" he said. "Well, I had the phone company run some numbers here. You been talking to some suppliers, all right, but they ain't dealing dresses."

Clip. Clip. Clip. Little bits of gray-white nail flew in every direction. One landed on the counter.

"I've worked here less than two months," Helen said. "I have no idea who Christina called. I told you everything I know."

Clip. Clip. Clip. More nail bits pinged on the counter.

"Maybe you'd like to tell it to a grand jury," he said.

Helen felt the fear grip her. Hansel saw it in her face and pushed harder. "If you lie to a grand jury, that's a crime. Or should I say another crime? You might want to think about what you'll be wearing then. Are two-piece suits in fashion?"

Clip. Clip. Helen didn't answer.

"The Broward County Jail's got some nice ones for their women prisoners. Sort of a beige-brown. That color would look good with your hair. On the back they say 'Broward County Jail.' How's that for a fashion statement?"

Helen said nothing. She was too frightened. Hansel put away his nail clippers, threw his business card on the counter, and walked out.

She used the card to scrape the nail bits off the counter. Then she tore it into pieces.

Dwight Hansel would keep harassing her until he found something, then he'd lock her up. It wouldn't matter that Christina had called those drug dealers. Helen would get the blame.

Meanwhile, she was getting death threats. She had stumbled onto something. She just didn't know what. The police, or at least Dwight Hansel, might think Christina was too much of a bimbo to blackmail people, but Helen knew better.

She thought there might be more secrets in the CDs. There was still one tower she had not examined. But she didn't want to stay alone in the store after closing, not after that creepy phone call.

Tara had called in sick that morning with the wine flu, so Helen was at the store alone. Business was slow. She decided she'd made enough money for Mr. Roget yesterday. She would take a break and look for the Dylan CD, the one that held Joe's secrets.

Helen put out the "back in 15 minutes" sign and pulled on her formal twelve-button search gloves. She checked every CD in the tower. Nothing. There were no Dylan albums.

There were two hundred forty CDs in those towers, and she was going to open every case if she had to. She grabbed one from the middle: *Music for Lovers*, a collection of love songs.

Wait a minute. "You Gotta Serve Somebody" might be in

a collection. Maybe that's why she couldn't find it. Five minutes later, Helen spotted the Dylan song in the "Sopranos" sound track.

She held her breath as she opened the CD. The photos inside were so sad she could hardly bear to look at them.

The first was taken at night. It showed a ramshackle boat loaded almost to the waterline with passengers. The people looked thin, brown-skinned, and miserable. Some were shivering, others were clinging to one another. A woman in the foreground was so weary, she seemed near collapse. Helen thought she was no more than twenty, but her eyes were much older.

The boat was aground near a mangrove swamp. What didn't show were the hordes of hungry mosquitoes and the rank stink of the murky water. Some passengers were wading in the dark water or helping others off the boat. Helen thought of sticking her own feet in that snake-infested muck and shuddered.

These were illegal immigrants. Helen knew it. She had seen too many scenes like this on TV, when their boats landed in Miami or Hollywood Beach. The INS sent them right back where they came from.

Then she looked a little closer. One of the men helping people off the boat was Joe.

Christina's ex was bringing in illegal immigrants. Maybe that was why he had no alibi for Christina's death. He could not tell the police he was handling an illegal shipment of people.

Unless Joe had another good reason for no alibi: he killed Christina that weekend. His ex had enough material to put him away for a long time.

Helen remembered Brittney and Christina sitting in the back of the store, cackling like witches and brewing revenge for Joe: "Immigration? No. Bad idea . . . Some guys in Miami would like to know what he's up to, though, and they aren't as nice as the IRS . . . When I finish, Joe will wish he was never born."

Instead, Christina had been destroyed.

The second photo looked like those 1890s pictures of New York tenements. More people than Helen could count were crammed in a high-ceilinged, windowless room. They could hardly move, it was so crowded. Stained, sheetless mattresses were on the floor. Four people were sleeping on one. Laundry was hanging across a back corner. Through the limp and tattered clothes, Helen saw a toilet. It was near a table with bread, a giant can with a knife stuck in it (peanut butter? meat spread?), and soda cans.

This wasn't a photograph of 1890s immigrant misery. These pictures were recent. The clothes and shoes were modern.

Illegal immigrants.

There was another photo of what was probably the outside of the same building. At least, the yawning doorways were similar, and the inside walls were the same dingy green. The building looked like a warehouse. The street number was painted over the front door. In the background were four giant candy-striped smokestacks, a Port Everglades landmark. Sailors steered their boats by those smokestacks.

Helen remembered the business story Christina squirreled away in the manuals. It said Joe's company had bought a warehouse near Port Everglades. What was that address? Helen stood up, heard her knees crack, and felt needles and pins in her feet. She limped over to the stack of manuals and found the dull story.

Now Helen found that story riveting. The addresses were the same.

Joe was mixed up with importing illegal immigrants, probably from the Caribbean, and Christina had the pictures to prove it. "You Gotta Serve Somebody" was another of her ugly jokes.

Immigrant smuggling was a lucrative business, if Joe's Ferrari was any indication, but you needed the morals of a slave trader. The immigrants paid high prices to be packed in leaky tubs and smuggled to America. The cruelest smugglers didn't even take their passengers ashore. They dumped them in the water within sight of land. Some never knew they'd arrived in America. Their dead bodies washed ashore.

Once here, the unlucky worked as wage slaves, making

far less than Helen's seven seventy an hour. Helen remembered Christina asking Tara about the kind of maid she wanted.

"Do you mind a Haitian?" Christina had said. "What about someone who doesn't speak English?"

"I don't care what they speak as long as they scrub my floors," Tara had said. "Brittney has a real gem. She pays her almost nothing but room and board. The woman is practically a slave."

They were slaves, chained to their low-paying jobs by their fake papers, their lack of education, and sometimes, their lack of English. They lived in little rooms in luxurious homes and were utterly isolated. Domestics did not hang around the yacht club or get a cappuccino at the local patisserie. They couldn't complain about their pay or working conditions or they'd be deported. They had no job benefits and no future.

Anyone who hired illegal immigrants broke the employment laws, but few of Juliana's customers wanted cabinet posts.

Joe was Christina's source for those reliable scrubbing slaves. Helen would bet the rent that Christina collected a fee for finding maids for her customers. Joe probably got a kickback, too.

When they split, Christina wanted revenge, and she knew enough to get Joe in big trouble. Maybe Detective Dwight Hansel wasn't so dumb after all, if he believed Joe had killed Christina. Helen had the motive right in her hand.

Helen dusted herself off, put away her twelve-button kid gloves, and called Sarah to crow about her discovery before she opened the store again. (Well, she didn't say which fifteen minutes she'd be back, did she?)

She was lucky. Sarah was home and answering her phone.

"I've got something," Helen said. "Something big. These have to be pictures of an illegal immigrant smuggling operation. And Joe's involved."

She described the photos.

"That's what you say when you see the photos," Sarah said. "Joe could say he was rescuing some poor strangers

when their boat went aground. Does the photo indicate these
are illegal immigrants?"

"No," Helen said. "But it's obvious."

"Why? Because they're not holding visas? You can't
even prove that boat photo was taken in Florida. It could
have been the Bahamas or some other island."

"What about those awful warehouse photos?" Helen said.
"One shows the striped smokestacks. That's definitely Fort
Lauderdale."

"Any date on those pictures?"

"No." Helen could feel her triumph slipping away.

"I didn't think so," Sarah said. "Joe could say the photos
were taken before he bought the warehouse. He's not in
those pictures, is he?"

"No," Helen said. "I have absolutely nothing."

"But you do. You have a place to start."

"You don't expect me to go to Joe's office and confront
him, do you?"

"Are you nuts?" Sarah said. "The cops think Joe did it,
too. Stay away from that man. He's dangerous."

"But I can talk to Brittney," Helen said. She remembered
those long afternoons the women spent on the black
loveseats, whispering their hatred for Joe, planning his
downfall. "Brittney had no love for Joe. She helped plot revenge against him. I bet Brittney has the dirt on that maid
business."

"What are you going to do?" Sarah asked.

"Something safe and smart for a change," Helen said.
"Brittney has the key to this. I have her address in our files.
It's time I paid her a visit."

Chapter 29

Fifty-five. Sixty. Sixty-five.

Helen felt around inside Chocolate, her stuffed bear, for more money. She pulled out a crumpled five dollar bill and two singles. Seventy-two dollars. That was all she had saved after the rent was paid.

The cab to Brittney's house should cost about twenty dollars round-trip, but you never knew. Peggy would have driven her, but Helen didn't want to drag Peggy into this. A bus was two bucks, but the next one wasn't until eight p.m., and the last bus left Brittney's neighborhood before ten. That might not give her enough time.

Helen put the seventy-two dollars in her purse, then walked to the Riverside Hotel on Las Olas and asked the doorman to call a cab. She gave him the two singles.

The cab driver had a heavy accent Helen could not place, but she understood one thing: he was rude. He listened to a radio station turned up loud. It sounded like French, but not quite. Haitian-Creole? He did not turn on the air conditioner. Helen amused herself by counting the acne scars on the back of his neck while the cab idled in traffic.

Brittney lived in Bridge Harbour, a high-priced neighborhood near the Seventeenth Street Bridge. It was an odd mix of architecture. The older houses were sprawling one-story places that knew how to hunker down in a hurricane. The new up-thrusting tract mansions were two- and three-story affairs, badly designed for high winds. The fake Spanish tiles would turn into Frisbees. The balconies, cupolas, and other gewgaws would sail off into the storm. The builders swore the tall windows were hurricane-proof, but that claim had not been tested yet

Helen could not admire the view. New houses were popping up like zits at prom-time in Bridge Harbour. Magnificent mansions overlooked the aqua Porta-Potties of the construction site next door.

Brittney lived in a two-story white cube. It looked starkly expensive, like the offices of a top-notch plastic surgery group. Helen could see a swimming pool with a waterfall. A Hatteras cabin cruiser was tied up at the backyard dock. Parked in the driveway was a black Land Rover and a red Porsche. Brittney had a few bucks. Why was she dating aging mobsters? Or was that how she got her money?

Luxury cars were common as Hondas in this neighborhood. Helen wondered how the neighbors tolerated the old gray beater next door. Its rusted trunk was tied with twine. A tired woman in a white uniform heaved two bags onto the seat and drove off. The beat-up car must belong to a servant.

"This is the house. Stop here and wait, please," Helen said, yelling at the driver above the Haitian radio station.

"You pay me up front now," the driver said. He did not put the car in Park.

"I'll pay, but you have to wait for me," Helen said. She counted out the fare to the exact penny.

"You didn't tip me," the driver said, indignantly.

"I won't, unless you wait," she said.

Only then did he put the cab in Park. He was going to wait.

Brittney's house looked bigger and more impersonal as Helen approached. The flower beds had spiky plants and bristly bushes growing in rocks. The bronze front doors belonged on a museum. The pet flap cut into the garage door looked too ordinary for this place.

A chunky brown-skinned woman in a snow-white uniform answered the door. Helen wondered if this was the wonderful wage slave, Maria.

"You wait here, please," the woman said.

The inside of Brittney's home was all white: white marble floor, white textured walls, angular white couches like ice floes next to ice shards of glass tables. White orchids were the only living things in this ice palace, and they looked made of wax.

The walls boasted a lesser Picasso. Helen thought the colors were drab.

The air conditioning was set so low, Helen was shivering by the time Brittney appeared. She walked languidly, as if she was drifting in a dream.

Brittney wore a white string bikini. Helen had flossed her teeth with more material. Brittney was almost nude and absolutely perfect. She was not cold in that getup. She was the princess who ruled this ice palace.

"Helen, from the shop. What brings you here today?" Brittney said. Her whispery voice was clear and cool, like a breeze from a cave. She did not offer Helen anything to drink or ask her to sit down.

"I wanted to ask about your maid," Helen said.

"Do you need one?" Brittney said. Was there a hint of contempt? Helen couldn't tell. As usual, Brittney showed no emotion.

"No, a customer does," Helen lied. "Tara raves about your maid, Maria."

"Christina made the arrangements," Brittney said. "And Christina's dead."

"Do you know where she got the maids?"

"Why do you ask?" Brittney did not deny that she knew.

"Was it Joe? Was he part of an illegal immigrant operation?"

"I don't know what you mean," Brittney said.

She did, Helen thought.

"I think he helps bring them in and keeps them at his warehouse."

"I wouldn't know," Brittney said.

"I think you do," Helen said. "The police believe Joe killed Christina. Don't you care?"

"Of course I care," Brittney said. But a look at the ice palace showed Brittney did not care for any living thing except herself. Helen tried to appeal to her self-interest.

"You and Christina were plotting against Joe," Helen said.

"Why do you say that?" Brittney whispered.

"Because I heard you. If Joe found out about your plans, you may need protection. I could put you in touch with a homicide detective."

"And get myself in trouble? No, thank you," Brittney said.

"I'm sure you could get immunity for hiring an illegal alien."

"I'm not worried about that," Brittney said. "Telling the police about Joe will get me killed. Do you know the kind of people he deals with? They would put me in a barrel."

"Who are they, Brittney? Tell me, if you're afraid to tell the police."

"They're—"

But Brittney never finished. A big ball of white fur streaked into the room, then stopped at Helen's feet. It was a cat with golden eyes, a cuddly gray-and-white body, and front feet the size of catchers' mitts.

"Thumbs!" Helen said.

"Mrrrrr," the cat said, rubbing against her legs.

"His name is Mittens," Brittney said.

The maid came running in. "Sorry, missis, sorry. I know you say lock him in, but the cat he got out. He opens doors. He is very smart."

"Don't stand there jabbering, Maria," Brittney said. "Get him out of here."

Maria picked up the big cat. It struggled to get free, scratched her arm, and jumped down.

"Here, Thumbs," Helen said. The cat tried to run to her, but Maria tackled the animal, this time successfully. She carried him into the depths of the house.

Helen had no doubts now. "That's Thumbs. That's Christina's cat. The one the police can't find. You killed Christina."

"Killed her? That's ridiculous. You are accusing me of murder because I have a cat?"

"A six-toed cat," Helen said. "Just like Christina's."

"Polydactylism is not uncommon," Brittney said.

"You wanted Christina's cat. You tried to buy it from her. I was there."

"You better watch what you're saying," Brittney said. Ice crystals seemed to form in that cold whisper. "I can slap you with a lawsuit."

She was almost naked in her string bikini, but her nudity gave her a greater authority, as if clothes were for lesser mortals.

"If you're going to accuse me of murder, you better prove it. Now get out before I call security and have them throw you out."

Chapter 30

Brittney did not deny killing Christina.

Only when she was back in the hot cab did Helen realize this. Only when she was watching the driver's evergreen air freshener swinging from the rearview mirror did Helen understand.

Brittney never said "You're crazy!" or "How dare you?" or "I didn't kill her," or anything else an innocent woman would say. Instead, she threatened to sue Helen and call security. She wanted to either shut Helen up or get her out of there.

By the time Helen understood this, the cab had peeled out of Brittney's circular drive. Helen was so rattled, she wasn't sure how she got out of that icehouse. She didn't know who opened the massive front doors. Seeing the dead Christina's cat was like seeing a ghost. She knew that was Thumbs. How could she forget those enormous feet?

Helen had accused Brittney of murder in her own home. Did she really believe that?

Yes. Why else would Brittney have that cat? Who would murder Christina and give the cat to Brittney? What killer would waste time corralling a cat and packing its litter box and food?

Brittney killed Christina. It was the only explanation that made sense. She wanted Christina dead. And she wanted the cat.

But *why* did Brittney kill Christina? Blackmail was the only answer. Except Helen couldn't find the evidence. She had to have a reason. She also had to prove that was Christina's six-toed cat.

While the cab driver blasted her with Haitian talk radio, Helen rehashed the unpleasant scene. She was disgusted with herself. She was such an amateur, blurting out an accusation of murder. But Brittney—or rather, Brittney's cat—caught Helen by surprise.

Still, Helen wished she had not behaved so stupidly. Brittney had money, and that meant she had power. Helen, who used to have money, knew this. She was just a dress shop clerk with no money and no connections. She couldn't accuse a woman like Brittney without good reason.

Even worse, Brittney had connections outside the law. Her mobster ex-boyfriend, for instance. Would he do Brittney a favor for old time's sake?

Lord, I've opened up my big mouth again, Helen thought. It got me in trouble in St. Louis, and now I'm in deeper in Florida.

Helen was so unnerved, she thought she saw a black Land Rover, like the one Brittney drove, following her cab about three cars back.

Ridiculous. Paranoid. SUVs were all over the roads in Florida. An SUV was barreling toward the cab now, high beams blinding Helen. She could not make out the color in the dark. Was it dark green? Black? Maroon?

She didn't know the make, either. It honked at the cab, flipped off the driver, and passed on the right side. It turned out to be a black Cadillac Escalade. But Helen could not be sure it was the same SUV she'd noticed several blocks back.

"Do you see a black Land Rover following us?" Helen asked the cab driver.

He shrugged and turned up the radio. It was a sensible response. U.S. 1 was clogged with SUVs.

Helen looked anxiously into the darkening night. Now three huge SUVs were behind them, and another one was alongside the cab. It was like traveling in an elephant herd.

A Chevy Tahoe was gaining on them. A monster Toyota

Land Cruiser was next to the cab, but it was dark gray and driven by a man talking on his cell phone.

When the cab turned off Las Olas to her side street, Helen no longer saw any SUVs. She must have imagined the black Land Rover. It was her own guilt following her, not Brittney.

She was relieved to be home. The Coronado looked like a tropical dream tonight. Flood lights highlighted the old palm trees. Bougainvillea spilled drifts of purple blooms on the sidewalk and into the turquoise pool. The air smelled cool and fresh.

I can't believe I live in a place so beautiful, Helen thought.

When she passed Phil the invisible pothead's, she smelled the burning weed. He had already lit up for the night. Helen was beginning to think the man was nothing but smoke.

It was only ten o'clock, but Helen was dead tired. Once in bed, she could not sleep. She kept thinking of her humiliating scene with Brittney. She tossed and turned until eleven. The bed squeaked when she moved. Tonight, the mattress felt like it was stuffed with green cantaloupes. They rolled every time she turned.

This insomnia called for desperate measures. Helen decided to clean her apartment, a once-in-a-blue-moon activity. If nothing else, it might shock her system so she'd fall asleep.

She scrubbed the bathroom. (Was she going bald? Where did all that hair on the floor come from?) She cleaned the kitchen. She threw out some vintage lasagne in the fridge. By one a.m., she had dusted the furniture, mopped the floors, and stacked the magazines for recycling.

That's when she saw the *Best Friends* magazine from Sarah's house. Helen sat down in the Barcalounger to finish the article on theater cats, when a more lurid story caught her eye: "Hair-Raising Convictions! When Cats and Dogs Are the Witnesses, Their DNA Is the Evidence."

The police were using the same DNA techniques on animal hair that they used on human hair, the story said. They'd solved several murders with animal DNA. A line about a long-buried murder victim jumped out at Helen like a frisky pup: "When they dug her up, she had a single dog hair on her socks. Sure enough, it matched the transvestite's puppy."

In another case, cat hairs on a murderer's jacket proved that the killer had had contact with the victim's cat—and the victim. The man was convicted, thanks to the cat hair. The police officer who'd used pet DNA to crack the case won an award.

Did the police find cat hairs on Christina's body? Helen thought Detective Karen Grace said they did. She knew they'd found a grooming brush filled with cat hair in her penthouse.

Helen had the solution to her problems in her hand. She could prove that the six-toed animal was Christina's cat. She would solve Christina's murder.

She'd call Detective Grace first thing in the morning.

She reached up and turned off the light. As she drifted off to sleep on the Barcalounger, Helen was spending the twenty-five-thousand-dollar reward.

Helen was dreaming about barbecue. Expensive barbecue, using only the finest wood. It smelled delicious.

Then the wind shifted, and the smoke was right in her face. Helen woke up coughing and choking. She still smelled barbecue, but there were nasty odors underneath it now: burned electrical wiring, hot metal and melting plastic. Her eyes stung and watered. The room was filled with smoke.

Helen's apartment was on fire. The blaze had started in the bedroom. The chenille spread was a sheet of flames. Black smoke boiled up to the ceiling. The bedroom rug was on fire. She could not see the sliding glass doors. Helen could not get out the back way.

She tried to remember what she was supposed to do. Don't stand up, she recalled. Crawl to the nearest exit. The front door was only fifteen feet away.

She dropped to the floor and began crawling. The crawl seemed to take forever. She couldn't see. She tried not to breathe. The apartment, which barely seemed big enough to turn around in, now went on for miles. It was filled with deadly smoke and fumes. What if she got lost? She stuck her right hand out and felt for the wall. Follow the wall. Follow the wall.

Her hand hit a table, and something fell on the floor and shattered. A lamp? A vase? She didn't know.

I'm getting closer, she thought. I can't be more than five feet from the door. I can almost reach up and touch the door knob, if my lungs don't explode before I make it. The air was so hot and thick it was almost solid. Helen pulled her T-shirt up over her mouth and nose, to shield her lungs from the hot smoke. And she kept crawling.

Helen could hear sirens now. Someone must have called the fire department. She reached up and found the skinny panes of glass in the jalousie door. She was gasping and choking, stupid with smoke. She felt for the door knob. The door didn't open. Helen had locked and dead-bolted it.

Helen pulled herself up to her knees and struggled to un-lock the door. The deadbolt key was in the lock, but the door would not open. She pulled at the lock with all her strength. She tried to turn the key, but it wouldn't move. She was trapped. She could not breathe. She felt her vision close in and darken until it was as black as the smoke.

As she fell to the floor, she heard glass shatter. Cool air poured in the broken door. Helen coughed and gagged. Smoke boiled and roiled and twisted itself into dark phantoms.

Helen's vision cleared a little. She felt strong hands pull her outside. She gulped in fresh air, faintly tinged with burning pot smoke. She saw three words floating in the blackness: "Clapton Is God." The white letters stood out like a celestial message in the smoky dark. But before Helen could figure out what they meant, everything went black again.

Chapter 31

The sun was shining in Helen's eyes. Someone had his hand clapped over her mouth. Then Helen realized it wasn't a hand. It felt hard, like plastic. She tried to pull away from the thing over her mouth and sit up.

Strong hands pushed her back down. A woman's voice said, "Take deep breaths now. Steady . . . steady . . . relax. You're going to be fine. You're breathing nice and easy. Another deep breath and I'll take off the oxygen mask. Do you understand? Nod your head yes."

Helen nodded. That wasn't sun in her eyes. It was overhead lights. She was in a hospital emergency room, lying on a narrow gurney.

The oxygen mask was removed. Helen's lungs hurt. Her mouth was dry and ashy. She couldn't get rid of the taste of smoke. Her clothes and hair smelled like a fireplace. She would never eat barbecue again.

"What's your name?" the doctor asked.

Helen almost giggled. The doctor's name was Curlee, and she had wild frizzy brown hair pulled into an unruly ponytail. She sounded brisk and competent.

"Helen Hawthorne."

"What day is it?" Dr. Curlee said.

"Saturday," Helen said. "Wait. It's after midnight. It must be Sunday."

"Who is president?"

"That bozo neither one of us voted for," a loud voice said. "She's fine."

It was Helen's landlady, Margery. She was wearing another purple shorts set. This one was turned inside out, with the tag in front. Margery must have dressed in a hurry.

"I've come to get her out of here," Margery said. "Hospitals are full of sick people. She'll catch an infection."

"Are you next of kin?" the doctor asked.

"I'm her aunt," Margery said. Helen stared. Her landlady lied without a qualm. "And I'm paying her ER bill."

"No, I have money," Helen said.

"So do I," Margery said. "And don't argue with me, young woman, or I'll tell your mother."

That was the only threat that could quiet Helen. She shut up about the bill.

"She's suffering from smoke inhalation," Dr. Curlee said. "Helen does not appear to be burned or injured except for a cut on her arm. Luckily, it won't require stitches.

"We're doing some basic lab work to make sure she's OK, and we'll check her electrolytes. We need to keep her for observation for awhile. Then, if everything is all right, she can go home."

"How much longer will it be?" Margery said.

"Another three or four hours, if all her tests go right."

"I'll stay with her," Margery said.

The doctor's beeper went off, and she left Margery and Helen alone in the curtained cubicle.

"Is Cal with you?" Helen said.

"Cal? Why would Cal be here?" Margery said.

"Because he pulled me out of that burning apartment. I thought he might have come along with you. I wanted to thank him for saving me."

"Cal didn't rescue you," Margery said. "Phil did."

"The invisible pothead? I finally saw him and I don't remember?"

"I wish you'd quit calling him that," Margery said, testily. "I see that boy all the time."

Helen felt groggy and thickheaded. "I saw something else, too," she said. "These weird white lights or letters spelling out 'Clapton Is God.' It was like a vision."

"Vision, my sweet Aunt Fanny," Margery said. "You saw Phil's favorite T-shirt. It's black with white letters. He got it from Ed Seelig, a guy who sold Clapton some of his guitars. It's his prized possession. I'm surprised Phil risked it to save you."

Helen put her head down on the thin pillow and tried to remember. She recalled Phil's hands, calloused and strong. But she could not see a face above that T-shirt.

She also remembered the boiling smoke and the bed with sheets of flame. Her funky little apartment was gone. Helen felt a sharp stab of regret. The funny boomerang table and the exuberant Barcalounger were ruined. The squeaky bed was no big loss.

"Oh, Margery. Your beautiful apartment. It's all my fault. I'm so sorry."

"It's not your fault," Margery said. "The fire marshal thinks it was arson."

"Arson!"

"Somebody wanted to burn you alive," Margery said. The landlady's shrewd old eyes bored into her, and Helen felt like she was in the sixth grade and had been caught smoking in the girl's bathroom.

"Now, you better tell me what you've been up to. All of it. Because it's no longer your own private business. They set fire to my apartment building. It's my business now."

For the next two hours, the two women stayed in the chilly, uncomfortable cubicle while Helen talked about Juliana's: the blackmail, the drugs, the illegal maids, even the banned biopolymer injections. She finished with the reappearance of Thumbs, the dead woman's six-toed cat.

Margery had something of her own to add. "A police detective, Karen Grace I think her name was, came by yesterday, asking where you were the weekend Christina was murdered," Margery told her. "I said you went on a date with Cal Saturday night, moped around the place Sunday, and went to work on Monday like always. Peggy and Cal told her same thing."

"Did she talk with Phil?"

"He didn't answer his door. And he had the good sense not to light up while she was there."

Occasionally someone would come in and stick Helen with a needle or make her breathe into a machine. But mostly the two women were alone. They talked until Helen ran out of things to say.

"Now, who do you think set fire to my apartment?" Margery said.

"Brittney," Helen said, without hesitation.

"You don't think it could be a drug dealer? Or Joe?"

"They would have just killed me. They wouldn't fool around trying to burn me. It was Brittney. She never denied killing Christina. She knew that was a mistake, and I'd talk. She had to shut me up. The timing is right, too. Brittney followed me home, then came back and started the fire."

"Are you going to the police?"

"And tell them what? That a rich, well-connected woman tried to kill me because I saw her cat? I haven't a shred of evidence."

"It's their job to get the evidence," Margery said. "You should tell them."

"I tried that once," Helen said. "Dwight Hansel acted like we were a bunch of bimbos. He thinks only men are smart enough to murder."

"You can't pretend nothing happened," Margery said.

"I'm going to search those CD towers again. Then I'll try to prove that cat was Christina's. I found a way. At least, I thought I did. I had this magazine story about how some police are using cat DNA to solve crimes. But now it's burned up with everything else."

"I don't think so," Margery said. "You had a magazine clutched in your hand when you were carried out. In fact, it was the only thing you saved."

"Terrific. I left my purse and good clothes in the fire and saved a magazine."

"Your clothes are fine. They smell like smoke, that's all. The insurance company told me where to send them for cleaning. We'll buy you some things in the meantime. Insurance will cover it. The firefighters found your purse. It's OK. But your teddy bear was totaled."

"Poor Chocolate," Helen said. "Well, at least I got his stuffing. That's where I kept my money. I still feel terrible about what happened to the Coronado."

"Relax," Margery said. "I've got insurance up the ying-yang. I might even get new air conditioners and a paint job. And you'll have all new furniture in your apartment."

"But I loved the old," Helen said.

"Then you shall have it. I've got a storage room full of that stuff."

"A new bed might be nice, though," Helen said.

"I think we can swing that."

"I'm going to have to find a place to stay while my apartment is being fixed."

"You can have 2C. That fraud Daniel is gone. I told him to pack up and get out."

"Didn't you have to give him thirty days' notice?"

"Not if he was cheating old ladies. Took off like he was on fire."

Helen winced at Margery's choice of words. She looked down at her soot-streaked shirt and shorts. "What am I going to wear to work tomorrow? I mean today."

"Today's Sunday," Margery said. "You don't have to worry about going to work. It's five in the morning. If the hospital ever lets us out of here, you're going straight to bed."

One hour later, Dr. Curlee said Helen could go home. Margery began issuing orders. Someone brought Helen's belongings in a plastic hospital bag: her tennis shoes, which looked like two charcoal briquets, and a singed copy of *Best Friends* magazine.

Helen was exhausted. Margery seemed to be gaining energy. She rounded up the papers to sign, then tracked down the nurse with the obligatory wheelchair and loaded Helen into her car.

Helen was so tired she stumbled up the steps to Daniel's old apartment, 2C. She tried to help Margery put fresh sheets on the bed, but her landlady said Helen was in the way and shooed her into the shower. Margery left out fresh towels and a T-shirt for a nightgown. Even after Helen washed her hair twice, it still smelled of smoke.

"You look better," Margery said, when Helen came out of the bathroom. "Well, cleaner, anyway. There's coffee in the cupboard. Open the miniblinds when you get up, and I'll bring you breakfast."

Helen thanked her landlady and crawled beneath the sheets. Just before she fell asleep, Helen realized that she was in Daniel's bed at long last.

She woke up at noon. Everything smelled like a dead fire and tasted like smoke. Her throat was dry and scratchy, and she had a nasty cough. Helen opened up the blinds, and Margery came over with orange juice, a bagel, and a purple shorts set.

"I think these are your size," she said, "but you're stuck with the blackened tennis shoes until we hit the mall. Do you want to see your apartment?"

"I don't think I'm ready," Helen said.

Her purse smelled like a smoked ham. Her money was usable, but Margery wouldn't let Helen spend her own cash. "Let insurance pay for it. I've been making premiums on this place since before you were born."

Margery bought Helen two suits, two blouses, underwear, shorts, T-shirts, and shoes at the Sawgrass Mills Mall. They had lunch, although the chicken salad had a slightly smoky flavor to Helen. But she finally felt fortified to face the damages at the Coronado.

The sickly smoke smell hit Helen at the door. The living room and kitchen weren't bad. They reeked of smoke and were covered with greasy black grime, but they were recognizable. Helen could even use the cosmetics she found in the bathroom, although she drew the line at barbecue-mint toothpaste. The broken jalousie door was boarded up. That made the room darker and hid some of the damage.

But the bedroom frightened her. The bed was a blackened mass, burned to the bedsprings. She felt queasy just looking at it. She could have been part of that unrecognizable charred horror.

The fire marshal thought so, too.

"The way you had the pillows and covers arranged, the

arsonist must have thought someone was in the bed. You're lucky they didn't see you sleeping on the Barcalounger."

"There's no doubt this was arson?" Helen asked.

"None," the fire marshal said. "We found the burn patterns, and we found potato chips."

Potato chips? Helen thought she'd heard wrong. But the fire marshal told her that some professional arsonists used potato chips as the perfect fire starter. Chips were oily, highly flammable, and consumed by the flames.

A trail of chips would lead to the main fire starter. "The individual slid open your patio doors and splashed barbecue starter all over your carpet to the bed. Then the individual lit the chips and had time to get out before the fire really took off. Except this arsonist didn't quite get it right. We found some chips left behind unburned in the damp grass."

This was no pro, the investigators decided. Still, there had been enough fire to kill Helen. If she had not fallen asleep in the living room, Helen would have roasted in her own bed. Its blackened, burned-out skeleton taunted her.

Helen felt rage, hot as the flames of the night before. Brittney set that fire. She was not getting away with this.

Chapter 32

Helen could hear the phone ringing as she struggled to unlock the green door at Juliana's. It was an angry, impatient ring.

"The boss is calling, and he's not happy," Helen said, sprinting for the phone. "I can tell by the ring." She was back at work but still recovering from the fire the day before. She ran a little slower than usual.

"You're silly," Tara said. "Phones sound the same."

But they didn't. Helen knew this call sounded angry, and Mr. Roget usually called from Canada when the store opened.

"You've sold up a storm. Why would Old Tightwad be angry?"

Helen caught the phone on the fourth ring and prayed Mr. Roget had not heard Tara call him Old Tightwad.

Mr. Roget didn't bother to say good morning. "Helen, I want to talk to you about that champagne showing," he said.

How could he be angry about that? Helen thought. I did a month's worth of business in three hours.

"I see you bought three bottles of champagne for forty dollars each," Mr. Roget said.

"Yes, sir. Piper-Heidsieck Extra Dry."

"You realize that comes to one-hundred-twenty dollars. U.S. dollars, not Canadian. Who authorized you to spend that?" he said.

"No one, sir. But look how much I sold."

"You are supposed to sell. That's your job. It is not your job to waste good money on overpriced swill. I'm docking your pay at the rate of one dollar an hour until you pay for the champagne." He hung up without saying good-bye.

Helen slammed down the phone. She'd made Old Tightwad thousands of dollars, and he'd demoted her to six seventy an hour.

"What did he do?" Tara said.

"Docked me a dollar an hour to pay for the champagne."

"That's heinous," Tara said. For once, Juliana's favorite word fit the circumstances.

"It is heinous," Helen agreed. "It will take me three weeks to pay off that champagne. But you know what? He's never going to get that money from me, because I'll be at my new job. That was the last straw. I will find a job, no matter what."

"When you go, I go," Tara said. "I won't work for him a minute longer."

After Mr. Roget's reprimand, Helen did not care about selling clothes, but the customers bought anyway. She had to work hard not to take out her anger on them. In the slow times, she typed out a new résumé. She printed it on the office equipment, using store paper and envelopes. Take that, Mr. Roget.

Helen was angry. Angry at her cheap boss, who would not spend money to make money. Angry at Brittney, who was getting away with murder. Angry at herself, for not finding the evidence to nail Brittney.

When Tara went to lunch, Helen stood in the stockroom and stared at the two towers. Somewhere in those CDs was the evidence against Brittney. Where was that stupid Don Ho album? Helen would have to go through every album in both towers—all two hundred forty. She put out the "back in fifteen minutes" sign to make sure she wasn't disturbed. If Mr. Roget lost business, too bad. Then she pulled on her twelve-button search gloves. The endless stacks of CDs seemed to taunt her. Nothing in her life was working out right. Nothing.

Helen was so frustrated, she took the closest tower and

shook it. She heard an odd rattle near the base. It sounded different from the shaken CDs. Helen got on the floor and examined the base. A small drawer slid out of the bottom of the tower. Inside was a cassette tape, a ninety-minute Memorex with a label in Christina's bold, black handwriting: "Wedding Song."

The tape Niki wanted for sentimental reasons.

Helen wondered what kind of music Niki wanted for her wedding. Would she pick something as cloying as her perfume, like the Carpenters' "We've Only Just Begun"? Or did a woman who'd been naked in *Playboy* want to walk down the aisle to Mendelssohn's "Wedding March"?

Helen couldn't resist. She popped the tape into the store's sound system and got a blast of static. After adjusting the dials, Helen waited for the music. Instead, she heard a doorbell, then a clicking noise, like high heels on a hard surface, possibly marble or tile.

Helen moved out into the store by the speakers, so she could hear the tape better. There was the sound of a door opening, then Christina's unmistakable voice. It was eerie hearing the dead woman speak. Christina said, "Niki, how are you?"

Niki?

There was a rustle of expensive fabrics. Helen could imagine the air kisses and practically smell Niki's perfume. Niki clicked her way inside and said, "Is that your kitty? He's so cute." They must be in Christina's penthouse.

Niki cooed over Thumbs. Christina got her a glass of Evian. They sat down on something soft and got down to business. At times, the recording sounded like it was made from the bottom of a well, but Helen could figure out what was going on.

"Did you bring it?" Christina asked.

"Fifteen hundred today, the other half later," Niki said. "Three thousand total. I still say that's expensive."

"I can get you somebody for five hundred," Christina said. "The kind who brags in bars to his friends, then rolls over the first time the cops put on any pressure. Buy the best and only cry once."

"That's why I put it in a Neiman Marcus bag, since I'm

buying the best." Niki giggled. "You want to count it?"
Helen could hear paper money being snapped and shuffled.

"When's the wedding?" Christina asked.

"He marries that bitch a week from Saturday."

"You're sure?" Christina said.

"I checked with his best man. Jason has always liked me. He can't understand what got into Jimmy."

"He's thinking with his little head," Christina said. "Don't worry. We'll fix it. It will look like a carjacking."

"You know what's really funny?" Niki said. "Jimmy is paying for this. I sold some jewelry he gave me to get this money. He won't miss it. Three thou is petty cash for Jimmy. He'll never know that he paid to get Desiree out of his life."

Niki's girlish giggle made the hair stand up on the back of Helen's neck.

"You know you'll be the first suspect when she goes. Do you have a solid alibi?" Christina said.

"I'll be visiting my mother in Greece until after their wedding."

"The wedding that won't happen," Christina said.

"Right. Once Desiree is dead, I'll fly home to comfort my poor Jimmy."

"And then you'll be the bride."

"But we won't be going to Belize for our wedding," Niki said.

They laughed. It was not a pretty sound.

The tape ended with a snakelike hiss. Helen wondered why Christina made this tape. She could never go to the police with it. She'd go to prison along with Niki. Maybe the tape was insurance, so Niki paid the rest of the fee.

Unless Christina wasn't threatening Niki with the police. The thought hit Helen like a punch in the face. Suppose Niki's new husband found out his wife had arranged the murder of Desiree—and he'd been fool enough to finance it?

Jimmy the Shirt would dump her without a penny. If Niki was lucky. He might kill her or have her killed. The boyfriends of Juliana's regulars had interesting connections. Christina knew that.

Niki had married a T-shirt baron who threw money

around like confetti. Thanks to this tape, she would be a little cash cow. Christina could milk her for the rest of her life.

Too bad Christina didn't live long afterward. She was as
dead as Desiree.

"Wedding Song," indeed. That was another of Christina's
little jokes. Niki sang herself into a nasty little trap.

Helen went back to the stockroom and turned off the
hissing tape. She checked the drawer in the bottom of the
other tower. Empty. She stared at the CD towers. All her
searching, all her work, and this is what she had to show for
it: not one, but two reasons for Niki to kill Christina. She
still had no motive for Brittney. Helen could not find that
blasted "Tiny Bubbles" CD.

It was hopeless. Helen was sick of looking. She was sick
of working for a boss who didn't appreciate her. She was
sick of Christina and her greed and the trouble it created.
She was sick of all the ugly things she'd seen and heard
here.

The twin towers seemed to taunt her with their secrets.
She gave the closest one a kick. It wobbled and swayed.
Helen tried to grab it before one hundred twenty CDs spilled
onto the stockroom floor. She missed. Plastic cases flew
everywhere, splitting open, cracking, sliding across the
floor. As the tower toppled, she saw one CD was hidden
under its base.

Don Ho's "Tiny Bubbles."

She picked it out of the square of dust under the tower.
She didn't want to open it. She knew the dead Christina had
hidden another horror behind the Hawaiian crooner.

Inside were four photos.

The first looked harmless. It showed Brittney and a dark-
haired man on a big white boat. The Hatteras cruiser docked
behind Brittney's house? They were both so small and perfect, they looked like dolls on a wedding cake. Brittney was
trying to kiss the man. His face was turned toward the camera, as if he was avoiding her kiss. His hands were pushing
her away. He seemed drunk, or high, or both. So did Brittney. She was holding a champagne bottle by the neck.

The photo was taken before she'd had her biopolymer injections when her face could still show emotion. Brittney looked angry.

In the second photo, Brittney was swinging the champagne bottle like a club. The short man was cowering in the corner with his arms up, trying to protect his face. Brittney was pop-eyed with fury. Her murderous rage radiated from the photograph. Helen knew she was seeing a man who was about to die. She felt a sick fascination, but she still reached for the third photo.

In that one, Brittney was heaving the man over the side of the boat. His torso was half over the railing, like a sack of flour. His hair was almost dragging in the water. Brittney was about to give him the final shove, into the water and the next world.

In the fourth photo, Brittney was on the boat alone, staring into the water and waving good-bye with one hand. She held the champagne bottle in the other like a trophy. Those tiny bubbles had packed quite a wallop.

Who could have taken those photos? And why?

Helen thought she knew. Brittney's good friend Christina had been on this booze cruise. The drunken Brittney had been enraged by Steve's rejection and bludgeoned him with a champagne bottle. Perhaps clever Christina had even egged her on. Christina certainly hadn't tried to stop her and save Steve. Instead, she'd snapped the pictures that guaranteed her a lifetime income.

Christina had been blackmailing Brittney. Helen had heard Christina on the last day of her life pressuring Brittney for more money in Juliana's dressing room. "I don't have more," Brittney had said in her strange hissing whisper. "I'm not made out of money."

Brittney had killed Christina and set herself free.

Helen checked the clock. Ten minutes before Tara returned from lunch. Time for a quick call to Sarah while she picked up the spilled CDs. Sarah's phone rang and rang, but she didn't answer. Helen left a message while she stuck the last CDs in their slots. Then she put the "Wedding Song" tape back where she found it and stripped off her search gloves. She removed the "back in fifteen minutes" sign just in time. Tara was coming up the sidewalk.

Sarah called an hour later. "I can't talk now," Helen said. "Can you meet me tonight after work for dinner? My treat."

They met at one of the few Las Olas restaurants Helen could afford, Cheeburger Cheeburger. While they wolfed down fries, onion rings, and big juicy burgers, Helen told Sarah about her finds. The blood dripping off her rare burger added the right touch to Helen's tale of murder and blackmail.

When she finished, Sarah said, "Niki is our killer. She has the best reason for murdering Christina. She was already being blackmailed for the jewel theft. After the Desiree tape, she'd have two reasons. Christina would squeeze her doubly hard for cash."

"Christina didn't have time to blackmail Niki about Desiree," Helen said. "Remember her weird filing system? There's no article about Desiree's carjacking hidden in the store manuals, because Christina probably died the same day as Desiree."

Sarah took a bite of burger, then said, "Didn't mean she hadn't started pressuring Niki for more money."

Helen finished the last bite of her burger and delicately licked the juice from her fingers. "That's the part I don't get. Christina was already blackmailing Niki for the jewel business. Why would Niki give her more ammunition by going to her for a hit man?"

"Because Niki was desperate," Sarah said, taking the last onion ring. "It had been years since she'd been in *Playboy*. She never became a model or a movie star. Nothing was going to happen to her, except she'd get old. Jimmy was her last chance to snag a rich man. If Niki had to kill to keep him, she would."

"Nice theory," Helen said, finishing the final french fry. "Except Niki's got an unbreakable alibi for Christina's death. She was out of the country."

"So what?" Sarah said. "I still think she could have hired a hit man."

"And I still say it's Brittney," Helen said. She counted off the reasons on slightly greasy fingers.

"One, Christina photographed Brittney actually killing

someone. That's better than a tape where Niki is just talking about it.

"Two, Brittney has no alibi for Christina's death.

"Three, Brittney tried to kill me when I accused her of murdering Christina."

"You don't know that," Sarah said.

"The fire happened right after I saw her. I don't believe in coincidence. Besides, Brittney has the mob boyfriend."

"Ex-boyfriend," Sarah reminded her.

"And four, Brittney has Christina's cat," Helen said.

"Prove it," Sarah said. "One cat looks like another."

"I will," Helen said.

"And I'll prove my theory," Sarah said.

"How?" Helen said. "Are you going to play that tape for Jimmy the Shirt?"

"Not this woman. I know about killing the messenger. Let's leave that tape right where it is, so the cops can find it if they need it. I'm going to get on my computer and start searching newspaper data bases. The key to this case is Desiree's carjacking. It's not easy to pull off a carjacking in a gated community. Someone had inside knowledge. Most gated communities have a TV camera at the gate. Either this one didn't or something malfunctioned."

"How do you know?"

"The police would have released a description of the suspected vehicle, a license plate number, or a photo of the driver. But there's nothing. I bet the hit man—or woman—has used that method before. I want to research carjackings in South Florida and see if I can find a pattern. When I do, it will lead back to Christina."

"Too far-fetched," Helen said. "The killer is Brittney. I know it. I'm showing those pictures of her swinging that champagne bottle to Detective Karen Grace. She'll have Brittney in jail before you start up your computer."

"I bet you're wrong," Sarah insisted. "I bet you anything the killer is Niki."

"What will you bet?"

"You like chocolate?"

"You bet," Helen said.

"Then I bet you a hot fudge sundae at Jaxson's."

"What's that?"

"You claim you like chocolate and you've never been to Jaxson's?"

"Never even heard of the place," Helen said.

"When you wrap your lips around their hot fudge, you'll think you've died and gone to heaven."

"Actually," Helen said, "I'm trying to avoid that experience—at least for another fifty years."

Chapter 33

"What do you mean, we don't have anything?" Helen said. Anger and disappointment made her voice rise. She sounded whiny, and that made Helen madder. She'd called Detective Karen Grace because she seemed smarter than her partner Dwight Hansel. Now Helen didn't want to hear Detective Grace's smart talk.

"Show me the connection to Christina," Grace demanded.

This wasn't how it was supposed to happen. On the phone, Grace had seemed interested. She told Helen not to touch the photos and drove straight over Tuesday morning. Helen had buzzed her through Juliana's green door. In her badly tailored gray pants suit, Grace looked out of place, like a computer dropped into a pink boudoir. Juliana's women were ornamental. Grace, with her lush figure and strawberry blond hair, could have been, but she lived by her brains.

Helen had been sure once Grace saw those photos Brittney would be arrested, and it would be all over. Especially when Helen told her about the visit to Brittney's ice palace, the six-toed cat, and the fire. Instead, Grace said, "What do these photos have to do with Christina's murder?"

Helen pointed to the photos on the stockroom counter.

"I see four good reasons for Brittney to kill Christina," she said. "She photographed Brittney killing the guy. Look at that one: Brittney is slamming the guy's head with a champagne bottle. And this one: She's throwing him over board. He's dead, or will be shortly. That has to be her fiancé, Steve, the one found floating in the canal.

"Look at this first photo again," Helen pleaded. "See how he's trying to push her away? He dumped her and she killed him. It's obvious."

"I'll tell you what's obvious," Detective Karen Grace said. "There's no connection to Christina."

"Christina took those pictures," Helen said. "That's how she was blackmailing Brittney."

"Prove it. I don't see Christina's name on the back of these photos. We didn't find any telltale photos or negatives in her penthouse."

"But you found a camera."

"So what?" Grace said. "Everyone has a camera."

"Christina used photos to blackmail people. I know that for a fact. I've seen those photos."

"Do you know for a fact that Brittney was being blackmailed? Did she tell you?" Grace asked.

"No, but . . ."

"Here's what we have: photos of Brittney hitting a guy with a champagne bottle. She looks drunk as a skunk. It doesn't look premeditated. Any good lawyer—and Brittney can afford the best—could argue diminished capacity. Brittney might get manslaughter. If there were enough men on the jury, she could get a medal. Florida juries have done stranger things. But I see nothing to link Christina with these photos of Brittney."

"I found the photos here in the store," Helen said.

"Where Christina worked. But you work here, and so does Tara. I'll bet your next paycheck the only fingerprints on those photos are yours."

"Mine!"

"That's right. You picked them up. Brittney could say you were blackmailing her, and you made up that wild story about her cat. You have no credibility. The homicide investigators will find out that your name isn't really Helen Hawthorne and that you're on the run."

Helen froze. She felt the blood draining from her face.

Her jaw moved up and down a few times before the words came out. "How did you know?"

"I'm a detective," Grace said.

"My life's over," Helen said. "My ex-husband will find me."

"Your ex is a creep. I'm not going to say anything unless it turns out you did it. My partner knows your story checked out. That's all he knows, and all he cares about."

Just when Helen felt herself breathing again, Grace said, "You should have told me about the phony aggravated battery at the store here. I don't appreciate your hiding that."

"What about Tara?" Helen said.

"What about her?"

"Well, she was the one who saw the guys with the guns. She, um . . . had reasons to hate Christina. . . . Uh, I mean, she had a past in Las Vegas where she worked as a . . ." Helen couldn't bring herself to say that Tara had been a prostitute, and Christina had blackmailed her. She liked Tara.

"I know she used to be a pro," Detective Grace said. "She wouldn't be the first Lauderdale lady to have an interesting past."

"She's got an alibi?" Helen said.

Grace rolled her eyes. "You watch too many cop shows. Tara is blessed with a nosy neighbor who watched her the whole time. Said no cars left the driveway. Even knew she and her boyfriend had Chinese delivered Saturday and Papa John's pizza on Sunday. The neighbor said her boyfriend never came out of the house until after three p.m. Monday to pick up the morning paper, and he was still wearing his bathrobe. Tara didn't appear until nine Monday night, and she sat in the hot tub for twenty-seven minutes."

"That neighbor must be one lonely old lady."

"Mr. Rodriguez would resent that description," Detective Grace said. "He's a lively seventy-eight-year-old with high-powered binoculars. He waits for Tara to go sunbathing in her bikini. She also likes to sit nude in the hot tub after dark. The old boy watches her like the Secret Service watches the president. He even keeps a diary."

"I guess you can find those things out when you're the police," Helen said.

"I hope you are not wasting your time playing detective. You don't have my resources or my training."

"No, but I find stuff anyway. Look at those." Helen pointed to Christina's other CDs with the blackmail material. She kept her promise to Sarah and did not bring out the Niki cassette. "And you were wrong. My fingerprints aren't on Brittney's pictures or any of the others. I've opened them up wearing gloves."

Helen showed her the pair of twelve-button search gloves, which were getting slightly gray at the finger tips.

"I didn't realize it was a formal search," Detective Grace said, as she pulled on her own gloves. They were latex, not twelve-button kid. One by one, she opened the cases.

"Quite a collection of individuals here," Grace said, after she finished. Helen thought "individual" was cop-talk for "scumbag."

"I'll alert our special victims unit about the sexual abuse of a minor. But all of these individuals have alibis for the time of the murder."

"You checked them?" Helen said. She was surprised.

"What do you think I was doing? Sitting on my hands? I checked out all the shop's regulars."

"So the only two without alibis are Brittney and Joe," Helen said. At least, that's what she and Sarah had managed to find out.

"I'm not at liberty to say."

"Maybe not, but I'm right. And I'll bet you don't believe in coincidence. I get death threats. Then I go to Brittney's house and see the dead woman's missing cat. I confront Brittney, and that same night somebody tries to kill me."

"I don't believe in coincidence," Detective Grace said. "But I need a connection. It will take time to establish one."

"I know a shortcut," Helen said. "What if I could prove Brittney has Christina's cat?"

"How? It's an alley cat."

"DNA," Helen said. "Animals have it, too. Were any cat hairs found on Christina's body?"

"Four or five," Detective Grace said.

"And you found cat hair in Christina's condo?"

"A whole brushful," she said.

"Then all we need is the cat, and we can get a DNA test."

"Two problems," Detective Grace said. "First, Sunnysea Beach is not going to pay for a DNA test for a cat. DNA tests cost thousands, and we don't have that kind of money.

"Second, even if they did, we'd need a court order to get Brittney's cat. There's no way a judge would give us one. It would be your word—the word of a woman on the run— against a solid citizen."

"Look," Helen said, desperately, "the last detective who used this technique was named Officer of the Year. He got a ton of publicity. You could get out of Sunnysea Beach and get a job with a better force. Get a decent partner instead of Dwight."

"And where do I get the money for the test?" Detective Grace said. She was considering it, Helen thought. A little more persuasion, and she'd say yes.

"The merchants association has a twenty-five-thousand-dollar reward for anyone who gives information leading to the arrest and conviction of Christina's killer. Put my name in for the reward, and I'll pay for the DNA test if your department won't."

"Deal," Detective Grace said. "But we still need the cat's hair."

"I can get it," Helen said. "Brittney's house has a pet door. The cat goes out at night. I'll grab it and get a few hairs." Helen didn't want to think about pulling hair from a live cat. A live cat with more than his share of razor-sharp claws.

"I don't want to know any more," Grace said. "Just don't call me from the Bridge Harbour police station."

"First, I have to call the animal DNA expert," Helen said.

Helen enjoyed running up Juliana's phone bill to track down the DNA expert. Dr. Joy Halverson was at QuestGen laboratories in Davis, California, four time zones and twenty-five hundred miles from Florida.

"Do you have cat-hair samples with roots?" Dr. Halverson asked.

"Detective Grace says a grooming brush filled with hair was found in the dead woman's penthouse."

"That's a good source. There should be root material," Dr. Halverson said. "What about the hairs found on the woman's body?"

"I don't know," Helen said. "Is it important?"

"Yes. There are two kinds of DNA testing in forensics. STR, short tandem repeats, is the most accurate test, but it needs nuclear DNA. You get that from blood samples, saliva, or hair with roots. A shed hair does not have a lot of root material. You might get lucky, though. One of the hairs found on the body may have a root. You need to check."

"What if it doesn't?" Helen said.

"Then the probabilities change drastically. If you get a match when you use STR testing, there is only one chance in a billion the test is wrong. That's fairly convincing evidence. If you use the non-root material, the chances drop to maybe one in three hundred."

The whole case was riding on a hair. A cat hair.

"If I go ahead with the test, what will it cost?" Helen said. "It's for you, not the police, right?"

"The local police department can't afford a DNA test for a house cat," Helen said. Neither can I, she thought.

"If a private person did it, the test would run about a thousand dollars," Dr. Halverson said. "If I did the test, it would take two to three weeks. The price goes up to two thousand or more if I have to testify in court."

The DNA test would take a huge bite out of Helen's suitcase stash. It's an investment, Helen decided. If I get the reward, I'll still have twenty-three thousand dollars. But I can't get anything without it.

"How much hair will I have to pull off the cat for comparison?" Helen said. She was not looking forward to this part.

"None," the doctor said. "I need a cheek sample. You can use a fine brush, like a baby tooth brush, or a cotton swab. Just brush it on the inside of the cat's cheek, and that will get the DNA sample."

Great. Helen had to steal cat slobber instead of cat hair. How was she going to stick a Q-tip in a strange cat's mouth?

"Do you have a court order for the cat?" Dr. Halverson said.

"No," Helen said. "I can get what I need by other means."

"Like climbing the fence?" the doctor said shrewdly.

"I'm hoping the cat will come out to the sidewalk," Helen said. She knew how hopeless that sounded.

Next, Helen checked with Detective Grace. "We have to be the only people in America who want cat hair," Grace said.

"Not just any cat hair," Helen said. "It has to have roots."

"I'll get back with you," she said.

Detective Grace called Helen back two hours later. "We're in luck. There's a root on one hair."

"Then I'm about to become a cat burglar," Helen said.

Chapter 34

"We better scout Brittney's place. I want to see what it looks like at night," Margery said.

"The same as in the day, only darker," Helen said.

"Not true. Every place looks different at night. Acts different, too. Trust me on this. I'm an old night owl."

Helen wondered what Margery saw at the Coronado after dark. Her landlady was providing the wheels for the cat caper. "Brittney goes to a different South Beach club almost every night," Helen said. "Wednesday nights she goes to the Delano. Usually leaves sometime after nine."

"Fine," said Margery. "We got a date tonight at ten. It's Tuesday, so we'll nail the cat tomorrow."

At ten o'clock, they pulled out of the Coronado and headed for the Seventeenth Street Bridge. Margery drove an old white Cadillac half a block long. Helen wondered if it was a state law that when you reached age seventy, you had to drive a big white car.

On the other side of the bridge, Margery made a left onto Bridge Harbour Parkway, and they were suddenly in the hushed, winding streets of the wealthy. Her landlady was right. Bridge Harbour was different after dark.

The huge houses looked more like hotels, with their two-story entryways. Huge, enormous, and giant described everything about these houses, except their lots, which were barely big enough for a modest ranch house.

"How come major mansions are built on such little lots?" Helen said.

"You can get land in Omaha," Margery said. "They want water. The fewer drawbridges your yacht goes through before you get to the ocean, the better. Bridge Harbor is only one drawbridge away.

"Now, can we skip the house tour and get to work? Did you see all these 'No Parking' signs? What are we going to do with this car? I can't park it. And look at these security patrols."

Bridge Harbour houses were built along a system of canals. The security service had white patrol cars stationed at every little canal bridge.

"I counted six rent-a-cops on wheels," Margery said. "This is not going to be easy. Show me the house. And tell me it doesn't have a seven-foot wall, like every other place we've passed."

"Oh, no," Helen said. "It has a tall hedge, but a nice open driveway. The cab pulled right in."

But no car could get in at night. The driveway was closed by an electric gate. "That wasn't here during the day," Helen said.

"At least it's fancy wrought iron," Margery said. "The cat can slide through the curlicues. I don't like those security lights. Place is lit up like Times Square."

Helen thought she saw something white flitting through the bushes. Was the cat on his nightly prowl? It was hard to tell in the glaring lights.

"Let's get out of here before they notice my license plate," Margery said. "We've got planning to do."

They stopped at a Pollo Tropical and picked up dinner to go. Even the fast food in Florida was exotic. Where else in America could you get fried plantains at a franchise? They ate their chicken tropi-chops (three dollars and seventeen cents, with rice and beans) in Margery's kitchen.

"With all that security, we're going to need an excuse for wandering around," she said.

"I could be a jogger," Helen said.

"Security won't fall for that," Margery said, stabbing at

her chicken. "Did you see any joggers on those streets at ten o'clock?"

"No," Helen said. "Wait. What if I was looking for my lost cat?"

"I like that," Margery said. "It's almost true. It would explain why I was driving around, and why you were trying to catch a cat.

"Now we have to figure out how to get the cat. Are you sure it goes out at night?"

"There's a cat flap in the door. I thought I saw something white in the bushes. But I don't know how to get it to come to me. I've never had a cat."

"We need catnip and peacock feathers," Margery declared. "My friend Rita Scott grows her own catnip and makes these toys stuffed with catnip. Her cats go nuts over them. I'll get some, and a peacock feather, and meet you at my car at ten o'clock tomorrow night."

Helen spent all day Wednesday wondering if she'd get caught and spend the night at the Broward County Jail. She was glad it was a dark night with no moon. The two cat burglars met at Margery's car. Margery was wearing a purple velour jogging suit and mauve tennis shoes. Helen had on jeans and a black sweatshirt. She always felt so conservative compared to her landlady.

On the Cadillac's back seat was a peacock feather and a plastic ziplock bag. Inside the bag were fabric cat toys no bigger than Helen's hand. She picked one up and sniffed it.

"It smells like grass," Helen said.

"That's the most potent catnip in the feline world," Margery said. "Rita says you call the cat by name, none of that 'kitty, kitty' stuff. Then stick the peacock feather through the gate and wiggle it around. Cats love playing with peacock feathers. When the cat gets close to the fence, bring out the catnip toy. It will come running. No cat can resist Rita's catnip."

"What's in that paper bag on the back seat?" Helen asked.

"Our last resort," Margery said. "Do you have everything?"

Helen patted her fanny pack. "Yep. Q-tips in a plastic bag. Small Ziplocs for the sample."

"Let's go," Margery said.

Bridge Harbour looked different again tonight. Now it was not only rich but powerful. The tall gray royal palms looked like dinosaur legs, ready to crush them. The security guards waited at the canal bridges like spiders, poised to trap them. Helen felt the fear snakes crawling in her stomach. She could lose her job for stalking a Juliana's customer. If Helen was arrested and her name got in the papers, she might as well move. She'd never get hired by anyone, anywhere.

Margery drove slowly by Brittney's house. "The red Porsche is gone, and the house lights are off except for one in the back. I think she's gone," Helen said.

"Then let's go to work," Margery said. "I'll drop you off and drive slowly around the subdivision. I'll be back shortly."

Helen took a deep breath, then picked up the peacock feather and stuffed three catnip toys in her pocket. She walked over to the wrought-iron gate and crouched down in the flower bed. It was filled with sharp white rocks and spiky green plants with sawtoothed leaves. A lizard ran out of the flower bed, and Helen jumped. A spiky plant left a long scratch on her hand. Helen wondered if the cops could get her DNA from the blood on the white rocks.

"Here, Thumbs," she called, in a hoarse whisper.

Nothing.

"Thumbies," she called. "Here, Thumbs. Here, boy." Was that a rustling in the bushes?

Helen stuck the peacock feather through the gate and waggled it around. A white blur shot out from the bushes and nailed the peacock feather, leaving it twisted and broken.

"Thumbs!" Helen said.

"Mrrr," the cat said, switching his gray tail. In the security lights, he looked more like a stuffed toy than ever, except for those enormous six-toed feet. They belonged on a lion, not a cat.

"Look what I've got for you." Helen held up the catnip toy, just outside the gate.

Thumbs whipped a paw through the gate and snagged the toy from her hand before she knew what happened. Now she had another long, bloody scratch. Thumbs had the toy inside the gate, where she couldn't reach him.

"Thumbs," she pleaded. "Thumbs, come here."

The cat ignored her, as only a cat can. Thumbs was fascinated with the toy. He sniffed at it and batted it across the driveway. Then the dignified cat began leaping like a kitten. He ran around the driveway like a crazed hockey player, swatting the catnip toy with his paw, falling over it, doing back flips. She'd never seen a cat behave like that. Catnip was not a mellow high.

Thumbs jumped, ran, and rolled with the catnip toy, while Helen begged him to come back. Finally, he gave the toy one massive swipe and knocked it into the ornamental pool. He sat by the pool and stared sadly at his drowned plaything.

"Thumbs," Helen said, holding up another catnip toy. "I've got another one. Here, boy."

Finally, she had his attention. Thumbs raced over to the gate and tried to swipe the toy from her hand.

"Oh, no you don't," Helen said. "This time you are coming out here."

She held the cat toy two feet from the gate. Thumbs slid through a wrought-iron curlicue. She wasn't sure how a big cat could get through such a small opening. When he was on the other side, Helen grabbed him.

"Gotcha!" she said.

She was nearly blinded by the spotlight in her eyes.

"Would you come away from there, please," a voice said.

Oh, oh. She'd been caught. Where was Margery? Helen hung onto Thumbs. She was not letting go of this cat, not after all the trouble she'd had catching him.

"May I see some identification, ma'am?" the voice said. It was not a question. It was a command. "Do you live in the area?"

"No," Helen said. "I'm . . ."

More lights in her eyes, this time from another car. A door slammed and she saw Margery get out.

"Oh, good," Margery said. "You found Thumbs. That's our lost cat," she explained to the security guard. Margery reached into the bag in the back seat and pulled out a paper. "We've put up these flyers all over Lauderdale. One of our neighbors called and said she'd spotted Thumbs all the way over here."

The security guard read the homemade flyer like it was a court document. Helen could see the headline: "LOST!!!!! GRAY AND WHITE CAT WITH BIG FEET! ANSWERS TO THE NAME THUMBS. REWARD!"

Thumbs was starting to squirm. If he escaped, she'd never catch him. If he scratched her, she'd lose another pint of blood.

"Pardon me, sir," Helen said, "but Thumbs has been missing for a full day, and he needs his medicine. He has a bad mouth infection."

The guard backed away from the diseased animal. Margery pulled a bag of cat treats from her purse and said, "Here, I'll give him this and you give him his medicated swab."

When Thumbs opened his mouth, Helen ran the Q-tip inside his cheek, then quickly pulled it out. Margery popped a treat in the cat's mouth before he could protest. Helen stuck the swab in a Ziploc bag. The guard watched them.

"We really need to get him home now," Margery said.

The security guard walked them to Margery's car. "Glad you found your cat, ladies," he said.

"Not as glad as we are," Helen said. Margery elbowed her to shut up.

Margery drove to the end of the street and out of Bridge Harbour. Then she turned around and went back to Brittney's house.

Helen hopped out and dumped Thumbs over the fence. He looked up at her. He didn't want to go back to the ice palace, and he was wearing a fur coat.

"You're a good guy," Helen said. "But you've got to stay here if you're going to help us."

As she ran for Margery's car, she saw Thumbs padding

toward the house. It could be her imagination, but he
seemed dejected.

"Thumbs is such a nice animal. I hate to leave him,"
Helen said.

Margery swatted at the white cat hair swirling through
her car like a snowstorm.

"Are you kidding?" she said. "We brought most of him
with us."

Chapter 35

"Are you going to sit up all night watching a Q-tip full of cat slobber?" Margery asked. "It's three a.m. Your lights are still on. You should be in bed."

"I don't want anything to happen to it," Helen said. "It's my freedom from Detective Dwight Hansel. It's also twenty-five thousand dollars."

"I'll babysit the Q-tip while you sleep. I'll even fill out the FedEx form."

Helen's landlady was wearing her purple chenille robe and red curlers. Margery's toes were a vibrant red. Somehow, this made her look trustworthy.

Helen was tired. She'd spent the night staring at the Q-tip, as if it would self-destruct.

"I guess I can do that," Helen said.

"I don't know why you didn't just drop it in the FedEx box this evening. Then it would be safe."

But would it? Helen worried that the heat would ruin the DNA sample, even though she knew that was ridiculous. The police got DNA off soda straws that had been sitting in alleys. She watched *Law & Order* and *CSI*. She knew her forensics.

Still, Helen worried. What if a car ran into the FedEx box? Or it got hit by lightning? Or vandals started a fire? She knew all these possibilities were incredibly remote. She

also knew she would hang onto the cat DNA until five-forty-
five Thursday night.

Then she would walk over to the parking lot behind the
bank, drop the envelope in the FedEx box, and wait until the
driver picked it up at six p.m. After that, it would be out of
her hands until the test results were ready in two or three
weeks.

At nine the next morning, she stopped by Margery's for
the FedEx package. She noticed that Margery had used her
own credit card number for the billing.

"I'll reimburse you," Helen said.

"Forget it," Margery said. "Wednesday night was the
most fun I've had in years, which should tell you something
about my life."

Helen spent a miserable Thursday looking at the clock
every fifteen minutes. The hands moved so slowly, she was
sure it was broken, so she kept calling Time & Temperature.

At noon, she called Sarah. "The cat DNA goes off to the
lab today," she said. "Then I'll have my proof that Brittney
did it."

"You're too late," Sarah said. "I've already found the pattern that will nail Niki. Do you know there have been three
carjackings in the last two years where the grieving spouse
remarried quickly? We're talking less than six months."

"So they were a little hasty. So what?"

"Those hits were made to look like carjackings," Sarah
said. "Someone was yearning to be free. And in one case,
witnesses saw a gray Toyota Camry leave the scene."

"Shouldn't be too many of those in South Florida," Helen
said.

"Go ahead and laugh," Sarah said. "You'll eat your
words. And I'll eat a Jaxson's hot fudge sundae."

Helen hung up laughing, until she looked at the clock. It
was twelve-oh-five. Time stood still that afternoon, while
Helen paced and fussed and checked the clock. When it was
five-forty, she and Tara could stand it no longer. Tara promised to lock up the store. Helen grabbed the package and ran
all the way to the FedEx box. It was exactly five-forty-five
when she reached it.

She was reading the FedEx airbill once more, making

sure all the little boxes were checked and the spaces were filled in, when a car came squealing into the lot.

It was a red Ferrari convertible, the same color as Margery's toenail polish. It pulled up in front of the FedEx box at an angle, almost pinning Helen to the box. She stared at the car's flat predator's nose. The headlights looked like evil eyes.

Another predator was driving. Joe, Christina's ex-boyfriend, got out. He was dressed in black Hugo Boss from head to toe. He had something black in his hand, but it was not a cell phone. It was a gun. A Glock nine.

Uh-oh, Helen thought. She looked around. The lot was deserted. The bank building had no windows on this side. She was alone in the middle of the city.

"Why don't you give me that package?" he said.

Joe thought she had his blackmail photos. All Helen had to do was explain, and he'd calm down.

"This has nothing to do with you," Helen said. "This is DNA from Brittney's cat. It will get her convicted. It will exonerate you. You hate Brittney."

"She always said you were dumb," Joe said. "Now give me that package."

At long last, Helen understood. It was the cheater's oldest trick: pretend to hate the one you love. Her ex, Rob, swore he hated their next-door neighbor, Sandy. Helen believed him until she found them naked together. Brittney had pretended to hate Joe, and gullible Helen had believed her, too.

"You were cheating on Christina with her best friend," Helen said, then wished she hadn't.

"I wasn't cheating on her," Joe said. He sounded stung. "I told her I wanted to drop her after Key West."

"When you brought her that cat."

"Don't mention that stupid animal. I caught hell on both sides for that. Christina rammed my ass for giving it to her."

"Reamed," Helen said.

"Whatever," Joe said. "Brittney did the same thing because I *didn't* give it to her. She's crazy about that cat.

"Look, I was very up-front. I told Christina I didn't want to see her any more. That's when she started blackmailing me. She didn't want money, like she did with Brittney. She wanted me to marry her. I refused, and she started cooking up these crazy plots to get even. Good thing Brittney was there. She kept me inundated on those fruitcake plans."

"You mean updated."

"If you know what I mean, why say anything?" Joe said, waggling the Glock at her. "I'm getting tired of this. I'm trying to tell you something. Brittney thought it was OK to kill Christina because she said she kept the blackmail photos at her penthouse. But she lied to us. We didn't find out until too late."

"Imagine that. Christina lied to you," Helen said. "And you were dumb enough to kill her before you had the photos."

"I didn't kill her. All I did was put her in the barrel and dump it in the bay. Brittney did the killing. I wanted to shoot her. Keep it simple. Brittney thought the doorman would remember me if I showed up in my red Ferrari, and she was probably right. It's a 550 Barchetta," he said, as if Helen should be impressed.

"Brittney said she'd handle it. She knew a way to sneak into the building that no one would notice. She borrowed this old gray beater and dressed like a maid. She carried the body out in a wheeled trash can. The dumb spics who worked there helped her put it in the car. Can you believe that? That's what happens when you don't speak English."

Helen didn't think Joe spoke it, either. This was probably not the time to say so or mention that she found his language offensive. But she had to say something, or he'd shoot her and take the package with the cat DNA.

"How did you know I found the photos?" Helen said.

"Brittney talked with Sharmayne. She said you found Christina's photos in the store. We tried to scare you into giving them to us."

"You made that threatening call," Helen said.

"That's right. But it didn't work. Brittney set the fire, but you got out of that, too. So you're going to give me that package, and then you're going to tell me where those photos are."

Helen knew what would happen after that. She didn't

have the photos. The police did. But Brittney and Joe would not believe her. They would torture Helen until she begged them to kill her. Then Helen would go for a barrel ride in Biscayne Bay.

Helen turned and dropped the FedEx package in the slot. She had nothing to lose.

"Hey!" Joe said. "Get that out of there."

"I can't," Helen said. "No one can get into that FedEx box."

Joe pointed the gun right at her face. She was looking down the black barrel. "Then we're going to wait right here until the driver shows up. You are going to ask for it back. And if you try anything funny, I'll shoot you and the driver."

The next minutes ticked by slowly. Cars passed on the street, but no one stopped. No one dropped off a last-minute package. Joe kept the Glock hidden in his jacket pocket. Helen wondered if Joe would really shoot out the pocket of a Hugo Boss suit. She looked at his face and decided he would.

At six, the FedEx truck pulled in. The driver was a muscular blond man in shorts. He had great legs. Helen would hate to see him shot.

"Ask," Joe hissed. "And remember what I said."

"Hi," Helen said brightly. "I dropped my package in there, and I need to get it back. I don't want to send it after all."

"I'll get it for you, ma'am, but I need to see your airbill and some identification."

Helen reached into her purse. Joe was watching her. She saw the gun move in his pocket, a reminder that he'd shoot the driver. Helen felt around in her purse. She could not find her pepper spray.

"You're taking a long time, honey," Joe said. "This nice man wants to get going."

Helen grabbed her wallet, the airbill and her house keys.

"Here," she said to the driver.

Then she threw herself on the Ferrari. She was spread-eagled on the long, slanting hood, holding her door key pointed like a dagger over the perfect red paint job.

"My Ferrari," Joe screamed. "Don't hurt my car, you crazy bitch."

"Shoot the driver and I'll rip a strip right off the car hood," she said. "Shoot me, and you'll put a bullet through the engine. You'll kill two hundred thousand dollars worth of car."

"It's four hundred ten thousand dollars," he said. "There are only one hundred twenty Barchettas in the U.S."

The FedEx driver was edging toward the truck. She could hear him on his cell phone, "Possible domestic dispute. The guy's got a gun."

She touched the key to the paint job, ready to scrape it down the shiny hood.

"Don't!" Joe howled, as if she was about to gut his first-born. "Don't hurt it."

"Then put the gun away, and get out of here," Helen said.

She heard the sirens, and so did Joe. He ran for the Ferrari. He didn't even open the door. He just jumped in. The powerful V-12 engine rumbled into life. Helen could feel it vibrating under her. She also realized she was still on the hood. Joe shifted the Ferrari into reverse, swung out into the parking lot, and Helen slid off the hood. Her key left an inch-wide gouge the whole length of the hood, down to the yellow prancing horse emblem.

"Aggghhhhh," Joe screamed in agony, but kept driving.

The FedEx driver was yelling into the cell phone, "He's escaping. It's a red Ferrari. I think it's heading west on Broward toward I-95. He's got a gun. He's armed and dangerous. He nearly ran over a woman."

The driver turned to her. "Are you OK, ma'am? Do you need an ambulance?"

"No, I feel terrific," Helen said. She remembered how her key had dug into the Ferrari and left that long brutal track down the hood. She hadn't felt so good since she took a crowbar to Rob's SUV.

"I can get that package for you now," the driver said.

"No, thanks," Helen said. "I definitely want to send it."

Chapter 36

Joe was clocked going one hundred eighty miles an hour on I-95.

He had to slow down dramatically when he encountered a white Lincoln Continental driven by Mrs. Geraldine Fitzhammer, age seventy-six. Mrs. Fitzhammer was going forty-five in the fast lane.

Joe's Ferrari glanced off her rear bumper and went spinning into the concrete highway divider. He suffered two broken legs, a broken wrist, and a broken collarbone in the collision. Unfortunately for Joe, he remained conscious.

Mrs. Fitzhammer was unhurt but mad as hell. Her late husband's 1983 Lincoln did not have a scratch on it until Joe clipped it. Mrs. Fitzhammer was so angry at this desecration of her husband's memory that she returned to her car and retrieved the foam box containing the remains of her early-bird special. Joe was hit with potatoes lyonnaise, half a grouper filet, broccoli florets, and a buttered Pepperidge Farm roll, then beaten with the box.

Mrs. Fitzhammer did not stop until the police arrived on the scene. She was delighted when Joe was arrested. She wanted the police to handcuff him, despite the broken wrist.

Brittney saw the Ferrari chase on TV. She was arrested later that evening at the Miami airport, boarding a flight for Rio. Brittney had always admired Brazil. It had such innovative plastic surgeons. Brittney might have made it to Rio, if she hadn't taken time to pack twenty-two pieces of Fendi luggage, including a cat carrier.

Detective Karen Grace called Helen to tell her about Brittney's arrest. "What happened to the cat?" Helen said.

"I'm trying to figure out what to do with Thumbs," Detective Grace said. "Brittney doesn't have any family. I can't take him home. My cat would throw a fit. I'll probably take him to the Humane Society."

"I'll take him," Helen said.

"What if Brittney wants her cat back?"

"Then I'll give him back." But Helen was sure Brittney would not be free for a long time.

Helen did not allow Thumbs to roam free, but she did walk him on a leash by the pool every night. Since pets were not allowed at the Coronado, Margery now had to ignore Pete *and* Thumbs. The cat and the parrot ignored each other when Thumbs went for his nightly stroll by the pool.

He'd been at the Coronado for a week when the six-toed cat was bitten by a spider. His huge paw swelled to twice its size. Peggy drove Helen and Thumbs to the emergency animal hospital. Helen had always thought that small animal doctors looked rather like small animals. But Dr. Richard Petton looked like a shaggy Mel Gibson.

Helen was impressed with the way Dr. Rich gently handled the hurt, angry cat. "Easy, big guy, we're just trying to find out what's wrong here," he said, as he examined the grossly swollen paw. When Thumbs lashed out, the vet deftly dodged the slashing claws. Helen noticed Dr. Rich was not wearing a wedding ring but that did not always mean anything in South Florida.

Dr. Rich called the next day to check on Thumbs' progress. That's when he asked Helen out to dinner for Saturday night.

"We'll go Dutch," Helen said warily.

"No, my treat," he said. "I asked you out."

Rich and Helen had a lovely dinner and a walk on the moonlit beach. They talked and talked, until he kissed her in the silvery light by the soft ocean. The evening went so well, Helen asked him out Wednesday night—her treat. That one went even better. They had another date for tonight.

"So how was your evening with Dr. Rich?" Sarah asked. They were at Jaxson's Ice Cream Parlor in Dania. Helen had won the bet and was about to claim her prize, a hot fudge sundae. Sarah swore it was nirvana on a spoon. Sarah was wearing something turquoise and gauzy that set off her curly brown hair. On her wrist was a silver bracelet with an oval turquoise stone. Sarah had plump, pretty hands, and her jewelry showed them off.

"We're going out again tonight," Helen said.

"And this is your second date?"

"Third," Helen said. She thought of Rich's kisses, and a pleasant little sizzle zapped all other thoughts.

"Earth to Helen," Sarah said.

Helen blushed and quickly changed the subject. "So this place has been around awhile?"

"Since 1956. That's ancient for South Florida. They make their own ice cream." The walls were an appealing jumble of old license plates, odd gadgets, and antique ads. Helen watched the man behind the counter put the finishing touches on her hot fudge sundae. He was huge, and his skin was as dark and lustrous as the hot fudge he ladled out. Good. Helen did not trust a thin man in an ice-cream parlor.

A waitress in a candy-striped outfit brought the towering creations. Each was topped with a thunderhead of whipped cream and had a side dish of extra hot fudge.

"I'll never eat all this," Helen said.

"Wanna bet?" Sarah said. "And since we're discussing betting, I should say congratulations. You were right. I was wrong. Brittney killed Christina."

"Didn't your carjacking investigation go anywhere?"

"It hit a dead end, pardon the pun. What do you hear from the police?"

"Not much more than you're reading in the paper," Helen said. "You know Joe's going to testify against Brittney."

"I thought they had such a hot romance."

"They did. But now Joe is looking at a long date in the federal pen for illegal immigrant smuggling. He decided to save his one true love—himself.

"By the way, Joe claims Christina took those pictures of Brittney whacking her fiancé with a champagne bottle, so I guessed right. Joe told the police that she stood on the deck and kept shooting photos while Brittney bashed the guy. Christina bragged to Joe about how she didn't flinch, despite the blood."

Sarah winced. "That's cold."

"I think it runs in her family."

"How's the store?"

"Not good," Helen said. "With Christina's murder, plus Joe's illegal immigrant and drug mess, we're up to our hemlines in law enforcement. You never know when some cop or federal agent will walk in."

"That must make the boyfriends of Juliana's regulars nervous," Sarah said.

"Sales are way down. Ever since Venetia's child-sex scandal broke, we haven't had any serious customers, just sightseers in flip-flops. Did you hear the press conference Venetia's lawyer gave? He said she did those terrible things because she was on Christina's pills."

"Ouch," Sarah said. "Look, I don't want to make you feel worse, but do you listen to the Crazy Cracker Morning Show? He called Juliana's the Little Dress Shop of Horrors. Said it had a real exclusive clientele. Only murderers, child molesters, and pill poppers were allowed through the green door."

"We can't survive that kind of publicity. Juliana's is done for," Helen said.

"I saw Tara on TV a couple of times, but you've never been interviewed. How did you avoid that?"

"It wasn't easy. The reporters were camped in front of Juliana's for a week. Each morning, I went inside wearing dark glasses and a headscarf and carrying a bag of cleaning supplies. I told the reporters: 'No spik English.'"

"And they believed you?"

"Sure. I have dark hair."

"I love it. How's your job search going?"

"It's not. I can't find a thing. It doesn't help when I tell them where I work."

"Helen, I don't want to nag, but I can get you a good job at a decent company."

Helen couldn't accept Sarah's generous offer. She had to stay out of corporate computers. Rob would find her.

"The cat DNA test results came back yesterday," she said, switching subjects with the subtlety of a sledgehammer. Sarah, deep into her hot fudge, did not seem to notice.

"The tests proved the cat hair found on Christina's body, the cat hair in her penthouse, and the cat at Brittney's home were the same animal. Sunnysea Beach is taking credit for the whole thing. They're bragging about their pioneering investigative techniques."

"But it was your idea," Sarah said.

"I don't care. They're picking up the bill for the DNA test. Two tests, actually, since I got the first round of cat DNA without a warrant. They want a second test that will stand up in court."

"That is good news."

You don't know how good, Helen thought. She'd planned to pay for that DNA test out of the twenty-five-thousand-dollar reward for finding Christina's killer. But she could not claim the money. The merchants association insisted on media interviews, including *USA Today*. Helen could not risk nationwide publicity. Her ex, Rob, or the court might find her. So she turned down the reward. It was the price she had to pay to stay in South Florida.

Helen could not suppress a sigh as she thought of the lost money.

"See, I thought you'd like Jaxson's," Sarah said. She thought Helen was sighing in delight over her sundae. Helen realized she was scraping the last of the fudge out of the side dish. She'd eaten the whole thing.

"That was a terrific lunch," Helen said. "I'm glad we skipped the sandwiches and went straight for the sundaes. No point wasting good stomach space on ordinary food. Now I have to go back to work. Just drop me off at Federal Highway and Broward. I need the walk."

It was nearly one o'clock on a sunny winter afternoon. Flowers bloomed. Palm trees rustled like taffeta dresses. Passersby looked trim and chic. Even the signs in the store windows were attractive. Especially the one in the window of Page Turners bookstore. It said, "HELP WANTED. Immediate openings for booksellers."

Helen went straight in and asked for the manager. Gayle was small and blonde and dressed in black, like a Juliana's regular, but she wore Doc Martens, a shoe that never trod Juliana's carpet.

Helen breathed in the smell of hardbacks and reveled in their colorful covers. She saw a sign announcing that Burt Plank would be signing there Saturday. A real bestselling mystery writer. No more empty-headed bimbos. Helen knew she would like it here. Then she remembered what the other manager said on her first interview at Page Turners.

"Will I have to clean toilets?" Helen said.

"Not if you work days," Gayle said.

Helen could live with that, especially after Gayle went upstairs to talk to the owner about her special circumstances. She was back in ten minutes.

"He says he can pay you six seventy an hour in cash," Gayle said. "That's twenty cents less than our other booksellers make, but he says it's really more because there are no taxes and withholding." Gayle looked like she did not believe this. Helen said the money was fine. She wanted out of Juliana's.

"When can you start? I'd like to begin training you today," Gayle said.

"Let me make a phone call. I'll be back in half an hour."

Helen felt no loyalty to Mr. Roget, not after he'd docked her pay for the champagne. Dead-end job workers were powerless. They were yelled at by customers and abused by cheap bosses. Their hours were changed without notice. They were fired for no reason.

They had only one weapon, and Helen was about to use it. She marched into Juliana's. "Tara," she said. "I'm calling Mr. Roget. You'll want to be here for this."

Tara waited expectantly, rocking from one dainty foot to the other, while Mr. Roget's secretary found their employer. Finally, he came on the line.

"I'm quitting," Helen said. Tara's eyebrows shot straight into her hair. She could hear Mr. Roget sputtering and protesting.

"When? Right now. What? You'll give me a dollar-an-hour raise? No, thank you. Don't worry about sending me this week's pay. I'll take the money out of the till before I leave. I'll also take the money you docked me for the champagne. I know you weren't serious. You couldn't possibly be that cheap."

Tara let out an audible snort.

"Stealing? I don't think so. But you can report me if you wish, Mr. Roget. Of course, you'd have to explain our unusual financial arrangement.

"You want to speak to Tara? She's right here, Mr. Roget."

Helen handed the phone to Tara, who listened for a moment and said, "No way. I'm outta here, Old Tightwad. Get someone else to work for your miserable money."

Tara hung up the phone, laughing. "Free at last," she said.

Helen paid Tara her wages out of the till, then took the money she was owed, but not a penny more. She balanced the cash drawer and put it in the safe, turned off the lights, and turned on the alarm.

As she was locking the door, a skinny woman wearing a Harley T-shirt and missing two teeth rang Juliana's doorbell. Two weeks ago, she would never have dared.

"I'm sorry, ma'am, but we're closed," Helen said. Then she shut the green door for the last time.

Epilogue

Juliana's never reopened after Helen shut the green door.

The store is now a wood-fired pizza restaurant. The pizza place kept the painting of the notorious Juliana, bought at the Episcopalian rummage sale. The red-lipped, hard-eyed Juliana looks down disdainfully on chicken-and-artichoke pizza. The green door has been painted tomato red.

Helen still has Thumbs. Brittney wanted Maria to care for the cat. If Brittney had arranged for her slave-maid to have the proper papers, she might have had her wish. But Maria did not have a green card. She was too busy worrying about the INS to concern herself with a cat.

Helen is still dating Dr. Rich, although she is no longer sure whose turn it is to pay for dinner.

"Is this serious?" her landlady, Margery, asked Helen one evening as they sat by the Coronado pool.

Helen thought of their last night together and smiled. "It's too early to tell," she said. "But I may have found the one single man in South Florida who's not a deadbeat, a drunk, or a druggie."

"We'll see," Margery said. She still had not forgiven the male species for Daniel, the divinely handsome con man, not even when she read that he'd be going to prison for his frauds.

Helen lived in Daniel's old apartment, 2C, for ten weeks while her home was repaired. Margery threw a party when

Helen's place was ready. Her apartment looked just the same, only better. The boomerang table and the Barca-lounger were back in their usual places. The new bed did not squeak. Sitting on a turquoise chenille spread was a brown teddy bear with a slit in its back. This was indeed a stuffed bear. It was stuffed with a hundred dollars. Margery claimed not to know how the money got inside. Helen loved everything about her new place except the faint odor of smoke, but she only smelled it on rainy mornings.

Everyone at the Coronado attended Helen's party except her neighbor Phil. Helen had tried to thank the invisible pot-head several times, but he never answered the door. One night, she left double-stuffed Oreos and two quarts of Cherry Garcia ice cream packed in dry ice on the doorstep and yelled, "Thank you, Phil."

The cookies and ice cream were gone in the morning.

Tara and Tiffany did not have to reveal their imperfect pasts to their boyfriends. Tara's return to her old job-free life had one unfortunate side effect. Her neighbor, Mr. Rodriguez, suffered a mild heart attack when she stepped nude into the hot tub at three in the afternoon.

Tiffany with the bad eye job still has the same boyfriend, Burt, but she did get a new pool service.

Although the hit man who killed Desiree Easlee was never found, Niki was arrested for her murder. Under Florida law, the person who joins in a crime is as guilty as the one who pulls the trigger. Niki was charged with first-degree murder and conspiracy to commit first-degree murder.

Her husband, Jimmy the Shirt, hired the best criminal defense attorney in Fort Lauderdale. He got Niki out on bond. Jimmy put up the money. At a press conference, he said his lovely wife could not possibly be guilty of this terrible crime, and he stood behind her one hundred percent.

He was standing behind her a month later when she slipped and fell off his one-hundred-foot yacht, but, alas, he was unable to save her. The sea was rough, the night was foggy, and so was Niki after five margaritas. Her body was recovered three days later. Niki was cremated and her ashes were scattered on the beach in Belize.

Detective Dwight Hansel received a commendation for his investigation of Joe's illegal immigrant and drug smuggling ring. He was hired by the Miami Palms police department.

Joe was tried and sentenced to twenty years in the federal penitentiary. His Ferrari 550 Barchetta was totaled, leaving only one hundred nineteen in the United States. Joe's insurance company refused to give him the full replacement price of four hundred ten thousand dollars, saying the car was not in good condition. They cited a long scratch on the hood, which was not the result of the accident, and food stains on the leather seats. The insurance check was confiscated by the federal government under the RICO racketeering laws.

Detective Karen Grace was named "Florida Law Enforcement Officer of the Year" for her innovative murder investigation using animal DNA. She was offered a job with the Broward County Sheriff's office at a substantial increase in salary.

Brittney was charged with the murders of Christina and her fiancé, Steven. Helen was relieved that Brittney was not charged with trying to burn down her apartment and kill her. That meant Helen would not have to testify. She could continue to escape media attention.

Brittney denied everything. She hired Oliver Steinway, the same attorney Daniel used for his fire extinguisher scam.

The prosecution felt it had a good case, thanks to Detective Karen Grace. She spoke to Emmanuella, the Haitian housekeeper who worked next door to Brittney. She drove the battered gray car with the twine-tied trunk.

Emmanuella said Brittney wanted to give her fifty dollars to borrow her car and her uniform. Emmanuella said no. She had to go to her niece Merline's wedding all the way up in Deerfield Beach, and she needed her car. Brittney threw in two hundred dollars for cab fare. It was pocket change for her, but nearly a week's pay for Emmanuella.

The frugal Emmanuella had a cousin who worked for a limo service. He gave her a special deal, and she got a limousine cheaper than a cab. Emmanuella put the difference in her savings account and pulled up at the church in a limo bigger than the bride and groom's. There was no question about the date. The entire family remembered when Emmanuella the housekeeper came to the wedding like a rich lady.

At the trial, the whole story of the murders came out—or at least the parts that the prosecution could piece together. It started with a man. Brittney found out her fiancé, Steve, had been planning to dump her for a blond ten years younger. The blond was named Kevin. Kevin was married then, and didn't dare go to the funeral or to the police.

If Brittney couldn't have Steve's love, she wanted his money. Steve had not changed his will yet. If she killed him, she would inherit everything.

Christina offered to help Brittney with Steve's murder. She was on the Hatteras on that final cruise. She also took the incriminating photos. When Brittney inherited Steve's money, Christina began blackmailing her. Just a few "loans" at first, but then Christina's greed grew until Brittney killed her.

The prosecution said Christina insisted that Brittney deliver the blackmail payments to her penthouse after work on Saturdays. The front desk records showed Brittney usually visited Christina once a month.

The last time, Brittney came prepared. She buttoned the maid's shapeless uniform over her dress and put a big plastic trash can in the battered gray car. Then she wheeled the trash can in the service entrance at One Ocean Palm Towers, right past the Hispanic staff on their smoking break. No one challenged her.

Brittney took the service elevator to the penthouse, took off the maid's uniform, and left it and the wheeled trash can in the fire stairwell.

Once inside, Brittney found some excuse to get Christina in the guest bathroom and clobbered her with a heavy jar of bath salts.

Brittney wiped up most of the blood, but enough seeped

into the white tile grout that the police suspected murder. When they found bits of bone and brain matter, their suspicions were confirmed. Brittney may have worn a housekeeper's uniform, but she did not clean like a pro.

Brittney hauled Christina's body out of the condo in the wheeled trash can. The Hispanic staff who hung out back remembered that the pretty blond maid struggled to get the heavy trash can into that old gray car. They helped her tie the trunk with twine. That night, Joe put the body in a barrel and dumped it into Biscayne Bay. It was supposed to look like a mob hit.

It didn't. But Brittney still might have gotten away with murder if she hadn't taken that cat. She thought she'd cleaned the penthouse thoroughly of any trace of Thumbs, but she never found the grooming brush deep in the cabinet. That brush and one rooted hair on Christina's body were enough to turn the investigation toward her.

Brittney had to fight DNA from three separate sources. There was the cat DNA, which proved she had the victim's cat. Also, a crumpled tissue was found in the guest bathroom wastebasket. Brittney had blown her nose and left her own DNA at the scene. On the same tissue were small amounts of Christina's blood. The police found Christina's blood and hair in a wheeled trash can at Brittney's home and in the battered gray car.

Still, the reporters thought Brittney would not be convicted. "A Kleenex, a cat hair, and three people who barely speak English isn't much of a case," one of the pundits said. Joe testified, too, as part of a deal for a reduced sentence, but he was dismissed as a "lying goombah."

Most reporters secretly felt Brittany would go free because she was so beautiful. The men on the jury could not stop staring at her. They could not take their eyes off her lovely face.

But to everyone's surprise—except Helen's—Brittney was found guilty.

The foreman told reporters why the jury voted to convict her: Brittney showed no emotion throughout the trial.

Join Helen Hawthorne on her next
dead-on funny adventure in

Murder Between the Covers

A DEAD-END JOB MYSTERY

by Elaine Viets

Available in December 2003
from Signet

COMING IN JUNE 2003 FROM SIGNET MYSTERY

COLD SLICE
A Terry Saltz Mystery
by L.T. Fawkes   0-451-20835-8

I want to tell you a story. It's about friends, hard work, good love, bad love, and murder. My name's Terry Saltz.

It started like this. I got drunk in a bar one night, trashed the place, and went to jail. As a result I lost my job, my wife, my truck, and my mobile home. Losing that truck was the part that hurt the most.

When I got out, I figured I had to start again at the beginning. I walked into Carlo's Pizza and got hired as a night delivery driver. Relieved to be back on someone's payroll, I was making new friends and having more fun than expected...until one of the other drivers turned up dead. The cops got nowhere fast, so me and my new friends decided it was time to go looking for the murderer.

ACT OF MERCY
A Sister Fidelma Mystery
by Peter Tremayne   0-451-20908-7

In the year 666 C.E., Sister Fidelma embarks on a pilgrimage to reflect upon her commitment to the church and her relationship with the Saxon monk Eadulf. Seabound to the Shrine of St. James, she encounters her first love Cian, who abandoned her ten years earlier. But before she can sort out her feelings she must discern if a murderer has also set sail with her.

To order call: 1-800-788-6262

BUBBLES UNBOUND
by
Sarah Strohmeyer

WINNER OF THE AGATHA AWARD FOR BEST FIRST NOVEL

It doesn't help that her name's Bubbles. Or that she's a gum-snapping hairdresser with Barbie-doll curves pinched into hot pants and a tube top. Or that she's saddled with a sleazy ex-hubby, a precocious daughter and a shoplifting mother. What can a beautician do to add new highlights to her image? For starters, trip over a corpse, and implicate a wealthy town socialite in the crime. Now, with a well-muscled photographer by her side, Bubbles is playing star sleuth.

0-451-20544-8

"Meet Bubbles Yablonsky, beautician-reporter-sleuth and blazing star of Strohmeyer's entertaining, establishment-bashing debut." —*Publishers Weekly*

"Pennsylvania's answer to Erin Brockovich." —Jennifer Cruise, author of *Tell Me Lies*

To Order Call: 1-800-788-6262

S578